SONIC ATTRACTION:

RAE OF SUNSHINE

SONIC ATTRACTION:

RAE OF SUNSHINE

BY:

LAURA CHRISTIAN AND GIHAN SALEM

RAMBLING RHODESY

PUBLISHING

ISBN: 979-8-9871415-6-4 (Paperback)
ISBN: 979-8-9871415-7-1 (E-book)

Rambling Rhodesy Publishing
PO Box 3164
Sugar Land, TX 77486-3164

www.ramblingrhodesypublishing.com

First printing, July 2024.

DEDICATION

For the dreamers, the fans, and the kids hiding out in adults and gasping for breath…

Revel in those dreams!

Live those fantasies and make no apologies!

And to all the artists that have inspired us:

Thank you for living your lives out loud.
Thank you for all the interviews you've done,
for the creative contribution you've made to the collective psyche,
and the impact you've had on our lives.
Thank you for giving us a place to escape from the real world.

Lastly, a special thank you all of the people in our lives who have loved us through the crazy stages of this writing process and have listened to us yakking for hours on the phone debating the plot. Your support was a critical part of this writing process.

BONUS EXPERIENCE

Listen along to some of the music that inspired this story.

PROLOGUE

Rae spun her wedding ring down to her knuckle as her friend/coworker, Kendra, drove her home. She rotated the claddagh ring several times, assessing the scratches that had accumulated over the years.

At twenty-nine, she was sitting in the passenger seat of her friend's car at 1 a.m., on her way home from her bartending job. The club had been so dead, they'd closed early. Her legs and feet ached from standing all night, and not even her "slutty" outfit had boosted her tips. Said outfit was stowed in a locker in the employee area at the bar. If her hubby, Alex, had seen her work uniform, he would have gone spare…lost his mind, she corrected. Alex hated when she used her "Rebel Gloss" speak as he called it.

She couldn't help it. Rebel Gloss was the band that had seen her through the loss of her parents nine years ago. And the band was British. Their vernacular had become part of her.

Honestly, Alex had supported her through the entire ordeal too. He was quirky and sometimes difficult to get along with, but he was under a lot of pressure at work. His coworkers were all out to get him, and as his wife, it was her job to support him. As he'd been her proverbial cheerleader since high school, it was the least she could do in return.

"Are you sure you don't want to stay at my place?" Kendra asked. "I could keep on driving."

Broken from her reverie, Rae shook her head. "No, I'm good. He's my husband and my biggest fan. What's not to love?"

"Um, the way he makes dirty passes at all of us when that freak drops you off at work." Kendra glanced from the road to her.

"He's no worse than our customers," Rae excused. "He's playing. That's how you know he likes you."

"What is he? Five? Hair pulling at this age is relegated to kinky bedroom stuff and bullies. And your vanilla status makes him a bully."

"Stop," Rae protested. "You don't know. What we do in the bedroom is plenty."

"Only because you have nothing to compare it to."

Rae made no response as Kendra stopped in front of her house.

Kendra threw the car into park and squared off to look at her. "You know you're always welcome in my car, but the fact that he won't let you drive—"

"That's my choice. And we can only afford one car anyway, so what's the point?"

"Girl, unless you've got a crack habit I don't know about, you can afford a car. You make at least $500 a week in tips alone on a slow week."

Rae had been saving up in hopes of having a baby. So far, it hadn't panned out, and her sour mood curled her mouth into a frown. She reached for the door handle.

"Thanks for the ride." She rushed out, unwilling to risk the sound of the engine waking her husband. She pressed the car door shut softly and scurried up the walkway.

With practiced ease, she turned the lock tumblers silently and twisted the knob. Its gears made almost no sound as she pressed it open wide enough to shimmy inside. She was about to congratulate herself for her stealthy entrance when she heard a groan.

"Yeah…there."

The deep voice didn't sound like Alex. Maybe he was dreaming. Craning her ear towards the sound, she heard fleshy, sensual noises.

She rested her keys in the key bowl and crept to the bedroom. It might be kind of sexy to watch him have a happy dream.

"Did you hear that?" This voice was female, and Rae's entire body tightened.

Rage filled Rae, and she scrambled to the open bedroom door. In the semi-dark room, it took her longer than it should have to identify what she was seeing. A tangle of limbs and bodies occupied her bed. There were too many arms and legs to process.

One thing was clear: Alex was naked and buried inside another woman. A second woman was groping a strange man between her husband and the other woman. A distinctly large and hairy hand clasped one of Alex's butt cheeks, two fingers lodged between them.

The divorce papers she was served on her thirtieth birthday cited "*irreconcilable differences.*" It sounded more amicable than *infidelity*. But Rae wasn't about to quibble over terms. She just wanted out.

She had some wild oats to sow…wishes to fulfill. She would never be suckered into a relationship again—she had served her time. Commitment was a trap. From now on, this was the Rae Show, and she was the star.

Rae finished up in studio three and grabbed a bottle of water from the mini fridge in the boss's office. The owner of Lakeshore Studio, Bernie, kept it stocked for employees; everyone else had to use the vending machines in the hallway. The perks were few, but the cold water would be liquid heaven in the concrete courtyard in the center of the building.

She adjusted her earbuds and untangled the cords as she walked. The volume drowned out any other sound, and her whole body sagged with relief. Once settled onto one of the four stone benches, she closed her eyes and focused on the music filling her ears.

One song was her self-imposed break time. Officially, she got fifteen minutes twice a day plus a thirty-minute lunch. Unofficially, like everything else at Lakeshore, she was lucky if she got a fifteen-minute lunch, much less five minutes between bookings.

At least she got a little sun in the pseudo-Japanese rock garden when she could snag a breather. Other than a lone cherry blossom tree along the back wall and a shelf of bonsai near the door, nothing lived in the garden. The scattered benches were bleached in full sunlight, but the blistering rays kept Rae from being the pastiest woman in L.A.

It wasn't the work she minded; it was more that she wanted to finish at least one song uninterrupted. Maybe relax for more than two minutes. Most of her coworkers wouldn't be caught dead in the sweltering space.

Sure as God made little green apples, halfway through the first song, someone was tapping her shoulder. She popped her earbuds out. Anger roiled through her tight jaw, ready to snap at the offender. Unfortunately, it was her favorite client, Derek Reed, and she couldn't lash out at him…the jerk. Damn his perfect Hollywood smile and brilliant blue eyes. Thank God she'd gotten over her childhood crush years ago. Shading her eyes, she wrinkled her nose as she squinted up at him.

"What can I do you for, Big D?"

"Checkin' in to four; need another pair of hands to set up," he replied. His white teeth flashed even though he was almost featureless in shadow. "When you're ready."

She enjoyed his company more than the interrupted music and offered him a genuine smile.

"I'm ready." She hopped off the bench and began winding her cords.

Out of all the producers and musicians that came through Lakeshore, regulars and drop-ins alike, he was one of the few who treated her with any kind of respect. After two years, most people still treated her like a glorified gopher. Inevitably, the lower on the food chain they were, the poorer they acted.

The women were the worst. None of them knew what to make of her. Was she a star fucker or a lesbian with penis envy? Why else would a "pretty little girl" want such a butch job? They couldn't understand that the nuts and bolts of the music industry simply fascinated her. She loved seeing how tracks were recorded and mixed; how each piece came together to form the whole.

Her love of music and the industry started when she was a girl in Tulsa. As the bass player for a local band and a session musician, her dad was practically a local legend. Every summer, he would smuggle her into the studios to listen to him work. When she was old enough, she picked up a part-time job there then switched to full-time after graduation. Being a tech made her available to pick up the odd session bassist job when her father turned it down.

"Just you today?" Rae asked as she followed Derek inside, "Or you got a crew with you?"

"It's your lucky day." He smirked, leading her down the avocado green hallway, shuffling through the shag carpet. "You got me all to yourself. Plus—for a nominal fee—Bernie let me have you all to myself for the rest of your day…and all day tomorrow, too."

"You…really?" Rae stammered. In Tulsa, Rae had been regularly requested. In two years at Lakeshore, this was a first. "Thank you!"

As they set up, he detailed his current project, a demo for a potential collaborator. After soundchecks, he adjusted the mixing board levels to his liking.

"So…you booked a day and a half? Must be a big deal or a short deadline," she guessed.

"Why, Rae! I didn't know you liked fishing," Derek teased. "Can you give me a line on the backup mic?"

She wondered if he'd realized the door he'd opened. Rae never missed an opportunity to harass him about his days in The Legends, a boyband he'd been part of as a teenager.

"*Your love is like a time machine, rocking me to and fro,*" she sang drawing out each word then sticking her tongue out. Singing their old songs back to him was her favorite way to tease him.

The first time she'd met him, she admitted that she used to be a fan just to watch his fair skin flush pink. Over the past two years, it had become an inside joke. Something about their sibling-esque antics was comforting. He was the closest thing to family she had.

"Brat." Derek laughed, eyes twinkling as he scrubbed a hand over his dark auburn buzz cut. "Now on the main, something else?"

Obligingly, she sang a riff from Rebel Gloss's *Fresh Spirit*. When he nodded, she went to the guitar and played a chord.

"You play any instruments? I mean…really play?" Derek's question came as she plinked a few notes on the keyboard.

"Bass, and *just* for relaxation," Rae replied. When her parents had been killed by a drunk driver, she couldn't even touch her bass without bursting into tears for five years. The only person to hear her play since was Kendra.

"Why?" Alarm bells flared in her head, certain his question hadn't been as innocent as it sounded on the surface. She peered at him through the glass.

"I could use some help layin' down the tracks. And in L.A., you never know who's doubling. But hey, run the board for me, maybe do some back-up vocals, I'll forgive you for holding out on me. I can do rhythm on the keyboards."

"For you? I'll bring my bass tomorrow," Rae promised.

Derek's head snapped up at her serious tone. His lips quivered strangely, and his Adam's apple bobbed along his throat.

"Thanks." His eyes slashed to the console.

Two hours later, they were slouched on the brown leather couch in the control room, bickering about the project as they ate the sushi he'd had delivered.

"Dude," she complained around a mouthful of eel roll, "I can't tell you if it's what you're looking for if you don't tell me who you're trying to impress."

He stirred wasabi into soy sauce at the bottom of the takeout container. "I'm *not* trying to impress. Either he likes it or doesn't…I want it to be representative of how I flow," he groused.

"Save it for someone who hasn't watched you bleed your heart out for the last two hours, Reed," she murmured. "This is…I've never seen you like this before."

Derek frowned, sipping his water. "It's…he's got a lot of juice," he replied slowly. "Not as much as he used to, but this could either make my name or *bury* me."

"You've worked with high rollers before. Why is this one so different?" Popping another slice into her mouth, Rae chewed thoughtfully. He was more nervous than she'd ever seen him, constantly running a hand over the short bristles of his almost-shaved head and gnawing on his upper lip.

"It's…I don't know," he sighed. "A gut feeling."

"Eat your sushi, Big D," she said softly. "If whoever this cat is isn't blown away by the stuff you've already done, he has no ear."

"Yes, Mom." Derek smiled wryly. "You do know I'm older than you, right?" He garnished a slice of dragon roll with ginger and wasabi before shoving it ungracefully into his mouth.

"Bah, two years." She chuckled. "Doesn't count."

When seven o'clock rolled around, they were wrapping up the third song, barring the bass tracks. She hated to leave him alone. She was in the groove now. Her fingers were itching for her instrument, her brain swirling with ideas. However, she was due at *The Oubliette* where she was scheduled to tend bar.

When she'd come to L.A. at 25 with her then-husband Alex, she couldn't get her foot in the door at any of the studios. So, she took a short bartending course and got a gig to supplement his computer programmer income. She'd tried to quit when she found a place at Lakeshore, but the club refused. She'd been bartending weekends ever since.

"You should come by tonight," she suggested as she slung her bag over her shoulder. "It's Friday; lots of people to network with. Plus, there's some live acts you could check out. Dante Amato's there tonight. He's kinda…folksy…for your taste, but he's got a good set of pipes, and he's been in the business almost as long as you. You might like it."

"Rae…" Derek protested, wrinkling his nose.

"Come on. Lots of chicks'll be there; you could pull *easy*. Plus, first beer's on me. Please?" Rae batted her lashes, her dark brown eyes wide and hopeful.

"Maybe I'll stop by. When's your boy playin'?"

"Not *my* boy." She chuckled. "I mean, I have one of his CDs, but let's say I prefer the work of someone he used to sing with." She sighed wistfully and clasped her hands under her chin thinking of Jacob Hunter and his sultry tenor. She snapped out of it when Derek chuckled. "It'll be a good palate cleanser, and I'm gonna be so *done* with drunk people by the time he goes on…"

"Aha! You don't care if I hear this guy! I'm moral support!" Derek laughed, shoving her shoulder.

"Damn skippy," she replied, grinning.

"Well, if I can shift plans, I'll see you there, but no promises," he conceded.

"Fair enough." Rae headed out, clutching the bag of bar clothes on her shoulder.

As she walked the seven blocks to the club, she unwound the bun at the nape of her neck, letting her wavy dark brown hair fall to her waist in a ponytail. Luxurious, long locks made for better tips.

Slipping in the back door, she went straight to the bathroom to change into black leggings and a silky red blouse. With half an ear to soundcheck, she slicked a dark red gloss over her lips, added black mascara, and deposited her bag in the bank of employee lockers. She spotted several people connected to the performing bands milling around the VIP loft on her way to count out a register to help Kendra set up for the first wave. Given her seniority, she was sure she'd be stationed in the VIP area.

Kendra bumped her shoulder from behind. "Look out."

Rae followed her gaze to the steel stairs to see their coworker thundering down from the VIP loft, an almighty scowl marring her face.

Tessa, a considerably newer hire related to one of the managers, was squeezed into a silky pink bustier that left little to the imagination, and her blonde pigtails bounced perkily with every stomp.

"What's the dealio this time?" Kendra muttered.

"That bitch Suzie won't let me do VIP. It's got to be her," she complained, pointing unabashedly at Rae. "It's not fair. You can't make any money working general admission. Who'd you blow to keep VIP all to yourself?"

Rae threw an apologetic look at Kendra. There was nothing to be gained by engaging with the younger woman. At least she would be a whole floor away from her vitriol. With a death grip on the drawer, she sneaked up the service stairs to the VIP lounge.

Her favorite manager, Suzie, met her mid-flight. The woman touched Rae's arm lightly, her expression serious.

"Look, you've worked VIP before, so I don't have to give you the big spiel, but…there's a *Somebody* up there and—"

Rae cut her off with a sharp nod. "Got it. Diva or wallflower?" she asked, balancing her till on her hip.

"He's a blender that never will because…well, see for yourself. And for fuck's sake don't stare," Suzie ordered.

Rae made her way to the loft bar and set up. Presumably she'd see whoever it was, but if he wanted to blend, her best course was to play business as usual.

A few patrons in her zone already had beers with open tabs. She eyed the tickets, trying to match customers with drinks, and her mouth went dry as she read one of the credit cards: Jacob Hunter. It was ironic that she'd mentioned him to Derek in a roundabout way less than an hour ago.

No wonder Tessa was pissed.

She easily picked her celebrity guest out of the crowd, looking wistfully over the railing as if he wanted to be either on the stage below or in the growing crowd.

Orders started flying in, and she had no spare time to think about the most gorgeous, talented man she'd ever seen. Her section was filled to capacity, and Rae ensured they were all furnished with exactly the drink they wanted with a smile and a wink. She fell into the rhythm of mixing, shaking, and serving. When the music tapered off, Rae found herself humming a beat as she worked. She realized, with a smile, that it was Derek's demo. A tiny shiver of pride ran through her.

"What's that you're humming?" a soft, yet unmistakably masculine voice asked.

"A song a friend of mine is working on," she replied, glancing up. A startling pair of silver-blue eyes stared back. Her throat went dry, and her voice cracked as she asked Jacob Hunter, "What can I get you?"

"I'm cool," he answered, "but when Dante gets up here, he'd probably like a Heineken."

"Can do," she offered, lips quirking into a smile. "And how will I spot Dante?" she asked, putting on her best bartender front.

"Oh, right." He chuckled softly, and it took every ounce of self-control for Rae to stop herself from biting her lip as he continued.

He turned to the stage and pointed. "Lead singer. Old friend of mine."

"Gotcha," she replied. She began clearing empty glasses and swiped a rag over the bar, signifying the end of their conversation. It was standard VIP etiquette, especially for the shy ones.

To her surprise Jacob remained, watching.

"Something else you needed?"

"No…well, okay this is gonna sound dumb, but…could you sing more of that song?" His eyes were like saucers, and he leaned his forearms on the bar to be closer.

Rae wanted to cup his cheek at the adorably shy expression but clenched her hand on the bar rag instead and smirked.

"So you can snake it?" Rae balked. "Not a chance. I could give you the songwriter's card though."

He smiled brightly at her, and she swore his eyes raked her from head to toe and back.

Trying not to blush, she raised both eyebrows, waiting for his answer.

"Sure, yeah…that'd be cool," he responded, still beaming.

She dug one of Derek's business cards out of her pocket and handed it to him. Somehow, over the course of knowing Derek from Lakeshore, she had taken it upon herself to promote him at every opportunity. She felt obligated, as a vintage fan, to campaign for his career.

Looking over at the stairs, she saw Dante and his band approaching and retrieved the previously requested beer from the cooler.

"Put it on my tab," Jacob requested, then pushed off the bar and left to greet his friend.

Rae stared after him, despite Suzie's warning. When he reached Dante, he pulled the glasses from his friend's face and put them on, staring at the card she'd handed him. Even from the bar, she could see his brows furrowing before he slipped the card into his wallet.

Rae's chin hit the countertop. He'd put the card in a safe space rather than trusting his open pockets. Like he was serious about wanting to know more. Rae allowed herself a tiny squeal before she turned to the customer in front of her. Her mouth was asking what drink she could mix, but her brain was plotting a way to get her phone from her locker and send a text to her boy about the transaction.

Kendra relieved her for her break, and the moment she reached the back room, she texted Derek to let him know what had happened. Her phone rang almost immediately.

"You got Rae. Speak," she answered, trying not to smirk.

"I got your text," Derek announced. "Start from the top and explain why you'd give my card to a boy-bander."

Taken aback by the sharp tone, Rae blinked. "Uhm…this is Derek Reed, right? Former boy-bander?" she snapped. "I did you a favor. Deal with it. So, I was humming your song, and he asked about it, but I'm not about to sell you out. So I gave him your card. And anyways, I think you guys would work well together. I mean, it's a long shot that he'll even call, but he put your card in his *wallet* instead of his pocket, so…"

"So…if I worked with him…" Derek prompted.

"I would buy copies for me and as many people as I could afford." Rae chewed her bottom lip. "I'd understand if you didn't want to, though. I know how important rep is in this town. But if he calls, give it at least half a thought?"

"You wouldn't make me give you freebies?" Derek asked warily.

"Hell, no!" she retorted. "I'd want this bitch to make bank, man. I wouldn't cut into your profits like that!" She looked at her watch and frowned. "You coming tonight?"

"I don't think so. I'm leaving the studio now, but I'm wiped," Derek answered tiredly. "This project is kicking my ass."

"Okay, well, I'll talk to you tomorrow then. I gotta get back to work. Get some rest, okay?" After his murmur of assent, she hung up and stared at her phone. She allowed herself to imagine the two of them working together then shook her head, dismissing it. After an ugly divorce and eleven years living in Hollywood, she'd stopped believing in serendipity. She knew better than to waste energy on fantasies.

Shrugging off Derek's foul attitude, Rae chugged an energy shot and headed back to VIP, weaving through the crowd and ignoring the drunken gropes of the bolder customers. The night flew by serving drinks and entertaining the rambunctious crowd. Swept up in the spirit of the evening, she and Kendra performed their *Cocktail* routine, flipping bottles and entertaining the crowd with their expertise. The tip jar overflowed.

At last call, Rae was swamped with guests flocking to make one last order and close their tabs. Jacob was among the last stragglers to reach her.

"Thanks." He smiled as she handed over the bill for him to sign.

"That's a first." Rae smirked. "Most people don't thank me for taking their money."

Laughing, Jacob traded her the bill for his card. He leaned one arm on the counter, smirking as he fussed with his wallet. His platinum eyes rolled up to her face. "Well, maybe I was thanking you for the eye candy."

"Then you are very welcome, and thanks yourself," she answered then winked and turned to the next customer. Watching him leave out of the corner of her eye, her body felt as though it was floating. Had he called her eye candy? *Her*? It was the best "tip" she'd ever gotten.

Rae was on autopilot as the club emptied and she tidied her station. When she placed her tip jar in front of Kendra in the back office, she wasn't entirely sure how she'd gotten there. She took a seat at a nearby table to count out her drawer.

Suzie sat across from her and cleared her throat.

"Yeah?" Rae asked without looking up from her task.

"I need you to come in next Thursday afternoon and run VIP," Suzie murmured quietly.

She paused in counting her twenties. "Afternoon?" Rae repeated. "I can't, you know I'm at Lakeshore from seven to seven on Thursdays."

"Look. It's a private party. You and Kendra were specifically requested, probably because of that little routine you did earlier on the bar. Which I still do not approve of for safety's sake! All I need is a broken bottle and a stupid customer." Her forehead relaxed as she leaned forward on her forearms. She met Rae's eyes. "Think about it? Please?" Suzie stood and squeezed Rae's shoulder.

"I'll talk to Bernie, okay? But no promises." Rae went back to counting her till. What was *with* today? First, Derek's thing, then Jacob-freaking-Hunter called her eye candy, and he snags Derek's card from her…now this?

"Is it a full moon tonight?" she asked aloud to the room.

"No," Kendra laughed, "but I'm guessing there was a high roller in VIP tonight. There's two Benjamins in here…one with my name in black marker, and one with yours."

"You have *got* to be kidding," Tessa whined, looking up from wiping off tables.

"Look, Tessa…I was working here for like two years before I got to work VIP," Rae soothed. "Give it time, huh? Your turn will come."

The younger woman stormed around as she collected remaining bottles from tables and pitched them into a large trash bin so hard, they shattered.

At 6:59 a.m. the next day, Rae stepped through the studio's back door, moaning in relief at the blast of air conditioning that welcomed her. She waved through the window of Bernie's office as she started toward studio four.

"Rae, can you come in here?" Bernie called.

"What's up?" Rae asked, worried by the serious look on her boss's face.

"Have a seat," Bernie replied, gesturing to the leather chair opposite his desk. He shuffled papers and smoothed a hand over his bald head as she did so, then steepled his fingers.

"You know we've been getting fewer clients, what with so many people able to use their computers to make albums at home and—"

Rae's stomach dropped, and she sensed what was coming. His awkward delivery wasn't softening the blow.

"Say it," she grumbled.

"I've got to cut the studio's hours by half, and the staff, too." Bernie sighed. "I would've kept you if I could, but I had to go by seniority to be fair."

"When, uh…do…that is…uh…" she stammered.

"End of today, but everyone gets a month's severance out of my own pocket," Bernie murmured, handing her a check without meeting her eyes.

She barely heard the rest of his words as she clutched her things and stood, nodding as if everything he was saying was reasonable and sane. She caught bits here and there about managers being bumped down to techs and offers for references as she stuffed the check into her pocket and headed out of the room to find Derek.

"Hey, Rae," Derek hailed with a broad smile as she entered the control room. He was pressing bits of masking tape under the controls, writing in what part they would play for the recording with his left hand and waving at her with his right.

"Gimme a minute or ten to feel human, Big D," Rae mumbled, setting her gear on the floor.

He gave her a glance then said nothing else for an hour.

Rae busied herself hooking up the leads trying to not to think about the rug that had been pulled out from under her. Once they'd completed soundcheck, she sat down with her bass to warm up. The strings were hard against her fingertips, the vibration keeping her present in the moment. Muscle memory led her straight into one of her favorite bass driven melodies, an older disco funk song by Rebel Gloss.

She stretched her fingers when she'd finished. The music had calmed her breathing and taken her to her happy place like it had when she lost her parents. This was nothing more than a job, she reminded herself. And not her only one. She would be fine.

"Got any notes?" she questioned.

Derek's jaw hung open, exposing all his teeth to her. He blinked. "I…damn, Rae! You been holdin' out on me!" He whistled.

"Holdin' out?" Rae's brows wrinkled.

"You look trashed, girl…like somebody locked you in a trunk and drove you out to the desert…but your warm-up was fire," he expounded.

Rae didn't much like compliments, but when it came to her playing, she knew deep down she had earned that.

"Been playing since I could hold a bass," she confessed with a shrug. "Daddy taught me. As for looking trashed…half the staff got laid off including me." As the words left her mouth, she realized how they could be interpreted, and she backpedaled. "You'll get a hundred percent from me, don't worry."

The muscles of his jaw twitched. She could see the questions in his eyes.

His concern made her eyes gloss over, and she swallowed the emotions back and plucked a string absently. "Can we just…not talk about it yet?"

He sucked in a breath and nodded, slapping his knee sharply. "Sure, man. Of course."

After discussing his outlines, they began working out the rhythms. In no time, they had a good basic line for each of the two songs and laid down the tracks.

Two hours later, her fingers were raw, and Derek was laid out, spinning slow circles in the desk chair.

"Alright, I need a break," Derek grumbled. He stopped spinning with one toe to the carpet when he faced her. "Pizza?"

She nodded curtly as she fiddled with tuning her instrument. She expected him to whip out his fancy phone and start ordering, but he remained still, eyes trained on her.

"Rae…about Bernie and the studio…"

"No, Big D…it was fair. He went by seniority. A couple of the managers got demoted to tech and their secretaries…" Her chest felt tight at the thoughts, and she waved it off, forcing a bright lilt into her voice. "Anyway, he gave me a month's severance and tried to get us all jobs at other studios, but they're doing layoffs too, so…" Rae shrugged.

"Well, I'm paying you scale for the bass work, and if I need you tomorrow it'll be the same," he insisted.

It felt like charity, which she hated accepting, but necessity forced her to allow it.

"And," he continued, emphasizing the word and leaning forward in the chair, "if I get this gig Monday, I'll need you…please?"

Overwhelmed by his kindness and tired, her eyes filled with tears, and her throat tightened. Rae's head dipped in ascent, and with a hard swallow, she scrubbed her eyes then gestured to his phone.

"Right, food." Derek smiled crookedly.

After they ate, they worked for another four hours before Derek demanded another break. Rae was starting to flag, and she timed her yawns behind his back. She fished an energy drink out of her duffle before she sat next to him at the mixing board.

"Well, damn," she sighed, flexing her fingers. "I haven't played this much all in one go since…well, it's been a long time."

He turned her wrist to display her palm under the console light then released it. "Here…I have some ointment," Derek offered. He tossed her a small tube from the satchel on his other side.

As she worked on her hands, Rae scanned the room.

"You know," she announced, "part of me is kind of glad about getting laid off. Is that bizarre?" She ran a hand across her forehead.

"I don't have enough information to answer that," he deferred.

"It's just…barring you, Luke, and Bernie, everyone here were just…asshats on parade, you know? After almost three years, the only time I enjoyed being here was when you came in. I started wondering if I should go back to Tulsa. Like, maybe I'm not cut out for Hell-A."

"Don't be stupid," Derek scoffed. "You can't go! Who'd put me in my place if you left? Peter? Leo? Hell, we sit around and puff up each other's egos."

Rae chuckled at the mention of former members of The Legends. "*Somebody* needs to keep your ego in check." She sighed, the humor going out of her as her thoughts continued spiraling. "I'm starting to wonder…what have I been working myself crazy over for it all to just…I don't know, Big D. I'm 36, and I still don't know what I want to be when I grow up!"

The corners of his mouth hinted at a smile. "Well for now, you're my go-to bass player and if—"

"*When*, dammit!" Rae corrected. "Maybe I'm supposed to bust you down when you get out of hand, but not letting you shit in your own cereal is also part of my job, nimrod!"

Derek held up his hands defensively. "Yes, ma'am," he countered.

Standing, Rae crossed the room and touched the door handle connecting the control and tracking rooms. "Seriously, man! In all the time I've known you, this is the best stuff I've heard you do!"

"Okay, okay," he laughed, throwing his hands up in surrender. "*When* I get this gig Monday, I'm gonna insist you back me. I won't be able to pay you much over scale, but…" Derek shrugged.

"So, no upping my schedule at *The Oubliette*? I gotta pay—"

He drew back, frowning. "Not only no, but *hell* no," he insisted. "I mean…you got a month's severance, right? I need you available."

"And it'll take two to three weeks before my next paycheck starts at the next job, and I still gotta eat."

Derek's expression remained unphased by her plea.

She sighed. "Look, there's a private party at *The Oubliette* on Thursday afternoon I gotta take. My girl Kendra and I were specially requested. Plus, I gotta do my regular hours. I'll give you two weeks after that to be on-call before I have to have something solid," Rae offered.

"Fair enough." Derek nodded. "Now let's bust this bitch out." He gestured for her to get back to her bass, and she chuckled, obliging him. It was good to be recognized, and the way he was treating her amplified her need to please.

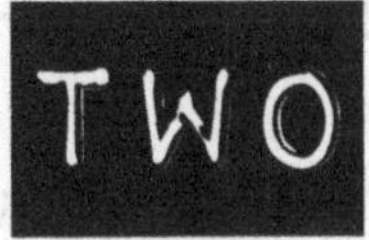

Jacob Hunter followed behind a young waitress as she led him to the table where he was meeting his collaborators. He kept his head down in hopes of not being recognized. After more than a decade in the spotlight, he had adopted an unhealthy obsession with privacy. He'd had his clothes ripped straight from his body more times than he could count, and his scalp tingled at the mere thought of all the hair that had been yanked out of his head over the years.

His new agent, Meyers, hadn't seemed happy about his request to schedule lunch on a Monday afternoon to meet a potential producer. Part of him wished they could've met at the agency in a conference room with a tray of deli sandwiches. But Meyers had insisted on treating him to lunch. And then, out of the blue, he got an email the night before saying his agent wouldn't even be at the lunch. He pushed his frustrations aside and followed the hostess to his table.

He sighed relief when none of the other patrons paid him any attention. So far, the only person who had shown signs of recognition was the hostess.

"This is your table," the young lady pronounced, beaming at him as she motioned to the table where another woman was seated.

He thanked the hostess quickly, relaxing when she darted away. He pulled out his chair, evaluating the impeccably dressed woman in a pale purple suit. The lines followed sharply and modestly around her body, making her look a little square, and certainly formal. He almost felt underdressed in his loose jeans and casual t-shirt. At least he'd grabbed his pinstriped sports coat on the way out the door.

She stood and smiled broadly, extending her hand.

"Mr. Hunter." His name on her lips was more a statement rather than a direct address, and he chuckled at the formality. "I'm Grace, Mr. Meyer's assistant."

Jacob squeezed her hand firmly without breaking her fingers. She was trying very hard to appear professional; she must be new to the industry. She looked harmless though, and he appreciated the effort on his behalf.

"Pleasure to meet you. And please, call me Jacob. I'm not old enough for a mister yet," he offered before taking a seat.

"I'm so glad you were able to make the meeting. Unfortunately, Mr. Meyers was detained out of town and won't be back till tomorrow. He asked me to take his place introducing you to the producer since this was a casual introduction."

"Excellent," Jacob answered, chuckling inside at the thought of this being Grace's casual attire. "It's about time Meyers got himself an assistant. The man overextends himself, and sometimes, I'm not totally sure he gets what I'm saying anyway. Age difference and all."

He shook the linen napkin into his lap and settled his silverware in its correct placement on the table. Friends called him fastidious; he called himself refined. He caught the assistant watching his routine with the hint of a smile and noted her silverware was seated as properly as his.

"I'm incredibly grateful to be working for him," Grace added. "LA is not a city where languishing without work favors anyone."

Jacob nodded his agreement. "So, you're new, I've guessed. How long have you been with Meyers?"

Her cheeks and ears went slightly pink, and she fidgeted with her menu. "What gave me away?" Grace asked.

He chuckled. "You've been nothing but professional, but the last time I saw a suit at a meeting like this, there were lawyers involved." He suppressed an involuntary shiver at the memory.

"Oh no," she mumbled, folding her menu and drawing it into her lap.

She looked lost, and Jacob scrambled to reassure her. "It's okay. You look very professional. I'm not used to anyone taking us all so seriously anymore. It's refreshing."

She smiled, the pink on her cheeks deepening. She glanced at her iPhone, and a frown twisted her mouth. "It's lovely to see someone so prompt, but it appears that perhaps our…" Her eyes darted past him, lips stopping mid-word. Her professional mask slipped as something akin to horror passed over her features. Before his brows could finish furrowing, her serene expression returned, smoothing out her face.

Jacob followed her gaze across the room near the entrance, seeing a man of average height with a buzz cut. From the way he seemed to be gesturing toward the hostess, Jacob assumed he was looking for them.

"Never mind. It looks like our producer has arrived," Grace said, confirming Jacob's theory. Her eyes were glued to the newcomer as he approached.

They stood as he arrived, and she extended a hand to him. "Welcome, Mr. Reed," she greeted.

The man looked momentarily confused as he returned her handshake. "Thank you," he mumbled, adjusting a small satchel over his shoulder.

Before he could introduce himself, Grace took charge. "Allow me to introduce Jacob Hunter. Jacob, this is Derek Reed, the producer that Mr. Meyers wanted you to meet."

Derek swallowed visibly, staring at their hostess as though Jacob wasn't there. He held out a hand blindly toward Jacob.

Jacob glanced at it suspiciously, wondering if these two had a history. The concern evaporated as Derek turned his full attention back to Jacob as they shook. He had a perfect handshake, Jacob noted.

"Great to meet you," Derek replied.

The three sat, Jacob and Grace politely ignoring Derek's fumbling as he arranged himself and his satchel.

As soon as he appeared to be relatively settled, Grace spoke again. "As I've told Jacob already, Mr. Meyers was unable to make today's meeting, and he sent me to facilitate. I understand that Jacob is looking for a producer, and Mr. Meyers thought that Mr. Reed might be a good fit."

Sunlight from the overhead window caught the producer's hair, turning it fiery red as he turned to the woman in charge. "Please, call me Derek," he insisted.

Derek reached for his bag again, smoothly extracting a digital music player complete with a set of studio-grade headphones. "I brought a sample of some things I've been working on lately." He held the items out to Jacob.

Modest, I like it, Jacob thought. He's prepared and eager, and confident. If his work is good, I can definitely work with this guy.

Jacob slid the headphones over his ears as Derek tapped the screen on the player. A sonic playground of melodies and beats enveloped him, and he closed his eyes, tuning out all other stimuli. After a moment, he noticed his breathing had synced with the rhythm, fingers unconsciously tapping out the unusual, but organic timing.

This was the sound he wanted for his next album but hadn't been able to describe. It was part pop, part funk, part dance music. He understood its core, enjoying the twists and turns from verse to chorus. He'd heard what he needed and slid the headphones off.

"Wow! What *is* this?" he questioned. He realized he sounded a bit keen and pulled back. Maybe this guy was only taking the meeting as a favor to Meyers. Maybe he didn't want or need new clients.

Derek shrugged, absently winding the cords and tucking the whole lot into his bag then relaxed in his chair. "I was noodling. Sometimes I get these ideas in my head, and they don't let me rest till I get them out. I find that in this industry, it's hard work that sets you apart from the rest. And a little talent helps, too."

"I completely understand that," Jacob commiserated. "There are times when I look up and it's 3 am, and I completely lost track of time. Forgot to eat, haven't talked to anybody. I'm completely absorbed." His mind was still whirling with the demo tracks he'd heard, and a feeling of camaraderie settled over him.

"Exactly." Derek snorted softly and tilted his head. "Granted, Rae, my studio tech likes to remind me by locking up the studio and turning off the lights."

Jacob laughed at the notion. He'd been almost locked in a studio more than once. It was why he had installed one in his home to avoid such tedious schedules. He was already imagining how Derek's sample would sound on his home system.

"Dude, that music's got some chops. I like that electro trance direction you were heading. I've been wanting to experiment more with that myself."

"I am pretty open to all kinds of music. I've worked with pop, hip hop, EDM, K-pop, you name it. I'm inspired by all kinds of music. I like to think my flexibility is an asset. I truly believe that each artist has their own unique sound, and I want to showcase that."

"He's so modest," Grace cut in. "He's worked with Matte Boys, Sherry Halo, AndrEa, and a bunch of others."

Jacob had forgotten for a moment that anyone else was at the table. He glanced at the administrator on his right. The names she dropped were big, and he wondered why the producer hadn't dropped them himself. He knew them all by reputation but hadn't had the opportunity to work with them.

"That's right," Derek agreed softly.

Jacob wanted to know more, especially about the actor Grace had named. "Sherry Halo, really? Wait—she did that telethon for the homeless. You were in on that?"

"Actually, I *was* that, but I don't like to admit it. I'm proud of the work we did, but the admin side of it went totally south. It didn't do what we'd hoped it would."

It had been a massive collaboration enlisting a number of Hollywood's elite, recorded and produced at a breakneck pace. He wondered how the modest man before him had started such a big project. "How did you manage that?"

Derek shrugged. "I ran into her at some function. I hardly even remember what it was anymore. We got to chatting about paying our dues, and it sparked the idea for her. She's a nice woman."

Jacob's mind reeled. "I remember that, man," Jacob mused. "We were supposed to be involved—you know, me and the Harmonizers. But we were so busy with the group and stuff, we couldn't pull ourselves away."

"I vaguely remember hearing about that. We pulled it off, but it would've been better with you. I wanted to do something big, but I think we lacked the right promotional structure."

"I hear that. Know a lot more about it than I'd like to," he sympathized. After his solo career didn't reach the heights he'd planned, it took a long time to understand that it was the marketing, not his talent that let the project down. Jacob swallowed back the rising bitterness. "It's amazing how something so pure and right as music can be spoiled by people who know nothing about it so quickly."

Derek nodded empathetically. "It's a crime."

His words confirmed the deal for Jacob. "Well, I don't wanna be a downer, especially considering this work you brought today. I feel like we might be speaking the same musical language. I'd like to schedule some time together. Ideally, I'd like to move kinda fast, and it sounds like that's in your wheelhouse. I've got a few tracks I've been kicking around—some lyrics, but it feels incomplete. Thought we could work on that and see if anything comes of it."

"That sounds great," Derek agreed.

Jacob's brain was already scheduling. He would be on a plane in a few hours to finish some legal obligations and do an interview with an up-and-coming blogger. He couldn't believe how far he'd fallen from *Rolling Stone* to this not-quite-a-celebrity interview. In moments, they were comparing calendars on their iPhones.

A waiter appeared to take their orders, and then, the war stories started. He was shocked at the similarity of their tales even though Derek's limelight had been a mere flash a decade before his. Before long, they were in a heated discussion about the latest specs on microphones, mixers, and more as they picked at their food. Jacob glanced at his cell phone and frowned.

"Hey, man. I've enjoyed meeting you. I think Meyers was right about us. I'd like to get this thing started. Let me give you my deets." He searched for something to write on and spotted Grace's leather-bound notebook sitting between them. He reached for it, glancing at their hostess. "May I?"

Brows thatched, Grace nodded. "Sure."

Unceremoniously, he pulled the pen from its elastic band and scribbled the details on a sheet before he ripped it out of her book and passed it to Derek.

"I hope you can read this. Mom always complained about my penmanship. Shoot me an email or a text, and we'll find some time next week or so to sit down at a studio together."

"I'll plan on it," Derek agreed, folding it neatly without looking at it. He extracted a paper CD sleeve from his bag. "If you'd be interested, I brought you a sample. And I left my card inside."

"Awesome!" Jacob exclaimed, snatching it from him greedily. This man was impressing him at every turn. It felt like magic. "I'm digging this, but I've got this plane to catch, and I have this thing about commitments."

Derek shook him off as they all stood. "Never apologize for your success."

Jacob held up the CD, waving it gently. "I'll have a listen on the plane. I hate to excuse myself, but if I don't get moving…" He turned first to Derek and extended his hand. "I'm looking forward to working with you." After a quick shake, he turned to Grace. "It was a pleasure meeting you. Tell Meyers I said you are always welcome to take care of my business. It's great to have you on the team."

She dipped her head, smiling politely. "He'll be pleased to know you're so happy with the firm."

Jacob took her hand, shaking it firmly without releasing it. "No," he corrected. "I mean, tell him that I liked working with *you*. You were the perfect facilitator. Meyers gets too involved. But don't tell him that last part." He patted her hand as he released it, flashing his celebrity smile and made a hasty exit.

His skin buzzed with excitement as he walked to his car, already humming what he could remember. Maybe he had finally found the musical partner he'd needed. The universe was sending him a message he was reading loud and clear. How else would the hot bartender at his friend's gig give him the card of the producer he had flown in to meet?

He thought of the vixen who had given him Derek's card as well. He hoped that song she'd been humming with her plush, red lips was on the CD in hand. His smile widened. Maybe, when he got back into town, he'd go back to *The Oubliette* and find her—take her out for dinner, dancing, and more if he was lucky.

THREE

Monday afternoon, Rae shifted from one foot to the other as she waited for Derek outside the bar he'd proposed. She peered around the corner near the minuscule parking lot in case he had somehow managed to sneak in without her seeing. She wished he had called her instead of texting, wanting to hear in his voice how his meeting went.

Suddenly, a pair of arms snaked around her from behind, lifting her off her feet.

"Holy crap!" she squeaked. It had to be Derek, she rationalized, recognizing the move. Wriggling out of the embrace, she whirled around and socked him lightly on the arm. "No sneaking up on me!"

"Sorry," he chuckled, sounding anything but as he led her to the building and held the door for her. "It was too perfect a setup."

She sent him to the bar for drinks while she grabbed a booth and settled in. She watched him leaning over the counter as he asked for drinks. He was well formed—sexy even. He was clearly excited. There had been a time she'd have entertained the thought of finding out what was beneath his skinny jeans, but the thought of it gave her the icks now. He was like the brother she never had. Almost fatherlike the way he looked after her at the studio.

She waved him over when he turned, hands full of drinks.

His deep blue eyes were wide, and he was chewing his lips. But the corners of his mouth kept inching up. He was buzzing with excitement as he set a draft beer, a vanilla screwdriver for her, and two shots of top shelf whiskey on the table. The glasses clinked as he slid into the opposite side of the booth.

Rae focused briefly on the mass of drinks in front of her. "Oh my!" she exclaimed. "This looks like a celebration." Touching a finger to the rim of her glass, she tasted her favorite vanilla vodka and grinned. It was nice to be known and spoiled.

Derek nodded. "Meeting went well, but more importantly…I have a *fan*," he informed her, picking up his beer by the neck and taking a swig to hide his grin.

Trust Derek to bury the lead, but she played along as he told her about the strait-laced assistant who had been a surprise replacement for his agent. As his hands gestured her shape and her suit, Rae bit her tongue. He may not know it yet, but he was already infatuated. For as many hours as they'd spent in the studio recording, it was interesting that he was prioritizing telling her about this stranger over the news they were here to celebrate.

He finally raised a glass to toast, and Rae lifted hers in solidarity.

"To getting attention and getting in with them." He slugged his whiskey shot as Rae stared at him.

The words pinged a familiar song in her brain, and she froze, drink forgotten between her fingertips. A lyric from Jacob Hunter's most popular solo song. Surely, he hadn't intended to imply the artist's identity. And if he did mean what she thought he meant, did that mean that the demo she'd taped her fingers for had seen the inside of Jacob Hunter's ears?

After a minute, Derek raised both eyebrows, "Were you planning to drink it? Or are you showing it off?"

Woken from her stupor, Rae slammed back the shot and set the empty glass next to his. She wanted to wipe the smug look off his face but couldn't formulate words. Why hadn't he told her?

Sipping her tall drink, another thought railroaded into the fore of her mind. He wanted her on the project; he needed her to keep cool. Nodding once, she folded her hands on the table, staring at him as her mental gears clicked into place. He had kept Jacob's identity a secret because he hadn't trusted her.

He held up both hands as if reading her mind. "Yes, okay? At first, I didn't tell you because I thought you'd mock me until the end of time. Then…I didn't want to jinx it," he grumbled.

She decided to skate over this spiraling issue of trust with her pseudo-sibling and switched tactics to put him in the hot seat. "So…this fan of yours, when do I get to meet her?"

"Never," he laughed, fidgeting and picking at the collar of his shirt. "I don't need the pair of you ganging up on me!"

"Cute?" she quizzed, sipping her drink.

"Yeah, but not my type. I mean, she was wearing a suit! A freaking lavender business suit! You know?"

Rae eyed him with a pensive smirk. "Your type?" She paused for effect, leaning into the table on crossed arms. "What is that, exactly? Sex-pots? Is it fulfilling or satisfying for more than fifteen minutes?"

"What? You think I should date someone like you?" He smirked.

"God no!" she laughed. "We'd kill each other in less than a day! And I get it to a degree." She gestured from his head to his toes. "You're hot. You're youngish…sex should be fun. But I meant that maybe you should widen your parameters. Unless…fifteen minutes of happy is all you need."

"Oh tell me about all your *parameters*, Miss Advice?" he shot back.

"Been keeping myself too busy to look since the divorce." She smiled ruefully. "And I don't know. I guess I don't want to give someone that kind of emotional access anymore, you know?" She shivered, remembering the night she'd caught her ex-husband cheating. She popped her neck and raised an eyebrow.

Derek emptied his beer bottle and set it down with a forced belch, then changed the subject. "Well, I'll make sure to keep you busy with this Hunter project," he promised, clearing his throat. "And any other project that comes my way. Bass especially, but also tech work. At least that'll be one less thing to worry about."

"You don't have to—"

"I know," he cut in. "Let me do this, alright?"

Rae nodded and, finishing her drink, gestured to the bar for another.

In the quiet between rounds, her brain offered her a series of images of Jacob in various states of dress from his lifetime of media before plummeting her into the pit of unworthiness her ex had created.

Derek couldn't know how she felt. Telling him would only validate his reservations about her working with Jacob. She could be professional, she vowed. She could stare at her bass and perform without raking her eyes over the singer's tight body. But it wouldn't matter if she did ogle him unabashedly. He wouldn't want her anyway. There was a sick relief in that.

Unwilling to wallow in her thoughts, she changed the subject. By the time Derek had settled the bill for the night several hours later, Rae was sufficiently lubricated with vanilla vodka to answer when Derek asked what "Rae" was short for. They were leaning against the building and partly on each other as they waited for the cab the bar had called for them.

"Desirae," she told him then frowned as he snorted.

He coughed out, "Stripper," behind his hand. "Why don't you go by your middle name?"

"Sage?" she supplied, realizing only too late that she'd now divulged her full legal name. She and vanilla vodka needed to have a chat about this. "Not only no, but hell no. And don't tell anybody, for God's sake." She wagged her finger inches from his nose.

"Desirae Sage Duncan," he caroled. His face lit up, and he lurched closer. "DeeDee! Why not that? Why Rae?"

She scowled as the cab arrived.

Derek held the door for her before falling in behind her.

"Because," she groaned, drawing out the word and dropping her head on his shoulder. "DeeDee is at least as strippery as Desirae. And…my ex called me that. My parents always called me their little Rae of sunshine."

"Alright then, Sunshine," Derek murmured. "Rae it is. I promise."

~ ♪ ~ JACOB ~ ♪ ~

Comfortably ensconced on the plane at cruising altitude, Jacob pulled out his laptop, plugged in his headphones, and inserted Derek's CD. He let the groove pull him in, appreciating it as a whole before he dissected it. He listened to it twice more before taking notes on the portable device. The intricacy and consistency of the rhythm excited all his senses, and the production values were far higher than he expected for a demo. Derek's style of composition suited his voice.

He had been thinking if he started small with a couple of singles, he might find his way into a full album again. After hearing the demo, he was ready to dive all the way in. Somewhere in his soul, a knot unraveled. Derek had the musical chops, and the connections to go with it. How had this guy never crossed his radar before?

The answer was simple: he'd assumed his team of trusted experts was on top of everything. When they told him they had promotions under control, he believed them. If the producer said his work was sub-par, he believed it. In hindsight, he saw that the label had intentionally botched his solo launch in favor of his band mate, Jason.

Someone he thought of as his brother stole all their attention: the tours, the stadiums, the record, the movie deals. He wasn't sure if he was more hurt by his younger colleague out-achieving him or the label that had dropped him like yesterday's news. He pushed the negative thoughts away and tuned himself back into the music pulsing through his headphones. He would do it right this time.

Derek's bassist had to stay, and he wanted the backing vocalists and synths, too. The drums sounded electronic, and he made a note to find someone. If he was lucky, he could find a session band to record that would also be open to touring if the album got that far. Jacob spent the rest of his flight sketching out plans for the album.

One of the songs on the demo was the one the bartender at Dante's gig had been singing! For the length of the song, he was lost in thoughts of coffee-colored eyes and wide, full lips as he pictured her curvy hips swinging to the music tantalizing his ears. He imagined dancing against those hips, letting her know just how hot he thought she was.

Once he'd checked into his hotel, Jacob researched Derek on the internet. He found clips from his old TV show, laughing at the past antics of his new producer. They had more in common than he realized. No wonder they had hit it off so easily. They shared a shorthand that could only come from having lived similar experiences.

Like Derek, he had cut his teeth as a teen in an ensemble group of actors, actresses, musicians, and dancers called The Tree House Kids. He missed a handful of them as well as his "brothers" from the Harmonizers. He tried calling first Danny, then Blake, but neither one answered. At least his new people made time for him, unlike the others.

His brain returned to the demo, playing it again. He needed to brainstorm with Derek. He found the producer's email from Meyer's meeting invitation and shot off a proposal for a lunch meeting on Friday.

~ ♪ ~ R A E ~ ♪ ~

In LA, Rae crawled out of bed and to the tub, filling it with scalding water as she peeled out of yesterday's clothes. The light from her digital clock lanced pain through her head, and she left the overhead lights off. She soaked in the dark until the pounding in her brain and the roiling in her stomach had subsided. Once dry, she slipped into a beige tank dress and dialed Red Dot to have them deliver Gatorade, saltines, and ibuprofen.

"I hate you, Derek August Reed," she whispered into the darkness of her kitchenette. It was his fault she'd drank like a twenty-year-old.

She tipped the delivery boy exceedingly well and spent the rest of the afternoon tiptoeing around her hangover. It wasn't until dusk that she looked at her phone to find Derek had texted. It was the most important single sentence she'd ever read.

> **Big D:**
> Jacob demands we use my bass player for his album.

She read the words a dozen times. They were simple enough on their own, but the idea they implied was too surreal to be believed.

She'd thought Derek was being kind, a good buddy, when he'd complimented her skill in the studio the day after she'd been laid off. However, when someone who didn't know her, wasn't in any way invested in her happiness, and was known for perfectionism, *demanded* she play bass on his album, it reignited her belief in herself. Her fingers flew over the phone, texting Derek for details about the meeting. Not a minute later, he called.

The ringer triggered the return of the headache she thought she'd conquered.

"Talk softly," she whispered. "I'm mostly recovered but my brain's still a bit tender. I haven't tied one on like that since…well, a long time ago."

"Heh, I understand," he chuckled softly. "I sweat the nasty out earlier."

"Huh, if I'm ever stupid enough to get that drunk again, I'll keep that in mind." She smirked, rolling onto her stomach.

"Anyway, we've got a brainstorming session with Hunter on Friday at lunch," Derek murmured. "I'm thinking the ball might get rolling Monday or Tuesday."

Rae veritably grunted her approval. She sat up sharply, wincing in pain and clutched her forehead briefly until the pain eased. The shock of this new project nearly shook her out of it, but the vanilla vodka's magic carried too stiff a punishment.

"We?" she repeated.

Derek laughed. "I was wondering if you'd catch that. Yes—he asked me to bring my bass player. Best to get introductions done early and make sure we can all work together before the project starts."

Rae was trying to wrap her brain around it. She frowned. "You think we won't get along?"

"No, didn't say that. It's always a good idea to introduce everyone early," he soothed.

Her glitchy brain began cobbling bits of information together. "So, he's back in LA? I thought he was out of town," she reasoned.

Derek paused. "Um, I don't know. I guess so. I guess we need to pick a place. I was a bit overwhelmed by how fast he responded. Lunch on Friday sounded like a great idea."

"Devil's in the details," she mumbled.

"I'll work out the plans with him and let you know. I'll pick you up if you want a ride."

Anything that involved Rae not extending effort was well-received.

"Great. What time?"

Derek faltered again. "Um, we didn't discuss that either. Lunch is you know…lunch time."

Rae found the energy to chuckle. "You need an assistant," she suggested. "One of you does. 'Cause you both suck at making plans."

"I guess I'm used to other people taking care of all that for me. They say lunch on Friday, and it comes with all the details. But I can manage them. I'm not completely incompetent. I'll send him an email tonight. You go get some rest. Keep hydrated, and I'll get you the details. I thought you'd wanna know."

In the dark, alone in her place, Rae smiled to the room. "I did. That's exciting. My ego thanks you."

"It's welcome."

The phone had barely disconnected before she flopped onto her back, kicking her feet in the air with excitement. Screw her remaining hangover! This was worth the ache! Her heart clenched, thinking how proud and delighted her dad would be, and she sighed wistfully. Maybe angels did exist, and her parents were still looking out for her.

FOUR

Nestled safely in a Boston hotel room, exhausted from the day's travels and road food, Jacob stared at an email from Derek. When he had proposed lunch, he hadn't thought it through any farther than picking a day, but now staring at Derek's message, he grumbled at himself for not thinking of the details. Derek had suggested a Thai place on Sunset, but which one? Sunset was a long street, and he wasn't familiar with every restaurant it hosted. And what time was lunch? He rubbed his eyes sleepily. He was sure he did not have the brainpower to handle this now. But he knew who would.

He grabbed up his cell, scrolling to find Meyers in his contacts. He was pleased when the agent answered.

He got straight to the point. "Meyers, my man. Thanks for hooking me up with Reed."

"It's working out then?"

If he didn't know better, he'd think his agent sounded surprised. "Absolutely. In fact, it's so good, I want to meet again. Could you set that up? We've talked by email, but we're no good at making meeting arrangements."

The agent made a knowing sound. "We can take care of that for you. Why don't you call the office and talk to my assistant. She'll make it happen."

Jacob sighed relief. "Great, that'd help a lot. I appreciate you letting us borrow her."

"Not a problem. That's what she's there for. By the way, how'd she do at the meeting today? She said everything went well."

"It did. She had a knack for details and kept us on track. Very professional."

"Glad to hear it. You know how it is with new employees. Always good to hear feedback."

"Yeah, she worked out great. Knew a lot about the producer too, which was extremely helpful, 'cause I gotta say, I'd never heard of him before."

"Really?" Meyers questioned. "Well, that's why you keep me on as an agent."

"Yeah, it is," Jacob replied. "Listen, I gotta go, but thanks for the help. I'll call the office. How late is Grace there?"

Meyers hesitated for a moment. "Oh, she's always available. Let me text you her cell so you can text or call. She's always checking her messages."

"Perfect," Jacob added, and the phone dinged a moment later. "Got the text. Thanks. Talk to ya later." Without any further pleasantries, he hung up, dialing the phone number. It took three rings to get an answer. As Jacob was preparing to leave a voice message, a harried Grace answered.

"Hello?" she gasped.

"Hi, is this Grace?"

"Yes, it is," she replied. "How may I help you?"

"Grace, this is Jacob Hunter. We met at lunch on Friday."

"Yes, sir. I remember you. How can I help?"

"Well, I need your help setting up another lunch for me and Derek…and his bass player. You did such a great job at lunch that Derek and I are going to pursue this project. However, it's become incredibly clear to me that neither of us have your skill for arranging lunch meetings." He rubbed his forehead, some of the day's tension releasing.

"Glad I could bring something to the table. Do you know when you want to meet?"

"This Friday lunch for three people," Jacob replied, relieved that someone had agreed to do work he was simply too lazy to tackle himself.

"No—four with you. See? I can't even tell you who's going to be there," he groaned. Did Grace need to be there? It seemed rude to ask her to plan and not invite her. Besides—she'd been so helpful the first time.

She chuckled as his thoughts rambled. "It's not a problem," she assured. "I'm happy to help."

And he believed her. She proceeded to ask all the right questions, including "dietary restrictions." He would never have thought of that on his own. She promised to make all the arrangements and send details by email.

"So you'll have it all in writing," she finished.

"Spectacular," he replied. "I appreciate it. We've traded like four emails, and we couldn't get it done. It's nice to have it all taken care of."

"You're in luck. I excel at lunch," she teased. "I'll have that for you this evening. I'm actually in the car right now, and—"

"You're driving?" he interrupted, horrified. "Hang up right now. No sandwich is worth risking your life for. I'll look for your email later tonight." Without waiting for a reply, he ended the call. The idea of using a phone while driving spiked his anxiety.

He paced for nearly half an hour, checking his phone every few minutes. He had no idea how long she would be on the road, or how long it would take to make the reservation and send the email.

He began plotting what they would talk about Friday. What if Derek didn't have an appropriate drummer or guitarist? Maybe that's why he'd phoned it in with the machines. They'd need to hold auditions. Maybe Grace could set that up too. Meyers would definitely be able to provide him with some candidates.

A polite text requesting a call as soon as she was not operating a motor vehicle calmed his nerves. His phone rang almost immediately. What sorcery was this?

"Grace? Not driving?" he asked, answering with a big smile stretching his face.

"No, sir. How can I help?"

"I need a drummer and a guitarist." He sighed. "I know you're new and all, but you knew an awful lot about Derek's music and, unless I miss my guess about you being a thorough kind of lady, mine, too. So, if you could get with your boss or someone and get me a list of about five musicians for each position that Derek and I could check out, I would be eternally grateful. Especially if we could have that list by Friday's lunch. Oh, and please call me something other than *sir*. That's…you know, my dad." He chuckled nervously. Why was he nervous?

"Mr. Hunter, I don't know how to…what I mean to say is, wouldn't you rather talk to Mr. Meyers about this?"

"Well, the last time I asked him for help he sent me to you," Jacob reasoned. "Figured I'd go straight to the source this time. Besides, he should have info on all his clients that you would have access to, right?"

"Well…yes, I…" she ventured carefully.

"Thanks, Grace, you're a gem! Remind me to buy your lunch when I see you on Friday!" Jacob grinned, hanging up.

~ ♪ ~ R A E ~ ♪ ~

Rae practically bounced into *The Oubliette* Thursday night for the special party she and Kendra would be hosting.

"GURL!" Kendra called, swatting her towel in Rae's direction.

Barely skirting the faux assault, Rae giggled, jogging out of harm's way. "Gotta make those tippies," Rae replied, throwing her hip sassily to one side. She straightened and shrugged. "Studio laid me off."

She struck a pose, showing her costume to advantage. Her pigtail braids brushed across her exposed flesh, intended to draw eyes down her body. A tank style corset cradled her goods like a pair of white chocolate bon-bons, and she felt like a display case. The outfit was finished off by a pair of red leather hotpants. Her severance pay would only cover expenses for a month, so she had resorted to changing up her wardrobe as a last resort opportunity to boost tips. She looked like a tramp next to Kendra's tasteful cleavage.

Kendra squeezed her around the shoulders. "Oh, honey. I'm so sorry. I didn't know it was so bad over there."

"Me either," Rae retorted with a scowl.

Rae swore that Suzie danced out of her office at the words. All of the manager's teeth were sparkling between her curled lips as she clapped her hands. "Did I just hear the sweet news that your availability opened up?"

"Don't get too excited," Rae scoffed. "My buddy Derek has booked all my free time to work on a project for him as tech and bassist."

Suzie's face fell, then looked confused. "You play?" she asked.

"Rae'll call me a liar, but she's one of the best you'll ever hear," Kendra piped up, grinning. "Glad you plucked up to play for someone other than your mirror and me!"

"Kiki…" Rae warned. If she had known Kendra would spill her secrets, she'd have never played for her.

"Rae Rae," Kendra challenged, crossing her arms over her chest.

"Anyway," Suzie sighed, waving the pair to the bar. "It's all one tab, by the way. Some industry thing."

Nodding her understanding, Rae scooched behind the bar, dropping her bag into a safe cranny out of sight. "Will there be entertainment?"

"Not tonight," Suzie answered. "And I'm going to schedule you for more hours next week."

"Don't," Rae begged. "I don't want to have to bail on you. I have a meeting tomorrow to see what Derek has planned. Let me just get through that first, okay?"

Shaking her head, the manager frowned. "Another musician. Why are they all musicians?" she grumbled as she walked away.

Sharing a laugh, Kendra and Rae began prepping glasses and sundries, working around each other with the ease that only time and experience can produce.

"So, do you know the artist he's working with yet?" Kendra grinned.

"Technically…sort of?" Rae giggled. "We officially meet tomorrow for lunch even though I've served him here." If he had called her *eye candy* at Dante's gig, what would he call her now? Heat crept up her bodice and made her neck and jawline itch.

"Okay, hoe. What aren't you telling me?" Kendra demanded.

"Can you keep a secret?" Rae asked, suddenly serious.

Kendra squeezed a bar rag between her palms and inched in close. Her brown eyes were wide over her berry lips. "Of course!"

"Cool, me too," Rae laughed, dodging a playful slap. She scooted a foot away, dragging the cutting board with her as she finished slicing limes. "Seriously? I don't want to jinx it, okay? Even just being a session player on this could open a ton of doors. Maybe even get me an agent."

"Alright," Kendra accepted. "You'll tell me when you can." Her knowing smirk looked more like an order than a concession.

Twenty minutes later, the private party descended on them, and it was nothing but work until 2 a.m. when the last of the party goers exited the building and cleanup began. She had hoped when Suzie said she and Kendra had been requested for a special event that Jacob Hunter or Dante had been the instigator. It had turned out to be an unknown exec. He tipped both of them generously, but as part of the tab at the end of the night which meant everything was taxable. When she crawled into bed at 4 a.m., she wondered how much longer bartending was going to work for her.

She had a limited number of years where all it took was a pair of laces and a metal cage to look twenty again. She was an excellent bartender with an excellent memory and stellar people skills. But that didn't bring in tips like tits and ass. If she did well on this project with Derek and invested wisely, maybe she could start relying on her talents and not her looks.

A spiral of self-realization and a fitful sleep was all that stood between her and lunch with Jacob Hunter. Half her wardrobe was in piles across her futon and floor by the time Derek arrived to pick her up for lunch. He'd said the lunch was casual, so she'd opted for black capris, a green poet blouse, and sandals. She hadn't bothered with makeup besides a light gloss. More than that was for bar work or concerts.

Late Friday morning, Rae hurried down her apartment stairs toward Derek's car as she finished re-braiding her hair. She wrapped the elastic band around the bottom of her braid for the final time then pulled open the door of his BMW. She was keenly aware of his eyes on her as she settled into the passenger seat.

"You didn't dress up," Derek murmured as she buckled her seat belt.

"You said it was casual, Big D," she frowned. Her blouse flared over her lap, almost reaching her knees. She wasn't wrinkled, and she was perfectly dressed for an LA luncheon.

He pulled into traffic nearly silently. "Yeah, it is. I thought you'd wanna dress to impress."

"Why?" Rae blinked, confused. She wasn't there for eye candy—this was business.

"Never mind," he replied, turning on the radio.

They arrived at the restaurant five minutes early, and Jacob was already seated, sipping an iced water and perusing the menu. Rae took a deep breath and Derek squeezed her shoulder before leading her to the table.

She couldn't help but fix her gaze on Jacob, nearly swallowing her tongue when he looked up, his silvery blue eyes sparkling.

She exhaled in relief when his eyes lit on Derek, and Jacob set down his menu with a smile. He brushed his hands on the legs of his cargo pants and stood as they approached. His eyes flickered to her and away several times, and a tiny frown curved his lips.

Bet he thinks I'm a date, she thought.

His lack of recognition eased her tightly wound nerves a fraction.

Derek stopped in front of the table, placing Rae beside him with a hand in the small of her back. She froze to the spot.

God, Rae thought, *how can anyone be that handsome in an orange and pea-green plaid sweater-vest? That's obscene! Oh my Lord! His shoes match!* If he were her man, she would bring his wardrobe into the current century. She started dressing him up in her brain, trying out different style choices than golf nerd.

They shook hands.

"Jacob, hey man! This is Rae, my bass player," Derek introduced.

"You're a girl," Jacob blurted, cheeks flushing immediately.

Rae glanced at Derek. The producer's eyebrows were in his hairline.

Jacob squeezed her hand and drew himself to his full height, tucking his hands awkwardly in his pockets for a moment. "Sorry, I…it's just…uh…" he stammered, then rushed to pull out a chair for her.

"It's okay," Rae chuckled as she sat, less intimidated after his faux pas. "Rae's kind of an either/or name, and there's not a surplus of female musicians."

While the men seated themselves, a waitress appeared at their shoulder asking for drink orders.

Rae studied Jacob as he gave his order, fumbling and pointing to the menu finally for a light appetizer. She had never laid eyes on anyone so beautiful who looked so incredibly uncomfortable. In her experience, that level of discomfort came from a lack of self-confidence, and she knew that couldn't be his case. Assuming he was embarrassed by his earlier statement, she patted his shoulder once they were alone again.

"Really, it's okay, Mr. Hunter. You didn't offend me," she murmured when he wouldn't meet her eyes.

Jacob blew raspberries and waved her off. "Come on, now. Mr. Hunter's my dad," he retorted.

"Get used to it," Derek commiserated, looking up from his menu. "It was months before I could get her to stop calling me Mr. Reed at the studio."

"Hush it, Big D," Rae scolded. Heat raced up her jawline toward her scalp.

"I see it wears off eventually," Jacob noted. He looked between the pair. "How long have you been working together?"

Derek's lips pursed in concentration. "Geez, it feels like a lifetime because we have this great rapport...but it's only been...what? Two years, Rae?"

She nodded, mentally calculating the time from her divorce until present day. She even managed to keep the majority of the bitterness off her face. "That's about when I started at the studio. Derek is there a lot."

"I'm a little surprised you haven't invested in a home system," Jacob mused, eyeing Derek.

The producer shrugged. "I thought about it. Tried it, in fact, but the studio's not that expensive, and I don't have to use my mixing deck for a coffee table anymore. You know how apartments in LA can be a bit tight."

Rae hid a grin behind her hand as Jacob nodded sympathetically. She knew damn well he had no memory of cramped living conditions. Before the conversation could stray any further off course, their waitress reappeared with drinks and took their entrée orders.

"So," Derek began, pulling a notebook and pen from his trademark satchel. "We need what to get this ball rolling? Drummer and guitarist?"

Rae snatched the notebook and pen from him, poking out her tongue at his surprised face.

"Yeah, Grace sent me a list of prospective musicians, based on her knowledge of our work," Jacob replied, handing over his phone with the aforementioned email open.

"Grace?" Rae asked, tone carefully neutral as Derek accepted the proffered item.

"Our agent Meyers' assistant," Jacob answered. "I've highlighted a few I know by reputation."

Rae clapped her hands softly together and leaned toward Jacob. "Oho! Is that *the* Grace?" Rae cooed. "Your fan?" She poked Derek in the ribs, then peered at the screen.

"Hah!" Jacob exclaimed. "And here I thought she was just well-prepared! So, Grace is a fan of our Derek, is she?"

Rae liked the thought of having an "our" with Jacob, and she looked fondly at Derek in time to see his mouth gape.

She wasted no time jumping in, looking conspiratorially at Jacob. "And he thinks she's cute," Rae divulged.

"Well, she hid her fandom admirably," Jacob commented.

Rae didn't miss the flash of unease that clouded his face for a second. She guessed he must have had some extremely bad experiences with stalker fans, as big as his career with the Harmonizers had been.

"Only until you left, and then it all gushed out," Rae explained "Derek told me all about it after your meeting."

"Cute, huh?" Jacob grinned, bumping shoulders with Rae companionably. "Too bad she couldn't come today."

"Well, she's not his *type*," Rae stage whispered, holding a hand ostensibly to cover her mouth. She put it down as she continued, glancing distinctly away from both her table mates. "Although…you know what they say about those strait-laced girls…" she trailed off then, seeing the sour look on Derek's face, and changed the subject.

She looked at the list on Jacob's phone more closely, reading names. "Wait, Joe Andrews? He's brilliant."

"Andrews come into Lakeshore?" Derek interrupted, frowning slightly.

Her brow furrowed, briefly surprised that she had to explain. "No. He played for Rebel Gloss a while, before Mike Rodgers came back," Rae replied, shaking her head sadly that they needed the explanation. "Anyway, for drums I recommend Joe Andrews. But, if you're gonna want him for touring, you'll need a stylist. He was a bit rough-looking last time I saw him live."

Jacob sat up a bit straighter and sipped his water. "Well, I was hoping that whoever cuts the album would be touring too," he mumbled. "Would you be okay with that? I mean, sharing a bus and stuff?"

Rae blinked, then looked over at Derek. Her? Go on tour? She was still getting used to the idea of being an LA session player and now she was being asked to go on tour?

"As long as I'm on whatever bus she's on," Derek insisted. "I'll take care of her."

Rae looked down at her hands and pressed her lips together, trying not to laugh. She had only known Derek for a few years now, but she knew him as the talented pro sitting beside her. But the earnest promise to look after her reminded her of the boy from The Legends all those years ago who had needed someone to look out for him.

Jacob's face contorted into a frown before his features smoothed out. "Are you two…" Jacob trailed off.

Rae understood him perfectly and sneered at the thought. "To clarify, he's like a brother to me so, ewww," Rae retorted, shuddering.

Derek's matching shiver drew a chuckle from his client.

"Glad you are in agreement," Jacob mumbled.

The server delivered Jacob's panang beef, Derek's grilled seafood, Rae's masaman beef, an order of deep-fried purple yams, and pork spring rolls. After she left, the three spent a couple of minutes inhaling the savory scents before tucking into their meals.

"So, I was thinking maybe Monday we could hold auditions for the other two band members," Jacob mumbled around a yam, hastily chewing and swallowing. "Real jam-sessions if Rae doesn't mind joining in." A trail of oil ran over his lip onto his chin, and he swiped at it with a napkin.

Rae hid a grin behind her hand. There was absolutely no reason for the warm fuzzies that welled up in her throat as he sucked down his food, and yet, here she was, trying not to blush. "Yes, yes. I'd be happy to," she replied.

"Money," Derek agreed.

Rae scratched down the plans as she ate as the two men tossed ideas back and forth rapid fire. Despite her lunch getting cold, a grin curved her lips as they flew from concept to concept. She felt Jacob watching her intently as she did and forced herself not to fidget.

"You guys need a secretary," Rae interjected when both men paused to eat while their food was still warm. Setting her pen down, she flexed the fingers of her right hand. "Or an app on your phones to record conversations."

"Sorry," Jacob blushed. "Guess we got caught up in the moment."

"It's cool," she murmured. "My fingers need a break, is all."

"I think we've taken it about as far as we can without the rest of our band," Jacob announced. "Put your pen away before you run out of paper," he teased.

"Thank you, *Master*," Rae laughed, stretching her fingers for another moment before folding her notes away into her bag.

Jacob smiled, setting down his fork. "I think this is going to be a lot of fun. I think we all get along great so far."

Derek nodded avidly, placing his napkin on the table and grinning mischievously. "Speaking of getting along…my buddy Peter and his wife are havin' a cook-out tomorrow. You should both come."

"Peter?" Rae gasped, eyes wide. Was he inviting them to a Legends party? After two years of begging? "As in, Peter Day? Is Leo gonna be there, too?"

"Yes, that Peter," Derek replied. "And I think Leo's still in the Apple."

He turned to Jacob. "Do you think we could get Meyers to loan Grace to us? Rae's right about us needing an admin. We can't have our bass player ruining her grip taking notes. Maybe we can charm her away from Meyers."

Rae burst out laughing. "Charm her out of her *attitude*?" Rae waited to see if Derek caught the reference to one of The Legend's more "lurid" songs. One that he took lead vocals for.

Derek blinked, mirroring Jacob's confused expression.

"Are you going to *indulge her fantasies so fleeting*?" Rae squealed as she quoted another Legends lyric, covering her mouth and biting down on her thumb. This helped stall the laughter bubbling in her throat, but it did nothing to stop excited tears from squeezing out the corners of her eyes.

Derek groaned. "Please forgive her. She likes to mock my past with obscure song lyrics from when I was a teenager."

Jacob shook his head. "Not cool, man. We all had to start somewhere." He turned to Derek. "Where did you start again?"

"*Only Legends need apply*," Rae squeaked, laughter pealing from between her lips. She was about to break out into one of their songs, but the expression on her friend's face warned her off.

A growl emanated somewhere from the back of Derek's throat. "I got my start as a member of The Legends. We used to wear shirts that said, '*Only legends need apply.*'"

"That's funny, dude!" Jacob chuckled. "You'd be surprised at some of the stuff I had to do for the Tree House Kids. It's a different scene when you're trying to be a teen pop star."

Rae quieted as Derek cut her a sharp glance. "But getting back to the subject at hand—maybe we should seriously consider *hiring* Grace away from Meyers."

Jacob gave a slight nod. "I'm not sure how I feel about that. She's been great so far, but are you sure you want a fan working so closely with you?"

Rae recoiled at the insinuation. "Plenty of bands do it. Fans are the most loyal employees you'll ever find."

"Whoa!" Jacob held up his hands defensively. "All I meant was that fans aren't usually objective."

"That depends on the fan!" Rae continued.

"I hadn't given it much thought. I think of her as my agent's secretary, you know?" Derek clarified.

Jacob nodded. "Yeah, true. We'll think about it. Maybe we should get to know her before we decide. If we tour, we're going to need someone to coordinate. I detest tour plans. I've seen how much work is involved. And I guess it'd be good to have someone who thinks like a fan to avoid some of the scams and protect our privacy."

"Makes sense," Derek replied. "It's up to you. We know she'll stay in the loop as long as we get Meyers to approve it. I mean, we *can* be pretty needy, and he has too many other clients to be on call for little old us."

"You'll probably have to hire her away from him if it gets to a point where we need her a lot," Rae interjected. She nearly choked on her tongue at the use of the word *we*. No one seemed to notice as the conversation continued.

"Well, we can cross that bridge when we come to it," Jacob replied, effectively ending the discussion. He looked to Derek. "Hey, can you email me those details for your friend's party? It's been a while since I got to hang out somewhere. It sounds nice."

"Sure, man. Not a problem. In fact, I'll copy Grace on the email."

"Whoa, that's secretary speak," Jacob teased. "Yeah, get her in on it. It's always a good idea to get to know people before you hop into bed with them."

Rae burst out into nervous laughter at the thought of being in bed with Jacob. Damn him for being gorgeous as hell. To her good fortune, Derek sounded like he was choking, and she realized delightedly that he must've been thinking of hopping into bed with his fan.

She squeezed his arm to bring him around then patted his shoulder. "That's a proverbial bed, Big D," Rae clarified. "We're teasing you. You're a big, strong guy. You can take it."

Derek did not seem to appreciate the gesture according to the fiery scowl he shot her direction before plunking his napkin on the table beside his empty plate.

Jacob smirked, then pushed himself to his feet. "It was good to see you again, Derek. Nice to finally meet the bass player and put such a pleasant face with the name." Jacob looked at Rae first, shaking each of their hands in turn. "Got a few things to get done today, but we'll get that jam session together before the end of the week, you think?"

"Sure, man. Let's get this project moving before we lose our hot iron," Derek replied.

"Cool, me too. See you tomorrow. Text me those party deets!"

Jacob took his leave, and the moment his back was turned, Rae laid herself full out across the table. "He's just…beautiful."

Derek laughed softly, muffling the outburst behind his hand. "Maybe we shouldn't tell him you're such a fan," Derek suggested. "At least not till you've proved your point. He didn't seem too keen on fans."

She bristled instinctively, righting herself. "I take offense to his thought train," she stated. "It's so…narrow minded. Spoken like someone who's been far too isolated from the real world."

"Or someone who's had his fair share of run-ins with the loonies. You gotta admit that some of them can be little overzealous."

Rae considered his words before a grudging nod of agreement. She knew the stories about stolen pets and children harassed in their own backyards.

"Why you gotta go and side with him, man? I needed something to dislike."

"Besides that sweater vest?"

Rae snickered. "Are you sure you're not gay?"

Derek rolled his eyes. "One hundred percent not gay, despite living with four other guys as a teenager in a TV apartment with no bedrooms."

Rae pranced from foot to foot, skipping along beside him on the way to their parking spot three blocks away. Now that the stress of the meeting was over, the resulting nervous energy surged through her limbs, sparking childlike glee. She harbored her share of demons on any given day, but not today. Today she'd filled her head with Jacob Hunter, so close she could smell his cologne, stuffing things into his mouth.

~ ♫ ~ JACOB ~ ♫ ~

After their enormous lunch, Jacob had passed out on his couch. Upon waking, he paced his LA house, rehashing the entire conversation and plotting before he called Grace.

"Hello, this is Grace," the personal assistant answered.

"Grace, it's Jacob. Not driving I hope?" He intended the words to show his concern, but he realized belatedly that they had sounded more like a scolding.

"No, I'm not. How can I help you?"

He chuckled. He'd talked to Grace several times now, but he still wasn't used to the almost impersonal tone she spoke with, despite trying to ease her into a deeper level of comfort. "Well, I don't need anything. First, I wanted to thank you for that list of musicians you sent and for setting up the lunch. Perfect choice again. And I wanted to give you a heads up."

"Oh?" she asked.

"Yeah, I met with Derek and Rae his bass player today. And we hit it off. Props to Meyers again. And Derek invited us to this thing tomorrow, and we're hoping you can come. It'd be cool to get to know the people involved in this. It's not a work thing—it's a fun thing if you don't have plans." He wasn't sure why he was rambling. Something about her quiet demeanor made him want to fill in all the gaps.

"Um, yeah, I could do that," she replied. "Can you give me the when, where, why, and what?"

"That's what I like about you, Grace! Attention to detail—coordinating in your sleep. But I, uh, don't have them. Derek's gonna send you an email with the finer points." He leaned back onto his camel-colored leather couch, stretching lightly and pulling up a yoga video on the 97-inch television in his living room.

"That sounds great," she mumbled. "Thanks for the heads up."

"Sure. I think it's a good idea, you know? Have a little fun before all the work gets started."

"Right," Grace replied.

Jacob could almost see the smile in her voice as she continued.

"Well, see you there probably."

"Cool, see you later." Jacob smiled as he hung up.

He stood and stretched before playing the video and losing himself in the peaceful exercise. Years of dancing had strained his muscles and joints, but this was his go-to when his tensions were high. Completing the routine was virtually impossible, his mind wandering down melodic roads and feeling tiny branches of ideas splintering away. When he completed the routine, he scrambled to his feet and down to his studio to begin recording all the seeds he'd collected.

His phone rang several hours later. He recognized the number and made a mental note to save it. "Derek," he greeted. "What's up?"

"Hey, man. Sorry to interrupt, but I have a favor to ask if it's not too soon."

It was soon. "Well, I can try. What is it?"

"Well, because Pete's my best friend and all, I got roped into setting up early. Chairs and the like. And I was supposed to bring Rae, but I don't want her prepping. She'll be bored. So…" He trailed off, and Jacob thought he heard snickering in the background. However, he also heard the sound of a cash register beeping, so the laughter could've been anyone.

"Any chance you could pick Rae up on the way? It'd be a big help to me, and then you don't have to arrive alone. Win, win."

Jacob wanted to pick up Rae… He let the rest of the thought trail off before it found its way into his reply. "Sure. Text me the address."

"That's great, man! I owe you one!"

~ ♫ ~ **RAE** ~ ♫ ~

When the knock sounded on her door late Saturday morning, Rae was almost ready. Clad in jean shorts and a yellow tank top, she padded barefoot to answer. It was unusual for Derek to meet her at the door when he gave her a ride. He texted from the street to tell her to hurry up. He must need to use the facilities.

She prepared to wave him in as she opened the door, but in the producer's place, she found Jacob instead. His posture was relaxed as he stood tall with a friendly smile splitting his face.

The bratty remark she had for her pseudo-brother died on her lips, and she blinked in confusion. "I'm uh, not ready," she finally mumbled, mentally cursing herself for not at least greeting him first.

Jacob's smile waned. "Oh, well, um…Derek said he had to go early and asked if I could pick you up on my way. He didn't tell you?" Jacob asked, shifting from foot to foot.

Doing her best to collect herself, Rae attempted to shrug it off. "No, he didn't, but come on in. Have a seat." She left the door open as she went to tug her sheets off the futon and raise it for him to sit. "Sorry the place is a mess." She laughed nervously, clutching the sheets and their contents in a ball to her chest. "I never have guests."

"It's your Bat Cave. I can dig it," he offered with a smile as he sat.

"Soda? Water? OJ?" she called over her shoulder as she walked a whole five feet to enter what could only loosely be called a kitchen.

"Oh, juice sounds great," he replied. "You don't have to beverage me, though."

"Every guest gets beveraged at my place," she informed him, head already in the fridge. She carried a glass of orange juice to him, doing her best not to touch his fingers as he accepted. *At least it was mostly neat*, she sighed internally. There was no wasted space, with nothing but a few mismatched rugs on the pale hardwood floor.

She could feel him watching her putter around, pulling her wealth of hair into a ponytail.

She looked up wide eyed when he asked, "So, how long you been playin'?"

"Since I could hold a bass," Rae answered. "My dad played; taught me everything I know. Of course, when he died there was a while there where I couldn't look at my bass, much less pick it up. I'd not played in front of anyone but my best friend and the mirror for years until Big D asked for help on this demo." She perched on the corner of the couch, keeping as much distance between them as she could manage while she pulled on a pair of socks and canvas tennis shoes.

"Wow, that's…sorry about your dad, but I'm glad Derek got you playing again," he murmured, biting his bottom lip.

"Me too," she whispered, standing. She had made the mistake of looking into his devastatingly gorgeous face, and her stomach filled with butterflies. "I'd forgotten how much I missed playing with people, you know? Um, I'm gonna go finish up so we can get moving."

"Sure thing," he beamed.

In the privacy of her bathroom, Rae contemplated all the ways she was going to harm Derek when they got to the party. Sending Jacob over to her crappy apartment? And God! What must he think about her efficiency? It had never bothered her before; it was a place to crash and get ready for going other places. Now though, with Jacob sitting on her lumpy futon, it looked like a dismal little hole.

She cracked the bathroom door silently to peek. Jacob sipped the juice, absorbed in his phone seeming perfectly at ease. And dammit if he wasn't the prettiest thing in her apartment in his khaki shorts, tight green t-shirt, and brown flip-flops.

~ ♫ ~ JACOB ~ ♫ ~

When he'd finished his juice, Jacob carried it to the kitchen. His plan had been to set it in her sink, but he stopped himself. He couldn't be the only dirty dish. All the tools were there, and before he knew it, he was washing the cup and placing it on the nearby drying rack.

The whole place smelled sweet and lightly fruity like pie, and his belly wriggled in anticipation. The space was cozy like his friend's apartment in New York City. After the Tree House Kids got canceled and before he'd met the rest of the Harmonizers, he'd crashed there for a bit, and he appreciated the economy in her furnishings.

"I'm ready," Rae announced as she breezed past him to the oven.

Jacob slipped out of her way as she opened the oven door and reached. He was about to offer help, but she had already pulled a giant aluminum foil pan out of the oven.

That explained the smell! "That smells heavenly," he complimented. "I thought it was a candle somewhere. This is better."

Rae cast a sidelong glance at him as she set it on the stove top to close the oven door.

"Family recipe," she explained. "Always a hit at family reunions when we were still doing those."

Jacob prepared to carry the hot pan for her, but instead of handing him the oven mitts, Rae grabbed one corner, slipped the other hand beneath, and was off to the races.

"Let's go," Rae instructed.

He trailed after her, barely making it outside before she'd slammed the door shut with her toe.

"I can hold that while you—"

Rae shook her head, thrusting one hip at him. "Keys," she ordered.

A dangly keyring protruded from her hip pocket, and with trepidation, he pulled it free.

"Lock up," she added, then barreled down the stairs ahead of them. He stared at the fob in his hand, looking from her to the door and back. Thankfully, she only had three keys, and he guessed right on the second try. By the time he had locked the fiddly door, Rae was waiting at the base of the stairs.

She followed him to his car, and he held the door open. "I can hold it while you get settled."

Stubbornly, Rae shook her head, and Jacob looked away as she dropped into the seat and balanced it on her lap.

For the briefest moment, their eyes met. Her cheeks were pink, and his belly flipped at the sight. Satisfaction he didn't fully understand settled somewhere deep inside him. Shaking his head lightly, he gently closed her door.

Once behind the wheel, he smiled over at his companion. "Seat belt?" he questioned.

Rae fumbled, starting to release one corner of the pan, but it drooped, and she caught it again. "Um…this pan may not have been my smartest choice. I wasn't accounting for how heavy this would be."

Without hesitation, Jacob leaned across the car, trying not to smoosh her as he grabbed the belt buckle. The fabric whizzed loudly in the quiet space, and Jacob's hands shook as he plugged the safety belt into place, fingers brushing her hip.

"Sorry I didn't think to do this when you got seated," he mumbled, when she shivered a little.

"It's fine," she squeaked as he settled back in his own seat and buckled in.

Jacob had preloaded the GPS to stop first at Rae's, and he tapped the start button to begin leg two of the route. With a glance, over his shoulder, he pulled smoothly into traffic. The scent of the pan she clasped was distracting, but also a safe topic, and he dove in.

"So, what is the delicacy you're cradling?" he asked.

"Peach cobbler," she murmured, sounding almost shy. "My mamma taught me how to make it when I was about twelve. The recipe has been handed down in her family since the 1800s."

"That's amazing, to have that kind of history," he enthused. "I was dropped off at a police station when I was born…" he trailed off, wondering why he had mentioned that. Being in foster care until he aged out of the system was a matter of public record thanks to his past celebrity, but it wasn't something he usually chose to discuss in casual conversation. He blamed her homey story and the comfort food in her lap.

However, if it wasn't for the foster family he'd had at age fourteen, he would never have auditioned for a role on The Tree House Kids. Growing up in the system had its challenges. Most of the people weren't horrible, but he was never their first priority. He had gotten lucky with the last family. They treated him well, more like a distant cousin's kid rather than their own. And they had put all his earnings into a savings account for when he turned eighteen. He squeezed the steering wheel gratefully, realizing how it could have gone so differently.

Their conversation died with his admission. What could anyone possibly say to follow that up other than that they were sorry. Any follow up questions would have been invasive, and he scolded himself for sharing his trauma with a near stranger. He scrambled mentally for another topic and realized she was humming along to Derek's demo CD. He had taken it everywhere on repeat, picking out the lyrics and enjoying the raw tracks.

There was something familiar about the way her shoulders swayed and her head bobbed along, and recognition dawned on him like a ton of bricks landing on his sternum. She was the hot bartender at Dante's gig! She was also one of the backing vocalists! What were the odds?

He worried that she was bartending. Did that mean she wasn't committed to the project? He was being silly. Everyone in the industry had to pay the bills somehow until their ship came in. Bartending paid well, but it should be easy to give up.

"So tell me about your musical influencers. Feel free to go into great detail." He glanced at the GPS. "We have at least thirty minutes, and it's this or awkward silence."

She chuckled, launching into all the artists that inspired her. Some of her choices he'd never heard of, and she took great joy in educating him. By the time they arrived, she had barely scratched the surface and was fully engaged in trying to convert him into a fan of Rebel Gloss and their infamous bass player.

"I'm not saying I don't like them," he argued. "I'm saying I don't know most of their work."

She pouted as she scanned the streets for a parking space. "I can't believe you don't know who Nigel Davies is. He's a crucial part of my upbringing."

Jacob chuckled. "Are you sure that isn't more about his looks?"

She huffed. "Don't even start. I can appreciate him on multiple levels without taking away from his influence on my playing."

"Well, I'm glad for it either way. You do him credit," he complimented.

This seemed to appease her, and she pointed out a spot. He gunned the engine, executing a perfect parallel parking move with a satisfied smirk.

FIVE

As Rae and Jacob walked to the back gate of Peter Day's home, she spotted Derek immediately standing with Peter and a woman in a pastel purple sundress. Her eyes snapped from her first sight of Derek's former band mate for the first time to Derek staring at the woman by his side. Every instinct in her wanted to race to him and do everything in her power to turn his cheeks blistering red. After sending Jacob her way unannounced, he deserved it.

"Big D! A little help here," Rae yelled, balancing the giant aluminum pan of cobbler. When he didn't immediately come running, she called to him again. "This is warm, and the tray's flimsy!"

Derek rushed to the gate to open it, allowing her and Jacob inside.

"Thanks man," Jacob greeted, smiling at the producer. He handed a bag of serving spoons and a bottle of wine over. "I was going to get it, but she's fast!"

Rae rolled her eyes.

"I've met her," Derek acknowledged with a laugh. "She can do about anything on her own. Come in! Meet everyone! Get some food!"

Peter joined them with a smile, taking the tray deftly from Rae's hands as though it was a stack of paper plates. "Here, let me have that. I'll get it to the buffet. It looks heavy."

Rae shrunk back, feeling strangely naked without the pan to hide behind. She straightened her spine, throwing off the moment of weakness.

"Welcome, Rae!" Derek greeted hugging her quickly.

Peter adjusted the tray once he had control of it, but nearly dropped it as Derek said her name. "Wait…*you're* Rae?" he asked, swirling to face her.

At her nod, he bumped her shoulder. "I'm Peter. Come with me. We have tons to discuss. I've been looking forward to meeting you."

Rae blinked in shock, some of her frustration about her surprise chauffeur abated. Seeing Peter at a distance had not prepared her for the thrill of excitement at finally hearing him speak to her. For two years, Derek had been taunting her with his old band mates but had never offered to introduce her, despite repeated requests.

"Anything for a Legend," she giggled, looking from Derek then back at Peter.

"Great hosting skills, Pete," Derek sighed, ushering everyone out of the gateway. "Dude, this is Jacob, my partner in crime for the next while."

"Oh!" Peter rested the tray against his chest and extended a hand to his other new guest. "Sorry, man. I smelled food and lost my brain. Welcome. Have a beer! There're burgers coming off the grill and tons more." He gestured over his shoulder toward the buffet. "My wife's a fantastic cook. Help yourself."

"Cool." Jacob grinned. "Although I might be contractually obligated to eat Rae's cobbler first," he added, nodding at the tray. "I've been smelling it the whole ride here and salivating."

Heat flared in Rae's cheeks, and she nodded then changed the subject. "Do what you want, but I am having some of that heavenly meat I smell first, and you'd do well to do the same, Mr. Hunter." Wagging her finger at him, she turned and followed Peter to the table.

Two long folding tables bowed under a variety of dishes till she could barely see the tablecloth beneath them all. To her delight, there was a giant crockpot of pulled meats slathered in sauce as well as burgers and brats coming off a nearby grill. Peter introduced her to the grill master then instructed her to fill her plate and ran off to retrieve another tray of raw patties from the house.

Rae didn't realize how hungry she'd been till she reached the end of the table and barely had room for her thumb to hold her plate steady.

Peter was back shortly, gathering a plate full of salty snacks. "This is my second round," he confessed. "But there's food that wasn't here before. Like cobbler."

She laughed, finding the cooler full of assorted beers under a pop-up canopy.

"You need a hand?" Peter questioned.

"Neh!" Rae answered happily. She picked out three beers: one for her, one for Jacob, and another for Derek with her left hand and held them aloft. "Bartender by trade. I got this."

"Nice work," Peter complimented, grabbing one of his own and following her.

She searched out Jacob and Derek, tracing the shadiest path she could find to join them.

"Eye Candy!" Jacob's voice rang out over the crowd, and Rae's head snapped up.

Her grip on the bottles slipped, but she clamped down. He remembered! She may not believe him, but she liked it all the same, and her hips swung saucily.

She realized she was a beer short with the woman standing between Derek and Jacob and called over her shoulder at Peter. "Hey, I need another beer for…Grace, I assume," she requested.

Peter followed her gaze and nodded. "Good guess," he complimented as he handed her the item. She slipped it into a sneaky hold with the other three.

Rae leaned in closer and lowered her voice, "If what I've heard is true, Grace is a fan, too. She needs to be in on our little talk."

"Right. Once everyone gets food, I'll whisk you two away," Peter promised.

Armed with frosty beverages, Rae headed over to the group, a nip of jealousy stinging her at the sight of the pretty woman tucked against Jacob's side. She sternly told herself to suck it up; she wasn't in the market, no matter how gorgeous the guy. Relationships were nothing but trouble and heartache. Besides that, she was about to be working with the guy, and dating co-workers was bad juju.

"Grace, this is Sunshine," Derek introduced.

Rae wiped the smile off his face with an elbow to his arm. The chuckle died on his lips transforming into a pout as he rubbed the offended spot.

"Hey." Rae smiled, handing out beers. She dried her free hand against her shorts as Derek took the remaining beers, opening each and passing one back. She extended a hand to Grace. "Cool to meet a fellow Legends fan. We're thin on the ground anymore."

Grace nodded, accepting the gesture as she stepped closer to Derek. Rae tilted her head, wondering if she'd misinterpreted their coziness. "Nice to meet you as well." With a smile, Grace accepted the beer. "How do you know the guys?"

"I work with Derek," Rae beamed. "I hear you're responsible for introducing these two?"

"Nah, I just paid for lunch," Grace shrugged.

"You remembered my order." Jacob grinned, clinking his Heineken to Rae's bottle before taking a sip.

"I did," Rae replied, and her brain recalled how he looked leaning on the club bar all over again. She fanned herself twice, blaming it on the sun.

She tore her eyes away, looking past him and spied Peter near the back door of the house, waving to her. She stretched up on her toes to wave back then looked at her new companion with a devilish grin.

"Oh look, Miss Grace! Mr. Day is beckoning! Let's go!" Without waiting for a reply, she hooked her arm through Grace's and led her away, beer in one hand, plates balanced in the other. She slowed her pace once they were a few feet away.

She offered Peter a smile as they approached.

"So, ladies," Peter began, smiling down at Grace and Rae. "Legends fans, hmmm?"

"Well, yeah," Rae answered. "Y'all were a must for me! Five cute boys singing, dancing, and being adorable dorks?" She lifted her head to the sky for a moment, trying to contain the word vomit she felt gathering on the back of her tongue.

"I mean, I tease Big D that I liked Leo best, but I didn't have a favorite. It was too much fun to even think about stuff like that. Besides,

I already had my celebrity crush on Nigel Davies from Rebel Gloss and that boy over there when he was on the Tree House Kids."

The moment her finger landed on Jacob across the yard, her eyes widened, and she shook her head. "Nope, forget you heard that!" she gasped.

He laughed. "You are among friends with very bad hearing," he teased. "I've been plotting what embarrassing stories I could tell you both from the moment I heard you were fans."

"Well, don't let us stop you. We have *excellent* hearing," Grace ribbed.

Rubbing his hands together, Peter beamed. "Perfect. Right this way." He led the ladies up the few stairs from the backyard into the kitchen. It was small, but efficient, accented in sea-foam green which played well with the mid-century design, and Rae instantly felt at home.

"I thought I'd start with the nickel tour since you all have never been here. The restroom is that way," he pointed down a short hallway leading to a bedroom. "Our bedroom is past there if you want to leave your purses—I'm sorry—*handbags* inside. Nancy's always on me about the difference. I don't mean to offend."

"I am not that fancy," Grace chuckled, waving off his apology as she headed to the room.

Rae laughed as well. "I'm a bartender," she explained, flashing a hint of her driver's license from her hip pocket. "I learned how to get along without that ages ago."

Peter gave the pair a thumbs-up and once Grace returned, ushered them into the dining room. He sat down, gesturing for them to do the same. "And that concludes the nickel tour." He began munching on a mixed plate of chips and pretzels as Rae and Grace started on their lunches.

"So, you work for D's agent?" he asked, looking at Grace.

"I do, for a little over four months now. Feels like the first day and a lifetime."

Peter laughed. "I know that feeling."

Rae almost rolled her eyes. She didn't mind small talk, but that was not what she'd been holding her breath for since Peter had rescued her at the gate. She was finished with niceties and interrupted quickly.

"So, tell us all about Big D when he was a Legend." She picked up her sandwich and delved in, full grin and bright eyes blasting at Peter.

"Let's see—what can I tell you that won't get me pummeled…" he trailed off. "D was an amazing prankster. He had the best poker face. But he sorta grew out of that."

"The baby face or the pranks?" Rae asked between bites. The meat was grilled so perfectly that she had to stifle a moan.

"Both! It's hard to remember how young we were back then. But especially Derek. He was the youngest of all of us even though he and Leo were the old pros. It was so hard to keep up with them."

"My inner fangirl is so excited that you two stayed friends. Whatever happened to the others?" Rae pressed.

Peter shrugged. "We still see Leo sometimes, but he's got a lot of irons in the fire living in New York, so he's been MIA for a while. Ryan is hard to reach with his wrestling career. And we still have no idea what happened to Ben. He's probably on a beach somewhere with an acoustic guitar. Maybe he even learned to play it."

The girls laughed heartily and listened as Peter recalled an incident during their single concert tour where the bus had left a pit stop and left Ben behind.

"Someday," Peter continued, "You should get D to show you his collectibles. He's got a whole room. I have no idea how he got all this stuff. I used to make fun of him for it, but the longer ago it was, the more precious it gets. There's a legacy somewhere in there." He looked momentarily wistful.

"And what about you? I noticed you left yourself off," Rae prompted. She looked around the room. "Looks like you're doing good, and we see you married well."

He smiled, a dimple popping on one cheek as he grinned proudly. "I've been working on a men's fashion line. It's still a startup, but I'm getting a lot of buzz. Still a long way to go before I become a household name."

Rae nodded, sampling the different food on her plate. "We know you have all the juicy stuff fangirls like us need to know. So, spill the beans. Best prank D ever pulled and best one pulled on him," she prompted.

Peter began regaling them with stories and had been going on for nearly thirty minutes before his wife's voice hailed him from outside. "We were absolutely not hiding in the house," he told the ladies, snatching up his plate and sprinting for the door.

Rae and Grace both followed, disposing of their plates in the kitchen trash on the way out. They watched as Peter found his way to his bride, winding his arms gently around her waist and kissing her jaw.

The girls were barely down the steps before he returned to finish his story. "I heard you were a fan, Grace," Peter egged. "You're awfully quiet."

She smiled clutching her cup. "Oh, I am. I freely admit it. I basically can't think of any burning fan questions I could ask that wouldn't be wildly inappropriate."

Peter laughed at this. "Okay. I can work with that." He smiled wickedly and met her eyes. "Boxer-briefs. No, he does not shave his chest. And, yes, he's single and very straight."

Grace's eyes flew wide open, and Rae belly laughed, first clutching Grace's arm, then reaching for Peter's.

"I adore you," she cackled, relishing the way Grace's face went beet red. Something in her knew that the woman needed to be yanked out of her comfort zone, like she had when she was with Alex. Kendra had done it for her, and it was her job now to do so for Grace.

She hoped the secretary wasn't in a horrible relationship like she had been, but she had all the markers of someone who was being taken advantage of in some way. If she could coax her out of her shell, she could be a powerhouse. They had only met that afternoon, but Rae was already invested. How had she grown so attached so fast, when she had been eyeing the woman jealously less than an hour ago?

Peter interrupted her thoughts. "Derek's like my little brother, you know? All I want is to see him happy. It's weird. I remember meeting him at auditions. I did not think either of us were going to make it when I saw the competition. But we clicked the first day, and here we are all these years later. We got pretty lucky. It's rare to find that sort of friendship in this town."

"It looks like you got double lucky between Derek and Nancy," Rae beamed, as she nodded in agreement.

Peter lit up like Christmas had come early. "D introduced us. He met her when he was a waiter over at Planet Hollywood."

Grace arched an eyebrow, and Rae's breath caught at the back of her throat, abrupt tears threatening to overrun her vision thinking of her musical partner in crime serving sodas to tourists and celebrities. His life was so nearly wasted. She found a smile of pride curving her lips as she followed Peter's gaze.

"I guess the universe isn't always out to destroy us," Rae offered.

"It's a roller coaster. It's sure easier to hang on when you've got someone in the car with you," Peter replied.

Grace chuckled. "You are both too deep. I'm not sure I have anything to offer at this rate."

Rae shook her head. "Are you always on?" she asked Grace, noticing the woman checking the phone in her hand.

Grace shrugged. "It pays the bills. And I don't always have to be in an office at eight."

"Sounds like pretty steady work. That's hard to find around here," Peter complimented. The conversation shifted away from the history of the fandom, and Peter peppered them both with questions about their own lives including how long they'd been in LA and what part of town they lived in.

"Peter," Nancy called from near the buffet. "I need another bag of ice, please."

"Duty calls," he offered, then disappeared into the house.

As the conversation buzz between Rae and Grace fizzled, Rae followed Grace's gaze to where Derek and Jacob were eating. They appeared to be pulling food off each other's plates like teenage boys and laughing, elbows and bits of food flying.

"What on Earth are they doing?" Grace whispered.

"Trading desserts like little boys at school, it looks like," Rae giggled. "Look, Jacob's taking all my cobbler." She flushed with warmth. Oh sure, she planned on teasing Derek about not liking the one thing she could cook, but Jacob wanting all of it turned her squishy.

"Good for you, Sunshine." Grace nodded to her.

Rae chuckled. "You know that's not my name, right? It's Derek mocking me. *Rae* of sunshine?" she enunciated.

"Oh!" Grace chirped, frowning at first, then laughing. "Oh—that is clever. Actually—Sunshine wouldn't be the most unusual name I've heard working here. Sorry about that."

Rae waved it off as the pair made their way over to the guys. "No big. He thinks you're cute, you know," she tattled.

"What?" Grace blinked, taking a step backward.

Seeing the distress on Grace's face, Rae steered her over to the makeshift bar. Peter's wife Nancy was manning the station, laughing as she passed out beers and waved bottles of liquor tantalizingly at her guests.

"May I, Mrs. Day?" Rae asked. "Miss Grace needs something a bit more fortifying than beer."

"You're the pro, sayeth D." Nancy smiled, stepping away. "Give me a yell when you want out."

Rae nodded absently and gave her a thumbs up as she took quick stock of the supplies. "So, you're a personal assistant to a talent manager," she murmured to Grace, smiling as she started mixing a daquiri. "What's that like?"

"Exhausting, but occasionally cool," Grace replied, gesturing around the party and tipping her hand toward Derek, Jacob, and Peter.

"How did you get into that?" Rae asked, slipping into bartender mode. All she wanted was for Grace to feel comfortable, and the amiable tricks of the proverbial trade began to work their magic. If she ever wanted to put someone at ease, she always asked them about themselves.

"Oh…well, I was a secretary back in Chicago for years. Got tired of all the snow, rain, and tornadoes, so I put my resume on the internet and my house up for sale." Grace shrugged as though the decision and process had been a no brainer.

"Smart. Brave too," Rae commented, setting down the daquiri and a shot of vanilla vodka.

"I don't know about that," Grace demurred. "Are these both for me?" One eyebrow lodged firmly in her hairline. At Rae's nod, Grace took a deep breath, braced herself and knocked the shot back. She sipped the daquiri and hummed. "Wow, that's the best thing I've ever tasted!" She took another quick sip while Rae started mixing another drink. "What about you? How did you get here?"

Rae gave Grace a condensed version of her life story while she mixed drinks for guests as they wandered up. Occasionally, she interrupted herself to shout out to her hosts to bring her more ingredients. Rae didn't meet Grace's eyes, pretending to be focused on her bartending as she wrapped up the story.

"So, he traded me out for a fancier model, and I have no idea what he's up to now. I'm ecstatic he's gone." She was skimming over her divorce when she felt the back of her neck prickle.

"He sounds like an idiot," Jacob murmured, coming up behind her with Derek and joining the conversation. Her years of experience as a bartender kept Rae from jumpstarting at his arrival. Nobody looking would even know how her heart rate sped up in response.

She rolled with the conversation, her hands continuing to measure, mix, and pour. "Well, he thought he was marrying a future rock star," Rae explained, then shrugged indifferently. "When that didn't pan out, he felt justified to screw around."

Derek laughed, throwing an arm around her shoulders, squeezing them. "Ah but you *are* gonna be a rock star! And *then* he'll be sorry!"

She let herself relax at the comfort Derek's touch had provided. "I don't care as long as his alimony checks keep coming in. I'm grateful we didn't have kids. I don't know if I'd have been able to leave him." She bit her tongue at the confession. She hadn't meant to tell that part.

"You're such a softie," Derek teased. "And you'd have done what you needed to protect a child—especially your own. LA hasn't made you *that* tough."

Rae stuck out her tongue and pushed Derek away.

"You two are worse than my sister's kids," Jacob commented.

Derek leaned toward Rae nearly setting his head on her shoulder.

"Jacob wants to whisk you away to make him cobbler forever," he sang. Edging around the bar, he draped an arm around Grace's neck and stage-whispered into her ear. "I don't think we should let him, do you?"

Jacob and Rae both rolled their eyes.

"There will be no whisking," Rae drawled. How much had Derek had to drink?

Her thoughts were interrupted as Nancy joined them. "Hey! How long have you been behind this bar?" Nancy shook a finger at Rae. "Go, mingle! You stay back there any longer, I'll have to pay you, and we can't afford your services."

Properly admonished, Rae scooted out from behind the bar, Jacob right behind her.

"There's some shade over there," Jacob pointed out. "I'd hate for these cold beers to warm up before their time."

"Oh, shade sounds great," Grace mumbled, hurrying in that direction.

The quartet pulled up lawn chairs and settled into a breezy nook near the bushes. Derek and Jacob started discussing new music they'd heard recently and which songs they liked the best. Before long, Derek had pulled out his digital music player and Jacob had produced the latest cell phone so they could compare notes, grooving in their chairs and debating the finer qualities of each.

Rae hung on each word, joining the conversation as she could. The afternoon passed in a pleasant fashion, and before they knew it, the sky had taken on a crimson tone.

The distinct clinking of silverware to a glass called a halt to conversation. Everyone looked around for the source and found Peter standing precariously on a cooler that was a little less than level.

Nancy turned down the music and joined him. "Get down from there before you break something more than a bottle," she teased.

When everyone laughed, Peter hopped down and raised his bottle to everyone. "Before all the games start, I wanted to thank everyone for coming. I know some of you have other obligations, but while we're all gathered, I…well, Nancy and I…wanted to share some news."

"And I got tired of everyone trying to push a beer on me," Nancy added. The guests chuckled again.

Peter wrapped an arm around her waist and pulled her gently to his side. "It wouldn't be very responsible for a pregnant lady to drink for the next several months."

The announcement was met with cheering, and a rush of guests surrounded the couple.

Rae barely knew them and refrained from joining the fray to give her congratulations like Derek. She looked over at Grace and Jacob, realizing they both must be feeling like the same awkward outsider as she did. In the next moment, Grace disappeared.

She glanced at Jacob. He was staring at his phone. Her hand itched to grab his and squeeze it to let him know she understood how he must be feeling. Before Rae could think of something to say, Grace returned with her handbag and a glass serving bowl.

"Well, it's been a great afternoon. I don't remember the last barbecue I went to," Grace piped up, smiling. "It's getting dark, and I should get going. I wanna get to my car before dark. You know how it is in LA."

Seizing an opportunity, Rae hopped up from her chair, reaching for Grace's wrist. "Oh! Would you mind giving me a ride? I'm sure Derek'll wanna help clean up, and Mr. Hunter's driving kinda scares me," she requested. She wilted under Jacob's exaggerated offended face.

"Hey now!" Jacob pouted. "I'm an excellent driver!"

"For the Indy 500," Rae teased, poking him in the shoulder. She turned to Grace and added, "Please? I'll gladly give you gas money."

"Oh, well. Sure. No gas money required."

Jacob popped up from his chair as well. "Oh, I'm not letting you ladies walk out to the car alone. It's LA after all," he added. He gestured to Derek. "D! I'm walking them to the car. They're leaving."

Derek looked startled and surprised. He held up a finger to his friend then trotted back. "It's so early," he pointed out. "Are we boring you with the music talk? I promise we can stop."

"No, you can't." Grace smirked. "And honestly, that's not it. I have some things I have to get done before getting to the office tomorrow, and I don't like to drive around here in the dark when I don't know where I am."

"I'll walk with you," Derek answered.

~ ♪ ~ JACOB ~ ♪ ~

As Derek and Jacob walked back the three blocks to Peter's yard, the night was surprisingly quiet but for the sound of cars passing. Relaxed from good beer and great food, Jacob glanced at the shorter man. There was no more appropriate time than this to ask what had been on his mind a good portion of the day. The sun was setting quickly now turning the skyline full red, purple tinging the sky ahead of them.

"So, what's the score on Rae's ex?" Jacob asked.

Derek's answer was delayed. "She caught him cheating, so he served her with divorce papers on her thirtieth birthday." He pressed his hands deeply into his pockets as they walked.

"He served her because *he* cheated?" Jacob yelped then froze in place. "Wait. Did you say thirty? You're pulling my leg. She's twenty-five at most!"

His companion stopped too, turning three quarters to look back at him with a chuckle. "Tell her that, and she will love you forever, man. She turns thirty-seven this year."

"Now I know you're messin' with me! No way she's two years older than me," Jacob laughed.

"My hand to God, I swear," Derek replied, lifting his hand skyward.

"I never would have guessed," Jacob murmured. After a beat, he wondered aloud, "So, she single?"

Derek looked him up and down.

Jacob looked around, then back at his companion. "What?"

"Once, when I asked her if one of the Lakeshore techs was her boyfriend, she said, and I quote, '*I don't shit where I eat, Mr. Reed.*'" Derek turned and started again toward the party.

Jacob started to protest, but Derek held up his hand. "Dude, I can see you dig her. And that's cool. You seem like a great guy. But please don't mess with my little sister. She won't have it, and I don't want anything to get weird."

"Fair enough," Jacob surrendered. He couldn't pretend not to be hurt by the advice, but this was why he had asked. Better to be rejected by his friend than the woman he had been ogling discreetly all day.

SIX

acob headed straight to his studio when he got home from the barbecue. Derek's demo had been playing in his car the whole time, and his brain was toying with some of his own lyrics on top. He wanted desperately to tweak the arrangements and chop it up differently, but the CD didn't give him the freedom. He needed the producer's raw tracks. It took a phone call and less than an hour for Derek to join him.

Jacob's body uncoiled as they worked, and ideas flowed between them. When they emerged from the studio for a break, birds were chirping, and the early morning sun burned their eyes.

"Man, I am fried," Derek moaned, leaning against Jacob's kitchen counter and closing his eyes. "I haven't gone full out like that in a while." He stretched with a yawn.

"It's good though." Jacob smiled languidly. It felt like they'd built an entire album between the two of them in a single night even though he knew they hadn't. "Foundation laid and all that." He forced his eyes open and hugged his arms around his chest.

"Yup," Derek agreed. "Gimme a few minutes, and I'll head out; let you rest."

"I got guest rooms, dude," Jacob pointed out. "Crash here."

Derek looked at him like he'd grown a wart between his eyes. "You sure?" he mumbled.

"It would make me happy. And selfishly—we can start again after some rest."

Both men chuckled, Jacob's morphing into a yawn. He pointed the producer to the nearest guest room.

"Sleep. We'll talk later."

Jacob barely remembered falling into bed when he woke hours later. First thing on his list was to shower. Water pelted his scalp, cranking up his whirring brain. It had been the most productive session he'd had in years. But it meant they needed new basslines. Some of Derek's demos had found their way into the recordings, but most of it was tracks from his own holding tank that had made the cut. Derek took one listen and made the most life altering tweaks that took his music from mediocre to mouthwatering.

He buttoned up his jeans and dialed Rae's number and listened to it ring on speaker as he slipped a shirt over his wet head. Pride filled him at having stolen the number from Derek the night before with the excuse of needing to give her details to his accountant for payroll.

Her sleepy greeting sent chills through his gut. He could picture her in bed—her warm, naked body tangled in the sheets, inviting him to explore.

"Did I wake you?" he worried, walking down to his studio.

"No," she yawned. "I'm waiting for the coffee to brew. These late nights at *The Oubliette* get harder every year."

He chuckled. "I had one of those nights myself," he confessed as he roamed his studio. He picked up dirty napkins and paper plates, shoving them inside the empty pizza box. "Hey, if you don't have plans today, I was hoping you might come over. Derek and I were up most of the night working on some new stuff, and we kinda need some revisions on the bass tracks."

She cleared her throat. "Oh, sure. Can I have like an hour or so?"

"Take your time," Jacob encouraged. "We're not in a big rush, and D's still asleep. Whenever you can get here is fine."

Butterflies danced in his stomach as he hung up. He gulped as he remembered the producer's words the previous evening about not messing with her. What was he thinking? It was like he couldn't help but be drawn to the woman. He kept cleaning until the doorbell rang, then rushed to let her in.

She looked amazing. Her hair was pulled back into a long braid that swung as she stepped into the foyer, carrying the nectar of the gods and a bag of bagels. A soft, black guitar case was slung over her shoulder.

He took the coffee from her and led her to the kitchen, trying not to glance back at the tight red jeans hugging her legs and black tank top that outlined all her curvy features in excruciating detail. He'd have to turn up the thermostat so she wasn't so cold or he'd definitely get caught staring.

He seated her at the island, doctoring his coffee and peppering her with questions about her studio work and her favorite bass. After the coffee, he fidgeted with the bagel, producing butter knives and plates for them. He felt like a spaz bouncing around the kitchen and had finally stilled himself on the bar stool opposite hers when a half-asleep Derek stumbled in.

"Hey, Big D!" Rae saluted. "I brought sustenance in the form of coffee and bagels."

He rubbed his palm against his eyes and blinked at her. "What are you doing here?" he grumbled, shuffling over and taking the cup Rae held out to him. He plopped onto one of the barstools and began doctoring his coffee.

"Jacob called and said he wanted to noodle around with beats," she replied, shrugging and taking a bite of the round bread.

Derek eyed the younger man warily and sipped his coffee.

"I got here ten minutes ago," Rae chuckled. "We were talking equipment when you came in."

"D and I were up after dawn recording," Jacob explained. "Maybe we should start by playing you what we did last night?"

"Let's finish our brekkie first," Rae chuckled. "Maybe the ferocious gleam will have left y'all's eyes by then. You both look like big cats hunting."

Grunting, Derek tipped his coffee cup in salute and dropped one leg to the floor. "Let's do this." When no one budged at his call to action, he sat back down and laced his fingers around the cup of wake-up juice.

Jacob, however, was wide awake and launched into the whirlwind of thoughts cluttering his mind. Rae was listening quietly, pinching off bites delicately to press between her cherry lips. Part of him wished she would tear into it like an animal, losing all control, and he faltered in his explanation.

Luckly for him, Derek chimed in with opposition. "If we keep going the new direction we agreed to last night, I don't think it needs to get so big. I really think we should see how the bass line feels before we try turning a corner. I have a feeling it will fill in the gaps," Derek countered.

Jacob looked from Derek to Rae as she popped the last bite into her mouth, one cheek bulging as she tamed the chunk inside, and he choked on the coffee he'd sipped. All the music in his brain curled around her shape, caressing her cheeks and tangling its fingers in her hair. How was he supposed to think about music with her so close? He cleared his throat as though he hadn't just imagined her cheek bulging with other things in her mouth.

"Derek says you can hear a beat and anticipate it like it's no big deal," he prompted, relishing the blush that bloomed across her cheeks.

"He's exaggerating," she mumbled, sweeping the crumbs from the bar onto her empty plate.

"Really?" He smirked. "He also says you can play any Rebel Gloss song."

"That's because I've loved that stupid band since I was ten years old," she chuckled. "I studied Nigel's technique until my fingers were raw."

Without thinking, Jacob grabbed one of her hands, turning it over cheekily, inspecting her smooth fingertips. His heart thrummed anxiously at the contact, wanting more.

"Hey, hands off, pretty boy," Rae snapped. She tugged her hand back and wrapped it around her coffee.

The pink flush crawling down her throat into her ample cleavage was intoxicating. She might protest, but only for appearances. He wondered if they were alone if she'd accept his ministrations differently.

"Hey now," Jacob said with a laugh. "I haven't been pretty for a long time! Ruggedly handsome maybe..."

Rae almost fell out of her chair laughing. "Facial hair does not equal rugged," she managed to choke out. "It means you can't find your razor!"

Jacob blew raspberries at her and went back to drinking his coffee. He tried to act offended, but the corners of his mouth twitched up into a smile. Working…playing with these two was going to be a blast. He hoped the two band members they had yet to find would be as much fun.

Breakfast complete, Jacob led them to the studio. Rae stood at the threshold and stared. Her pouty lips pursed in confusion. He looked to Derek for an interpretation, but the producer's eyes were wide.

"What?" he questioned, following their gaze. Had he missed something in his cleaning mission?

"I thought you guys worked until dawn," Rae murmured. "Why does this place look untouched?"

"Uh, I picked up a little while I was on the phone with you," Jacob blushed. He hadn't felt his cheeks heat like this in over a decade.

"A little?" Derek squeaked. "Did you even sleep?"

"It's not a big deal," Jacob defended. "We're not pigs."

"Hush," Rae cut in. "It was very nice of Mr. Hunter to clean up for us. Gives us a fresh start." She raised up on tiptoe to kiss Jacob's cheek.

His skin tingled where her lips had been, but the way she called him Mister confused the hell out of him. The kiss felt dirty, like she'd shown him the same affection she would her grandfather. He looked to Derek for sympathy.

"She's ridden in my car and still with the mister?" he complained. Why wouldn't this woman calm down around him? He didn't like the cold shoulder.

"You'll get used to it," Derek encouraged, patting Jacob's arms and pushing past them both.

Clearing his throat, Jacob headed to the console, pulled out a chair, and offered the alluring woman a set of headphones.

The foam ear pads swallowed her face, but her grin sandwiched in the middle was nothing short of adorable. Derek slipped on his own set and was already down to business. He tapped a button and sat back.

Jacob watched in silence as her eyes closed. Her body began to rock, and Jacob guessed which song she was hearing based on the bopping of her head. Her hips joined the party, and then tears slipped from the corners of her eyes. After a couple minutes, she yanked off the listening device and jumped up, chair toppling backwards, in her fury.

"You assholes!" she shrieked. The noise turned into a growl, and she yelped again, whirling on them both. "Why haven't you worked together sooner?"

He wasn't sure what reaction he had expected, but it certainly wasn't this. Her words were complimentary, but her tone was fire. No—he realized—it was passion. He eyed the other man for a clue on the appropriate response.

"We're...sorry?" Derek suggested, blinking with the same shock Jacob felt.

Rae took several jagged breaths, fists clenched at her sides. Her lips moved silently counting numbers as she inhaled and exhaled a few more times. Then, she righted her chair and dropped back into it. She glared at them for a moment before shoving the headphones back on.

Derek caught Jacob's gaze over her head with a twinkle in his eye. He rolled his chair to the couch and freed Rae's bass from its confines then rested it in her hands.

Her eyes flashed open, and she adjusted her grip. His heart pounded as she went still again and then her fingers were plucking at strings. At first, he recognized the riffs she strummed, then gradually, the rhythms and progressions shifted into all new territory. She was composing!

Jacob snaked a line from the console to her instrument.

Derek was a flurry of activity behind her and held up a thumb to indicate he was recording.

As she opened her eyes, Jacob stared into their depths, imagining her hands on him instead of the bass. The music delved deeper, more sensual, and she didn't break their gaze.

~ ♫ ~ R A E ~ ♫ ~

Rae forgot Derek was there until he bumped her shoulder as he reached for a fader next to her, tweaking levels and hunched over the console. She pushed away from them a few inches to give the producer room to work. She snorted out a laugh at his intense expression.

Jacob was crouched in front of her, fingers stroking the lead he'd plugged into her bass. His body was perched between her knees, and for a moment she imagined his plug in her jack.

Two very different sets of blue eyes turned to her, and she burst out in giggles and continued playing. She rocked her hips animatedly, giving her very best rock god impersonation.

Joy bubbled out of her as she assessed this never-in-a-lifetime moment. She sprung out of her chair to play, letting the heady experience influence her hands as she let the music flow through her. She didn't know where the notes came from, but she followed the rhythm in her mind. By the time the song was over, she was gasping, and they were applauding, screaming her name in unison.

"That was…I don't…" she stuttered between breaths, eyes shining. "You guys!"

"Derek said you didn't compose," Jacob murmured, his gaze fixed on her.

"I've never done it before." She shrugged, still beaming. "When we were putting the demo together, I played riffs I knew until he heard what he wanted and gave me instruction." She pointed at Derek.

"And she was born in laughter and joy." Derek smiled.

"Born?" Rae asked, eyebrows raising.

"Jacob and I were talking about it last night, how the first time you compose is like being born into a new world," Derek replied.

"How very…existential," Rae teased.

"Yet true," Jacob chimed in. "Now, let's see if we can't do something about the rest of the stuff we've got cooking!"

Rae thought she might be the luckiest bassist on the planet pacing the studio and bouncing from a chair to the couch, into the tracking room and back. Even when Jacob ordered food, she found herself clutching her bass between bites and plucking out accompaniments to the arrangements. At six that evening, she apologized as she excused herself to go home and prepare for her shift at *The Oubliette*. She had tried to call for a cab, but Derek wouldn't hear of it and hustled her to his car.

"I'm not completely broke, you know," she grumbled when they stopped at a light.

"That's not the point, Sunshine," Derek countered. "It's not spending money when you don't have to. Besides, I needed to leave. Don't want to burn out on the first day."

"I didn't mean to break up the party," she apologized.

"It's cool," he assured.

The car was quiet but for the muffled sound of tires on pavement beneath them as he accelerated. His trademark smirk was nowhere to be found, and as he spoke, Rae shrunk into a coil of anxiety. She braced herself for an attack.

"Look, there's something we need to talk about," he broached, making an extra fuss as he checked for oncoming traffic before making a left turn.

"Okay," she drawled, waiting for him to tell her they didn't need her, and that she was out.

"I realized that the prank I played on you yesterday was not funny."

She bristled. "You're right. It wasn't."

"I was paying you back for pushing me towards Grace. So, no more meddling in each other's love lives. You lay off about Grace, and I don't send Hunter on any more surprise visits."

"Yeah," she sighed. "Talk about embarrassing. Do you know how shamed I felt having him in my shabby little postage stamp of an apartment? What a hard luck case he must think I am. I mean, I could have a bigger place, but I'm not there to do anything but sleep, so…"

"Rae, I'm so sorry. I didn't even think about that," Derek whispered when she trailed off.

She tried to smile as though he was forgiven, but the memory reared its ugly head. "I just…I could see he was checking the place out and…there wasn't much there, you know?"

"He doesn't think less of you," Derek insisted as he pulled up to her building.

"I guess," she frowned.

"I had to tell him about your no-dating-co-workers rule after we walked you guys to the car," Derek mumbled.

Rae froze with her hand on the door handle. Why would he tell Jacob that? The thought was like being doused with iced water then boiled alive.

"Sunshine? You alright?"

"Five by five," she sputtered, mind still reeling. She threw open the door and jumped out to extract her bass from the back seat.

"What?" Derek called.

"I'm good, D," she replied, rubbing her forehead and storming into the courtyard of her complex. So…what? Jacob thought she was *more* than eye candy? That didn't compute. Someone that gorgeous thought plain ol' Rae from Tulsa was…what? Date material? She shook her head to clear it. Derek must have jumped to the wrong conclusion. She nodded to herself as she began to dress for work. Yes, that was more like it. Derek must have gotten his wires crossed.

~ ♫ ~ JACOB ~ ♫ ~

Hiding in the studio once he was alone, Jacob listened to the work they'd recorded that day. Derek had been wrong about Rae being born as a composer in laughter and joy. Unless he missed his guess, she'd been born in desire. It seemed fitting for a bass player, a mistress of rhythm. Born in desire and baptized with laughter and joy. Oh, yes, he was definitely going to enjoy making music with her.

His revelry was interrupted by a ringing phone. He answered quickly, not even checking the caller ID. "You got Jacob."

"Jacob, it's Meyers. I wanted to follow up on that lunch."

"It's Sunday, man," Jacob said with a laugh, knowing there were no weekends in the biz. "Don't you have a family?"

Meyers laughed on the line. "Yes, but I just married off the last one. Gotta make up for lost time. How did that list of musicians work out?"

"Oh, it's great. We're going to hold auditions. Our bass player's pushing for Joe Andrews, and I trust her judgment. Still wanna talk to the others to be sure he's the right fit."

Meyers hesitated. "I don't remember putting him on the list."

"Hey, it's great that you did. She got really excited and vouched for him. Sounds like he's got some great cred. But, hey, I'm glad you called though. Been buried in the music until about like an hour ago. For those auditions, do you think you could spare Grace? We keep having these meetings, and I need someone who can coordinate this for me. Take notes, call people, and stuff. I want to go full steam ahead, and I need someone organized like her."

"Well—I can definitely get her to set up the auditions," Meyers hesitated.

Jacob could hear his agent formulating ways to say no. "I'm only in town for like a week. I feel like I can trust her."

"A week?" Meyers repeated.

"Yeah," Jacob answered, pacing the studio. He began coiling the lead from Rae's bass.

"You know, I've got a great pool of secretaries at the office. I can send someone your way."

"Well, that's cool, but she already gets along with Derek and Rae. It already feels like she's part of the team."

"She does?" he questioned.

"Yeah—we hung out at a barbecue over the weekend. One of D's friends' places. It was real casual. Nice to forget the celebrity for a bit."

Meyers was quiet for long enough that Jacob wondered if the call had dropped.

"Did I lose ya? Is that cool?"

"Sure. I can make arrangements for a week. You know she's my personal assistant? This is a big ask, Jacob."

"Yeah. You're the best, man. That's why I switched to you. It's a whole team of people supporting me. You know I didn't get that with my last agent. I know you're always there for me. You've got my back." Jacob was laying it on thick, but he was beginning to see an unflattering picture of this man.

"Of course. I'm always here for you."

"Awesome. Hey—I think Derek's going to be sending you some

paperwork next week. We wanted to draw up a little something to make sure we're all protected and stuff. Makes it easier to get past all that petty stuff and get on with the work. I can have Grace send it over to you, and make sure it's all good. That'll help a ton!"

"Sounds like it will. I'll let Grace know. Is Monday too soon?"

"No, that's perfect. We've been working all night already, so having some help will pick up the pace. Keep us focused. I'll be in touch. Thanks!"

Jacob disconnected the call, having achieved what he wanted from the conversation. Agents were a necessary evil. Most wanted to get their fingers in business that wasn't theirs, and he wished he didn't need one.

He was snatched out of dreamland Monday morning by the incessant ringing of his phone. He answered, voice rough and groggy.

"Mr. Hunter," Grace greeted. "I hope I'm not calling too early."

"A little, but it's my fault for working so late. What time is it?"

"About 9:30."

Sitting up and scrubbing a hand over his face, he realized it was a very reasonable hour to phone someone who wasn't a night owl. "Wow, okay, what's up?" Jacob replied.

"Well, Mr. Meyers said you requested my services for the week. I was hoping you might let me know where to meet you."

"Right, right." Jacob yawned loudly, then gave her his address.

"Perfect. Is it okay if I head over?" Grace asked, her professional tone tinged with worry.

"Oh, sure!" Jacob smiled at her thoughtfulness.

"Shall I bring breakfast?"

"Ooh, yeah, coffee would be magical. You're an angel!"

"How do you take it?"

"Three sugars and about half cream," he laughed. "I think Derek takes his black. I have sugar and stuff at the house if not."

"Perfect, I'll see you soon."

"Well, not like ASAP. Take your time so we can be ready when you get here."

To Jacob's mind, barely five minutes had passed before a ringing noise brought him back to consciousness. In fairness, he had gone promptly back to sleep after the call. It took him a moment to recognize the tone: the front doorbell. Most people knocked. But it was Grace, he reminded himself, tugging his flannel sleep pants up another inch as he tied the drawstring. Of course, she would ring the bell like a stranger. He wondered who had damaged her in life to treat everything with such formality. He pulled the door open and backed up with a smile but no words to admit her.

Grace stepped delicately over the threshold, laden with what looked like two mountains of gear. He watched her head flicking from side to side as she navigated the entryway and took pity on her as he closed the door. "Go on through to the kitchen. We can set up in there."

"Thanks," she replied, heading through the open concept floor plan to the kitchen counter. She set a giant striped catering bag on the table next to the fancy coffees in a gray drink carrier. The moment her hands were free, he watched in astonishment as a heavy bag slipped from each shoulder simultaneously into her hands before being gently eased to the floor. She twirled to face him, low heeled shoes moving effortlessly over his tile floors.

"I had them put a J on your cup and a D on the other," she explained. She touched the catering bag lightly. "I brought some hot and cold items since I wasn't sure what you'd like. I can set it up here on the counter if you point me to where the plates and silverware live."

Jacob blinked, hand still on the doorknob from closing the door. "You've got so much energy! Did you drink more than one espresso on the way here?"

She laughed. "No. I hate coffee. I'm a morning person."

He frowned as he made his way toward the caffeine. "Inhuman," he replied. As promised, one cup had a giant J on the side, and he reached for it greedily. The first taste of it was reaching his lips as she began buzzing around the kitchen, asking what he needed. What he needed was to digest his coffee. He excused himself politely to find his phone.

Jacob blinked again, swallowing the sip with appreciation. It was right. And all he'd had to do was answer the door. Maybe she was ungodly perky for this hour of day, but he assumed she hadn't pulled an all-nighter either.

He'd met people in the industry like Grace many times. They usually took no notice of him or anyone else around them. All business, all the time. She was in a dark business suit today, pants this time instead of the skirt from their initial meeting.

He reached for the cell on his nightstand. One text from Derek.

> **Derek**
> Just got up. Ready to roll when you are.

Well, maybe he *was* the lazy one. He dialed Derek back. "How are you already awake?" he asked by way of greeting when Derek answered.

Derek chuckled. "You called me, so I'm not alone."

Jacob was incredulous. "You couldn't have gotten home before four," he argued.

"I don't know what to tell you. I try not to sleep past nine most days or I'll lose the whole day. Speaking of—are you ready?"

Sighing, Jacob acquiesced. "Yeah. Grace is here. She brought you a coffee. And enough pastry to feed an army."

"Grace is there?" Derek asked.

"Yeah. I asked Meyers to borrow her for a week. It looks like she's moving in."

"Dude…" he chuckled. "But she brought coffee?"

Jacob laughed. "I see what drives you now. Yes. There's one with a giant D on the cup for you. She's not even drinking coffee."

"She probably wasn't creating the world's next mega sensation at 3 in the morning either. Okay. Let me gather my stuff, and I'll head right over."

"Cool. I'll leave the patio door unlocked, so come around back and let yourself in."

"Got it. See you then."

Jacob debated whether to take a shower or go to the kitchen and get started for the day. A quick sniff check indicated a shower was in order, and he made quick work of it. By the time he emerged, he found Grace engrossed in a document on her laptop at the end of the kitchen island. He was glad to see she had shed the jacket; it gave the hint that maybe she was relaxing. She had barely noticed his arrival.

With very little direction, Grace had a slew of administrative tasks underway. She was coordinating contracts, setting up audition space, and making distribution lists—whatever that meant. He wasn't entirely sure. The important thing was that he could return to the studio.

Jacob slouched onto the couch with his laptop perched on his knees, headphones spanning his damp head. He didn't bother turning on the lights, preferring to work by glare of the screen. He pulled up the tracks, playing with levels on Rae's new bassline in the software.

Unexpectedly, the lights flipped on, and he nearly dropped the laptop. Clutching the machine to his chest and tugging the headphones off, he glared, finding Derek smirking in the doorway.

"You scared me," Jacob accused.

The grin on Derek's face looked anything but apologetic.

"Clearly." He entered the room gesturing for Grace to follow. "You realize you left her out in the kitchen and didn't tell her where anything was including the bathroom."

Jacob's face scrunched as he looked at her. "My mother raised me so much better than that. Sorry!"

"I took care of it," Derek assured as he eased into a seat at the mixing console.

Grace waited in the doorway for instructions.

"I think we should bring in Rae if we're going to keep recording today," Derek suggested as he flipped on the controls. Lights flickered to life and blinked on the board with each motion.

"That's a great idea," Jacob agreed.

Derek tapped his phone, and in moments, his speakerphone was ringing. He passed it to Grace who jumped like he'd tossed a hot potato.

Jacob suppressed his snicker under Grace's withering gaze.

Rae answered on the second ring. "You got Rae."

"Hello, this is Grace. We met at the barbecue over the weekend."

"I remember. You're the other fan," she teased. "What's up, buttercup?"

"Mr. Hunter has procured my services for the week, and I was calling for two reasons. First, he and Mr. Reed are working on some music and wanted to know if you could come over to work with them. Also, they asked me to set up auditions today. Which leads me to my second question. As I recall, you work as a bartender at a club. Do you think it would be possible to rent the club today to hold the auditions? Hopefully it wouldn't interfere with their regular business since it's during the day. Or is that too short notice?"

"Well, first, yes. I'd love to head over. In fact, if you send one of the guys to get me, I can have your answer to the second question by the time I arrive, if that sounds copacetic?"

"Well, they're a little bit busy, but if you give me the address, I'll head your way," she replied.

Jacob waved his arms to get her attention, and Derek jangled his keys. Each of them pointed out themselves, and Jacob mimicked a steering wheel in the air.

Grace's face twisted into a snarl, and she turned her back to them as she finished the call. She passed the phone to Derek with a self-satisfied smile.

"You know one of us could have gotten her," Jacob groused. He'd already imagined the way she would roll her eyes at his driving and squeal as he took corners without slowing down.

"It's better if I pick up Rae. You'll be able to get down to business sooner, and I'll be back shortly. It's what I'm here for."

"Oh. Of course. Thanks." Jacob smiled brightly, masking his disappointment. Grace was, of course, right. But he wanted to spend a little more time getting to know the bass player. His cheeks warmed slightly at the knowing look on Derek's face.

"Hopefully when I return, I'll have Rae and a venue for the auditions. As long as the candidates are free, we should be ready to rock and roll."

Jacob shook his head. "It's been like, five minutes? Are you made of rocket fuel?"

She chuckled. "I wish. See you in a bit." Without further ado, she was out the door.

Staring after her, Jacob whistled. "I am not used to this level of support," he hummed.

Derek patted his arm. "This is what it's supposed to be."

Jacob turned slowly back to the console. "You were offering to go get her too."

Shrugging, Derek started opening software on his laptop. "I brought her in, and I knew she didn't drive. I had just assumed I'd have to transport her all the time." He smirked. "So thanks for getting us some help. It is pretty nice to just focus on the music."

Nodding, Jacob didn't respond. He wished he was focused on the music and not the woman playing their bass parts.

SEVEN

After fussing over what to wear to Jacob's house for ten minutes, Rae selected a white, ruffled top that bared her shoulders and hugged her curves with a pair of low-rise boot-cut jeans. Strapping on white sandals, she braided her brown locks into one long tail. Her mind had been working over the best way to get *The Oubliette* to agree to let her friends use the club that afternoon. Her best bet was Suzie, and she sighed relief when she was the manager to answer.

"Suzie," she greeted. "How's it going?"

"Better if our most dedicated bartender would come back," the manager answered.

Rae fought a groan. "I'm sure Kendra's giving you all the time she has."

"You know I meant you, goober," Suzie sassed. "If you're not calling to beg for more shifts, I'm busy."

"A friend of mine needs space to hold a few auditions today," she blurted, "and I was wondering if they could do it there." She held her breath, awaiting the answer.

"I don't know about that," Suzie hesitated.

"Oh, come on, Suz! It's a Monday," Rae cajoled. "It's your slowest night. There's no bands playing, and you barely break even opening the doors."

Suzie sighed. "It's not fair to use your knowledge against me."

"Who said life was fair?" Rae quipped. "You'd be doing us a solid. And they're willing to pay."

"How deep are the pockets?" Suzie prodded.

Rae had her now, and her body relaxed as she stopped pacing. "Deep—but this is more a personal favor to me."

"This about that project you and K were talking about last week? Where you actually play bass?"

Biting her lip, Rae cringed. She squeezed her eyes shut as she replied. "Yes."

"Oh, this I gotta see. I tell you what. I'll let you use the space today. We should be dead at 2:00. And I won't gouge your friend on the cost. But—if I do this favor at the last minute like this—you guys gotta play your first gig here."

Her heart thudded in her chest. Her first gig…the idea was surreal. "Throw in some waters and soft drinks, and you've got a deal."

By the time Grace arrived, Rae was bouncing out of her skin. The strap of her gig bag chafed her shoulder as she rocked lightly on the sidewalk while she waited. Her hips begged to swing back and forth in excitement, but she kept them in check, white knuckling the case strap instead. This was the beginning of the next phase of her life. All the heartache and hard work had led her to this moment. This was the moment of truth.

Grace's flashers signaled her pending stop, and the moment the tires came to a halt, Rae yanked the rear door open and laid her bass on the seat. She flashed a bright smile after settling in the passenger seat and reaching for her buckle.

"Good morning."

Grace smiled, turning off the flashers and glancing at her GPS.

"Is it still morning?" she teased.

"Oh, stop," Rae smiled, surprised at how quickly they were back on the road. She glanced at her companion. "So, Jacob got you for the whole week, huh?"

Grace nodded, navigating the streets. "He did. And what's your coffee of choice?"

Rae blinked. "Nectar of the gods. I am not that picky. Wherever," she replied, suddenly thinking of coffee. "And thank you! How did you know?"

Grace smirked. "Derek did. He said it would quote, 'Make you human.' End quote."

"Rude," Rae groaned. "True, but rude."

She described her favorite coffee as Grace located the nearest drive thru. Within ten minutes she had a caramel macchiato in hand, and she barely noticed time passing until they arrived at Jacob's. She could get used to being spoiled like this.

"When Meyers told me I'd be working for Jacob last night, he did not tell me that I'd be working out of the home of one of The Harmonizers," Grace mumbled as she pulled into the driveway and around to the back of the house.

With half of her coffee perking through her blood stream, Rae felt the statement in her gut and chuckled wryly. "That must have been a surprise."

"Yeah, I thought I had the wrong address. Never been so freaked out by a doorbell in my life," the other woman confessed.

Rae pictured it and snickered, eyeing Grace's business attire. Derek had described it well at their celebratory drink fest, but he had left out the part about her owning it. It had good potential for role play, she thought with a wicked grin. As quickly as the idea came to her, she abandoned it, the idea of Derek reciprocating giving her the willies. If she let that thought continue, she'd have to say goodbye to the sweet cup of caffeine clutched in her left hand.

Grace gestured to the side of the house as Rae freed her bass from the back seat.

"We should be able to get in around the back," the assistant instructed. "It was unlocked for Derek this morning. We'll go into the kitchen."

Rae grinned, following as the heat of the day began creeping over her shoulders. Her long braid swayed with her stride. The sight of Derek's BMW lit the fire in her belly knowing that the two men were already working.

In the studio, Derek was at the console, fingertips on two different faders, eyes closed and head listing to one side as he listened. Jacob was in the recording booth, belting out a note into the microphone. His fists were squeezed as he pressed his forearms to his side. His lids were closed as well, as though he and the music were the only things that existed.

Rae and Grace stood frozen in the doorway, staring at the tableau.

"Should we tell them we're here, or wait for them to see us?" Grace whispered.

"We might not live that long," Rae reasoned.

She stepped into the room, setting her gig bag on the couch and then slipping into the second chair at the console. She rolled over till her chair bumped Derek's.

He turned his head and grinned. "Morning, Sunshine. Give us a minute, k?"

Rae nodded and scooted to the couch to begin unsheathing her instrument.

"I'll be in the kitchen if anyone needs anything," Grace murmured from the doorway.

"No, don't. It'll be nice to have an audience," Rae encouraged. "Someone who could maybe see the forest for the trees."

"But I have to call all the musicians," Grace argued. "It's super last minute asking them to be at the club at 2:00 today."

It sounded like excuses to Rae as she yanked the zipper of her instrument case all the way around. She didn't understand why Grace resisted being drawn into the group. If she liked Derek as much as she claimed, she should be jumping at the chance to rub elbows with him at the console. She pinned the assistant with a sharp look.

"I'll be back in a bit," Grace conceded.

"I'll hold you to it," she vowed. Her index fingernail caught on a string, and she cussed a blue streak as the tip ripped away. "Can she not see I'm trying to include her? I mean, it's hard to show off without an audience."

"And yet you manage," Derek ribbed.

Rae nearly dropped her bass as she connected the strap behind her to the nub at its bottom. "Nope," she protested. "Not today." She took a seat beside him to secure the fussy strap.

In the recording booth, Jacob pressed a hand clutching a journal against one ear of the headphones and closed his eyes as he poured himself into the ballad-like vocal. She stared at his mouth as he enunciated each word, the passion practically dripping from his lips.

The lyrics were provocative, and when he opened his eyes after a particularly long note, Rae was rooted to the spot. Her body flushed, and she blindly grabbed her bass as she ran into the tracking room to join him.

She allowed the music to flow into the instrument from her hips, as her fingers plucked a counterpoint to his words. Eyes locked on him, she inched forward instinctively, matching his moves and licking her lips. Even separated by a wall of glass and plaster, it was as if Rae could feel Jacob pressing against her, telling her all the things he wanted to do to her. As the song ended, and he stopped singing, she realized she was out of breath, and she fought not to moan.

Jacob bounded out of the booth, fire and promises in his eyes, virtually stalking toward her. She swallowed hard, almost baring her neck to the singer in supplication.

From his seat behind the console, Derek coughed and muttered, "Save something for the stage, guys."

Heat blossomed up her neck till her earlobes itched as she and Jacob settled down on either side of Derek in the control room. Rae cradled her bass to herself, looking studiously anywhere other than Jacob.

"How was it?" Jacob prompted, looking at the producer.

Derek nodded. "You were definitely in a groove. Let's try it again, but if you can hold back some of that passion…Rae, you should hear it from the top. Try letting it build until closer to the end. If we can get the crescendo in the right spot…" Derek lifted a thumb on one hand while the other tapped buttons and turned dials. He looked at Jacob. "Can you do another take?"

"Yes, but lemme fiddle with the lyric in the first verse a second. I had a little inspiration when Rae joined in."

Rae looked up through heavy-lidded eyes. "Glad to be of service."

"Alright now—no talk of servicing anyone," Derek scolded, but the snicker that followed negated his words.

"Stop," Rae teased, pretending to punch his arm.

"I didn't start it!" Derek protested. He pushed Jacob gently and looked at Rae. "Go plug in so I can record this time. I'll play the beginning while you set up to give you a feel for where it's going. See if you can join in early and play through."

Rae did as instructed, plucking a few notes to test the volume. Derek played back the beginning, stopping and starting several times. The tune was fast and beat driven, and she tested out her counter rhythm again with a few tweaks. Grace was now sitting beside Derek. Their lips were moving, but she couldn't hear what they were saying. The shy smile on Derek's face was unfamiliar. They were already down bad for each other and didn't even know it.

Derek gave Rae a thumbs up. "You guys ready?" Derek called through the speaker.

Jacob looked up promptly from scribbling in his notebook and nodded. He slipped the pen into his back pocket, studying the sheet as he bounced from foot to foot. "I'm gonna go for it here. Let it all out."

Rae listened along as the music began, riffing the bass line until she found the right groove and leaning into it. Her eyes roamed over Jacob's back, watching as he swayed in time. He had a perfect ass, just the slightest bit round, and she imagined what it would sound like to slap it.

When Jacob began singing, Rae closed her eyes, allowing herself to feel his words as they washed over her. With her sight deprived of input, his vocals surrounded her, breathy, as though he was whispering in her ear. His voice dipped into a lower register than normal, and her body responded with a groan that almost escaped her lips. Derek had suggested she let the pressure build, and she allowed herself to wallow in the languid bassline.

As they approached the chorus, his vocal changed, becoming more urgent, and she matched his intensity as they reached the first chorus. By the end, the song was frenzied, and Rae poured herself into the bass as her eyes snapped open. Jacob gave one last powerful note, letting it die on his lips until all the air had left his lungs.

Derek was poised in the studio, with a finger over the laptop. He tapped one key to end the recording then clapped furiously. "That was amazing. You guys definitely fed the chemistry into that beast."

"You killed it. You were all the way in there," Jacob crowed.

Rae paced in small circles, not making eye contact for a moment. "That was amazing. You," she pointed first at Derek then at Jacob, "are both amazing." Her eyes lingered on him. The things he had sung she had been living in her head. Her fingers were almost numb from the experience, but she couldn't say any of this. She wondered if he realized he was sex on legs.

"Those lyrics," she whispered.

His tongue darted over his lips. "It's not too much?"

She bit her lip and shook her head. "Not at all."

"Grace?" Jacob asked.

Rae followed his gaze to Grace. She was unnaturally still, blinking in discomfort and looking at a spot on the wall past them.

Her voice was tinny over the open channel Derek was holding on the console mic. "Yes?" she squeaked.

"What's wrong?" Jacob asked.

"Nothing," she answered, hopping up. "Anyone need anything?"

"We need the truth," Derek chided.

She gulped, looking away briefly. "Well," she began, worrying her hands before tucking them into her elbows. "It's very…well, it's all sex! You can't play that on the radio." At this, her hands flew out to her sides, her eyes bugged, and her mouth hung open. It lasted barely a second before she folded in on herself again.

The words stung, but it didn't make them ring any less true. The thoughts she'd been having while sinking into the bassline had been pure lust. She looked to the singer to see how he'd taken the feedback.

Hurt. Deep hurt contorted his face. Maybe he had heard this before. Given his solo project, she assumed he had ignored his nay-sayers.

"Not every song has to be played on the radio," he countered.

She nodded. "I get that. It's just…it's strong, guys." She paused, then doubled down. "It just…it kinda sounds like a soundtrack for porn."

Rae's chin hit the floor, and she saw Jacob and Derek's do the same. Their music might have been sensual, but she would never classify it as porn.

Derek was the first to speak, head shaking derisively. Unless Rae missed her mark, he looked disappointed.

"Too much for you?" he taunted.

Rae's spine straightened, gripping her bass as she moved toward the glass. The spark that had been developing between them seemed to be on the brink of extinguishing. Despite her promise to Derek not to interfere, she couldn't help herself from jumping in.

"This is exactly why I asked her to join us," Rae defended. "I like something sexy as much as anyone, but we need somebody to keep our heads in the game. She's right. If we want to be successful, we've got to remember our audience." She turned to Grace. "Subtlety, right? It should be more like…foreplay instead of the main act. Leave them wanting more, yes?"

"Something like that," Grace mumbled. "Also, I wanted to let you all know that I confirmed the place and time for auditions. Thanks to Rae's connections, we can get rolling in an hour to find you guys a drummer and guitarist. We'll be going to *The Oubliette*, but with the caveat that they want to be the first place you play live."

"Oh. Right. Auditions," Jacob mumbled. He scratched the back of his head. "Well then, I guess we'd better go."

Once they were all outside, Jacob unlocked his car with a beep and reached for the driver's door.

"Why are you driving?" Derek frowned.

"Because no one else here has already driven to and from *The Oubliette*." He smirked. "Rae, you can sit in the back so my driving doesn't scare you."

"Cool. Now Grace and I can whisper about y'all," she teased back, sticking out her tongue.

Grace stopped short. "Actually, I need to take my car. In case we run long, I need the flexibility. I'll meet you there."

"Yes!" Rae crowed. "Mind if I join you? This way we don't have to whisper!"

At Grace's slight nod, she stuck her tongue out at the guys once more and slipped into the passenger seat. Once on their way, they settled into a companionable silence. About halfway there, Grace's phone rang.

There was no place to pull over. Grace quickly answered the call and tapped the speaker button. "This is Grace," she immediately answered. She held a finger over her lips as she looked at Rae.

"Grace, it's me. Have you got a minute?"

Rae assumed it was Meyers, and he sounded almost jovial, but in a way that made the bass player's skin crawl.

"Certainly. How can I help?" Grace replied smoothly.

"Well, I wanted to check on how it's going and how those contracts are coming. It's after noon, and I was hoping to get those back by close of business today."

"Right, yes, I recall," Grace replied. "I spoke with Mr. Hunter first thing this morning, and he's passed them to his lawyer to review."

"Did you relay to him the timeliness of this? You guys shouldn't be working today until they're signed."

"Yes, sir. I understand."

"Well, what are you doing right now? It sounds like you're driving. Are you even with Hunter?"

Grace took a deep breath. "I set up auditions so they could find a drummer and a guitarist, and we're on our way there now in separate cars."

"Where did you find space on such short notice?"

"*The Oubliette*. Rae works there part-time and they allowed us to use the space and even asked if the band would play their first gig there."

"Grace, you didn't tell them yes, did you?"

Rae looked out the window and made a face. This guy was gross. His tone was oily. She shuddered at the thought of that nasty man being in charge of her career. She paled when she realized that everyone else's, including the musicians she was about to meet, was in his greasy paws.

"No, no, of course not. That's always up to you to work out the best plan. That's not my place."

"Right. Right. And the musicians were able to be there?"

"Yes, sir. I called and spoke to each of them. They confirmed they'll meet us there."

"And Hunter is happy?"

"Yes, sir. Of course."

"Great. Also, there's a bag of clothes at the back door if you could drop those at the cleaners when you come to get Oscar this afternoon. We need it to be done by Thursday, okay?"

Rae's eyes went wide. He had her doing laundry? What the hell? She wasn't his servant or slave! And who the fuck was this Oscar she had to pick up? Her heart sank for the woman next to her.

Grace didn't even flinch, nodding to the road ahead as she changed lanes. "Yes, sir. I'll get it back to you by Thursday."

Rae looked at Grace, chin virtually in her lap. "Today?" she mouthed. Was this her life?

Grace nodded, eyes on the left turn she was making.

"So, you'll get those contracts today?" Meyers insisted as if Grace hadn't already said as much.

"I'll do my best." The assistant's lips curled between her teeth, and Rae heard a heavy exhale.

"Good. Good. Well call tomorrow. You have my schedule."

"Yes, sir."

The call disconnected.

Rae couldn't hold her tongue for another second. She whirled on the driver. "Who the hell is Oscar, and why are you doing his dry cleaning?"

"Oscar is a French Bulldog who pisses all over everything when he's nervous. And I always do his dry cleaning. It's part of my job. About three or four days a week."

Rae frowned. "How are you supposed to make Jacob's lawyers work any faster?"

Grace shrugged. "I'll figure it out. Or I won't, and he'll either fire me or make me wish he would."

Rae watched the buildings pass and pedestrians walking their dogs and scurrying to their destinations. Part of her was relieved that she had never been treated that way by an employer. The rest of her was determined to rescue Grace from the indignities foisted upon her.

"He does this," Grace excused.

"And you're okay with it?"

Grace shrugged. "I don't have a choice. I'd make a terrible waitress, and I'm not an actor or a musician. I don't know what else I'd do. And I can't stand the thought of failing and having to go back to Chicago. I keep hearing that this town is going to either make or break you, and I'm not too crazy about being broken."

"Does Jacob know about this dog thing?"

She shook her head. "No. Why would he? I'm okay. I'm not sure what Jacob needs me for but I'll roll with it."

"Grace? Do you not see what you did today alone? There was breakfast and contracts, apparently. And you arranged the venue and called all these people to audition, and we're going to be on time in a city you barely know. And it's not even one."

Grace shrugged. "It's my job. And I'd have done some of this earlier, but I didn't know until about 10 last night that I would be here today."

Rae drew back, scandalized and hissed, "He calls you at 10 p.m.? You work weekends?"

"No, no. Banker's hours almost. Weekdays from 8:00 till 4:30."

"But he called on a weekend." Rae did not understand why Grace wasn't more upset.

"Sometimes. Or the evening if something's up. And again—it's a good agency. Big. Job security. Come to think of it, he did this last Sunday, and that's how I ended up in the middle of Derek and Jacob at a restaurant. It's hard to complain about that."

Rae offered a chuckle of agreement and a tight smile. Internally, she was fuming on Grace's behalf. She saw the worried look in her new friends' eyes, so she swallowed back further criticism. The tirade continued internally, however, all the way to the club. She stalked toward the employee entrance with her bass to expel some of the excess energy and nodded at the guys who were walking up as she knocked on the door.

As they filed inside, Rae introduced everyone to Suzie and Kendra, who had come in to help. Rae knew they were there to spy on her, and she threw some extra sauce in her walk as she passed them.

She hoped they were jealous of her company. In all her time talking about Derek on the weekends, they had never laid eyes on her old boy-band companion. And while she had outgrown any attraction to him, she knew how good he looked. Between him and Jacob, her hotness meter skyrocketed.

Suzie had absconded with Grace for a tour, and Kendra pulled Rae aside to the bar.

"Desirae Sage!" Kendra scolded, squeezing her coworker's arm and leaning in.

"Blasphemy! Don't say that. Anyone could hear you," Rae snapped at the use of her full name.

Kendra squeezed her forearm and pressed their foreheads together with a tiny squeal.

"What?" Rae blushed, knowing exactly what her friend meant. "I couldn't say anything until it was all official." She looked over at Suzie who was depositing Grace in the vestibule. "And I swear it's a coincidence that he's the one from VIP the other night. I didn't know he was Derek's new client, hand to God."

Kendra eyed both Jacob and Derek. "Either way, I almost swallowed my tongue when he strolled in." She gasped. "Dammit he's pretty! It's unreal!"

"Yeah, don't tell him." Rae laughed. "He'd much prefer being 'ruggedly handsome' instead of pretty."

"Tough titty," Kendra growled. "He's prrrrretty pretty."

"Like I don't know?" Rae sighed. "Just…keep it reined in, yeah? I so don't want to deal with him getting pouty, and he's already halfway there thanks to Grace calling us out on our bass-heavy porno sound."

"Your what?" Suzie asked, blue eyes narrowing as she sneaked up beside them.

"It's not…well, I guess there's a…chemistry happening, and it makes for exceptionally sexy music. I'm pretty sure it's my fault. He…inspires all the dirty thoughts in my head to go berserk." Rae saw Derek waving to her. "Anyway, I better get out there."

"Derek?" Kendra confirmed.

Rae nodded, freeing herself from the bartender's grasp.

"I can't believe you've never brought him out here before for all the talking about him you've done. He's single, right?" Suzie asked. The way her eyes raked over him left no doubt about her intent.

"Don't. Don't," Rae warned, slipping away from the two women. "Not for you and not for him. He's all music and literally nothing else."

"So, what you're saying is he's got some rhythm," Suzie teased, lifting her arms over her head and gyrating her hips.

Rae shook her head and pushed away from the counter.

"You're the one that brought up porn!" Kendra called after her.

~ ♫ ~ JACOB ~ ♫ ~

Setup happened so fast, Jacob nearly missed it. Grace had stationed herself in the vestibule out of sight. A semi-circle of five folding chairs faced the stage, and he and Derek were positioned in the two center seats. He remained silent waiting to be told what to do. With no effort, the candidates were filed in one at a time, starting with the drummers.

Rae accompanied each drummer that came in, and he hoped to hear some kind of rapport.

Jacob bit back the lascivious grin threatening to expose his train of thought as Rae played. It was like his own private show. She was trying so hard to connect with each of them, but it was nothing like she had performed with him at his studio.

Until Joe Andrews arrived. The synergy between them was palpable. The two were anticipating each other, and a surge of jealousy started to rise in his belly.

She followed his opening riff, and before long they were playing *Lifestyle* by Rebel Gloss.

Jacob turned his attention on the homely drummer with his thinning candy colored hair and Journey T-shirt. The drummer's grin was like a thousand-watt lightbulb as he played. He was showing off, Jacob realized.

He glanced at Derek to gauge his impression as they rolled into another song.

By the time they'd played the third one, both were sweating and laughing.

Jacob nodded his approval to Derek.

The producer was on his feet, practically skipping toward the stage. "Well, Mr. Andrews, it seems our little Rae of sunshine has found her rhythm partner," Derek announced. "Welcome to the family."

Jacob was grateful for Derek's ability to step in without being asked. At the moment, Jacob was not in the mindset to give even good news or welcomes. Rae's performance—her loss of control while playing was…indescribable. His jeans strained against his desire as he looked at her congratulating the drummer. Her chest glistened, and the barest hint of her midriff teased him, and all he wanted to do was kiss her breathless. Dead puppies. Toxic waste. Funerals. Grandma Mary. He tossed random thoughts at his brain to quell the desire.

"Now all we need is a guitarist," Rae breathed, chest heaving from the exertion.

And his brain was devouring her all over again. Jacob crossed his legs as she high-fived Joe and skipped back to the chairs, patting one for their newest member.

He shot a handshake to the drummer as he was seated then turned to the vestibule, calling for Grace. "We're ready for the guitarists now!"

A short, bald man strode brazenly through the door, his naked chest exposed as his leather jacket parted. He had barely made it two feet into the room before Rae was on her feet, fists clenched at her side.

Joe's hands covered his face, and Jacob heard the groan before Rae exploded.

"Absolutely not!" Rae screeched. Her eyes were wide and wild, but her mouth opened and closed as though trying to spit out words. Jacob thought she looked like she was about to vomit.

Grace's dress shoes were sliding on the club's floor as she scurried behind him. She reached for him several times but never touched him, her lips curling back.

The man did not stop walking, but he slowed his pace, lifting his wraparound sunglasses to rest on his bald pate. His jaw twitched, chin hairs bristling.

"I beg your pardon?" he snapped.

"No snakes on our team," Rae answered. "I know what you did, you creeper! Making porn starring fans is as gross as it gets. Walk away now," she snarled, pointing at the door.

The man raised his hands in confusion. "What's wrong with porn?"

Seeing Rae's reaction, Jacob was on his feet. He'd seen these types of tactics before and it never hurt to remind people that they weren't the biggest person in the room. He straightened his back, looking down on the considerably shorter man.

Grace met his eyes frantically. Her cheeks were flushed, and her voice boomed. "He's not on the list. I tried to stop him."

From the corner of his eye, he saw Derek moving toward him till they were side by side.

"If Grace says you're not on the list, you're not on the list. We're in the middle of an audition and barging in here is incredibly rude," Jacob pointed out.

"Meyers said you were looking for someone like me, and I know Joe," the guitarist argued, pointing at the drummer.

"We're looking for *our* sound," Derek replied easily. "And you're not it. We do have security if you'd like an introduction." He lifted a hand toward the staff milling around the bar.

Jacob fought the urge to follow the producer's hand. He hadn't been aware of security, and he assumed the man was bluffing.

The audacious stranger mumbled a string of curses, and Grace put herself between him and Rae.

"Are you serious?" the man groused.

"This way," Grace encouraged leading him to the doorway. Business suit and all, Grace was on his heels all the way out.

Jacob wasn't sure what was going on or who this older man was, but if both Rae and Grace who were polar opposites were having the same reaction, he trusted them.

He glanced at Joe again, who was staring at his shoes and scratching the back of his neck.

Rae was shaking, and Jacob placed a gentle hand on her shoulder. Her violently adverse reaction and accusations had come seemingly out of nowhere. He'd known a lot of musicians with some less than honorable treatment of their fans, but porn? He drew the line there.

Rae covered her face with her hands, limbs shaking.

They did need to move forward with the auditions, but he couldn't bring new people in with Rae in this state.

"You okay? Need a few?" he asked kindly.

"I'm so sorry, Rae," Grace called across the room as she returned. "He was past me before I could—"

"No worries," Rae cut in, leaning into Jacob's soothing touch. He pulled her closer, tucking her protectively against his side.

"It's…a Rebel Gloss thing," Joe explained. "He fucked a lot of shit up for a lot of people involved with the band. Members, staff, and fans, and he was so damn crass, he bragged about it."

Jacob eased Rae into a chair, rubbing her arm tenderly.

"I'm so sorry, guys," Rae whimpered. "That was so unprofessional of me. I just…I couldn't…there's no way I could have worked with him. I know it's presumptuous of me, but—"

"Rae, hush," Jacob soothed, cutting in. "We would never force you to work with someone that nasty. Not even if he was the best guitarist that ever lived!"

She relaxed, chuckling and cuddling deeper into Jacob's side.

"If you hadn't said something, I would have," Joe assured, then shuddered.

"I'm with y'all on this," Derek frowned. "Bad juju like that? No thank you."

Four more guitarists auditioned, and while Jacob couldn't say any of them were bad, they simply didn't gel. They were glory hogs showing off five-minute solos they'd perfected in the privacy of their bedroom pretending they were rock gods.

He could see the growing irritation as Grace announced their last hopeful: Carmen Luz.

She had dressed the part, and her turquoise guitar wailed as she played a medley of the most difficult guitar pieces from a variety of genres. Rae and Joe played along as though they'd been at it their whole lives. Halfway through, Derek was up and singing along. Recognizing the song, Jacob joined in. They felt whole, and Jacob counted his lucky stars that this last guitarist was the right one.

"Well hell, I think we've got our fifth, right?" Derek exclaimed as they finished.

"Hell yeah!" Jacob agreed.

"Oh, thank God!" Joe exhaled.

EIGHT

After the auditions, Jacob invited the newly formed band back to his place for an impromptu celebration. Rae's body was thrumming with adrenaline. She was practically bouncing in the backseat of Jacob's car the whole way, gushing about the nuances of the performances.

Derek smirked at her in the rearview mirror, but Jacob was silent as she rambled.

She was surprised to find Jacob had prepared for the event, and the beers and snacks were flowing within moments of walking through the door. Their new members felt like they'd always been there.

Rae dropped onto the couch beside Derek, handing him a bottle of beer and surveying their new band mates. Her nerves were settling, her limbs ready for a rest, and a buzz was beginning to take over.

"This actually feels like something real and true with Mr. Andrews and Ms. Luz on board," she mused aloud.

Derek rolled his eyes. "Sunshine, drop the honorifics. It's gonna get real awkward real fast otherwise. You're our *equal* in this. You're part of this," he insisted, taking a sip of his drink.

"I guess," she fretted, startled when Carmen draped herself across both their laps.

"Come on guys, join the revelry," the guitarist giggled. Rolling off them, she stood and pulled both to their feet. "Time for an ice breaker!"

Joe was rifling through Jacob's CD collection while the vocalist was powering on the stereo from where he sat next to it.

"What kind of game?" Rae asked, following them and feeling Jacob's heated gaze on her.

She shrugged. "Never Have I Ever?" Carmen asked.

Derek laughed. "Grace might die of alcohol poisoning."

Jacob growled. "She's not even here, man. Meyers has her on some mission."

Rae snarled, her previous anger returning. "She's taking his dog to a freaking groomer and picking up dry cleaning. And besides, she'd be the only one sober, D. You got your game mixed up. What about…Truth or Dare? That seems more evenly dangerous."

"I veto all these games," Jacob interrupted.

"On what grounds?" Carmen demanded.

"On the grounds that I am no longer thirteen years old!" Jacob insisted, handing her a beer.

Rae snatched the beverage from him, pulling her cell from her back pocket.

"Speaking of thirteen," Derek cackled. "Who are you texting so furiously, Miss Sunshine?"

"Grace," she grumbled. "I'm telling her to hurry the hell up because you guys are no fun."

She squealed when Jacob grabbed her from behind with one strong arm and plucked the phone out of her grasp with the other. Still in his grip, he spoke very quietly against her ear. "None of that!"

What Jacob had intended to be scary, made her legs go silly instead. Losing her balance, she toppled, bringing him down with her as they grappled for possession of her flip phone.

"Wait, wait, wait," Jacob roared, on the floor twisted up with the bassist. He held the device out of her reach to get a better look at it. "Is this a flip phone? Do these things even still work?"

Carmen squealed in offense, and Joe grunted.

"It's not so bad," he defended. "Not all of us can afford the latest and greatest." He and Carmen both lofted their own ancient cells in the air.

"I like it," Rae whined, finally finding an opening and snatching it back from him.

"I'll trade you, Rae," Joe offered, wagging his ten-year-old phone at her. "This thing's solid, but the reception sucks."

"How do you text?" Jacob prodded. His brows knit as he squinted at the cellular devices displayed before him.

"I don't." Carmen laughed. "Who needs text when I can dial you up and hear the dulcet tones of your voice?"

Jacob helped Rae to her feet as he continued. "But the new phones keep your calendar and music. There's all sorts of cool stuff you can do with one. You can even email," he offered, waving his phone at the others. He looked at the screen and pulled it back. "Ooh, I have mail."

"At least everyone has a phone," Derek quipped. "It wasn't that long ago none of us had one."

"Or they were those giant bricks that strapped you to a car," Joe added. "Wow, am I the oldest one in the room?"

Derek laughed. "Oh, thank God it's not me. It's always me now," he complained.

Jacob stared at all of them. "Nope," Jacob announced. "Nope. Not for my team." He began tapping furiously at his phone while the others stared at him.

"What is happening?" Carmen asked, looking at Derek and then Rae and then Joe.

"Friends don't let friends fall behind the times," Jacob insisted. "I am ordering phones now. Do you think I can ask Grace to pick them up tomorrow?"

"Sure," Derek answered. "You did ask for her help. And maybe it'll keep her from having to take dogs for a bath." He shook his head. "What a demeaning job."

Jacob stared at him. "Is it? I've heard of worse jobs."

Rae waved him off. "It's not the job. It's the people. You should've heard the way he talked to her on the way to the studio. Demanding to know what she was doing and something about laundry to pick up."

"Well, that's fair. He's her boss, right?" Carmen asked, heading to the kitchen for another drink.

"Oh!" Rae exclaimed, a realization dawning on her. "Oh. Oh! That snake! *He* sent that absolute turd to our auditions!"

Derek blinked. "Maybe he doesn't know. I mean, I didn't know."

"But you're not his agent," Joe replied, leaning back. "Agents know all your shit. And then they hold it against you. It's an ugly town. Who's surprised that there's ugly people in it too?"

Jacob stopped tapping his phone and looked up at the other musicians. "Done."

Rae couldn't believe her luck in getting to be a part of this band. Working with Derek had been a head twister. But he had called her an equal. Then came Jacob—a celebrity heavy weight that she had spent a fair amount of time drooling over in his heyday. And now, she was in the presence of a drummer who had toured with Rebel Gloss for a number of years. Her eyes went a little misty as they tracked Carmen, wondering what secrets she was holding back. Or maybe, this was the beginning of her meteoric rise to fame, and Rae could say she "knew her when."

Overwhelmed as Derek began peppering Joe with questions about his time on the road, Rae headed to the mini bar and started mixing up cocktails. The routine of preparing glasses and measuring ingredients calmed her mind. She gave the shaker a good workover, stopping when she felt the ice cracking in the container.

Jacob passed by her wordlessly and began rifling through the cabinets. Rae realized she was staring as she saw him opening one cabinet after another, peering inside. She stiffened a little when Carmen eased over to the counter and leaned against it.

"What are we looking at?" she whispered.

"Nothing." Rae sighed, turning her attention to the five glasses in front of her. Having musical chemistry didn't mean she had any claim on him. With practiced ease, she divided the mixed drink among them evenly.

Carmen's smirk as she pulled a full glass from the lineup comforted Rae as she collected one of her own. They passed out the remaining drinks, and Rae settled into the corner of the couch.

The guitarist stood in the center of the room as she took a healthy sip. "Hey—so now that we're part of this band...when do we get to hear what we'll be doing?"

"Yeah, of course! Let me show you the studio where we'll be working, and we can listen there," Jacob offered.

"It's not finished yet—we've barely gotten started," Derek cautioned.

Rae smiled softly, squeezing Derek's elbow. "No one is judging you."

~ ♫ ~ JACOB ~ ♫ ~

Jacob led the charge into the studio, his heart squeezing as the ladies grabbed their instruments to join. Joe ran back to grab his sticks, and inside a minute, the girls were huddled in the tracking room as Derek pulled up the files. Joe was tapping his sticks on his knees, filling the quiet.

Midway through playback, Rae picked up the bassline, and with blinding speed, Carmen began riffing on top. The ladies were already bouncing back and forth like they were long lost sisters.

"We picked good," Jacob muttered to his companion at the console.

Derek hummed agreement. "Should I record?"

Jacob shrugged. "I don't see why not. We might get something usable."

The producer was already flying through the software and tapping buttons. If they could reproduce this energy on stage, the entire audience would fall in love.

Movement in his peripheral vision alerted him to a newcomer, and he looked up in time to see a snow-white bag placed at his feet. He winked at Grace as she curled up on the end of the couch, opposite Joe.

"Hey, thanks," he enthused, recognizing the phone store logo. Digging into the bag, he pulled out a box and handed it to Joe.

The drummer stared at it for a long moment. "This is incredibly generous," he stated, staring at the box, as if afraid to open it.

"Neh, it's selfish. I can't video chat with other smart phone users," he admitted.

Jacob launched out of his seat, a box in each hand, as he bounded into the tracking room and passed a box to each of the ladies. "Merry Christmas," he offered, beaming. "Welcome to this century! You're going to love it here."

Rae squealed, hugging him around the neck before delving into the box to extract her shiny new toy. "Thank you!"

Carmen kissed Jacob's cheek and took her gift to a stool to sit while she opened hers.

Once all the boxes were open, Rae and Carmen bounded down the hall looking for outlets to plug in their phones, Joe trailing behind.

Jacob practically had to drag them by the ears away from the charging devices to lead them to the table for dinner once the food had arrived. Their baser instincts finally kicked in, and food was flying across the table as they loaded their plates. Small talk filled the space as they staved off their initial hunger.

"Thanks for picking up those phones," Jacob thanked Grace. "That was above and beyond the call of duty."

Grace waved a hand. "It's no big. It gives me a place to be until Oscar is ready for pickup."

"Wait, what?" Jacob questioned, fork mid-way to his mouth. "It's like 6 o'clock!"

"And?" Grace questioned. "Some days I'm at it late, and some days I do almost nothing. Although—those are getting fewer and farther between."

"Name the last time you had a whole day off," Jacob challenged.

"Last Saturday I…wait. No, the Saturday before last. I spent the whole day running errands for myself."

"Well, that sounds like fun," Carmen teased.

"Oh, come on. You guys all work all the time," Grace insisted. "Didn't you pull an all-nighter Sunday?"

"Musicians work best at night," Derek interceded. "And we might work for three weeks solid, but then we'll take a month-long break."

"Lies!" Rae scolded. "Lies! This one never stops working. You're about the steadiest client at Lakeshore."

Jacob chuckled. "Makes a good producer. Gotta love what you do. But dry-cleaning and pet care—that sounds awful." He frowned, again wondering how he could hire her out from under Meyers without it backfiring horribly.

Grace's brows arched. "It's a decent living. And someone's got to do it. We can't all be pop stars."

"Ouch," Carmen exclaimed. "Draw back the claws, girl. I think he's trying to say you work really hard, and he thinks you're getting taken advantage of."

Jacob pointed at the guitarist. "What she said. It's important to know your own value. So often people get bamboozled in this city, and I hate to see it happen."

"You're a good man," Rae complimented, looking up at him. She rested her chin in her hand and stared at him.

"Thank you," he swallowed. He hadn't expected the warm fuzzies that her approval irrationally sparked in his chest. The squirming that followed under her watchful eye, however, was becoming an all too frequent occurrence. It would be so easy to lean down and gently peck her lips, like the most natural thing in the world.

Before the conversation could progress, Grace's cell phone dinged, and she grabbed it hastily. After a brief glance, she announced, "I have to go. Oscar is ready."

"He can wait," Jacob assured. "If you're picking up a dog, I bet it's 'cause no one's at home, and they won't have any idea when that dog gets back."

"True," Grace conceded, then countered, "However, if the groomer calls them when I don't respond, then I'll be in the soup again. It's a lot of responsibility, but I knew that when I took the job, so can't much complain, right?"

She was answered by a series of grumbles.

After harassing Derek about his fondness for Grace, which he eschewed artfully, they devolved into picking apart the songs he had been working on with Derek and Rae. After which, Carmen, Joe, and Derek disappeared into the studio to put their new ideas into practice.

Jacob found himself side by side with Rae at the kitchen sink. They had cleared the table and now, she was setting the dirty plates into a rising clump of soap bubbles. In profile, he studied the curve of her nose and the point of her chin. He had a pretty decent view down her T-shirt as well, but he averted his eyes, mad at himself for not wanting to take advantage. So many other guys he knew would've appreciated the view. Instead, he was thinking about her fierce reaction to a skeezy guitarist who had crashed the auditions.

She touched his arm lightly, a knowing look in her eyes. "Ask," she invited simply.

He wasn't sure he liked being so easy to read, but her request opened the flood gates.

"This whole porn business disturbs me." He sighed, watching her face intently. His gut was churning unhappily at the thoughts swirling in his brain. Had she been one of his victims? That was the real question weighing on him as he dried the plate she handed him. "Why do you know so much?"

He was in knots awaiting her answer.

"There's chat rooms for fans. We connect and talk," she replied.

Her answer had not eased his concern. "I saw how it affected you. You weren't one of the fans, were you?"

"Eew, no!" she squealed. She gagged and pretended to spit into the sink as she rinsed suds down the drain.

He was quiet as he stacked the dishes in their prescribed cabinet, carefully deciding on what he would say next.

"I saw how you reacted at the audition when he walked in. Anyone who reacts that strongly usually has a reason, and I know it's none of my business. I hope no one hurt you that way…or any way. It's hard for me to fathom." He swallowed thickly, heart pounding as he contemplated it.

She shook her head. "I appreciate that you're worried for me. But no. Nothing like that. Let's leave it at porn with willing fans is the least of his sins and move on. That guy screwed over a lot of people, including band members and…" She worried the hem of her shirt. "I know it sounds crazy, but Rebel Gloss has been a big part of my life. And they're like family. I take it very personally."

He nodded, a smile tugging the corner of one lip as his heart eased. "You're the good one too," he murmured as he took the last dish and put it away. "Thanks for the help cleaning up. You didn't have to do that."

She shook her head. "Of course I did. I made the mess too. I should help to clean it up."

"By that logic, where is everyone else?"

After drying her hands, Rae left to join the others, and Jacob sighed heavily. What was happening to him? He groaned, scrubbing his face with his hands as his brain treated him to the image of Rae's ass swinging delightfully.

"Don't shit where you eat, Hunter," he warned himself. Maybe it had been too long since he'd gotten laid? Truth be told, he hadn't wanted sex for a while now. The first spark of interest he'd had was when he'd gone to see his friend Dante at *The Oubliette* and he'd heard Rae humming. That night, he'd had images of crimson lips on his and long, dark brown hair wrapped around his fist.

Rolling his eyes at himself, he pulled up a gross picture on his phone that one of his former bandmates had suggested for an occasion like this. Shuddering, he swiped out of the folder and headed back to the studio.

NINE

When the band broke for lunch the next afternoon, Rae lingered in the tracking room after the others left to straighten up. Truthfully, after their last session, her stomach wasn't ready for food. Her bass was crooked in its stand, and the cables were tangled. The studio tech in her couldn't handle the chaos. She reached to right her instrument but hugged it to her chest instead. Her eyes closed, holding back tears.

"Daddy," she whispered. "You were right. Here I am, playing like you always said I could. *Composing* with an amazing team, and it *does* feel like coming home. It's…the most terrifying…joyous…the most natural and surreal, the most…" Unquantifiable emotions roiled in her stomach. "I wish you and Momma were here to see this. I think…no. I know I made a new family," she whispered, a few tears slipping past her tightly shut eyelids.

There was a knock at the doorway. "You coming?" Jacob asked.

She snapped up, bass still cradled to herself. "Yep. Sorry. Cleaning up," she replied, voice falsely bubbly. "You can take the tech out of the studio…"

"I get it." He stared at her for a moment, and Rae worried he would see through her façade. If he asked if she was okay, she didn't think she had the strength to answer him without devolving into tears. She held her breath until he nodded.

"See you there." He tapped the doorway and spun on one foot to depart.

She relaxed her grip, and a wet tear tickled her cheek. If he'd seen it, he gave no indication, and Rae sighed relief. When he'd turned to leave, he'd given her a delightful view of his backside. Her brain liked this thought much more than missing her parents. She straightened her bass, properly coiled a few cables, and then raced down the hall to join the others.

An amicable bubble of excitement mixed with spells of quiet as the band devoured lunch. Derek was in the middle of a long-winded suggestion about where he thought they needed to go when the unmistakable woosh the patio door sliding open silenced them all.

Every head snapped to the doorway, some forks half-way to mouths and others in mid-chew. A strange man turned the corner into the kitchen with a friendly wave and jaunty, "Hello!"

Rae instantly disliked and distrusted him.

Jacob was on his feet in the next breath.

"Meyers," he called, intercepting him at the kitchen counter. "Surprised to see you. I didn't realize I'd left the patio door unlocked."

She went stiff at the sound of his name. Strike three. Her eyes flicked to Grace who was sitting incredibly still between herself and Derek. Her hands were folded primly in her lap, her face expressionless and pale.

She shifted her knee to touch Grace's under the table in a gesture of solidarity.

Meyers stared at the table, his eyes landing finally on Grace. "I saw all the cars and assumed it might be. Common thing in this working town. I hope you don't mind," he added with a chuckle, as if he and Jacob were old buddies from way back.

"Um, of course not. What's up? Everything okay?" Jacob smiled graciously.

Rae squared her shoulders watching Jacob's usually expressive face blank. He wasn't any happier about the man's arrival than she was. How dare this slimeball show up unannounced?

Meyers nodded, eyes flicking to his assistant. "Grace, you look comfortable. And you're part of a matched set."

He gestured to Rae, wearing the same Rebel Gloss T-shirt as the PA.

Meyer's smarmy grin and arched eyebrow made her skin crawl. She was sure it was all over her face, and she didn't care if it was disrespectful.

Her fork clattered against the plate as she dropped it. Carmen's echoed in the room simultaneously. Rae crossed her arms over her chest to hide her valuable garment from the intruder.

"My fault," Joe called, raising a hand. "They did it in my honor."

Grace swallowed visibly and nodded.

Fury filled her limbs, and she considered leaping across the table to strangle him. Or poke out his eyes. Or any number of other scenarios where she took him down for the way he treated one of her new favorite people. She bet Carmen would join her, and she shared a look with the guitarist, who lifted her chin defiantly, nostrils flaring.

"Yeah," Jacob chimed in. "And we begged her. The suits made us uncomfortable."

"Ah. How's it working out, suits not withstanding?" Meyers asked, looking back at Jacob.

Derek launched himself from his seat and stood shoulder to shoulder with the singer. "The collaboration is everything we hoped for. We're right on track to finish up as planned."

Nodding approvingly, Meyer's flashed a grin at them both. Rae thought he looked like a shark sniffing blood. "Great, great. Any chance I could hear it?"

"Oh, no. We're not ready for that. I don't want to jinx anything. Too many cooks in the kitchen and all that. You understand," Derek answered instantly.

Jacob glanced at the producer and back to Meyers. "Yeah, we get a little superstitious about stuff like that. Playing it close to the vest works best for me."

Meyers' shark-like smile deepened, and a shiver wracked Rae's body. She needed a shower!

"Well," Meyers hummed, "that's why I introduced you. Kindred spirits."

Silence answered him.

His smile slipped for an instant before he lifted a hand. "Let me know if you need anything."

"Will do," Derek answered.

"Yeah, we've got Grace," Jacob added. "I know she knows how to get in touch. Thanks for stopping by." Jacob extended a hand to his agent.

Meyers shook it heartily before exiting the patio door. Jacob waved, closing it behind him and locking it with a distinct clack of tumblers that echoed across the house.

He stared until Rae heard Meyers' car start and the crunch of his tires against the driveway.

Everyone at the table sagged with an audible exhale.

Jacob shook his head, ambling back to the table with his eyes on Grace. "You were right. No more leaving the door unlocked."

"Okay, I'll say it," Carmen grumbled. "What a fucking ass! What was he doing here?"

Joe shrugged. "He does this."

Jacob's brow thatched in wrinkles, and he squinted at the drummer. "He's done this to you before?"

Joe nodded. "Yep."

"Grace did warn you to lock your doors," Rae scolded, as the adrenaline seeped out of her.

"And she was right," Jacob agreed.

"How long have you worked with him?" Carmen asked, leaning toward Grace.

Her voice was shaky as she answered. "Almost four months now. It's still new," she explained. She sucked in a deep breath, smiled awkwardly, then stared at her plate.

"Quit!" Carmen yelled. "Quit now. And sue the motherfucker. How dare he talk about what you're wearing?" Carmen thundered. The knuckles of her clenched fists were white. Rae's thumbs rubbed gentle circles on Carmen's hands until her grip loosened.

"He's my boss," Grace murmured. "It's his purview to set the dress code."

Jacob's head was shaking sharply. "And this week, I'm your boss. And I say anything goes."

"So ass-less chaps tomorrow?" Rae suggested brightly, waggling her eyebrows at everyone.

The group screamed in surprised laughter, and Grace wiped the corner of her eyes so quickly she almost didn't see it. The secretary began clearing her plate as she stood.

"Go back to the studio," Grace encouraged. "I've got this. It's time." She tapped her wrist where a watch should have been but wasn't. "Go back and strike while the proverbial iron is hot. Please."

"The woman knows what she wants. Let's leave her to it," Derek ordered.

Rae smirked at him and then Grace before skipping behind the others.

~ ♫ ~ JACOB ~ ♫ ~

The rest of the week blurred together for Jacob in a vortex of late-night recording sessions and delivery. Friday night after the band had deemed itself in need of a stopping point, Grace was gathering the last of her gear from the corner she'd occupied for the week. The band was in the studio, breaking down their gear and clearing out since he was headed out of town for a previous obligation. They all needed a break after the intense week, and for the first time possibly ever, Jacob was looking forward to the interviews and photo shoot he was doing out of town.

"What am I gonna do next week without you?" Jacob complained. "You can't leave me."

Grace zipped her shoulder bag shut with a chuckle and waved him off. "You'll be fine. You're traveling anyway Tuesday. You won't have long to miss me, and you'll be gone."

He rolled his eyes. "Well, yes. But..."

"But nothing," she interrupted. "You'll do great. It's not like you've never done this before."

He tried not to grin at how comfortable she'd become over the last week. On Monday she couldn't even knock on the door. By Friday, she had taken over running his household. His fridge was stocked with beverages and light snacks that would last until he got back, and a delivery of fresh items was scheduled to arrive the day he returned.

He shrugged. "Yeah, but I need you to understand how essential you were this week."

Grace smirked. "Put it in the liner notes," she teased.

"Liner notes," Jacob laughed. He saw Derek leading the others to the front room and called out to him. "Do we do liner notes anymore?"

"If we have a shred of dignity left, yes!" Derek answered.

"Who needs dignity?" Carmen teased. "What are we talking about?"

"Whatever else ya'll are talking about, you need to stop acting like we'll never see Grace again," Rae admonished, leaning against the assistant's back and squeezing her upper arms. "She's part of the family, and I *know* she will come for visits."

"Actually," Jacob added, "We'll be working on this for at least a month. You think you could stop by after Meyers to soundcheck for us?"

"Um," Grace hesitated.

"Yeah," Derek agreed. "It's kinda nice to have an outsider's perspective."

Rae punched Derek's forearm. "Family is not an outsider."

Derek groaned, rubbing his arm. "You can't us hit old guys, Rae. All I meant was she has a different perspective. Geez," Derek grumbled. "Could you lighten up?"

Rae squinted one eye at him. "It's a good thing you're pretty," she acquiesced.

"You are," Carmen teased, hanging on Derek's good arm and making kissy faces at him. She pushed him away and trotted to set her guitar case on the couch.

Jacob laughed. Rae had spoken true when she called them family, and it surprised him how quickly and organically it had transpired without him noticing. It reminded him of the energy he felt during the early days of recording with The Harmonizers.

His gaze turned to Rae. He couldn't begin to quantify what he had been feeling for her. Her passion when she played was the worst sort of aphrodisiac—it wound him up tighter than a drum.

But he would destroy her, if his history had taught him anything about himself. At the beginning when she was new and shiny, he would devote himself to pleasing her—to deriving pleasure from her. And the moment he let down his guard, he would abandon her for work, assuming she wouldn't mind. He could only serve one master, and for now, it had to be music.

His obsession had fueled the recording, and he poured all the wanting into the songs. He stared at his producer in an effort to stop the memories of her fingers stroking the bass strings and her tongue swiping out over her ruby lips when she focused on intricate finger work.

He turned his attention back to Grace.

"I've really enjoyed having you here. If this goes where I think it could, I hope you'd be open to making this more permanent."

Grace blinked at him.

"Say yes," Joe encouraged, stepping up and wrapping an arm around her shoulder. He squeezed it gently and released her quickly. "Glad you were here. Hope to see you next week." He raised his hand to the others and waved his phone. "You know where I'll be. Call me when you're ready." Then, he let himself out the back patio door.

Derek laughed. "You gotta respect a man of so few words."

Carmen waved a peace sign at the group. "Same here. Be safe in Boston next week," she called to Jacob. "Rae, you want a ride?"

The bassist shook her head. "Nah, Grace already offered. I want to make sure she's not at the vet or the cleaners or anything. She promised."

Carmen chuckled. She wrapped Grace in a hug and squeezed her. "See ya." She too, exited the kitchen, rolling the patio door quickly shut.

Grace blinked. "I should've seen that coming by now," she mumbled.

"Oh, if we're doing hugs, it's my turn!" Jacob bounced toward her and wrapped her up, lifting her briefly off the floor like he did to his sister.

Grace shrieked to Jacob's delight. "Oh dear! Down! Down!"

He dropped her unceremoniously, snickering at her reaction. He should call his sister. There was something primal about unsettling a person who was so quiet. Her face had turned pink, and she swayed on her feet, but Derek was there to steady her with the slightest touch to her forearm. He shouldered her bags and guided her out the door. She looked like a duckling following its parent, close behind him and happy to be led.

When the door closed behind them, Rae spoke. "I'm not sure either of them has any idea how cute they are together."

Jacob laughed. "I think you're right. Not sure it'll happen though. They're both so bent on being colleagues they won't entertain the idea."

"Give me time," she promised. "I love a good challenge."

"Hey, it's what makes them such great partners. Someone's gotta take it seriously."

"Yes, but life can't all be work. You gotta live a little to have something to sing about." Rae coughed and looked at the patio door with haste. "And on that note, I better get to the car before Grace completely forgets I'm here." She squeezed his upper arm, adjusted her bass on her shoulder, and scurried outside.

He stared after the bassist, and a slow smile crept across his face. He wondered if she had given any thought to "living a little" with him? He whistled as he began to clean up.

"Give me time indeed," he hummed to himself.

~ ♫ ~ R A E ~ ♫ ~

Rae walked into *The Oubliette* still pondering her conversation with Jacob about living life. She shivered as she recalled the way he sometimes whispered in her ear, his voice low and tense. A thousand other glances and touches filled her mind, and she went through her shift on autopilot until a familiar voice screamed her name. She looked up, beaming at Carmen.

The guitarist was all sequins, vinyl, and belly button as she trotted to the bar.

"Hey, girl!" she shouted back, stretching across the bar to slap at the guitarist's shoulder. "I'm so glad you made it! No one ever comes when I invite them."

Carmen flashed a smile and posed. "You've never known anyone like me," she sassed.

"Promises, promises," Rae teased back, hands already discreetly in motion prepping a tequila shot.

"I wanted to see the famous bartender in action," Carmen explained, slipping lithely onto the barstool nearest Rae.

Rae poured a cold beer, garnished with a slice of orange then handed it and the tequila to the guitarist, without a word. It was an unusual request, but Carmen had been making it all week as they listened to the daily playbacks.

"You remembered!" she exclaimed.

"Of course I did." Rae laughed, rolling her eyes. She saw Kendra approaching and pulled her close to introduce the pair. A group of frat boys at the opposite end of the bar were causing a commotion, pulling Rae from her friends. It took a few dirty jokes and a round of pretentious beers before she could return. She folded the phone numbers she'd been forced to accept as she strutted back to Kendra, bumping the other woman's hip.

Kendra glanced at her, picking up a vodka bottle and a shaker. "You wanna?" she asked.

Rae glanced around. Most people had fresh beverages, and she smelled tips coming her way. She nodded, and the pair began slinging bottles and mixing drinks. She smirked as Carmen watched, jaw slack and eyes wide.

The guitarist howled appreciatively as they finished with a fist bump and began wiping down the counters. Rae chuckled and handed her a fresh beer.

"Forget that pretty boy and be my girl!" Carmen flirted. "I'd switch teams for that skill level!"

Rae felt Kendra's questioning gaze on her and rolled her eyes. If she hadn't known before how obvious her attraction to Jacob was, she knew now.

"Go find Gracie and bother her about Derek," Rae scoffed, throwing her rag at Carmen, who caught it mid-air.

Across the bar, Carmen looked at Kendra, and her smile sharpened. "Right! Girl's night at mine after you two hot ladies are done here," she insisted before sauntering off into the crowd.

"I like her," Kendra chuckled, bumping Rae's shoulder.

"She's pretty awesome," Rae agreed. "You cool with hanging out after?"

"So she and I can compare notes? Hell yes!"

The rest of the night went by in a blur, and Rae congratulated herself for no longer obsessing over Jacob. No, now she was worried about Carmen and Kendra teasing the life out of her.

Since she and Kendra had walked, they stuffed themselves into Carmen's pink Pontiac. Rae climbed into the back to accommodate her friend who was 6'2" in flats. Almost before she could buckle in, the car sped into traffic.

She covered her eyes, sending mental apologies to Jacob for making fun of his driving. If Jacob raced the Indy 500, Carmen was preparing for Le Mans, twisting between lanes and generally defying the laws of physics.

Carmen sashayed ahead of them when they reached her third-floor walkup. They passed an ancient hardware store on the first floor as they wound around the building to the metal staircase. Its windows were dark, and nearly every available inch of glass was covered in a promotional ad or old newsprint.

Three flights later, the trio tumbled into a spacious studio apartment. Their hostess rushed in ahead of them, throwing her keys on the bed directly across from the door.

Rae stared around her, biting both lips together. The exposed brick walls and galvanized piping gave it a worldly look. A nearly dead plant in a macrame hanger was gathering dust near the kitchen. The only interior walls she saw had to be the bathroom. Multi panel screens gave vague shapes to the spaces separating the kitchen from the living room from the bedroom. No two pieces of furniture matched, but Rae thought it looked loved because of it. Clothes were strewn everywhere, not rumpled but arranged in haphazard piles over chair backs and tables. The bed sheets had been sloppily thrown in place.

Her furniture consisted of hand-me-downs and flea market finds straight out of a 70s home furnishing catalogue. Bean bag chairs and a worn avocado green couch filled out the space in front of an old tube TV resting on a flat trunk that must have been from the 20s. Its leather surface was cracked, but the patina was beautiful.

The space was mismatched, but it was what Rae felt when she thought of the word *home*. She wanted to throw herself into the plush looking mattress but refrained.

"Home sweet home," Carmen announced, twirling with her hands in the air to show off her space.

"Wow," Kendra breathed.

"What she said," Rae whispered, pointing at Kendra and walking slowly around the room to take everything in.

"Make yourself at home," Carmen entreated, then disappeared into a massive closet Rae had overlooked behind the front door. The interior shimmered in glossy threads, sequins, and vinyl. Unabashedly, the guitarist shimmied out of her clothes and dropped a thin t-shirt over her head. Her shiny pants were soon replaced with a pair of cut off sweatpants. The jagged edges barely covered the bottom of her ass.

"With all those clothes I was expecting silk pajamas," Kendra teased, plopping into a wingback chair. She kicked her shoes off, stretching out.

Carmen smirked. "You'll slide right out of bed. I sleep nude, usually. I just thought I'd protect your eyes."

Rae squealed. It wasn't as though she was shocked by the thought of sleeping in the buff, it was how easily Carmen threw out the factoid. As though she just confessed to breathing air.

"My eyes don't need protecting," Kendra teased with a laugh.

"You ladies ready to get your drink on? I've got vodka spritzers all around!" Carmen offered.

Rae and Kendra waved their arms in the air to order.

"That has to be weird working a bar all the time and never getting to drink," the guitarist mused as she pulled glasses from one cabinet and vodka from the freezer.

"You get used to it," Kendra replied. "It's the sober flirting that's the worst part."

A glass clinked on the counter, and Carmen barked out a soft curse then a sigh. "Nearly had a man down."

"Unless you're Rae," Kendra accused. "She's all with the fake flirting these days. Way over the top."

"What are you talking about?" Rae asked, standing to help with the drinks.

"Keep your ass on that chair, missy," Carmen ordered.

Rae snapped her head toward their hostess, blinking. "What? I wanted to help. Carrying three glasses is rough for a non-professional."

"You wanted to avoid the conversation," Kendra retorted.

"If you must know, I'm worried about money without Lakeshore in my back pocket," Rae confessed. "My alimony runs out in a few years, and I don't want to be reliant on it. And my lease is up at the end of July and they're raising the rent."

"For what? Extra building character due to crumbling plaster?" Kendra balked.

Carmen and Rae snickered. "You could stay here, but I only have one bed, and I have a lot of sleepovers."

"How many is a lot?" Kendra questioned.

Depositing a glass in each of their hands, Carmen dropped herself onto a large beanbag. She hummed and sipped her drink. "I don't know. Four to six? I have to wash my hair some nights," she teased.

Kendra squealed. "That sounds juicy."

"It's not," Carmen replied with a shrug and emptied her glass.

Rae marveled at the woman's confidence. How was she going to compete with this on stage? And what was more, why in the world would Jacob look any farther than Carmen for his carnal urges? She had everything in one tidy, trim, and very available package.

"I wish I could be as…confident and uninhibited," Rae admitted.

"You can," Carmen encouraged. "You just have to make the choice. No one's going to react to you differently than they already do, but you'll feel better doing everything. Life's too short to be shy."

"Wise words," Kendra complimented.

Rae squirmed as her coworker turned an intense gaze on her. After a few moments, she tucked her arms over herself trying to take up less space. "What?" Rae snarled.

In unison, Kendra and Carmen scoffed and rolled their eyes.

"You know exactly what, Miss Priss," Kendra huffed. "You've been a whole new person since you met Mr. Jacob Hunter."

"She has?" Carmen asked eagerly, sitting up and giving the Amazonian woman all her attention.

"I have never seen her this alive," Kendra stage whispered. "Not even with Alex!"

Rae scrunched her face up in annoyance. Why did *he* have to be brought up?

"Alex?" the guitarist repeated, her gaze swiveling to Rae.

"My ex-husband," Rae groaned.

"I can tell the story if you want," Kendra offered tenderly.

"Nah, but thanks, Kiki," Rae refused. She held up her empty glass. "I might need another of these first."

Carmen was out of her seat before Rae had finished speaking and returned nearly as quickly with a full glass.

"I'm all ears," she prompted.

"So we met in grade school in Tulsa. The first time I saw Alex, I was in fifth grade. He was in sixth, and he and his friends covered a Rebel Gloss song at a school talent show. And I fell instantly in love with Rebel Gloss and Alex." She thought of the day after the show where she'd dragged her dad to the local record store and begged to buy every piece of Rebel Gloss sheet music and album she could find. He had mocked her endlessly, but otherwise put up no fuss. She and her father had spent endless hours debating how she compared to their bassist, Nigel Davies, as she practiced.

"But you digress," Kendra encouraged.

"Sorry," Rae apologized. "So for three years, he never noticed me at all. The summer before freshman year, I was working at the studio where dad worked, and I spent the whole time lugging around amps and other gear, swooning after the super cool kid a grade ahead of me. And I showed up on day one in a D-cup, all lean and fit from the summer work, and then he noticed me. We were in a band together. He could barely play the cymbals, but he looked hot doing it. He looked hot breathing."

Both ladies snickered, and Carmen gestured flipping her hair and pretending to be a hot young Alex for a moment.

"Stop or she'll be laughing too hard to tell us everything," Kendra sassed.

"So I was the best thing that happened to the band. We were winning competitions, and I was all excited to play at the first game of the season. And we did great, and I got a little solo on the bass, and I thought I was hot shit."

Carmen clapped. "A baby rockstar in the making."

Rae smiled wistfully. "Well, I got more attention than I wanted. So the whole team cornered me after the game making some really ugly remarks about how they wanted to see how my rhythm was during…other activities." She cleared her throat, remembering the terror that filled her.

"Kids are such dicks," Kendra interjected.

"Men are dicks," Carmen corrected.

"Everybody's a dick at some point," Rae added. "But then Alex bursts through the crowd, throws an arm around me, and they backed off. We were inseparable after that. He went to community college while I finished high school, and we got married after I graduated."

"Waaaaaiiiiiit," Carmen cut in, waving her drink around. "Are you telling me that you married your childhood crush? Bet you sowed a lot of wild oats after you were free of that cunt!"

"Nope," Kendra chimed in. "Our girl's practically been a nun for over a decade."

Horror crawled across Carmen's face, and Rae bit her tongue trying not to laugh.

The guitarist slammed back her drink and climbed into Rae's lap.

"Carmen?" Rae asked, arching an eyebrow.

The guitarist's arms wove around her, face snuggled into Rae's neck. Stiffly, Rae craned around to look at her hugger.

"I'll get you some quality dick," Carmen promised. "Can't have my new best girl be lonely."

Rae and Kendra howled with laughter.

Stroking Carmen's obsidian hair in a motherly fashion, Rae explained, "I'm celibate by choice, darlin'. And trust me…Alex and I did plenty of exploring together. I know my way around a *quality dick*." She finished with a wicked grin.

"Fine," Carmen grumbled. She stumbled to her feet, slinking to the kitchen. "I take my pleasure very seriously, and I think denying yourself relief is a sin. It's a skill like everything else in life, and you should be exercising it regularly."

Stunned, Rae stared after her.

Carmen searched around in the fridge for a moment before standing with beers in both hands. "Caught you looking. You're so hungry for it, you're practically starving if you're checking out my ass."

In fairness, Rae was unused to seeing anyone's ass wriggling so openly looking around a refrigerator. She had been mesmerized.

"So why'd you divorce? You can't tell me just half the story."

Rae shrugged. "Well, my parent's died," she started, but Carmen interrupted.

"No!" She launched herself at Rae again, embracing her and squishing beside her. "I lost my aunt, and it still haunts me. You are so brave to go on without your parents."

Rae gulped at the show of empathy, and her throat clogged for a moment. She couldn't speak and suddenly hated herself for pulling her parents into any story involving her ex. But it had been when the cracks in their relationship started to appear.

"I'm sorry," Carmen soothed, stroking Rae's upper arm. "Go on. What happened next with the dumbass of an ex?"

"How do you know he's a dumbass?" Rae questioned, grateful for the transition.

"Because I have eyes, and anyone who would leave you is clearly a dumbass," Carmen explained.

At this, Rae chuckled. "Well, afterwards I got depressed, obviously. And about a year later, I caught him fucking his boss's eighteen-year-old daughter. Like—*in* the act."

"Asshole!" Carmen yelled, sitting up to throw both arms in the air.

"Nailed it!" Kendra added.

She finished her story quickly. "I left that night and haven't gone to bed with anyone since. Don't worry about me. I can take care of my own needs no problem," Rae insisted.

"Sure, that's why you undress Jacob with your eyes every time you see him," the guitarist accused. "Or play. You want to *play* with him, *chica*! And he's ripe for the picking."

"Oooh!" Kendra cooed excitedly. "Now we're getting to the stuff I'm here for!" The trio talked until the sun began to peek through the windows then crammed into Carmen's bed and passed out.

TEN

For the first time since starting this project, Jacob was alone. He paced his open floor plan from front door to kitchen and back, glancing at the patio door expecting one of his new bandmates to walk in. Well—to knock now that Grace had trained them all to lock the door. But there was no knock. At least it was only a day.

Jacob opened the refrigerator, staring into the full racks, assessing his options. He missed Carmen cackling after she made an off-color joke. He wished Joe was perched on the couch poking around his CD collection and playing tracks he didn't even know he had. He missed Derek's musical insights and his constant positivity.

But if he was honest, Rae's absence was the most upsetting.

Everything about her filled up his home. The way she moaned when he pressed a coffee mug into her hand each day. It was so honest—so sensual. He shifted uncomfortably and thought of newspapers and landfills, but her hips swinging as they found the right groove in the studio persisted.

She didn't seem to have any shame about it. She laid her whole self out for everyone to see. Long lashes brushing lightly against her flushed cheeks as she played; tongue searching over her bottom lip; hips swaying perfectly on tempo. It was instinctual—organic—and exclusively for herself.

He groaned now, finding himself at her guest room door.

Her presence surrounded him, footprints still carving a path in the carpet between the bed and the ensuite. He imagined her stripping off clothes, throwing them haphazardly on the floor on the way to the shower. The memory of her soft laughter and smiling eyes as if she were there in front of him filled his mind, beckoning him closer, and he dropped into the bed. He smashed his face into her pillow where the scent of magnolia and fresh rain lingered.

The tension that had begun squeezing his temples eased, and he inhaled deeply. He knew he was being foolish. His ex-bandmates never spared his feelings on the subject. He could practically hear the indignation in Jason's or Blake's voices…and the laughter in Danny's and Craig's. This was his pattern.

"There he goes—falling in love again."

Of course he was. Rae *saw* him no matter how he hid or how many walls he put up to separate them.

The sharp knock from his front door pulled him out of the nap he was almost having. Maybe it was her!

He answered the door with a bounce.

Resting against the railings was his long-time friend, Danny Porzio. Gone was the boyish face he had met so many years ago, replaced by a few more pounds, but the gentlest and most sincere smile he had ever known remained. Crinkles outlined his eyes, underlined by a lopsided grin. There was a hint of gray starting at his temples, but he didn't seem to know or care.

Danny straightened as the door opened, and he adjusted the duffle slung over his shoulder.

"Surprise greetings from Florida!" Danny hailed.

While it wasn't Rae, Jacob's mood spiked at the sight of his best friend. He clapped a hug around his dear friend and beckoned him inside.

"What up, Jakey?" Danny asked as he pulled away.

"Stop calling me that, man." Jacob tried to frown, but his former band mate's infectious smile made his lips quirk up despite himself.

Danny dropped his bag on the couch as Jacob ushered him into the kitchen for coffee.

"Place looks good," Danny complimented. "I expected some kind of frat party with all these people that have been stealing your time and attention from your brothers." Danny looked around.

"We took a day off, and I called for reinforcements before you got here, hence the clean house," Jacob explained.

"Well my timing sucks," Danny pouted. "I was hoping for an ambush!"

Jacob chuckled. Danny did love to make an entrance, and a captive audience was his favorite.

"Nope! They're all mine! It's too soon to introduce you."

"Afraid they're gonna like me better?" Danny teased.

Jacob was most definitely not afraid of that. Afraid he might poison them accidentally? Yes. Afraid he might tell embarrassing stories? Yes. Afraid he might get called out for his attraction to Rae? Yes. But *like* him better? No.

Danny gasped. "Oh my God, you've got the hots for one of them!"

"I do not," he hushed. "Shut up."

"Please, Jake! You can't lie for shit, brother. But I won't push…yet," he warned.

"I'd appreciate that," Jacob replied.

Danny eyed his friend for a minute. "Hungry? We should go grab a bite. Knowing you, you haven't been out of this cave in weeks."

Jacob chuckled, groaning. "I've missed you, man."

Danny grinned. "Come on. There's some ribs out there waiting for us to tear them up."

Jacob couldn't argue with that, and the pair headed for the nearest barbecue joint. Halfway through the first rack, Danny began his interrogation.

"So, I'm not going to ask if she's pretty because that's a given. What's she like?"

Jacob groaned, wiping his hand on the spare napkins beside him. "I thought you said you wouldn't push."

"I said *yet*. And yet is now over so…spill." He tore a rib from the rack and stuffed his mouth.

"No," Jacob answered firmly.

Danny rolled his eyes, a sticky rib poised between his fingers, and he swallowed. It was difficult to take him seriously with barbecue sauce spread liberally across his cheeks.

"See, here's the thing. I don't actually believe that you want to hold this in," Danny explained. "I doubt you've got anyone here to talk to about it 'cause they're all too close."

Jacob sighed, appetite gone. Danny wasn't wrong. "It's sticky because we're working together, and it's probably nothing. It's too soon to call it."

"Okay, at least tell me what instrument she plays. I gotta have something."

"The bass," he replied flatly.

Danny's face transformed into a happy "o" of surprise. "Really?" He took a bite, chewed thoughtfully, then nodded at his friend. "I can see that." He took another bite and chewed more. "What you need is to see her outside of work. Surely you deserve a vacation after this."

Jacob tilted his head at the thought.

"Vacation," he mused. "That's not a bad idea." He returned to his plate with fervor now. "A deadline is a *great* idea. Otherwise, we could drag on and on."

Jacob may not have been ready to confess his lust, but the details of the recording slipped easily into the story of meeting Derek for the first time, to picking their final two musicians, and all the recording they'd done since. By the time they had finished their meal and signed at least five autographs, they were racing back to the studio to play the rough cuts.

When Jacob's phone rang the following morning, he startled awake.

"Hello?" His stomach rumbled uneasily.

"Hey, man, it's Derek. I'm at the patio door."

Jacob cursed softly. "Sorry, man. I had unexpected company last night, and I totally overslept. I'll be right there."

He ended the call, fumbling with the sheets and slipping to the floor in his haste. He limped to the patio door managing to get it open and stood aside for Derek to pass.

"Sorry, man. Danny came by last night, and we lost track of time," he explained.

Derek shut the door behind himself, locking the tiny latch. "Who's Danny?"

"Sorry. Danny Porzio."

"Really?" Derek quizzed. His eyes darted around the room, his beatific smile amping up an additional fifty percent. "Is he still here?"

Jacob nodded. "Sleeps like the dead. I haven't started the coffee yet, but maybe we should set up before the others arrive."

Derek chuckled, circling the air with one finger in Jacob's direction. "Why don't you get dressed before the girls and Joe get here, and *I'll* set up the studio. We can call the gang and beg someone to stop for coffee and Rae on the way."

Jacob shouted his thanks before dashing back to his room to get dressed. When he was finished, he stopped in the room where Danny had passed out. He smacked his friend's leg.

"Dude," he called, giving his calf another slap. "Dude, I need you to get up."

After a moment, a groggy reply answered. "No. Need 'nother hour."

"Dude, my band is on their way."

Danny rolled slowly over, exposing his face. He eyed his old friend. "Dude, I'm old. I need all the beauty sleep I can get. I'll be quiet, I promise."

Seeing his friend's bedhead and hearing his voice, he couldn't kick him out in good conscience.

"Fine." He moved to the doorway and turned to snap, "We won't be." He closed the door harder than he should have but doubted Danny even heard it.

Despite his late start, Jacob was impressed how ready the others were when they started the session. Rae hit her groove early, and Jacob struggled to keep up. He wondered what she would say if she knew who was asleep in one of the guest rooms.

Derek must have recognized his distraction and managed to fully immerse him by discussing backing vocals. "Hunter, give me thirds on the chorus," he instructed, managing the console like an octopus.

Focused, Jacob leaned into the session. He had a perfect take on his next try and was staring at Rae as they moved on to the next song. The best part of her playing with her eyes closed was that he could stare without her knowing, dreaming of running his hands inside her thighs as he sang.

He adjusted his stance, closing his eyes to pull the notes out of his toes. He opened his eyes on the last note to see Derek's approval, but instead, his eyes landed on Danny grinning like a clown and leaning against the door frame. His voice cracked mid-note.

Derek flipped on the intercom, his scowl pronounced as he barked, "What was that?"

Jacob pointed, matching the producer's expression. "It's Danny," he mumbled. Of course it was Danny ruining yet another take with his disrespect for the process. Jacob squashed the surly response deep down. No reason to air their dirty laundry in front of his new family.

Danny stepped fully into the room, waving sheepishly at the group. "Sorry to interrupt."

"No interruption," Derek forgave. "Our alarms are about to go off anyway." He stood and offered a hand to the newcomer. "Derek Reed."

Danny shook it swiftly. "Danny Porzio."

Jacob hung his headset on the mic stand and dropped his notebook on a nearby stool. He supposed they were finished for now, and he ushered everyone out of the tracking room.

"Who has alarms set in the middle of a recording session?" Danny asked.

"People who work with Grace, who insists that breaks are legally required and necessary," Jacob replied as all their phones began chirping simultaneously. "See? You have perfect timing."

Everyone dove for their devices to stop the ringing.

"You know there's a way to disable that," Danny offered.

"Probably," Carmen replied, bounding over to the new person. "But when a woman's right, she's right." She stuck out a hand. "Carmen. The pleasure is yours," she announced, then bounced out of the studio and down the hall.

Danny watched her leave, eyes following down the hallway appreciatively. His head snapped back to Jacob. "Who's Grace?"

"Our agent's assistant. She'll be by some time tonight," Jacob clarified.

"If Meyers ever let's her stop working," Rae grumbled.

Jacob recognized her protective tone and smirked. It was cute watching her talk big about how much she disapproved of Grace's treatment. He had a brief inkling that she would be a bear of a mother, and he wished his mother had fought for him that way.

"She's not spying on you, is she?" Danny questioned.

"Hardly. Not her job," Jacob replied.

"No but taking dogs to the groomer and picking up laundry is," Rae added, pouting more. She crossed her arms over her chest.

"Yes, and she signed up for it," Derek admonished. "Plus, you know she does a lot more than that."

"Well, yes. But I think she deserves better. Someone needs to set a break for her," Rae grumbled then ran after the others to the kitchen.

She jockeyed for position between Carmen and Joe, grabbing the last Dr. Pepper before they adjourned to the front room.

"Since when do you keep your fridge stocked?" Danny exclaimed.

"Since Grace," he answered. "She has food delivered on the regular. We kind of forget to eat otherwise." He took a bottled water for himself.

Danny leaned in close to Jacob's head and whispered, "Are you sure you chose the right one?"

Jacob drew back. "What?"

"Rae," he answered, turning back. He grabbed a bundle of grapes from a tray on the counter and began popping them in quick succession.

"Who said…" Jacob refused to finish the thought. "Not here, man," he mumbled.

Danny smirked then joined the others, peppering them with intrusive questions. They took it in stride, and a surge of pride filled Jacob. The band devoured Danny's attention, but despite their day off, their answers made it clear to him that they were still tired. Perhaps Danny's vacation idea wasn't so bad.

He eased into the room himself, finishing the last of the water he'd been nursing and crushing the bottle for recycling. The noise got him the attention he wanted as he parked himself on a dining chair pulled into the living room.

"So, Danny gave me an idea last night that I want to run past you all," he began.

The group turned first to Danny, then to Jacob, eyebrows quirked.

Jacob continued, "I feel like we're doing some great work. And I feel like we're gelling as a band."

There was a murmur of agreement from the others, but they remained generally silent, giving him the space to think.

"If this all goes according to plan, once we finish the album, the real work will begin. We'll be testing it out on some local nightclubs, first at *The Oubliette*. Thank you, Rae, for the connection," he saluted their bassist who grinned and nodded her acceptance. "So, I was thinking we should maybe plan a little getaway before the going gets rough."

Stunned silence answered him, and he worried briefly that they all hated the idea.

"Well, for how long, and where were you thinking?" Derek asked.

Jacob shrugged. "I don't know. A week feels too long. Five-day trip? Long enough to relax but not so long we're out of practice."

He studied their faces for some indication of their answers. Rae's face was tense, and Carmen, beside her, mimicked a similar panic. Joe had no expression.

"My treat," Jacob added, realizing what their hesitation meant. While he had been giving them a stipend for their work, it was nowhere near what they would earn during a tour. Right now, they were all still struggling with rent as far as he knew. Except maybe for Derek.

"Oh, I'm in," Danny interrupted, rubbing his hands together. "And this should be tropical."

Jacob laughed. "Not you, joker!" He shook his head, explaining to the others, "You've got to watch this one."

Danny was laughing, too. "Come on. You know I make any vacation better. Life of the party."

"Yes, but this is about us—taking time to get to know each other as a band. And, love you man, but you ain't part of that."

Danny produced an exaggerated sigh and waved off his friend, laying back in his seat. "Fine! Fine."

Carmen was squealing suddenly. "Yes. Yes—I like this tropical idea."

"Ooh!" Derek looked like a gear had clicked into place over his head. "We've got to try Tulum. They've got these amazing all-inclusive resorts. We'll be treated like royalty."

"I like the sound of that," Joe replied, suddenly a part of the conversation again.

"Where the hell is Tulum?" Carmen asked.

"South of Cancun. Like an hour south. But the beaches are nicer, and it's quieter. Less touristy," Derek answered, rubbing his hands together in anticipation.

"I like the sound of that," Jacob replied.

"Can Grace come?" Rae blurted out.

"Of course—I was kind of hoping she'd plan it for us," Jacob answered.

"Wait, wait, wait. Why does she get to go, and I don't?" Danny butted in, grin splitting his face in two.

"Grace sets our alarms, our contracts, got audition space on like two seconds' notice. She's pretty much magic on legs," Derek answered.

"Magic on legs," Rae squealed then snorted. "You said that out loud."

"Derek likes Grace," Carmen sang out roughly three times before the look on Derek's face curtailed the harassment.

"It's not like that," Derek insisted. "She's good at her job. Game recognizes game."

"Gonna make it out the door with that head?" Carmen taunted. "Way to compliment yourself there, Reed."

Derek's cheeks turned crimson, and he stood abruptly. "Okay. Break's over."

~ ♪ ~ R A E ~ ♪ ~

The band had gathered around the dining table during their last break of the day, debating their recordings, arguing about how to handle a sticky transition between the chorus and the bridge. Rae had long since given up being heard between Jacob and Derek. For as often as they were in agreement, they were currently at odds, and Rae was staring out the patio door waiting for the tie breaker.

She and Carmen ran from their seats at the dining table when Grace's car pulled into the driveway later that evening, racing each other to the patio door to let her in. Each of them held out their blistered hands as she tried to enter.

"How do you think this'll go with my bikini, Grace?" Carmen asked, nearly shoving her finger in the other woman's nose. "Maybe something in stripes?"

"I was thinking a sequined glove might be good," Rae countered. She turned her fingertips up next to the guitarist's, making sure her bloodiest appendage was exposed, blister weeping down her knuckle. "Maybe something in a tasteful green to camouflage in the tropics."

"Isn't hot pink more your color?" Carmen debated.

Grace swallowed audibly, shielding her eyes from the wounds. "I'm sure we can find a good salve for that."

Carmen's face lit up, and she displayed the gaping blister on her thumb as she considered the options. A flap of skin hung from it, and Carmen jiggled it.

Like a knight on a white horse, Derek swooped in between the ladies, pulling Grace away protectively. Rae chuckled, liking this side of him.

"Let the woman breathe, ladies!" With one hand in the center of her back, he guided her toward the studio.

Rae and Carmen were hot on their heels, and Rae snapped for Jacob and Joe to follow.

Derek's hand was still on Grace's back but so lightly, his fingertips barely made an impression on her blouse. "So, we're thinking the current song is off somehow, but we aren't sure if it's in the mix…"

"More bass!" Rae interrupted, impishly.

The look Derek shot her and Carmen quieted them to a mere smirk.

Derek cleared his throat before continuing. "Okay, so…it's either in the mix, or it's something else entirely. Would you have a listen?"

Grace settled into a chair and nodded. As Derek leaned across the young lady to start the music, she swayed closer like she was a flower and he was the sun. Derek sat back, eyes laser focused on the assistant.

After some waffling, Grace agreed Rae was right, suggesting it needed more bass and drums.

"Huh, you were half right, Rae-Rae," Joe chuckled.

"It's happened before, me being right," Rae countered.

Derek threw one thumb at her, headphones pressed tightly against one ear. "Hang on," he ordered.

Rae watched the monitor as he squished some tracks and lengthened others, re-layering them with lightning speed. When he played the song again, it sounded like an entirely different track. The right track.

She gawked at the couple at the console. Grace had barely said a word, but Derek's whole view had shifted, and as Rae listened to her bass line and Joe's expert beat soar in the mix, her stomach quivered. Even Jacob was pleased.

Grace disappeared moments after Derek mumbled his thanks with an excuse that did nothing to prevent Rae and Carmen from laughing at her red ears.

"I think she needs a moment alone," Rae teased. Carmen squealed, and they danced into the tracking room for one more take.

Derek nodded to them from the console and pressed his mouth to the control room mic. "When you're ready," he bade, voice unnaturally sultry and playful.

Carmen shivered, rubbing her chest. "I feel dirty," she snapped.

"Gross!" Rae agreed.

He winked at them both through the glass. "Got your attention."

"Yeah, I'm with them. We're not your audience," Joe concurred. "She's in the kitchen being domestic."

Rae screamed out a laugh and launched herself at Joe for a hug.

Derek waved both his middle fingers at them before counting down from three and starting the recording.

Jacob crooned through the entire take, and Rae closed her eyes again, letting her brain go to all the naughty places it wanted as she imagined the rhythm flowing through her fingers.

She was unaware they had an audience, till the end when the motion of clapping from the control room caught her attention.

She looked up to see Grace and Danny behind Derek.

"Danny's back!" Rae crowed. She bounded out of the studio to bump fists with him as Grace offered to order dinner.

"Wait a minute!" Jacob shouted from the studio.

Rae swirled, body clenching at the sound of his commanding tone. His eyes were narrowed at her, and she held up her hands in surrender.

"Jesus Christ, Hunter, what did I do?" she muttered.

"You called him Joe right away," he stated, pointing to the drummer.

"Yeah…it's a Rebel Gloss thing," she explained.

"And then you called *him* Danny just now!" Jacob accused indignantly.

She shrugged, waving him off. Her eyes shifted to Grace, mirth filling her at the thought.

"Well, yeah. I've never wanted to shag *him*," she chortled conspiratorially to her fellow fan, her words coming out in a rush.

A pin dropping on the carpet in that moment would have sounded like a sonic boom. Why had she said that? Not only had she admitted to wanting to have sex with Jacob, but she'd also indirectly confessed to having had similar thoughts about Derek…in front of the woman he fancied!

In the next breath, Rae's stomach crawled up her throat. She needed a rescue and looked first at Grace, then Derek.

The producer's face was dawning understanding. She had called him mister for a very long time when they started working together at Lakeshore. The formal greeting had put an appropriate amount of space between them so she could get to know him and thwart most of the thoughts she'd had about jumping his bones. Once their sibling relationship had developed, calling him by his first name was easy.

She stopped breathing, and blood thrummed past her ears as she clapped a hand over her mouth. Drawing in a ragged breath, she wheeled around and darted down the hallway and out the front door, Carmen's bold laughter following.

She was two houses away before Grace caught up.

"I've ruined everything," Rae whimpered as Grace touched her shoulder. Fat tears rolled over her cheeks, and her nose instantly clogged. "This gig is the best thing that ever happened to me, and I blurt out the most unprofessional…" She swallowed hard against the lump in her throat.

"You didn't do it on purpose," Grace soothed. "It's not like you made a pass at him."

"But…now D knows it was never Leo I fancied, too."

"What?" Grace looked confused.

Rae rubbed at her cheeks as she groaned. "I wouldn't call Derek by his name at first either. For months." She stared at Grace, waiting for the woman to connect the dots. She turned a half circle wondering how long she could jog to get away from the look on Grace's face somewhere between horror and nausea.

"Oh," Grace mumbled.

"At least I'm over that particular crush…GOD," Rae continued. She sighed into her hands before peeking through to look at her friend. "Oh, he's gonna give me crap, but at least I'm immune to him now. I'll bet Carmen is *still* cackling in there. Even Joe and Danny must think I'm a moron…God why me?" she wailed, sitting down on the curb.

Grace chuckled, tucking her hands into her elbows. "It's charming," Grace mollified. "It's not like we didn't already know about Jacob. But the longer you stay out here wallowing in it, the more shit you'll get when you get back. And you love Carmen, admit it."

Rae couldn't stop the smirk that tugged on her mouth as she looked up at Grace. "Could you stop being a mature adult and making sense?"

Grace sucked in a deep breath and pretended to staple one hand to her forehead. "The drama! The horror! You will never work in this town again," she cried into the distance.

Rae laughed, tugging on Grace's arm. "Oh, knock it off. I am so done for today. I am out of music."

Graced arched a brow. "I sincerely doubt that. Come on. I have to click *Place Order* on the website for dinner, or we'll all starve to death before you can die of embarrassment."

"No," Rae protested.

As they neared Jacob's house, Joe's voice beckoned them as he called their names from the porch, gesturing manically for them to return.

Grace gently tugged Rae down the quickly darkening street to the front door. Carmen met them, hugging them both.

"Well, I'm hurt. You could call me mister if you want to," Danny teased.

"NO!!!" Rae cried.

Grace squealed, hugging Rae tighter and pulling her inside.

Jacob shook his head and started to the dining room.

"Come on. Come on. Business meeting," he called. There was a flurry of activity as everyone was seated, Danny squeezing in next to Jacob at the head of the table on a bar stool.

Rae felt her stomach clench. *Here it comes. I'm out of the band, and Danny Porzio is going to witness my downfall.* Carmen and Grace sat on either side of her, patting her hands.

"So, Grace, we need your help," Jacob started.

The woman's dark eyebrows arched up in surprise, and she squeezed Rae's hand. "Oh?"

"We were thinking that we are about to need a vacation, and we were hoping you'd set it up for us."

Rae almost threw up in her mouth from relief. She looked at him and almost swallowed her tongue. Something in his eyes made her knees weak and her heart race. Where she had expected him to be annoyed, he was…unaffected besides sitting a little taller than usual.

~ ♫ ~ JACOB ~ ♫ ~

The next day, Jacob answered his phone on the fourth ring. He'd had a little fight with himself over whether to answer the call when he saw the caller ID.

Meyers.

He showed the display to Derek briefly then answered.

"Jacob," the agent greeted. "How is the album coming?"

"It's good. Like pushing a boulder uphill alone in mud while barefoot in the rain, but I think we're nearly there," he replied with false cheer, wondering what the man wanted.

"Good. Good. So, listen, Grace tells me that you've invited her to vacation with you."

Jacob hesitated at the phrasing. Was Meyers fishing for gossip?

"With the band," he clarified. "We got pretty attached to her when she helped us for that first week."

"Ah. Good. Because, you know I frown on relationships."

There it was.

Jacob laughed obnoxiously as if Meyers had said the funniest thing on the planet. "I can totally appreciate that. But I'm not putting the moves on her, and she's not putting them on me. No moves here."

The agent exhaled relief. "Good to hear. I am afraid she's getting the impression that she's your point of contact instead of me."

"Really? 'Cause like every time I call you to set an appointment or anything, or send an email, you always offer that she can help me instead. So…maybe I'm getting some mixed signals here."

"Well, yes, perhaps that is my fault. I like to keep things neat you know."

Jacob sneered at the backpedaling. He wanted Grace to do all the work, and himself to get all the reward. Slime. Jacob relaxed his vocal cords, recalling his acting work on the Tree House Kids and affecting an equally innocent tone.

"Of course," he replied. "So, I did ask her to make the arrangements for the trip. And since it's for a holiday weekend, we kind of need her to do that now before everything sells out. I appreciate her help. She's very easy to work with."

"Can't disagree with you there. You have to be very careful in this town. People get wooed by the fame."

"Sure," Jacob replied, frowning. "Hey, listen, is there more? We're about to get started for the day, and everyone's sort of on the clock for me."

"Certainly. Thanks for the update and for understanding Grace's role in all this."

"Sure. Sure. You're not going to keep her from going, are you?" he pressured. Jacob had always considered himself intuitive, and something about the agent's words made his senses tingle. Understanding Grace's role? On a vacation? As a person? He hoped the man was squirming.

"No, she's welcome to go wherever she likes on her own time. I'll work out the vacation time with her today."

"Perfect. Rae and Carmen would be bummed if she couldn't."

"Must keep the ladies happy," Meyers agreed.

"Great. Catch you later." Jacob didn't give the man another opportunity to pry or say goodbye. He looked at Derek next to him loading the tracks they would be using on today's session. "That was weird."

Derek nodded sharply. "Agreed."

Jacob let his vision blur as he pondered the call. "You've known him longer. Is he always this like, controlling?"

"He is an agent, man. That's sort of his job."

"Well, like, he sort of accused me of having a relationship with her. And then implied that Grace was overstepping her bounds."

Derek shrugged. "He does like to make what he calls suggestions about who you should associate with or how your project should go, but that's what he's supposed to do, isn't it?"

"He sounds insecure. I don't like it." Jacob wrinkled his nose and sat up straighter. "If he was half the agent he thinks he is, there's nothing Grace or anyone else could do to make me doubt him."

"So what's the deal? Is she coming or not?"

"He made it very clear that this is her vacation time." Jacob shrugged. "So...I guess so?"

"I hope he'll still let her plan it," the producer grumbled.

"I'm hoping he lets her go. Can you imagine the girls without Grace to pester? Plus—she's done an awful lot to keep us on track without actually being here or getting paid for it."

"I like to think that we're part of that, too." Derek smiled. "But I take your point. She deserves to go for the sheer number of times she's ordered us dinner."

"I'm surprised she has an ear for music the way she does. I did not expect her to help like this."

"Same. And I confess, I do like a clear schedule. It's easier to focus on the music when we're not wasting time trying to coordinate dates and order lunch."

Jacob agreed, watching the way Derek avoided eye contact. "Can I ask you something while it's private?"

"Anything. I'm an open book."

"Are you developing a thing for her?"

Derek cast a sidelong glance at him. "What would make you ask that?"

He shrugged. "You're both single. Close in age. And I dunno, I see the way you look at her when she talks."

"She's a nice woman. But I think getting involved with people on a project like this gets messy. And who has time for it? We see her practically every day. I'm not sure that we'd all want to or be able to see more of each other than we already do."

Jacob nodded, dropping the subject. If this was his idea of being an open book, he must be clueless. At least he was good at music!

~ ♫ ~ R A E ~ ♫ ~

A mere five weeks after starting this short-term turned long-term project, Rae was hunched over her bass and rubbing her eyes, exhausted. To be fair, exhaustion had become her default. Looking around the room, she noted that everyone else seemed out of gas as well. Her eyes landed on Jacob, and the corners of his mouth quirked up.

Her insides quivered at the possibilities of what that smile could imply. She wanted to squeal and pinch his cheeks at his adorable expression. Instead, she sat on her hands. How could he be so sexy and manly one minute and then so sweet she might go diabetic the next?

"I think that's it," Derek announced.

Her eyes snapped to the producer. Was that possible? Had all the agony finally ended? How was he certain they wouldn't need one more bassline? One more vocal?

"Really?" Jacob questioned, eyes wide and suddenly awake.

Derek nodded, turning from the console to face the group. One cheek rounded over his smirk, brooking no argument. "And right before vacation."

Jacob, Joe, and Grace cheered unabashedly. From the corner, Carmen gave a tiny rah-rah, and Rae produced a smile.

"I knew a deadline would help," Jacob declared.

"You're right about that. Three days to spare. Plenty of time to pack," Derek replied, standing and stretching. In moments, he was walking Grace out.

Carmen leaned against her in the tracking room, and they remained rooted to the spot. Her eyes were focused on the singer's animated face as he and Joe schemed about what they would be doing on the beach in a few days. When their eyes locked, she started stowing her gear.

Jacob began unplugging cables, and when Derek returned, he immediately joined in, breaking down the mics.

"Okay, guys," Jacob announced, clapping his hands lightly to get everyone's attention. "Sleep time. This can be done later. Guest rooms for everyone. You know the drill."

Like a mini horde of zombies, they groaned and shuffled after him, mumbling "thanks" as he opened a door for each one. Rae's room was the last stop.

"You okay?" she asked softly when they were alone in the hallway. "I mean, we got everything done. I wanna make sure you're going to rest. I'll help clean up in the morning, so don't get started without me, alright?" She rested her fingertips on his forearm.

"I promise I will sleep until I wake up," he vowed. His face twisted up at his own confused response. He tried again. "I mean, I promise to go straight to bed now and stay there until I wake up."

Rae offered an understanding smile. "Okay then. Sweet dreams," she murmured, before shutting her door and locking it.

Peeling off her clothes, she folded them neatly and slipped between the cool sheets, falling asleep almost instantly.

ELEVEN

When the airport transfer van finally stopped at their final destination, Rae peered warily out the windows. She could practically see the heat roiling in the humid air and waiting to assault her, just like it had on the tarmac during deplaning.

The line at customs had taken forever, Jacob receiving no special treatment even after a handful of travelers clearly recognized him and kept trying to snap photos. Next was the gauntlet of salespeople hawking tours and rides, etc. Grace had instructed her to clamp her hands over her ears and follow along which she'd done, but by the time they'd boarded their private transport, Rae was out of steam. She had begun pleading with any deity available to make the road smooth as they wound south through the jungle to reach their destination. Could Derek have picked somewhere farther away from the airport?

Their driver hopped out and moments later, the panel door slid open. A thick rush of humid air enveloped her in a breath, and Rae's stomach gurgled unhappily. She wiped the sweat gathering in her eyebrows and tried not to cry. Already motion sick from the ride, the humidity was about to bring the airplane food back for a visit.

She wanted to appreciate the lush greenery, but she squeezed her eyes shut and focused on keeping her food down. She peeked out the open van door and clenched in horror at the open-air lobby, a lazy fan rolling unsteadily in its center. If their rooms were equally equipped, she was going to die. She whimpered, curling in on herself from her seat and placing her head on her knees.

Tulum was getting negative stars from her so far, no matter how gorgeous everyone and everything was. How was she going to tell them she wanted to go straight back to the airport? She had kept silent on the journey, but the way they all eyed her, she wasn't hiding her discomfort from anyone.

Derek and Jacob exited the vehicle, their voices drifting in. She wanted to follow them, but she worried that the heat would finish her off. There were still a few whisps of air conditioning floating around her knees, and she breathed them in. The van shifted as the others jumped out, and she held back a groan as her guts rumbled.

The doors at the back of the van slammed shut. Even their luggage had exited before she had. She looked up slowly as a gentle hand cupped her elbow, a soft voice tenderly coaxing her with promises of a breeze.

"Come on, Rae. It feels better out here," Jacob encouraged.

She allowed him to extract her with one hand braced on her arm for stability. The moment her head cleared the van doors, a breeze cooled her skin, and she gasped, gulping at the fresh air. Damp tendrils of her hair fluttered in the gentle wind as she placed one foot on the ground.

She barely registered Grace asking if she would be okay, but she managed a nod and waved off her friend, holding onto Jacob's arm. She looked up gratefully into his silvery blue eyes when her equilibrium settled, biting her lip at the protective look in his gaze.

Moments later, Grace approached with a frozen pink beverage in one hand and five leather wristbands in the other. Her face was pinched as she stared at her feet.

Rae's stomach sank. "Something wrong?" she fretted.

"No, it was just…so easy." The assistant's face lit with a smile as she held out a hand toward them. "Here, wristbands for all. These give us access to literally everything at the resort."

"Frosty beverages too?" Rae asked, eyeing the dripping affair in Grace's hand.

"Yes, that too. In fact…" she looked over her shoulder, and Rae followed her gaze. A hotel staff member bearing a tray full of frozen drinks scurried toward them.

"Welcome to Tulum." The young man smiled.

Carmen snatched two glasses from the tray and passed one to Rae.

The first sip of the frozen concoction flowed down her throat like a soothing cascade, chilling her body from the inside out.

"Ah! The welcome drink! Our adventure begins," Derek cheered, plucking his drink from the proffered tray and holding it up in salute.

Everyone followed suit, and Jacob lifted his glass slightly higher. "To a well-deserved break after five sleepless weeks!"

"Amen," Rae heralded, clinking her cup to the others.

"Allow me," Jacob murmured, setting his glass on a nearby end table and reaching for her wrist.

Rae blinked at him as he wrapped the leather cord around her left wrist. His fingers gently worked the cord, knotting it securely. Despite the cool drink and steady breeze, heat pooled in her belly as she watched him work.

She took the second band from his fingers quickly and turned his wrist face up. She couldn't help running her fingertip over the veins on his tender white flesh. She knotted the ends of the wristband together, trying to ignore how ceremonial the gesture felt. Her eyes flowed from his wrist to his face. His cheeks and the tips of his ears were red, and she fought the urge to giggle.

Grace's voice broke the spell, and Rae gulped as she tuned to the group. If she wasn't careful, she'd let this man slip right inside the wall she'd carefully constructed around her heart.

"They're bringing a cart up to take us to our rooms," Grace explained. "We essentially have the building to ourselves. Derek, Joe, and Jacob, you're the odd side. Rae, Carmen, and I are on the even. We're on the *privileged* side of the resort…"

Rae focused on sipping her drink as Grace rambled about their accommodations. The frozen beverage calmed her nerves. Maybe she could make it through this trip. Maybe she could even enjoy it with a steady supply of ice and alcohol.

Two six-person golf carts rounded the driveway and Derek led the charge with his drink. "To the carts! I fully expect us all to be toes in the sand by the end of an hour. That means you!" he ordered, pointing at each of them and making eye contact.

"Yes, Dad," Rae sighed, following after him. She would have rather spent a couple hours sleeping off her travel woes, but she was determined not to be a grouch.

~ ♫ ~ JACOB ~ ♫ ~

Jacob waited on the porch outside his room, drowsy and content in his gray, long-sleeved sun shirt and matching board shorts that capped his knees. He was fingering the cord around his wrist. Two beads capped a flat rectangular plate bearing the hotel's logo on one side, and the word "Privileged" on the other. He could still feel Rae's callused fingertips as she secured it on his wrist. She had bound him to her.

Before he could contemplate the idea further, the sound of the neighboring door opening interrupted, and he lifted his sunglasses as Derek joined him.

"My God! You're shaming every man here, bro! What are you made of? Marble?" he asked, startled at the sight of Derek's muscled torso.

"This is what I do in my spare time." Derek laughed, flexing his biceps. As he showed off, the third door opened, revealing Joe in a baggy black *Journey* T-shirt and checkered black and white board shorts.

"Well, there goes anyone else's chances at being seen," the drummer grumbled.

"I know, right?" Jacob agreed. "Put a shirt on, dude. The girls might blow a gasket."

Derek scoffed. "Let's find out."

Jacob rose, dropping his sunglasses back into place. "I'm not picking them up if they pass out. This is on you."

They were chuckling as they rounded the building's corner to collect the ladies. Carmen was seated outside her room, using a straw to coax the last of her frozen beverage into her mouth. It was practically obscene, and Jacob looked away.

She waved a hand in greeting and pointed her straw at Derek. "Please note my compliance with the order to have fun in the sun." She set her glass on the outdoor table and rose to spin in her crocheted bikini.

"Bravo," Derek dipped his head in approval. "I like the dedication." He passed her and knocked on Rae's door. When she didn't answer, Derek knocked again. "Rae," he called. "You okay?"

"Go away, D," she replied.

Undeterred, he knocked again. "You said you'd come. You're cutting into my beach time," he complained.

"Can't I stay here?" she called through the door. "We can do lunch."

"Don't make me call the front desk to tell them you're unresponsive, and we need a health check," he threatened.

At this, the lock tumblers turned. "You wouldn't dare!" she huffed through the door.

It opened to reveal Rae in a tasteful retro red bikini.

Jacob's mouth watered as he took in the high waisted bottoms hugging her hips and leading him to the ruffled top. The fabric waved at him around her cleavage begging him to stare. A white beach robe fluttered around her body, sunlight playing peekaboo through the pattern across her creamy skin. Even her bare feet were begging him to touch them. Absently, he reached for his wristband.

"That is obscene!" Rae scolded, flicking a finger in Derek's direction. "Put that away."

A wave of relief washed through him at her reaction. "That's what I said."

"Daddy needs a tan," Derek grumbled. "Get shoes, and let's go!"

Sighing, Rae complied, stepping into a pair of white wedge sandals that brought her eyes level with Jacob's and closed her door behind her. "What do we do about towels?"

Jacob startled at the sound of Grace's voice, not sure when she had appeared. "On the way to the pool there should be a cart with towels we can use and exchange as we need," Grace explained. She was standing in front of her door in a short cotton dress, clutching a straw bag over one shoulder.

Rae turned to Carmen. "We have to find her off switch."

"Good luck finding it under the layers," Carmen teased.

Carmen and Rae took Grace under their wings, leading her from the porch.

"This way!" Derek called, jogging ahead toward the beach. He stopped at a bamboo cart under a small palapa where rows and rows of neatly rolled white beach towels were piled. Derek grabbed one and turned back.

"Heads up!" He lobbed one tightly rolled cloth back to Jacob as though it were a football.

Jacob picked it out of the air deftly. "Good throw." He passed the towel to Rae then called for more. Derek complied, and Jacob passed one to each of his companions, keeping the last one for himself. Then he set off to catch up to his bandmate. If he stood behind Rae any longer counting the polka dots framing her perfect behind, he might embarrass himself. Chasing after his new friend and getting into the water proved the perfect foil.

At the shore, Derek dropped his towel at a pair of chairs on the beach then shucked his shoes. He sprinted toward the shore slowing down when the water was up to his calves. Jacob strode into the surf behind him, allowing himself to adjust to the temperature of the water bit by bit.

"I am so glad you suggested this. I didn't realize I needed it until we got here," Derek called over his shoulder.

"I've learned that you have to play hard after you work hard so you don't burn flat out," he replied. He turned his gaze to the shore where the rest of the band had staked out a group of chairs and umbrellas and were nesting. He watched as Rae divested herself of her robe to drape over a chair. His thoughts immediately wished for her to peel off the rest, and he ripped his eyes away.

To her left, motion caught his eye, and he stared in shock as Grace pulled her dress off to reveal a bathing suit. He wasn't sure what he had expected to see after all the business attire, but the modest, purple one piece showed her to advantage.

"So that's what she looks like under those business suits," Jacob mumbled.

The man next to him was staring intently, and Jacob couldn't stop the chuckle that escaped his lips as he interrupted the interested gape.

"What?" Derek asked, cocking his head toward his friend.

"Dude—that's *Grace*. You are hardcore checking her out," Jacob pointed out. He glanced at Derek through the glass-like water. "And you'd better do something about *that* before she gets here. If you thought she freaked out about the sexy *music*…" he trailed off.

Derek muttered a filthy word and begged, "Tell me about your mom. Quick!"

Jacob answered by splashing him with the biggest wave he could muster. Derek responded in kind, and in moments they were fighting to see who could make a bigger splash between gentle waves pushed them apart.

He turned his attention back to Rae on shore as she stroked sunscreen all over her skin and groaned, starting another splash fight with Derek to divert his gaze until she finished. Part of him wished he had stayed on shore to offer to apply lotion to all the hard-to-reach spots.

Her squeal called his eyes back to her as the surf engulfed her toes. She clung to Joe standing patiently beside her holding out his arm. She paused when it passed her knees before inching deeper. She stumbled, and Jacob caught himself before he could lunge forward to take over.

She wasn't his, and he wasn't hers. They were coworkers at most, and Derek had been insistent that she would not welcome his advances.

But he knew that wasn't entirely true. Her secret was out after the incident during Danny's visit when she admitted to calling him Mister because she wanted to shag him. The desire was there, and she couldn't take that back. Of course, he realized sorely, she had done the same to Derek apparently when they first met. But they acted more like siblings than possible lovers.

When they were close enough, Joe released her, turning to float on his back. He drifted past Jacob and Derek with a groan of delight. "This is perfect."

Jacob trained one eye on Rae as the ocean rolled over her chest. He heaved a jealous sigh. She was almost in arm's reach, but her momentum stalled out.

"Little help?" she requested.

"Come on, Shorty," Derek mocked. "It's not that deep, and the water will carry you. I swear."

"I am not a swimmer, and you dragged me out here," she grumbled.

"She wins," Jacob defended, taking her fingers lightly at last to draw her closer. He could get used to this. She glided closer, and he considered letting their bodies collide and wrapping both arms around her, or possibly all his limbs.

Derek scooted toward the shore to be closer before resuming his sitting position in the buoyant waters and rolled his eyes. "Happy?"

"Yes, brat," she replied, sticking out her tongue.

Jacob looked past Rae and Joe, not yet letting go of her hand, and enjoying the way his fingers tangled with hers. "What happened to Grace? And Carmen?"

"Carmen is a sun goddess and is worshiping in peace at the altar. A direct quote," Rae replied.

"And Grace?" Jacob prodded, looking to shore. Carmen was sprawled on a lounger, as described, looking like a wet noodle already. He respected her ability to live in the moment. Beside her, however, Grace was hunched over her knees, but he couldn't see what she was doing.

"Meyers," Rae replied, rolling her eyes. "What kind of asshole is that dude?"

Derek scowled. "The effective kind, unfortunately. He does have a knack for matching people up and has a huge roster."

"But it doesn't have to be that way," Jacob grumbled. "You wouldn't believe the shit he gave me when I asked Grace to help that first week and again when I told him I wanted her here."

"But it's a holiday weekend!" Rae rationalized. "That's supposed to mean something for nine to fivers!"

"Technically she's using vacation days, or else he wouldn't allow it," Jacob explained.

"She's not *on* vacation, though! She's over there checking in with him now. Working on his schedule," Rae tattled.

"Nope, not having it." Jacob released her fingers reluctantly, trusting Derek to look after her in his absence and stalked to the shore against the current with surprising speed. He hadn't fought with his agent to pay for her trip and watch her work. He was putting an end to this now.

~ ♪ ~ R A E ~ ♪ ~

Rae's eyes were glued to Jacob as he barreled toward the shore. The waves pushed him in, his calves flexing strongly against the resistance. The protective gray sun shirt clung to his skin, outlining his muscles and his ass as he breached the surface.

Aware of Derek beside her potentially catching her, she spoke up.

"Do you think we'll actually get to tour?" The concept of realizing her dream was foreign. She assumed that if anyone would understand or know the answer, it would be her good friend.

Derek shrugged. "If we don't, it isn't because of our work. It's solid. It really depends on Meyers connecting us with the right label and getting local gigs. LA's a competitive town."

Rae cursed softly. "I see your point. But plenty of bands schedule gigs for themselves, and *The Oubliette* definitely wants us to play."

"Look, all the talent in the world doesn't guarantee success," Derek reminded her. "You've gotta understand that a 'no' doesn't mean the work is bad or that the project dies. It's either the wrong door or not the head of the household. We'll do what needs to be done. I think the odds are in our favor, but you could make yourself crazy guessing. We did the work. Now we refill the tank. We'll see how it goes Tuesday. So, for now, no more speculating."

The answer had been intended to reassure her, Rae knew, and it had. Still, a tear clouded her vision. Since when had the dancing teenager that had given her the swoons in her youth become so insightful? She swiped the tear away, chuckling at her sentimentality.

"I am so proud of you, Big D," she told him. "You've come such a long way. Look at you with these words of wisdom." She paused, glancing at the shore again where Jacob and Grace were trading bottles, and Jacob was smearing his hands over his face. "You're his new hero, you know?" she murmured.

Derek waved her off. "Hardly—he's had far more experience than I have."

"Not on his own. His type of experience is different. He may have had more popularity, but as you told me, that was about who you were surrounded by and not about talent. Don't forget, I've seen how hard you work. You and Grace are the hardest working people I know in Los Angeles."

Derek laughed. "That says more about the people you know, Ms. I-have-two-jobs." He tapped her foot with his toe. "Speaking of—when are you going to quit the bar? It's standing in the way of your brilliant career as a bassist!"

Rae laughed. "Bass player is my back-up career."

"Bullshit. After what you put into this album, you can't sell me that one anymore."

Rae shrugged. Despite the callouses on her fingertips, she hadn't quite made her peace with the idea. Something about it felt *so* right, though. She was drawn to it like a moth to a flame…which meant she could get burned.

Glancing at the shore, she saw Jacob's silver blue eyes riveted to her as he and Grace splashed toward them.

Talk about burning! She didn't look away, blessing the soul that invented padded swim cups to hide her arousal.

"What did we miss?" Jacob asked.

Derek burst out laughing. "What happened to your face, bro?"

Jacob touched his white-streaked nose. "This? Grace had a bag of goodies. I do *not* want to burn, so I used the zinc."

Grace chuckled. "I've never seen anyone so excited about zinc before."

"I grew up with this stuff. Life saver. You all can mock me for my shirt…"

"Nobody is mocking you for that skintight shirt," Rae drawled.

Jacob's face flushed beneath the sunscreen.

Her gaze sharpened at the reaction. Why was he embarrassed? He had to know how sexy he looked.

"Well," he coughed. "Skin cancer is no joke. Plus, it's saved me from many a scrape." Jacob spun in the water, dunking his head back to wet his hair.

"There's plenty of sunscreen in my bag if you want some, Derek," Grace offered.

He nodded. "I will soon. I need all the vitamin D I can get right now."

"Vitamin D!" Jacob crowed. "That is your new nickname. I can see it now." He peered into the distance, throwing his hands up and spreading them wide. "Tonight, for one night only—Vitamin D!"

When the splashing started again, Grace and Rae swam away from the boys.

Joe paddled after them. "I thought Vitamin D meant something else," he mumbled.

Rae screamed with laughter, nearly slipping under the water's surface.

Joe caught her deftly and set her upright. "That was impressive," he complimented. "Usually, you have to go under intentionally in the Caribbean 'cause it's so salty."

Rae sputtered and splashed. It seemed that a little salt water and a lot of teasing was all it took to lift her out of the travel blues. Well, that and the attention of a breathtakingly gorgeous man.

~ ♪ ~ JACOB ~ ♪ ~

Jacob relaxed in the salty water, allowing it to carry all the weight on his shoulders. They had barely arrived in country, and already the band was gelling. The album had been floating through his head ever since Derek had called it finished. Part of him was making mental tweaks, but the splash fight pulled him out of the trap.

He had been on the top of his game not that many years ago. He knew what success sounded like, and this group of people had it. *He* had it. There would be opening gigs to get their feet wet, but it wouldn't be long before they'd be headlining. It sounded like a lot of work. But if Grace worked half as hard for them as she did for his agent, it was doable. Maybe if he secured the person to track the minutia, he could finally relax in this beautiful setting.

He twisted to face his co-conspirator. "You good to talk to Grace now about working with us?"

Derek grimaced. "Man, we barely got here."

"I know," Jacob sighed. "But if we wait, we'll be thinking about it the whole trip."

"*You* will be," Derek retorted. "I will be tannin' and scannin'."

Jacob splashed him a little and laughed. "Scannin' what?" he mocked. "All you've been scanning is our future band manager."

Derek rolled his eyes. "Okay—it happened once. But it wasn't my fault. Who knew she was hiding *that* under a suit?"

Studying his companion for a moment, Jacob dropped his shoulders under the ocean surface. "Are you sure you'd be okay with hiring her once the ball gets rolling? I don't want it to be weird for you."

"It won't be weird unless you make it weird," Derek countered. "I'll go get her."

He watched the older man wade to the ladies, calling Grace over. Her cheeks were pink from her eyes down to her elbows, and he suspected everything submerged too. It was kind of cute watching the two pretending not to be smitten with each other. Grace slipped by Derek, and he watched the producer's gaze trail down her back. It happened so naturally, Jacob wondered if he even knew he'd done it.

He interrupted the exchange before Derek got caught. "So—I've been promising you this talk for a while, and I wanted Vitamin D here as a witness."

Grace giggled, covering her face.

He and Derek laid out their pitch.

Grace was virtually vibrating and staring at her toes, whispering, "Meyers will kill me if he catches wind of this."

"You don't have to say yes now," Jacob offered. "But I'm putting you on notice. I'm going to press Meyers to let you help set up at the club for our first gig, and I want you to put out feelers for other venues open to letting new bands play."

"Can I think about it?" Grace waffled. "It's not that I don't believe in you guys. But it feels very *cart ahead of the horse* right now."

"Take the time you need. But when we get back, Grace, this is happening. Think of it like a promotion," Derek encouraged.

She arched a brow. "You have my attention. But I'll need something in writing. Something that's fair to both of us."

"Done," Jacob answered.

Derek groaned. "Thanks. You know he's going to pass it to me to work out."

"Oh, keep your shorts on," Jacob refuted. "I have a lawyer for this kind of stuff."

Rae joined them again, screeching and laughing, "Who's taking off shorts?"

The sight of her smiling face erased the last fifteen years in an instant. He wanted to keep her in this state for eternity. Feeling like a teenager again, he happily threw his friend under the bus.

"Vitamin D," Jacob taunted. "'Cause he ain't got nothing else to take off."

She squealed, spinning in happy circles until she wrapped her arms around Grace and squeezed her.

"JOE!" Rae yelled. "Save us! I don't wanna see all of Vitamin D!"

Jacob laughed, launching in front of the ladies. "I'll take one for the team."

Derek swung both his arms wide, and in the next second, he had splashed them all with two giant waves.

TWELVE

Perched on her porch recliner late in the afternoon, enveloped in the stillness of her surroundings, Rae listened to the waves crashing against the shore and wondered why she had to be so heat-averse. She'd been skeptical when the location was suggested. Heat was not her friend ever since she'd spent all day out on Lake Sahoma and suffered mild sunstroke as a teen. Now, if she got too hot, especially if it was humid, her stomach twisted itself into knots.

She had dreaded stepping off the plane in Mexico at the airport. The walk between the terminal and the van had been oppressive enough to make her regret coming. However, now that she was at the resort, she was having a surprisingly good time outdoors. The constant Caribbean breeze was a life saver.

Watching Derek and Jacob in the water with Grace and Joe had been worth every drop of sweat. Both men had reverted to their teenaged selves she had idolized growing up. Her mind raked over her memory of Jacob flicking water from his hair and his nipples poking through his shirt. She had prayed he'd take it off at some point so she could memorize every sinew of his body—not that she needed him to. Her imagination was her best developed muscle.

As the sun lowered, its intensity decreased. It had been a good day. She squirmed in her seat, gulping down half a bottle of water before setting it aside. Unexpectedly, Jacob rounded the corner, and her insides shimmied.

"Feeling better?" Jacob murmured, stopping beside her.

He smelled like salt and coconut and something manly she couldn't place in her sleep addled brain. She realized with a jolt that he had asked her a question.

"Hmm? Oh, yes, thank you, Jacob."

"What?!" he gasped with a laugh. "Do my ears deceive me?" Jacob faced her with a goofy, pleased grin. "Are you finally comfortable with me?"

"Yes, smarty pants," she chuckled. "Tending to me when I'm unwell is a great way to skip the line." Her stomach did a happy little flip at his mirth. It was like a cool rain on her weary soul.

"What do you want to do tomorrow?" he asked, resting on the arm of her chair.

"Hmm, well after Vitamin D dragged us out to the beach today, I'm thinking massages and fruity drinks in the shade for me," she answered.

"Ooh, I like the way you think," Jacob whispered.

Her breath hitched as he stared at her face. Before she realized what he was doing, he reached out and tucked a curl behind her ear.

His voice lowered, and she could feel the heat radiating off his side, his finger lingering on her jaw.

"You should be forced to relax more often. Brings out the gold in your eyes."

Rae froze, heart pounding as desire shot through her. When had his voice gotten so husky? Why was his touch so electric? If he kissed her, how was she going to say no?

The sound of a door opening and closing gave her the distraction she needed to gulp. Jacob's hand flew away, and he launched to his feet.

"Hey, guys!" Grace waved from her door. Her ankle-length sundress floated around her body, hair blowing in the breeze. "Coming down for dinner?"

"Absolutely," Rae called back. She searched the pathway, finding it empty. "Is D with you?"

"Yep, he's got us a table already," Grace answered. "Carmen promises she'll meet us there, but I couldn't raise Joe."

Jacob's jaw twitched as he nodded. "I…uh…I'll be there in a bit," Jacob promised. He turned partway toward Grace. "You go ahead. I'll get Joe up there." He hurried around the corner, and Rae stared after him until she heard his door shut.

She shivered, looking at Grace. "Give me a minute to change. I'll be fast," she promised. She skirted into her room, stripping quickly on her way to her suitcase. She pulled free the first dress she could find and piled her hair on top of her head, avoiding her own eyes as she used the mirror.

Had he almost kissed her? What was he thinking?

"Get it together, Duncan," she muttered. Messing with people she might tour with was bad juju. It would be convenient, she rationalized: do a show, carry their stage chemistry on to the bedroom with Jacob, relax. Repeat. Until fans start throwing their bras at him—begging for the ultimate autograph. She would be insanely jealous. They would fight. He would leave. And if she was lucky and they kept touring, it would become a blur of rubbing the hurt in each other's faces. And the music would suffer. Or else he could kick her out of the band, and she would be out a lover and her dream job. And for what? A fling? A sensual, life-altering, ruin-her-for-anyone-else fling?

No, she scolded herself. You don't have time for affairs with your coworkers. It was messy at the best of times. She needed to keep it clean.

She scurried out to meet Grace and rushed toward the privileged dining area. Derek called their attention once inside, waving one arm in the air. Carmen was already seated, strategically leaving an open seat next to Derek, and Rae sat across from her.

Grace slipped into her chair, casting a frown first at Rae and then Carmen.

Rae waved at her discreetly with her middle finger and ordered a double shot of vodka with her water. She pretended to stare at the menu in her hand, but her mind was back on the recliner outside her room.

She could still feel the lingering sizzle of the path Jacob had traced when he tucked her hair back. Her memories focused on his lips as he'd complimented her eyes, and she visualized him inching closer and closer. His lips looked warm and inviting.

When the server set a drink in front of her, she grasped for it sucking on the skinny stir stick to keep from shooting the whole cup. The familiar burn focused her thoughts to a pinpoint of vodka on her tongue. She could do this. She was here for the music—not for the man.

She snapped her attention to Derek as his voice interrupted her train of thought. He was standing at the head of the table, arms wide.

"Please join my table with the bevy of sun-kissed beauties." Derek waved Jacob and Joe over, his lips parted in a broad smile.

"Dial it down, sun-god," Joe griped. "You know it comes up all over the world?"

"But not like it does here," Derek replied, beaming at them all. "You cannot be mopey in a place like this. The resort is beautiful, the view is beautiful, the people are beautiful. And the drinks are flowing."

Rae held her glass up in salute, then pulled the straw free and swallowed half the liquid as she stared at Jacob.

His skin practically glowed against the peach polo he sported. His plaid shorts complimented it perfectly with earthy sandals, and she realized her mistake. In their efforts to force Grace next to Derek, Jacob took the seat at the foot of the table directly next to her. She could practically feel Grace's smug reaction and ignored it.

"Drinks," Joe agreed, bringing her back to the present. "That's what's missing." Joe craned his neck, looking around for the nearest server.

In no time, food began arriving at the table, multiple platters of appetizers placed in the center piled with a combination of fried foods and seafood. Rae wasn't sure her stomach could handle the exotic cuisine after the day she'd had, and she eyed it warily.

Carmen started them off, reaching for a sample, and slowly, the others followed suit. Rae reached for a bite finally, nearly colliding with Jacob's hand as he picked out a morsel. She jerked away, her food landing on the table.

"You first," Jacob conceded, drawing his hand back.

"No, you," she murmured.

He stared at her, folding his hands on the table.

After a few breaths, she tried again, successfully snagging a bite.

Sounds of chewing filled the air, and Rae watched as Jacob bit into his food.

And she suddenly understood Derek's obsession with watching Grace eat. Her pulse raced as Jacob's tongue darted over his lips, and then he licked his thumb. It was a quick motion, so subtle that she would have missed if she hadn't been staring.

Rae cleared her throat and grabbed at another appetizer to distract herself. And Jacob's fingers rammed into hers, their food slipping from their grasp and over the plate's edge. She pulled away, wiping her fingers on a napkin and staring into her dwindling drink. She needed another. She needed to stop thinking about other things she'd like to put in his waiting mouth—things he could lick as thoroughly as he had his lips.

She glanced around the table. Joe looked like he was half asleep, swirling ice in his cup. Derek was stuffing his face. Grace was trying to cut a spring roll on a tiny plate with a fork and knife. Carmen was unnaturally quiet, looking across the table at everyone.

A few minutes later, the appetizers were cleared and their first course arrived. Rae stared dubiously at her plate. It didn't look anything like what the menu had described. Her stomach grumbled, both hungry and unhappy at the prospect of consuming the meal.

"Okay, guys," Derek spoke up, leaning in, barely managing to keep his chest out of his food. "What is with the silence?"

"Um? Maybe we're all tired?" Rae mumbled. It was certainly not that she could almost feel Jacob's lips on hers after the look he'd given her earlier. *That* couldn't happen. She picked at the straps of her garnet sundress uncomfortably.

Joe lifted his drink to her statement.

"Okay." Derek stared at her, reaching for his fork. "So just jet lag?" he prodded.

Rae groaned. Why was he poking her? Was he blind? Had he not seen how hard a day she'd had? She wondered if Jacob was having a *hard* day too. She needed a good spanking or scolding for her inability to put him out of her mind. She met Derek's gaze head on, challenging him to continue and pleading with him to let this go.

"It's been an eventful day, alright?" she snarled.

Next to him, Grace set down her silverware. One hand patted Derek's wrist quick as a flash and then it was hidden beneath the table in her lap. She worried her lips, eyes darting from Derek to her and back.

"It was a long flight, and I think the heat took a lot out of us at the start," Grace soothed.

Derek acted as though he hadn't noticed the woman beside him touching him. Grace didn't touch people, and Rae growled inwardly as Derek continued.

"Okay, but what's wrong?" He speared his entrée and sliced off a bite. His tone was almost casual. He lifted his fork, smirking at her as he added, "Being tired has never stopped you from running your mouth before."

Rae scowled, fingers forming an involuntary fist around her fork. If they were in the studio, and if she wasn't ready to pass out, and if they were alone, she might be willing to confess to the salacious thoughts that had been plaguing her since Jacob nearly kissed her. But she could not have this conversation with him now in front of everyone.

Usually, Derek was in tune with her emotions. The fact that he was misinterpreting her signals now was infuriating. Maybe the sun had fried more than his ears.

"I have a lot on my brain if that's okay with you," she retorted, wishing he would leave her alone.

"But it feels like something's wrong. I don't want it to ruin the trip," he insisted.

Rae's eyes narrowed, steeling herself against his obtrusive gaze. She gripped the arms of her chair. She wanted to throw it at him. Or maybe her plate of food. She imagined his face covered in ceviche and salsa.

"Drop it. Drop it right now, Reed, if you don't want to ruin the trip," she warned.

Carmen squealed, laying on the edge of the table to look back and forth between the pair. "This is juicy," she exclaimed. "Former lovers, right? I knew it—I see your chemistry."

Derek and Rae turned their glare on her, and Carmen curled away from them both, the smile disappearing from her face and her spine straightening.

Joe lay back in his chair, pulling the remainder of his whiskey away from the potential fracas.

"Not lovers. Ever. Gross. Why would I say that?" she asked, waving her hands defensively.

Grace snickered.

The sound was like nails on a chalkboard, and Rae's wrath turned on the assistant. "This isn't funny," she scolded.

Grace blinked, and her cheeks turned red.

"We're supposed to be having a good time," Derek argued. "Maybe it *is* funny."

"I am not having fun," Joe interjected.

Grace frowned, inclining her head toward Joe. "Sorry, man. We'll be better. Won't we?" she asked first Rae and then Derek.

"Why do *I* have to be better?" Rae growled. "I'm sorry if I haven't been able to wrap my head around what's happening here. I mean, we cut an album! And now we're out here celebrating like this is totally normal."

"It is normal," Derek agreed. "It's what bands do! That was a lot of work to write and record that many songs that fast."

"This isn't normal for *me*!" Rae objected. "Do you know what I've gone through in the last two months?" The turmoil of her life bubbled to the surface, anger bleeding into every word.

"I lost my job at the studio, then I gave up my job at *The Oubliette* to start playing with you guys, and I have no guarantee that this will be success. I'm losing my apartment, and I'm trying to put on a happy face for you all, but all I've done is lose things. Forgive me if I'm terrified of what happens if we fail."

Rae's breathing was rapid, cutting off the rest of her tirade. She had felt herself start to rise to look down on her seated friends and rain more fire down on their heads, but she'd kept herself together.

"We're all taking a risk," Carmen countered from across the table. "It's cool to be scared. It is scary. But that's why we do big, audacious things like this to release the tension."

"Especially when Daddy foots the bill," Joe added, looking at their patron. "Thank you, man. Argument aside, this is pretty nice."

Jacob flushed at the compliment. "Glad to do it."

Derek set his silverware on his plate and eased forward in his chair. "I, for one, am happy you lost all those other jobs," he declared calmly. "You were never going to take the leap on your own, and now you're all ours! No more divided loyalties between us and the club!"

Rae let her fork clatter to her plate.

"You want to talk about divided loyalties? At least I don't jump from job to job like you jump from woman to woman!" she accused. A tiny grin worked at the corners of her mouth as her thoughts swirled wickedly. If he wanted to play with fire, she was ready.

"Why is it you're almost forty and still single, hmm?" she accused. "Would a relationship divide your loyalties Mr. All-About-The-Job? Isn't that why you won't even let yourself look at a woman who might make you happy?" Rae threw a near imperceptible nod toward Grace.

Derek's jaw twitched. His next words rumbled low across the table. "That is not the same, Desirae."

Rae flinched as he revealed her given name. She had told him that in confidence. How dare he use it in a very public disagreement?

"Oh, we're telling secrets now?" Rae snarled. "How about how hard up you are for Grace, hmm?"

Derek slammed his napkin on the table and stood. "Walk away, right now," he ordered.

"Or what? You'll fire me from the only goddamn job I have left thanks to you?" She turned her gimlet gaze on Jacob. He had nearly kissed her, but now when she needed him, he was silent? Was she nothing more than a warm receptacle?

"And you're going to let him? Who's in charge?"

Jacob raised his hands in mute surrender and shook his head.

Her vision was going red at the edges. He was staring back, compliant and at her mercy. She wanted to grab him and still her rage crushing their mouths together, and she could almost feel his hands clutching the small of her back.

Rae stood up sharply, the chair scraping against the floor. The room fell silent, and she glared at everyone around the table before pivoting swiftly and storming out of the building.

She couldn't be here. While she had no interest in letting Derek think he'd won, he had been right. She needed to be alone before her raging heart burned down everything in sight.

Picking her way down the dark path toward the beach, Rae chose her steps cautiously using the radiant light from the restaurant to find her way.

She removed her sandals as she reached the sand, inhaling the salt air and digging her toes in the cool grains. It was rare lately to get a quiet moment to herself. She loved being busy, and she adored being around her friends, but the strain of having been cooped up with the group for months had been more stressful than she had anticipated.

Standing in the quiet, sucking in fresh air, she could admit she needed a recharge. Holding back the tears that threatened to fall, she squeezed her eyes shut and listened to the pounding of her heart until it finally slowed.

She stumbled to the shore, sighing in relief when her feet landed on the firm, wet sand. The occasional splash of surf against her ankles quieted her mind. The moon and stars were bright reminding her of nights in Tulsa. She stood, staring up at the celestial bodies, unobscured by smog and light pollution, as the gentle waves pulled sand from beneath her soles.

And as soon as she thought of bodies, Jacob flooded her brain. He was going to drive her completely insane. She wasn't sure how she had kept such a level head this long with him constantly showing her glimpses of his belly button and listening to him fall down rabbit holes with Derek when they talked. At least when they were playing music, she could immerse herself in the bass. On the beach, all she saw was the way the water glued his clothes to his body, flowed down his legs, and dragged her eyes all over his toned physique.

How was she supposed to be mentally competent when the sexiest guy on the planet was constantly nearby? His scent made her stomach quiver, and the way his eyes crinkled around the corners when he smiled, made her heart stutter.

His touch was like lightning seared through her veins even as her skin felt smoothed by the softest silk. His blue-silver eyes entranced her. How was he even real? Shaking her head to clear it, Rae settled onto a beach chair and closed her eyes, letting the sounds of the surf drowned out her thoughts.

~ ♫ ~ JACOB ~ ♫ ~

At a silent distance, Jacob followed Rae from the restaurant. From the way she had paused several times in the sand, he assumed she wanted some space. And while assumptions often made asses out of both parties, his hesitancy provided an opportunity to figure out what to say.

The debacle at dinner was ugly in the politest of terms. He had never seen Derek so furious. He had gone from Apollo to Hades inside half a dozen words, and Jacob hoped never to encounter that half of him again.

But that was Rae—she got under a person's skin. She had certainly wormed her way under Jacob's.

He watched from the shadows as she slumped into a beach lounger and dropped her sandals into the chair next to her unceremoniously. Her long, dark hair clouded around her like chocolate waves, the dark red dress teasing him as the evening breeze fanned every curve. It pulled up her hemline, revealing a creamy thigh, and suddenly, his pants felt two sizes too small.

The last time he'd gotten aroused that quickly was almost a decade ago. He knew he shouldn't even be looking at her like that, not with their working relationship. He had followed her to make sure she was okay. But it was as if he had no control over himself whenever she was nearby. Now, he wasn't sure if he should approach or not, and consequently stood statue still like a creepy stalker.

The way she strode through the edges of the surf had been enchanting. Moonlight glimmered off her ass with each sensual step. He *couldn't* stop thinking about her, not since the day he'd met her at *The Oubliette*.

At first, she was a pretty face, eye candy. There was no pretense with

Rae. Maybe it was her years as a bartender or her knowledge of a working studio that made talking to her as easy as breathing. However, the real magic moment, when he'd known himself lost, was when she'd composed for the first time right there in his private studio. Born in desire indeed!

As the thought hit him, Jacob shivered with the realization that her desire was for him. She wanted him as much as he wanted her. There was no mistaking the lust on her mouth when she was plucking the bass rhythm and ogling him. His body twitched with the memory, begging for attention.

With a groan, he changed direction, fast walking to his room where he wouldn't be overheard. Rae was on the beach, the others were in the restaurant. He would have to work fast if he didn't want to be caught releasing his pent-up energy, he cautioned himself. But the way his zipper strained, he didn't think speed would be an issue.

By the time footsteps sounded outside, his panting was beginning to calm, and he tracked the ceiling fan blades twirling lazily overhead. He was going to hell for this—he was sure.

The sound of a door opening and closing on the other side of his room alerted him that Rae had returned. Minutes later, he was tapping lightly on her door with freshly washed hands.

"Derek," she warbled, voice sounding like another explosion may be around the corner.

"Not Derek," he corrected. "Jacob."

"Oh." Rae's voice was soft, and he heard her scramble to the door, and it opened widely. "In that case, come in."

He stepped past her, assessing her rumpled dress and bare feet. "Good walk?" he questioned.

"Yes." She nodded, closing the door and leaning against it.

Jacob was keenly aware of her gaze on him, and he met her eyes.

"I'm sorry I exploded," she apologized. "I think today was more overwhelming than I realized." She slunk to her loveseat and melted into it with a sigh. "And Derek's my bro, but he does not know when to quit sometimes."

"I apologize on behalf of the entire male species."

Rae chuckled, easing into the small couch in her room. "Thank you."

"Maybe after being cooped up in a studio alone for this long, we might need a little space while we're here. I don't want you all to think I planned this to control what you do."

"I don't think anyone feels that way," Rae excused. "Well, maybe Joe. Unless we're playing music, I can't figure out what he's thinking."

Jacob chuckled, planting himself in the armchair.

She nodded her assent. "I destroyed dinner. And I promise not to do it again."

They were silent for a moment, the sound of the AC blower filling the space between them. Jacob spoke first. "So, I don't know about you, but I'm kind of starving, and that food did smell amazing."

Rae shook her head. "I cannot go back there now. Breakfast will be hard enough."

"Neh, different staff I'm sure," he teased. "So why don't we order room service? And we can be as quiet as you want."

"Wait, there's room service? Why do we leave our rooms again?" she questioned.

"Because, ocean. And also, you haven't seen a coati yet."

"What the hell is a coati?"

"It's a rodent, I guess," Jacob explained.

"Rodent? I need to meet a rodent?"

He sighed. "Well, okay, it's not a rodent. But it's like a ferret and a raccoon had a baby, and they're about the cutest thing you'll ever see."

She arched a brow.

"Trust me—it makes a little resort walk worth it. And the iguanas are pretty stellar around here." Jacob continued regaling her with tales of his travels with The Harmonizers and the exotic locations they got to experience back in the day while they waited for room service.

When their food arrived, he set everything on the rattan table, tipping the waiter despite fervent refusals. He hinted that it would be a great offense to be refused. As they ate, Rae picked up the conversation, describing her quiet Oklahoma upbringing. When she talked about watching the Tree House Kids where he had gotten his first taste of stardom, he was captivated.

A bottle of champagne later, Rae was bemoaning the fact that her apartment building was hiking up their prices.

"I'm torn," Rae whined. "The rate hikes are ridiculous when we barely have a working coin operated laundry. But finding a new place is a pain so I'll probably pay it, but if we're going on tour…I'd be paying for an apartment to store like a box of stuff and a futon."

"Well, you can stay at my place," he announced, making a duh face at her. "It will give you time to make a better decision. I've got plenty of room," he encouraged.

Rae stared at him, stunned into silence. She sprang from her chair and began pacing the room.

"It makes sense if your lease is up," he insisted, watching her jaw twitch. "You're there most of the time anyway. It's not like you're not used to staying there already."

"I'm not a charity case, Mr. Hunter," Rae replied stiffly. "All I said was that they're raising my rent!"

The sound of the word "Mister" was distracting now that he knew what it meant, but he focused on convincing her to move in.

"I heard you! I wanted to offer my place as an alternative until—"

"What?" she cut in. "Until I save up? I have enough to cover the bloody buggering rent!"

"I understand that!" he shouted back, holding up his hands in defense. "I'm fucking lonely in that house! We're working there most days and nights. I have the room, and if it's so goddamn important, I'll charge you rent!" He stopped, chest heaving.

She stared at him for a moment, then burst into startled laughter. He tried to frown, but the ridiculousness of the situation hit him, and he joined her laughter with his own. When they had exhausted themselves, he cleared his throat and tried again.

"Rae, since your lease is up, would you mind terribly helping me out by renting a spare room with an adjoining bathroom to be your personal, private space in my home?" He took a deep breath and sighed. "Please,

Rae? I never realized how big and quiet the house was until you and the band came and filled it with music and laughter. I'm—"

"Okay, okay," Rae cut in, holding up her hands in surrender. "Against my better judgment, I will. But we have to lay ground rules, okay? And I demand that I pay at least what I'm currently paying for my apartment."

"Should I have Grace write up a contract?" he teased.

"Oh, shush," she laughed, swatting his arm.

"Now," he chuckled, dropping onto the bed and patting the space next to him. Rae rolled her eyes and sat down. "What sort of rules?" he asked.

Jacob listened as Rae spouted a variety of rules about cleaning responsibilities, grocery shopping and half a dozen other mundane domestic woes that came with sharing living space with another person, but none of them mattered to him. He would live by whatever rules she listed, as tiny as they were, just to see her face every day.

With each stipulation, he agreed, and her body relaxed visibly when she realized he wasn't going to protest.

"So when do we move you in?" he pressed.

"Um...my lease is up in a month?"

"I'll start clearing out a room for you when we get back, but...can I leave the bed in the room? We can set up the futon as a couch or put it in the garage for storage."

Rae patted his shoulder. "That would be amazing," she slurred, trying to pour more champagne into their glasses. Only a few bubbles dripped out, and she pouted.

She set the bottle down, turning her tipsy grin fully on him, and Jacob braced for the change of subject he saw coming.

"So, now that I have you away from the others," she purred, "you can reminisce all you like about The Tree House Kids. I know you think all anyone wants to hear about is The Harmonizers, but that's not true. Well, I mean, I like those stories, but...they're not the only interesting thing about you, you know?"

"I..." He blushed, not prepared to discuss all the mistakes he'd made as a teen on the hit cable classic. "Maybe tomorrow?" he chuckled, yawning suddenly.

"Any time," she murmured, yawning reflexively. "Jakey?"

"Hmm?"

"I really am sorry I wigged out earlier. I didn't realize how pressured I'd felt."

"It's no prob—"

"Seriously," she cut in. "And thank you for coming to check on me. You're the best person I know."

She was a lightweight drinker, he noted with a smirk. "Come on; let's put you to bed. I think you're due for some rest." He helped her into bed, kissing her forehead tenderly once she was comfortable.

"Thank you for the chat." He smiled, her eyes already drifting shut. He took the remains of their dinner, setting it outside her room, put the *Do Not Disturb* sign on her door, and went to his own room, rubbing the spot on his chest over his heart. Why did it ache like that?

Jacob turned to find Derek walking to the door and his face pinched angrily. "She's asleep, no thanks to you."

"I was coming to apologize," the producer defended.

"Save it for tomorrow," Jacob insisted. "I thought better of you, man. Jabbing someone who's already down? Not cool at all." He stalked around the corner of the building to his own room and sequestered himself inside before Derek could catch up.

THIRTEEN

Despite the sun glaring through the blinds like an interrogation light at the crack of noon, Rae woke feeling dark. Everything she and Derek had shouted at each other at the dinner table came rushing back. No blue sky or tropical flower was going to relieve the shame seeping from her pores. She should never have let him get so far under her skin. However, Jacob following up on her and staying till they nearly passed out drunk had been a delicious consolation prize. She should feel guilty for thinking of him as such, but her brain continued posing him in increasingly deviant positions anyway.

She needed a walk to clear her head. Donning her cover up, she checked her texts. There was an invitation to breakfast and some details about spa appointments. She closed the door behind her slowly, tapping out an apology.

A nearby opening door broke her from her reverie, and she turned to see Carmen emerging from her room.

"Hey there, Sunshine," Carmen greeted. "Sleep off the oogies?"

"I am so sorry about that." Rae sighed, twisting one toe against the porch as another wave of shame washed over her.

"Nah, we were all exhausted, and he kept picking like a kid with a scab. Besides, nothing you said was a lie."

"I know, but to have dragged Gracie under the bus like that…like she was a grenade I could drop on him."

"She is a grown ass woman, and if she didn't know that D has the hotsies for her…well, she needed to," Carmen affirmed. "The real question is if you and our fearless leader are gonna take your hotsies to the next level?"

Rae rolled her eyes. "Clicking musically doesn't mean there's more there."

Carmen hung on the statement for a long beat, searching the sky and tapping her chin. When she leveled Rae with her gaze, one brow quirked up. "So you *don't* want to bang him into next week?"

Rae sputtered. "I…NO, of course not! He's basically our boss!" Although, she did have a point. She hadn't quite erased the images of the things she'd like to do to his body as the man in question rounded the corner.

Her eyes raked over him lasciviously, chewing her lip as the sun caressed the side of his neck, and she followed the light down to buttons on his blue Madras shirt. He was some tropical Adonis, lean legs swathed in a pair of white linen pants.

"Morning, ladies," he mumbled, rubbing his temples.

Rae saw movement in Carmen's jawline, and she scrambled for something to say before being called out.

The universe intervened on her behalf as Grace's door opened between them. The secretary emerged, looking fresh as a daisy, and for a moment, Rae hated her composure. She bet the other woman didn't struggle to keep her lust under control. But she didn't hate Grace—she couldn't after seeing how Derek reacted to her. She had never seen him legitimately squishy before.

Jacob nodded. "Anyone wanna go to lunch?" he asked. "I've gotta soak up this hangover with something."

Carmen laughed as she shook her head. "I ordered room service."

"I already ate," Grace declined. "And I scheduled four massages at 2:00 at the spa."

Jacob counted the ladies then brightened. "So, there's one for me?"

Grace nodded. "If you want it."

"I'm in," Carmen declared. "For the record, you've set the bar pretty high for breaks now, Hunter."

He shrugged with a chuckle, eyes crinkling above his happy mouth. "You're welcome. Whoever's coming to lunch, let's go. Don't want to be late for the spa," Jacob encouraged, stepping off the porch and onto the walkway.

Rae squirmed under his direct scrutiny. She felt suddenly naked in his gaze and froze to the spot. Why was he staring at her as though he expected an answer?

"Rae would be happy to make sure you don't get lost," Grace offered. "I know she didn't get breakfast." The secretary crossed her arms defiantly.

Guilt for using Grace as cannon-fodder against Derek the previous night evaporated.

"Come on then, Desirae," Jacob called, extending a hand in her direction.

The use of her full name shocked Rae into motion, and she started after him without another thought.

"It's Rae," she insisted as they speed walked towards the privileged dining area. He was two steps ahead, about to bound up the stairs. His stride was confident, and she admired the set of his shoulders as she followed him.

"As you wish." Jacob grinned over his shoulder and stopped to allow her to catch up. They were silent until they were seated with menus.

Rae sighed relief as she read over it slowly. She could barely focus with his cologne permeating her senses. What power did paella have over notes of pine and tobacco?

Jacob's soft voice interrupted her search. "You okay to share tapas?"

"Sounds great," Rae agreed. She snapped her menu shut, grateful not to have to pretend to read any longer. Her eyes drifted around the room, taking in the décor and the tropical plants, landing anywhere but on him. Parts of the previous night's conversation filtered through her fuzzy mind, and it took all her skills not to cringe.

She wasn't sure if she could face him in the cold light of day. He seemed to have no animosity toward her, but he could be relying on his years of experience with the press to hide it. She refused to believe that he was unaffected by their conversation.

It was time to put on her big girl pants and say what she meant.

"So…the elephant," she mumbled, chewing her bottom lip. "Did we agree to live together last night? Or was that a bubbly induced dream I had?" She was afraid he would answer, and she rambled on. "I mean, I'm still okay with it if you are, but I understand if you were just—"

Jacob reached across the table, resting his hand atop hers. Her mouth closed instantly as the contact radiated throughout her body, skin puckering, and she tensed.

"Of course the offer's still open," he assured. He released her hand and began adjusting his silverware. "But I think you were right about setting some rules. And about more than wild parties."

She swallowed hard, suddenly picturing bumping into him fresh from the shower, wearing nothing but a towel draped around his hips. She shifted in her chair.

"Right, right," she agreed as the waiter approached to take their order.

Jacob ordered quickly and confidently, and their server disappeared just as swiftly.

When they were alone again, he caught her gaze. "But we have time. We don't have to work it all out today."

"Of course," Rae agreed, relaxing in her seat. One corner of her mouth quirked up, and she stared at the tablecloth. His acceptance made her feel bold, and she saw an opening to needle him and barreled forward.

"So, it's tomorrow." She giggled. "You promised me Tree House stories!"

Jacob eased back in his chair, taking a deep breath. "Are you sure you want to talk about that? It was a lifetime ago, and I was a kid."

Rae rolled her eyes, reaching for her water glass. "Yes, I do. I grew up on that stuff, man! I have so many questions."

Jacob sighed. "Where would you like to start?"

"Auditions. I want to know who you met and if it was crazy. I want to know it all." She leaned against the table, cooing when their sangria arrived.

"Fine," he agreed. He launched into a vague description of how many people were there. He mentioned a few of the other "Kids" he met during the audition process and then how excited he'd been when he'd gotten the call to say he won the part.

As their tapas arrived, he regaled her with stories from various stages of his past fame, and they delved into lunch without hesitation. All the questions she'd been formulating for a lifetime came pouring out, and he fielded them with the professional detachment of a pro. He refused to say a negative word about anyone, and for a second, his answers began sounding like one of the countless interviews she'd heard over the years.

He licked a glob of sauce from one finger, then another, gently removing bits of food from his fingertips. Rae returned the favor, sucking one finger up to her second knuckle and holding his gaze as she did. Her line of questioning changed, unwilling to be thinking about him as a boy while licking her fingers, and she asked about things that had happened to him later in life.

Noticing a pattern to his stories, she interrupted. "Why is *Danny* in half these stories?"

He glanced away, fussing with the napkin in his lap before he met her eyes. "He's kinda my best friend. My brother."

"That's too cute, that you've been so close for so long," Rae murmured tenderly.

He shrugged.

Rae sipped her drink. The mixture of cool fruits and wines went down easily. "I guess you don't get to see each other much anymore."

He shook his head. "That's life, you know. Nothing to do with our friendship. You do big things with people, but then they end, and you move on and do other big things with other people. It's a good thing, I think, to move forward in life. You don't want to get stuck in a rut. After the *Kids* and the *Harmonizers* for the last twenty plus years, I haven't had much of a chance to be alone." He grimaced. "And now that I am, I can't stand it."

She winked. "I think we've got a bead on how to fix that."

The smile he gave her was mellow. "I think we might. I take it you're not so great at the being alone parts of life either or you wouldn't jump at the chance to move in with a virtual stranger."

She shook her head, suddenly fascinated by the crumbs on the tapas plates, and she picked at them.

He rested his elbows on the table, folding them comfortably and leaning in.

Rae looked up to see his expression change, a wicked grin curling his lips.

"So, I've told you my whole life story. It's your turn."

Rae narrowed one eye at him.

"No, no," he insisted. "Turnabout is fair play. You have all this knowledge about me, and I don't have nearly enough details on you, future Roomie. Let's start with your bass playing skills. When did you learn to play?" he asked.

The question was harmless on the surface, but he had no idea the pain the answer was rooted in. She closed her eyes, sucking in a calming breath.

"My dad taught me to play when I was six or seven," she answered slowly. "I was just big enough to hold the thing. He was a session musician at a local studio. It was Oklahoma, mind you, so there were a whole two places to record. But dad let me hang out there in the summers. I got to know some super talented musicians that no one's ever heard of."

Rae allowed herself to tell a few stories about her studio time with her father, surprised at how comforting it was to share her story with Jacob…as if her father was there with them, approving of her disclosure. With most people, she stuck to facts only, but she found herself telling him the minutia of some of her favorite memories of her father and the love for music that he'd instilled in her.

A ding on their phones interrupted the conversation.

Grace
ten-minute warning!!! If you're not at the spa, you should be!

"To be continued," Jacob apologized. He stood, placing his napkin on the table and taking a step toward the door. "Seriously, I want to hear more."

Rae agreed, frowning at her drink. Without a word, she swallowed the last of it in one gulp.

Jacob stared at her with a grin. "Nervous?"

She shook her head. "Didn't want to waste it."

He pushed his chair in, starting toward the exit. "They'll give you another at the spa."

She laughed. "I'm counting on that. We can't possibly be hung over if we never sober up." Her breakfast sangria had already begun to work its magic, the pounding in her head turning down several notches as she followed him.

"Madam, I like the way you think." He extended an elbow in her direction then tucked her hand to his side when she accepted. "To the spa!" he declared and led them away.

They found Grace pacing the lobby when they arrived, peering at different displays with a look of concentration on her kind features. She looked up when Rae gently cleared her throat.

"This is nice, Grace. Thanks," Jacob offered.

"No, thank you," she corrected sweetly. "*Your* treat."

Jacob shrugged with a bright smile, his cheeks pinking as he looked away.

Grace gestured to one of the employees with a smile. "This is him," she said.

The white-jacketed employee smiled. "*Excellente*. This way, Mr. Jacob."

"Oh. Thanks." Jacob waved a helpless goodbye over his shoulder at the ladies, trailing after his hostess.

Rae watched him go, her innards swirling at the sight of his grin. Unwilling to be caught staring, she turned her eyes around the room.

"Where's Carmen?" Rae asked.

"Already started," Grace explained. "I asked them to take Jacob right away so he's not out in the open for longer than necessary."

"Smart," she praised.

Grace dropped into a waiting chair along the wall, eyes closing and exhaling slowly.

"I was impressed that they were able to get us through the airport with so little attention yesterday," she complimented.

Grace laughed. "His hobo look helped a lot."

Rae burst out laughing, covering her mouth at the commentary. She had been thinking the same, and it was nice to have someone who understood.

"How was lunch?" Grace inquired while they waited for the staff to return.

In the stillness of the room, peaceful décor and soft cushions surrounding them, she sucked in a deep breath then spilled all the beans to see Grace's expression. "Well, we're moving in together, so you tell me." Rae wiggled her brows.

Grace's eyes flew open wide. "Like…living together?"

Rae shook her head, picking at one fingernail. "Roommates," she clarified. "My lease is up in a month and when we get back, I have to either renew or make other arrangements."

"Oh," Grace mumbled, brows crunching together, looking a bit guilty. "You hadn't told me about your lease ending. I could've helped maybe."

"I've been trying not to think about it." Rae shrugged. "Stresses me out. Plus, we've been sort of focused."

"Are you sure that's a good idea? I know you've been working together for a few months now, but that's vastly different from living with someone, even platonically."

Rae's nose scrunched at the question. The worry wrinkled between Grace's brows was like a punch to the gut.

"And…" Grace lowered her voice. "Are you sure you'll be able to keep it platonic? You can deny it all day long, but I know he twists your Twizzler. How are you going to stay apart when you're always together?"

Before Rae could answer, a concierge arrived to lead them to their massage rooms. Rae followed along, barely able to enjoy the treatment. The scent of eucalyptus and pine tugged at her troubled mind. Grace was right, she knew. She had a few days to get her libido in check. Or else she could put her few belongings in storage until she returned.

Derek met them as they exited the spa, begging them to join him on the jet skis. The way his eyes roamed over Grace sent her brain down a lewd path, and she was back on the Jacob train.

"I'm not going to ruin my massage with a bouncy water toy," she declined. "But I will take Grace's bag." She secured the secretary's bag, pushing her toward her admirer before searching out a shady spot on the shore.

The privileged beach did not disappoint, and she sprawled under a wide umbrella. She'd barely pulled off her sandals before a server arrived, and she ordered a huge water and a peach daquiri.

She watched the water lapping the shoreline. *Focus on the water, Rae,* she soothed herself. *Breathe in and out, like the surf.* The moment the servers returned with her beverages, she gulped down the water.

The daquiri was cool and sweet, and it melted against her tongue. In the distance, a pair of jet skis spirited across the water. She imagined Jacob's hair waving in the wind, water turning his shirt invisible and outlining every delightful bit of muscle covering his chest.

She reached for Grace's bag in hopes of something to distract her. Inside was a thick novel with the picture of a purple headed vampire jumping off the cover. She didn't care what story was held within the pages; she refused to watch Jacob out on the water being all...sexy. She forced herself to digest each word, but the plot could not compare with the reality of the man on the water. A shadow fell across the page as she reread the same paragraph for the third time.

"Whatcha reading?" Carmen asked, flopping onto the chair next to her.

"Murder and mayhem," Rae laughed, closing the book. "Something way too heavy for this gorgeous beach." She stuffed a napkin between the pages and dropped it into Grace's bag. "Get bored of racing the waves?"

"Nah. Tired. Everyone came in for a rest." The guitarist shifted onto her side, resting her head on one hand. "Quick; before Jay comes back with drinks. How was lunch?"

Rae arched a brow. "We chatted about our pasts. That's all," she replied primly.

"Lies," Carmen retorted, squinting at her.

"Who's lying?" Jacob asked, handing peach daiquiris to each before settling in the sand between them.

"No one," Rae snapped, sipping her fresh drink.

"Absolutely not Sunshine here," Carmen sassed.

"Is that Grace's bag of sunscreen?" Jacob asked, grabbing for it.

"Yes," Rae replied. "Where is Grace, anyway?"

"Oh, Derek has absconded with her to the pool bar," he burbled conspiratorially.

"That explains why you're rooting through her bag like it's communal property." She paused, watching him squirt sunscreen into one hand before dabbing it across his cheeks. She squeezed her eyes shut, forcing herself to think about Derek. "Think he's finally realized?"

"What we've all known for weeks?" Carmen laughed, standing. "About time. Now that they're sorted, I wonder who else will come to their senses…" she trailed off and wandered away, sipping her drink.

"She's weird." Rae giggled. "I dig that about her."

Jacob climbed into the recently vacated chair and sipped his drink. "Yeah, she's pretty cool. Seen Joe today?"

"Nah. Think he's still sleeping?"

"Man! He warned us!" Jacob cackled, his eyes crinkling up and disappearing with mirth.

"He did," she murmured, feeling the power of his smile hit her like a brick to the solar plexus. She needed to focus her attention elsewhere. "How are your sandcastle building skills?"

"Huh, I'm a bit rusty, but I wouldn't mind getting dirty with you." He sniggered like a teenaged boy and shot toward the beach ahead of them.

Rae sent a sharp look at his back as he searched for an ideal location to build. Half an hour later, they were flinging sand at each other, castle abandoned, and racing around like kids. Rae formed a ball of wet sand, cheering at the satisfying slap as it landed on Jacob's shoulder despite his noble dodge.

"Oh, you're gonna get it now!" he warned, tackling her into the surf.

Rae froze as his weight pressed her into the sand, his whole body melting into hers. His wet clothes warmed against her skin, and there was no denying his sudden reaction that twitched against her hip. An involuntary moan escaped her lips, and she squirmed to inch closer.

Jacob's fingers twined into hers, his knees parting around her hips. This was it. This was the tipping point she'd been both dreading and craving. The sound around them disappeared. Their eyes were locked in a gaze, and this time, she saw him inching closer. If their hands hadn't been entwined, she'd have grabbed his ass to pull him closer and feel his delicious desire pressing into her belly.

Without warning, a wave crashed over them. Rae gasped, mouth full of salt water, and they scrambled apart, sputtering and crawling to their knees. She burst out laughing, flinging her hair out of her face as she tried to regain her composure.

Jacob did the same, helping her to her feet and leading her to their shady beach chairs.

They collapsed into the damp canvas slings, heaving with laughter until she couldn't laugh any more.

Rae stared into the distance, then fiddled with the ruffle on her suit. She felt the urge to say something. Not an apology perhaps, but to discuss the growing attraction. At first, she'd thought her fandom was to blame. She had spent a long time following his career during her formative years and using his body as her ideal partner. Then she attributed it to the music, drawing them to each other like magnets. But here on the beach, when it was simply them and the waves, the desire she felt reached a fever pitch. There was nothing mixed about the signals she'd felt beneath his shorts. No matter how she spun it, the truth seemed like an exposed nerve that she couldn't bring herself to pick at.

Unable to bear the silence a moment longer, she excused herself to her room, feet pounding against the pathway. Once there, she locked her door and starfished on the freshly made bed.

Her brain roiled. Every swirling bit of logic ended in the same place.

"He…wanted me," she whispered to the room. Men like him— successful, talented, beautiful, humble—didn't want her. She didn't deserve even a fling. But she would be damned if she could walk away from him—from the band—from the taste of success.

She needed to talk to someone. Say things out loud to see how they felt. Needed someone to tell her she was right—or crazy, one.

It couldn't be Carmen for the harassment alone. She didn't know Joe well enough to burden him. And her two besties were busy with each other. Hopefully making out in a secluded corner by now. She sent Derek all her best juju—Gracie would be no easy summit to climb. She fired off a message to Peter about this development.

She stared at the phone after pressing send. Her favorite contacts stared back. Derek. Grace. Carmen. Jacob, even though they never called or texted. And Kendra.

She exhaled a sigh of relief, blowing kisses at the picture as the phone dialed the number.

Two rings later, Kendra greeted her. "Hey, babe! Bored with tropical paradise already?"

Flopping to her back, Rae closed her eyes, throwing one arm across the bed.

"Nah, I just…something happened, and I wanted your take on it before I spiral out."

"Uh-oh," Kendra fretted. "Is it safe to assume that this is about your silver-eyed singer? Or did you finally decide to take a bite out of that producer?"

The thought of touching Derek after she'd seen how he reacted to Grace was exactly the image she needed to cool her proverbial jets. "Gross. Why would you say that?"

"I've seen his ass. I'd bite it," Kendra purred merrily.

Rae's freehand clamped over her eyes. "No. This is definitely about Jacob. Jakey. That sweet boy from *The Tree House Kids* that gave me all my first tinglies."

"Oh, honey. Sounds like you're the one who got bit. Tell me all about it."

Slowly, Rae relayed the events as they'd unfolded with stuttering clarity starting with the most recent and rabbit trailing into a hundred tiny moments shared since they'd met.

Her brain began weaving together the threads to negate the fact that Jacob was interested in her as more than a musician.

"I mean, he gets boners in the studio all the time, but he's kinda…known for music getting his groove on, even in the middle of a concert or show," Rae rationalized.

"Are you twelve?" Kendra laughed. "Ask him."

"What?" Rae lowered the pitch of her voice, mocking the idea. "Hey, Jacob, ya wanna bone?" Rae scoffed, relaxing into her own voice. "You know I ain't that girl."

"No, stupid. Ask him out."

Rae gasped at the proposition, flipping over and curling into her pillow. She couldn't do that. He would surely say no. Unless he said yes…

Kendra continued, her no-nonsense tone ramping up. "You are, let me remind you, at a terribly expensive, romantic beach. Why waste this perfectly ripe opportunity because you're afraid it could get messy. Plus, it's the twenty-first century! If you don't make the first move, you will never know what you're missing out on."

Rae groaned. "But what if today was a normal reflex to being near any half-naked female? And then I'll have to watch him make googly eyes at fans when we're touring. Won't that make things weird with the band?"

"God you're thick! I am telling you: I saw the chemistry the day y'all held auditions. I mean, you were playing it pretty cool, but you were constantly looking to each other whenever you had an idea. Jacob's eyes were glued to you during every candidate. To be honest, I thought you'd call me a lot sooner about this."

Rae's mouth gaped at the recollection. She was doing the work. Absorbed in the music. Had Kendra witnessed all this? And if she had, did it matter? Did she want another fling?

"But the band—"

"Shut up! Screw the band! This is the literal man of your dreams!"

Kendra's words landed sharply, and Rae released a yell into her pillow.

"I don't understand," Kendra prodded softly. "I've known you a long time now, Rae. Is it Alex?"

At the mention of her ex-husband, Rae cringed. Her belly swirled with what felt like fire, and she threw a decorative pillow across the room. She wanted to rage on about how the two were nothing alike. But the similarities were truly quite striking.

"It wouldn't be hard to be concerned," Rae reasoned. "Alex was and *still is* a nobody, even though I didn't know it then. And he found a younger model. What makes me think that Jacob with his adoring fans wouldn't find a new one every night? What a fool would I be then?"

Kendra didn't answer.

"I think that's it," Rae reiterated. Tears burned at the corners of her eyes, and she swiped them away ferociously. "Alex always made this big show of telling me how great I was. And how inspired he felt around me."

"And Jacob says those things too?"

Rae searched her memory. "Well, not exactly. But he compliments me at every chance."

"And how does he treat you outside the studio? For example, how has he treated you during this chic vacay that he whisked you away on?"

"You know we're not alone here, right? It's the whole band all the time."

"Except for now," Kendra pointed out. "You're hiding in your room talking to me after you nearly had a very private moment in the surf like you're in some kind of movie."

Biting her tongue, Rae released her pillow, sitting up and hugging her knees instead. "Well, yes."

"And you said after the pretty producer made you so mad at dinner—Jacob came racing after you and tended you."

"We call him Vitamin D now," Rae interrupted, hoping to shift the focus of the conversation.

Kendra snickered. "That is stored in the memory banks. But getting back to you..."

"Must we?" Rae cringed.

"Darling, that's why you called. You needed big sister to blow the smoke out of your eyes and help you see this clearly."

Rae promised herself she wouldn't cry, and she leaped out of bed to begin pacing. "Fine. Be right, why don't ya?"

"I am here for you. But from what you've told me, you're the thing standing in the way of you having a life-changing experience with a man who has been taking care of you with absolutely no benefits besides the pleasure of your company."

Rae stumbled, catching herself on the sofa.

"I love you. Now, stop wasting time and go to him!" Kendra encouraged.

The line disconnected, leaving Rae ogling the phone as it returned to locked mode.

The words ripped through her mind on repeat. "Stop wasting time and go to him."

Drying sand crusty on her skin drew her attention as the mantra spun into an internal tornado. She had claimed all along that she was resisting the attraction for the sake of the band. She had blamed their chemistry on the music; on circumstance; on basic male urges.

But maybe it was all simpler than that. Maybe she didn't want to risk another confidante taking her for granted. When she'd met Alex, all her drive to make her own dreams a reality took a backseat to his. She'd poured all of herself into him and given him all her best ideas. It wasn't until she had the courage to divorce him that she had begun to rekindle the flame of her own aspirations.

It was easier to convince herself that Jacob was having an involuntary reaction to her. All boys did. Boys didn't like *her*. She was a warm body, and she should be grateful for whatever pleasure she could take from it.

Leaving a sandy pile of clothing in the corner of the bathroom, she stepped into a cool shower. The frosty deluge dragged her attention to the present. She shrieked as sand and water ran down her hot scalp and sent goosebumps across her body. The remnants of his touch washed down the drain with the salt.

If Kendra was right, and Jacob's nether regions had reacted to *her*, why hadn't he made a move? He'd had plenty of opportunities. His inaction gave her the impression he didn't want the entanglement and that it *would* interfere with band dynamics.

Her hand skimmed over her body, brushing away the sand from her thighs, and her next argument formed. She scowled as she turned off the water and wrapped herself in a towel. The mental gymnastics were exhausting. A knock at her door interrupted her thoughts. Grateful for the reprieve, she called to her guest.

"Hang on!"

She tugged a sundress over her head and finger combed her hair on the way to the door.

Derek waited on the other side. He was the last person she expected. He was supposed to be with Grace! If they had crashed and burned already, she had no chance doing as Kendra suggested and going after Jacob. And part of her was still mad at him for picking a fight at dinner which had led to this whole debacle in the first place.

"Hi?" she asked.

Derek sighed. "I shouldn't have picked a fight last night."

He paused, and she knew he was waiting for her to speak but agreeing with him felt like twisting the knife a bit too far.

His lips drew tightly for a moment, but then he squared his shoulders. "But I'm glad you're finally committed to this band because I think you'll be successful. And I want good things for you."

Her anger abated at his statement. "Thanks. And I overreacted. I'm sorry I made such a scene," she replied.

"We're cool. I've known you long enough. But um, I was actually hoping you might do us both a favor."

She arched a brow. "And here I was thinking you came to mend fences."

The endearing smile she'd come to love from him as a teenager lit his face. "I can't want more than one thing at a time?"

She chuckled. "Say what you want."

"I dropped off Grace in her room. She's…well, she might need some tending in a couple hours. Think you could bring her to dinner?"

"Why does she need tending?" she asked, eyes narrowing.

"Well, I got her at least three daquiris at the pool, and I'm getting the feeling someone slipped her a few more. Pretty sure she's already asleep."

Rae gasped, trying unsuccessfully to hide it behind her hand. "So, Goody Gracie is drunk? Why do I feel the need to record this for posterity?"

"I think you'd be bored. She's a little unsteady and sleepy. And giggly," he added.

She eyed him from head to toe. "So…you and Grace?"

"Not a word," he warned.

"I don't know why you're so prickly about it. I fully support this."

Derek shrugged as he pivoted away. "Thanks." In a few steps, he rounded the corner toward his room.

Well, at least someone was getting it right. And looking after the tightly wound assistant was the perfect excuse to avoid her own burgeoning feelings for their lead singer. And Rae was grabbing at all the straws.

ae relaxed in her room, napping and then styling her hair carefully before she went to check on her neighbor roughly an hour before dinner. She arrived with a bottle of water and knocked at her door.

A shockingly long amount of time stretched before the door opened. It was all Rae could do not to laugh. Normally so tense and wound up, she had never seen the secretary with rumpled hair and definitely not with a sunburn. Rae held out a bottle of water and smiled.

"I've come to help," she murmured.

Grace accepted the bottle warily, pulling the door open. In moments, she was guzzling the water down as Rae settled in a chair.

The chugging stopped when the bottle was empty, and an atypically guttural groan escaped the woman's lips.

Rae smirked as she watched the half-asleep assistant wobble around the room, clearly woken from her slumber. She insisted she take a shower and waited patiently as the woman did so.

She paced the room, peeking at the woman's baggage without touching a thing. Her cases were open on the floor, neat rows of clothing and matching underclothes waiting to be plucked up. The woman was built for efficiency. Her whole world was about to be rocked, and she hadn't the slightest clue. Love, done right, was messy and disorienting. But with Derek, she stood a chance.

Spying the beach bag near the door, she pulled the tawdry novel from its confines and distracted herself with a chapter as the shower ran. It took nearly twenty minutes for her friend to return, looking much improved. Unwilling to give Jacob any more room in her head, she prodded her for details about her drunken pool time with Derek.

Grace's face glowed red as she passed on snippets of their rendezvous, and Rae coiled deeper into the chair.

To Rae, they were already a couple, and she was growing increasingly frustrated as Grace eschewed the attraction. "You've spent this delightful day together, and you're attracted to him. What could possibly be holding you back?" Rae pressed.

A long sigh preceded Grace's reply. "Part of me worries that I'm into him because I've been a super fan for so long. Am I crushing on *him* or who he used to be?"

The words struck Rae's core, and she lowered her hand, sinking back into the chair. "I think I'm more worried that I'm trying to scratch an itch," Rae confessed.

"What happened while I was getting plastered in the pool?"

Rae's eyes lost focus, and she worried her lower lip between her teeth.

"Rae?" Grace questioned, head lowering and leaning forward. "Did you *scratch* the itch?"

"No," she snapped. "But he started to. Right there on the shore."

Grace dropped her brush. "How far did it go?" she questioned. "Not the blow by blow, but…are we talking clothes floating away on the tide? Or…"

In halting tones, Rae relayed the episode to her, leaving out the tumult of emotions coursing through her body. "I ran away," she confessed.

Grace reached for a bottle of water from the mini fridge and tossed one to Rae. "Wow. That's pretty intense."

Rae heaved a sigh. "That's putting it mildly."

Grace didn't turn from the mirror as she applied powder across her cheeks. "You're afraid of it damaging the band?"

"Yes. I think we're on the verge of something big here. Or exciting at least."

"Is that your only hang up?" Grace prodded.

Rae hesitated. There were thousands. One niggled in her brain, and she hoped that Grace could give her an answer.

"Why me?"

"Why not you?" Grace countered. She turned to face Rae. Her spin was rigid, and she spoke with authority. "Look, if Jacob wanted anyone else, he'd have had them already. And I'm beginning to think that avoiding it for fear you're going to break up the band is going to break up the band. So—and geez, I think Carmen is rubbing off on me—if you're going to go down in flames for it anyway, why not commit the so-called crime?"

Rae burst out laughing. "I think she is influencing you."

Grace joined her, then shook her head. "It's mutual, so I say go for it. It's got to be easier than pining for each other."

The thought of Jacob pining for *her* was absurd. Her baggage alone was enough to make him avoid any entanglement with her beyond coworkers. It had to be the music between them. The basslines she'd poured into the songs were sensual at their core and feeling drawn to each other was a natural byproduct.

With an exaggerated sigh, Grace caught her eye. "Is it me, or does it feel like being in high school, and we're waiting to be asked to prom or homecoming or something?"

"I'm worried Valley is going to beat us in the big game," Rae teased in a high-pitched voice, then burst out laughing.

Grace squeaked in agreement, collapsing on her bed. In the midst of their laughter, a group text from Joe dinged on both their phones.

> **Joe**
> I'm starving. I can hear Rae and Grace cackling. Anyone else ready for dinner?

Upon reading, the girls devolved into more laughing, and Rae shot back a reply to meet on the pathway outside their hut toward the restaurant in ten minutes.

~ ♪ ~ JACOB ~ ♪ ~

By the time everyone gathered on the walkway to the dining hall, the sun had nearly disappeared in the horizon, and the sky was painted in shades of purple, gold, and red. Derek held out an arm to Grace and lead the way to the restaurant.

"Oh, we're doing this?" Carmen giggled and held her arm out for Joe. He accepted with a curtsy and leaned against her shoulder as they followed the producer.

Jacob noted it was down to him and Rae. Sensing a prime opportunity, he held out his elbow. "May I?" he asked.

Blushing furiously, Rae placed her fingers lightly on his forearm.

Heat raced up his arm, and a flush swept over his neck. His jaw locked, preventing him from saying another word. He was in it now, though, and he guided her along the path. His hesitation had cost him an obvious gap between them and the pair ahead of them, but Jacob smartly did not rush her.

He held the door as they reached their destination, the heat of her body nearly scorching him as she passed beneath his arm with a knowing grin.

The fabric skimming Rae's behind was mesmerizing, his eyes tracing the wine-colored skirt over what appeared to be an unencumbered behind. Was she going commando? Was she trying to undo him?

As they seated themselves at the table, a conversation had already started, and Jacob forced himself to tune in to avoid being caught with another pant tent under the table.

Grace was all business as she expressed concern. "I can't stop thinking about booking gigs when we get back. You need to name the band. Because, if you don't give me one, I may be forced to book you as *Fart Bandits.*"

Rae burst out laughing.

"I take exception to that," Carmen groaned.

"Then give me something better," Grace encouraged.

The table burst into a cacophony of band names, none of which were good. Jacob knew he should be participating. It was about his band after all. A band he felt incredibly passionate about and had spent a small fortune on bonding with at this very resort. He vetoed a variety of bad choices, but he couldn't take his eyes off Rae.

Instead, his brain replayed the moments before the ocean rolled over him and his bassist. Her body had been warm and sandy beneath his, the friction gentle and overwhelming. In that instant with his body perched atop hers, they had been the only two people on the planet. His memory glided over her mouth again. He had been so close. Felt her bare thigh against his shorts. The way she had squirmed to get closer told him she was equally as affected by his nearness. Thank God the ocean had intervened. He had been ready to free his hand and slide it between them just to know she was smitten too.

In all his interactions with Rae, she had never shied away from speaking her mind. There was nothing subtle about her bass playing. But here in paradise, the universe had given them a cold shower, and she disappeared until dinner.

She wasn't ready, and maybe she never would be. Maybe he wasn't ready either. During his solo album spiral, he'd had a different woman almost every night—sometimes more than one. He'd acted out all kinds of kinky fantasies. Explored the depths of his sexuality he had never known were lurking beneath the surface. And all he felt was empty, no matter how many bodies piled around him.

Of course, he wanted to plumb those depths with Rae. She was sensual and uninhibited and open. His brain stumbled over the fact. Carmen was just as open and sexy, but he didn't lay in bed thinking about her wants and needs. Rae was a different story. He had to know more about her; had to at least try. He would never forgive himself if he let go of the first woman who had ever made him feel so seen.

As the band quibbled over potential names, the joy radiating from her had his body on high alert again. Rae was practically crawling onto the table, in the center of the discussion. Her cheeks were ripe apples under wide eyes, hands flying as she spoke. Each new idea she presented sounded like an epiphany falling from her lips, and her laughter released the tension that had been gnawing in his stomach since deciding it was time to make music again.

"Bah, this is hard!" Rae grumbled, a frown popping out her lower lip adorably, and Jacob wanted nothing more than to bite it. Rae stared at the secretary across the table, seemingly unaware of his attraction. "Any ideas, Gracie?"

"Oh no, no, no," Grace laughed. "This is all on you lot. I'm here for the food."

The table went quiet as steaming plates of tasty goodness were set in front of everyone. Then came moans of delight as the dishes were sampled. Immediately, Carmen and Rae were sharing bites and giggling like schoolgirls.

Jacob couldn't fight the comparison between the two women. They were night and day. One tanned and athletic, the other pale and soft. He watched as Rae's face melted in delight as her lips closed over the fork Carmen placed between them. Her eyes fluttered shut, and the moan that escaped was sinful.

Normally, he would have wanted to be sandwiched between them, passed back and forth as the treat everyone wanted. But his fantasy only extended to Rae, imagining ways to elicit the same response. What had happened to him? Did he really think one woman would be enough?

After desert, Derek dragged Grace from the restaurant with a wave to the others.

Rae sighed happily eyes following the couple to the door. She lifted her cappuccino to her lips and sipped. "Well, she has to know he's interested *now*," she observed with a chuckle.

The sentiment pulled Jacob from his reverie into the present moment. His brows scrunched.

"Wait? She didn't know?" Jacob balked. "You're making that up."

"Oh honey, oh sweet summer child," Carmen cooed at him. "No woman that smitten would know. Right, Sunshine?" Resting her chin on one hand, the guitarist rolled her eyes toward Rae.

"Correct," Rae sang.

"Come on, Luz," Joe interjected. "There's plenty of fault to go around.

Us guys can be blind too. It took Rae's meltdown yesterday to open Derek's eyes." He swirled his coffee cup pointedly.

"I'm never living that down, am I?" Rae retorted.

"Not any time soon," Carmen sassed with a chuckle. "I found it highly entertaining."

Jacob scratched the back of his neck awkwardly. His plan for the band to coalesce had clearly been successful, but he hadn't counted on them ganging up on him. When the guitarist and drummer abandoned their half full cups, he knew they were conspiring against him.

Rae's tongue darted across her swollen, red lips, and Jacob thought he should stop wearing zippered trousers. He stared at her across the table for a full minute before they rose in silent agreement to leave.

They ambled away from the restaurant, steps nearly silent across the footbridge leading to their hut. Warm lights cast a yellow glow over the ground, and Jacob fought to stare down instead of at his companion. However, if he didn't take a risk soon, he was in danger of her fleeing again. Their hut was in sight, and the opportunity window was closing.

"Nightcap?" he asked.

Her face snapped up, and the moonlight highlighted her brown eyes, caressing her cheeks softly, and he shoved his hands in his pockets to keep from tracing the path.

"Sure. Lead the way."

Jacob led her to a warmly lit hut secluded between the beach and the resort. Customers swarmed the open-air bar, bursts of laughter punctuating the flurry of clinking ice, blenders, and fast thrown orders. Four bartenders seemed to blur from one end of the counter to the other, calmly filling orders without breaking a sweat.

They squeezed into a vacant space, ordering Blue Lagoons, Rae humming the song of the same name with a tiny grin as a blender whirred.

Jacob studied her covertly. The silky skin on her shoulders glowed under the stars, and he wanted to shower them in slow, soft kisses and nibbles. The bartender winked at the pair as he pushed their drinks, complete with fresh pineapple and tiny umbrellas, across the counter then immediately turned to the next patron.

Rae gulped, and Jacob followed suit as much as he dared while avoiding brain freeze. The alcohol burned his tongue happily, grateful that the bartender had poured heavy handed. Maybe it would work its magic and smooth out his stuttering reactions.

"I had fun earlier," Jacob started. "I can't remember the last time I built a sandcastle." He scouted a patio table overlooking the ocean and pulled out a chair for her.

"Me either," Rae replied, easing into the seat.

He settled himself across from her, sipping his drink. He glanced at her, hoping her wandering gaze would land on him, but it didn't. He had grown used to her gaze directed at him beneath her lashes accompanied by smiling or giggling. The silence was unnerving. He had to put himself out there. She was worth it.

"So…" He cast a sidelong glance at her. "I feel like I should…apologize for this afternoon."

Rae licked her lips, then turned her full attention on him. Jacob shivered at the sternness of her expression, somewhere between pained and professionally pleasant. It reminded him of a horror movie villain.

"No apology necessary," she replied in a cool voice. "Nothing happened."

If there was any doubt of the necessity of an apology, it was clear now. He thought he'd been reading her correctly on the beach, but he had been wrong. Jacob shook his head, holding up a hand. "Right, but—"

"No, Jakey," she interrupted. "I mean it. *Nothing* happened."

He stared at her in the flickering candlelight from the table. "But it did, and all I want to do is apologize."

Rae looked away. Her fingers toyed over the now sweating cup in her hand. "Okay," she replied.

He pulled back from the table in his chair. How had he read her so wrong? She had been so pleasant at dinner as though she held no grudges. He hadn't tackled her with the intention of rubbing himself against her.

"Rae," Jacob tried again.

She held up a hand. "I get it. You're a guy. It happens. The wind changes direction, and nature takes over."

"It's not that." He sighed. "Listen," Jacob wasn't quite sure where he was going, but he had to pull this conversation out of the tank. "I think I...well," he stuttered, "I'm starting to think..."

"Really, Jakey. Please. Please stop," she begged. "We are grown adults who know better than to endanger the band."

Jacob opened his mouth to protest, but she placed a finger over his lips.

"Enough," Rae pleaded.

This was madness. But he would give her what she wanted. "When you're right, you're right," he murmured, sipping his own drink.

~ ♪ ~ R A E ~ ♪ ~

Rae tried to bury herself in her melting frozen blue drink as she changed topics with Jacob. His bumbling apology had been painfully executed and made her soul ache. It confirmed her suspicions that he hadn't wanted her at all. She was just curvy in the right places that piqued his interests. They talked a little longer, competing for who could come up with the worst band names before he walked her to her room.

Once inside, Rae stripped off her clothes and headed toward the shower, heart still hammering from their exchange. She didn't know if she wanted him to agree with her reasons for remaining apart or kiss her stupid instead, and that was *precisely* why they shouldn't. If they started, she didn't think she could stop. What would she do when he woke up and was over his little crush? The band, and her friendships with them all were most of her life now. When he decided he was done with her, she knew she wouldn't be okay.

The way he had clammed up and moved on with the conversation had been exactly what she'd asked for. So why did him closing the door hurt so much?

Twisting the knobs harshly, she held one hand under the cold flow, waiting for it to heat. Her brain continued spiraling. Maybe the temporary pleasure was worth the permanent pain. If she continued to deny him, could she live with the regret? She stepped into the hot water, squeezing her eyes shut as it burned her skin.

When Alex had served her with papers, it hadn't been a surprise— they'd been over a long time, but the finality of it all still gutted her, especially the timing. The process server had leaned over the bar at T*he Oubliette* with her oversized handbags, the strap rings scratching the surface. Rae was already grumpy about working on her birthday, and the seemingly drunk patron in a tube top and suspenders was past annoying.

"Someone said it's your birthday," the guest drawled before giggling like a maniac.

"Who said?" Rae questioned, considering if she should cut her off.

The woman wobbled on the bar stool, scanning the room, then pointed at the blonde waitress across the room.

Tessa. Of course it had been her.

"It's just a day," Rae avoided, discounting the sentiment.

"The big three-oh, I hear."

"You can see why I'd ignore it."

"Oh, sweetie," the client drawled, digging through her purse. "It's just a number. There will be more. Desirae Duncan, you've been served." She shoved a brown paper envelope across the bar into Rae's hands then snapped a surprise photo with her phone.

She grunted angrily at the memory, spluttering under the shower head. Alex had been her childhood sweetheart. Marrying him had been a dream that ended like a nightmare. Falling for Jacob now would be the same. Dreams in the waking world were merely red flags for future misery.

Unable to hold back any longer, she released the tears she'd been fighting half the night. She sobbed about what might have been, what *could* have been. She could taste every nook and cranny, wake up beside him, let him love her. And it would be beautiful and blissful, and kinky as hell if she had her way about it. Her knees turned to jelly as she mourned what had never happened, and she slid to floor. Hot water mingled with hot tears as her shoulders shook. She sobbed long after the water ran cold and her teeth chattered.

She thought she heard someone at the door, but she ignored it. Right now, she needed to be alone with her humiliation.

~ ♪ ~ JACOB ~ ♪ ~

Unfulfilled didn't quite do justice to the letdown Jacob felt after depositing Rae in her room. She was clearly hurting. Her cold refusal to discuss their afternoon on the beach still stung even as he closed the door to his room.

He picked up his phone to text Danny, to tell him how badly he'd screwed up. Everything on the beach had been genuine. Honest-to-goodness fun. He hadn't thought about how his body would react when he tackled her. Some part of him had reverted to his Tree House Kids days, and he'd forgotten their genders and simply enjoyed her company. Maybe it was the way she had dug through his past, treating every word like a treasure. His former band mates liked to pretend it never happened, even though Jason had also been a member.

Jason said talking about it was just bringing up stuff the other guys couldn't relate to and held the two of them back. Jacob should just move on and stop living in the past. In hindsight, taking advice from someone five years his junior might not have been his best play. But he was insecure, and that was the choice he made then.

Dropping the phone to the bed, Jacob sighed. Danny would just tell him to make his move anyway. Refuse to take no for an answer. That's what Danny did with every uncomfortable situation in his life: barrel through to the other side and clean up the wreckage after the fact.

The worst thing he could possibly do now was to push Rae. She was stubborn, even in the studio, locking her jaw and preparing for battle if someone told her no. The better approach, he had learned from Derek, was to suggest something to her and let her come to her own conclusions. Less friction, more forward motion.

Heaven only knew what she had actually suffered at the hands of her ex. No one walked away from a marriage without some baggage. He still carried some from breakups with girlfriends years ago. Her consent was everything.

The shower in her room behind his buzzed to life, and he tried not to picture her naked and soapy and wet. The water ran for an inordinate amount of time before another sound joined the soothing waterfall. Tears. Tears that began softly and ramped up.

Was she crying for him? Crying because he wasn't man enough? Crying for something he said?

He launched from the bed, reaching for the doorknob to go console her, but stopped himself. *You are not her knight in shining armor. You're her villain. You're the problem.*

Turning, he walked into his bathroom, the sound of the water louder. He pressed his body to the wall, listening as she sobbed. He wasn't sure where all the tears came from, but he rested on the floor, pressing his side to the wall. He might not be able to hold her, but he was certainly not going to shy away from her unhappiness. Maybe the dam may have broken, and she would feel better when it was over.

He fell into a fitful sleep, sitting in his shower, dry and listening.

FIFTEEN

The air in Rae's room was humid when she woke. The previous day's clothes were strewn between the door and the bathroom like an exploded baggage claim, and her stomach groaned.

"Come on, Duncan," she scolded herself.

Grumbling as she went, Rae collected her dirty clothes, kneeling in front of her suitcase on the floor. Piece by piece, she folded each article and pressed them neatly inside. There was no more room for messy in her life. It was time to take control of things within her power. She pulled her last fresh bathing suit out and shimmied into it.

Her unruly hair stared back at her in the bathroom mirror, challenging her to tame it. Refusing to be undone by it, a little water, a comb and some patience produced a tight braid that hung down her back. Fingers twining a rubber band around the ends, she pinned her reflection sternly.

"Last night happened like it needed to," she explained. "Today is a new day. A brighter day. And *dammit*, you're going to have fun."

She batted her eyelashes for effect. She didn't believe herself.

"He is our friend, our co-worker, and we will be adults about this. No more tears!"

Rae donned a cover-up, slipping into sandals when her phone pinged. The message was from Carmen demanding she join a girl's beach breakfast immediately. She and Grace were waiting for her on the porch and promised to pound embarrassingly on the door if she did not comply.

A smile rounded her mouth at Carmen's perfect timing. It was time to face the world again as though nothing had ever happened.

She exited the room, finding Carmen and Grace pacing tight circles on the porches and staring at their phones.

"Good morning," Rae caroled, ignoring their worried expressions.

Carmen wrapped her arm around Rae in a sideways hug.

"You can quit pretending," Carmen advised. "We're having a boy-free chat." Tucking Rae against her side, the guitarist hooked Grace with her free arm and led them toward the beach.

Rae squealed as Carmen started skipping. She hadn't skipped since she was in pigtails, and Rae barely even noticed when Grace broke free.

Endorphins flooded her system, and she sucked in the tropical air happily. The morning sun burned hot on her skin, but the rays cleared away the fog in her mind. It truly was a brand-new day, and she had the strength to move forward.

The shore was lined with a dozen four-postered beach beds complete with blue and white canvas awnings. While she was enjoying the brief encounter in the early morning sunshine, the shade meant she would be comfortable, and she squeezed Carmen's arm.

"This is amazing!" she complimented. "What a great idea!"

Carmen shook her head. "Thank Grace. She's ordered a private breakfast out here."

The pair stopped at the first shaded platform, and Rae reached for the post to balance as she removed her shoes. She looked over her shoulder to see Grace picking up speed.

"Come on, slow poke!" Rae goaded.

"Let's use a different one, like down there," Grace insisted, already speed-walking past them. She stopped three beds down, claiming one corner of it and crawling in, sandals and all.

Confused, Rae and Carmen shared a glance, but followed suit.

A server rushed past her, conversing with Grace.

Rae giggled, watching them. It was like a secret language between administrative staff, she thought. One spoke, the other nodded, and it continued back and forth until the server rushed first to Rae to ask for her drink order, and then to Carmen.

Shoes dangling from one finger, Rae curled her toes into the warm sand as she walked and flung the sandals at the foot of the new bed.

Carmen dove into the center, rolling to her back with a squeal. "How are we ever going to go home and live without this service?"

"I know, right?" Rae agreed. She adored being fawned over by the staff.

"Okay, you two are going to spill about your evenings," Carmen demanded.

"Nothing happened," Grace and Rae chorused simultaneously.

Carmen fixed them both with a glare and shifted up to her knees.

"Liars!" She pointed at them both in turn, her finger landing on Rae. "You first."

"There's nothing to tell," she promised.

"I heard you crying in the shower," Carmen prodded. "Something happened."

Rae sighed. "We had a conversation," she answered.

Carmen balked. "All those tears were from talking? What part of '*go for it*' did you not understand? Joe and I *both* told you to get after that boy who, I might add, would do anything you asked. And after we set you up with a perfect opportunity to be alone, I come back to my room and hear you sobbing all night."

She hadn't been making much noise, Rae told herself. Had she been wallowing in self-pity? Yes. But it was the reality check she'd needed. Her stomach flipped unhappily.

"You did not," she whispered, eyeing Carmen. "There's no way you heard me two rooms away." If Carmen was telling the truth, who else heard? Her room shared a wall with Jacob's.

"Oh, I did," Carmen snapped. "And Jacob and Joe did too because they were both in their rooms." Jerking her thumb at Grace, she added, "You're lucky this one and Reed were out doing the opposite."

Latching on to a possible topic change, Rae raised an eyebrow at Grace, whose face lit up like Rudolph's nose. "Opposite? What were you and—"

"Nope!" Carmen snapped. "You first, Missy." She narrowed her eyes at Grace. "And don't think you're off the hook. You're next."

Rae gulped down a rockslide in her throat, trying to find the words. After several false starts she shrugged. "I can't…it's…" she trailed off, tears springing to her eyes and choking her up further.

Her resolve to shed no more tears disintegrated under the interrogation, and she pictured Jacob's face as she had told him *no* in no uncertain terms. The words she had chosen sounded cold in the warm light of day. If she voiced it again, it would be for real, and she was not ready for regret.

"Please, not yet," she begged quietly.

"*Chica*," Carmen cooed, hugging Rae tightly.

The other woman's arms were like a vice, anchoring her to reality. There was no judgement involved, and Rae relaxed in the embrace.

The scent of savory food wafted into her consciousness, and she pulled away.

"Bacon?"

She sniffed the air, much to the delight of her companions as a host of servers appeared with an array of food. Like a virtual whirlwind everything was laid out on the bed, and the staff rushed away.

Carmen sighed, touching the back of Rae's hand. "Okay, I will give you a break, but only because it smells amazing, and I'm starving. I'm going to gain like twenty pounds by the time we go home."

"Same!" Rae and Grace echoed.

Without further ado, they set to demolishing breakfast.

Rae hummed in delight as her empty stomach found something to chew on besides her nerves. Fighting over the last pieces of bacon she could manage and weaseling a piece off of Carmen's plate filled her with satisfaction. The satisfaction she had denied herself the night before.

About half the food was gone before Grace piped up. "Are you okay?" She glanced between her plate and Rae's face.

"Yes," Rae answered, nibbling on a piece of salty meat. She may not be happy, but she could agree to okay.

At this, the assistant's posture shifted from subdued to stern. "Then explain to me what this crying jag was about," Grace ordered, crossing her arms and staring at Rae.

Carmen shrunk back at the intensity and reached for Rae's knee. "I think you'd better tell her."

Under both their gazes, Rae's defenses slipped. Her belly was full. It was a new day. It was time she owned her own decision. She didn't have to tell them all the turmoil that still wedged itself in her brain. She scrubbed the night's events down to the facts.

"We agreed that we didn't wanna wreck the band. And so we're friends. We're colleagues. We're okay."

"You so are not," Grace refuted. "What I truly don't understand is why you're both fighting it so hard. I mean, I get not wanting to put the band at risk, but let's be honest: you don't even have a name yet. So why are you suffering?"

Carmen squealed, looking between the pair. "Note to self: Do not fuck with Grace 'cause she will straight up lay you out."

Grace had not stopped glaring, and Rae's face scrunched in annoyance. She wasn't going to get out of this without another scene. One scene per trip was her limit.

"Because," Rae whined finally. She sighed and reached for sausage then bit half of it so she wouldn't have to talk again.

Grace did not catch her hint and continued. "Look, I get that you're afraid of what could happen, but there's no fear of rejection. You *know* it's mutual. You're scared of something that may never happen and that you have a lot of control over making work out your own way."

"You can't know that," Rae retorted. "I can't…I *can't*. He'll get tired of me."

Carmen crossed her arms, mimicking Grace, staring her down.

"He *will*," Rae insisted. "And I…I can't let somebody that close again!"

"Honey, he's not Alex," Carmen groaned. "He would never cheat. He's a good man. Stop assuming he's an asshole too."

"Can we talk about Grace now? This is making me tired." Rae sighed, taking a deep breath and curling up into a little ball.

Carmen relented, shifting the spotlight. Some part of Rae delighted in watching someone else squirm under the same, intrusive scrutiny. At least she wasn't alone.

Rae's insides squeezed. Derek had finally come to terms with his feelings. She made a mental note to congratulate him when she saw him next and promised herself not to poke at the tender, new feelings. Yet.

~ ♪ ~ JACOB ~ ♪ ~

Jacob woke with gritty eyes. His skin tingled in all the wrong ways, his head ached, and his heart was just…*broken*. He had startled awake in the middle of the night still sitting in the shower. Rae's room was silent, and he hauled himself to the bed.

How could he be heartbroken over a relationship that hadn't even happened? He rolled onto his back, growling sub-vocally at the overly cheerful sunlight lodged in his room.

Rae had reduced him to a teenager defeated by unrequited love. He remembered what it felt like when he was fifteen and had a crush on a girl he took classes with on set. He had convinced himself it must be love if he liked watching her do algebra problems on the white board. He had asked her out, and she had told him no. With many fewer words than he and Rae had exchanged. He was sad then, feeling rejected, but this was inherently worse.

He replayed the conversation over in his mind. He had been ready to confess his feelings to her, and she wouldn't even hear it.

Throwing the covers aside, he stomped into the bathroom, took a hasty shower, scrubbing himself raw. Once dressed, he clomped over to her room. She didn't get to decide this alone. He should never have agreed to her refusal. They belonged together, dammit.

He pounded a fist on her door, his balance oscillating from one foot to the other as he waited for her to answer.

"The girls are at the beach," Derek called.

Jacob startled at the response. He had thought he was alone, but he saw Derek at the corner of the building, damp-headed and freshly clothed.

Derek's face pinched in concern. "Woah, what did she *do* to you?" he probed.

"What did she *do*?" Jacob repeated with a growl.

"Okay, buddy," Derek murmured, hands out as if he were approaching a wild animal. "Let's go talk this out over breakfast, hmm?"

Jacob nodded, stomach grumbling hopefully at the mention of food. Given the other man's defensive pose, he backed down, releasing a sigh. "Yeah, okay. Breakfast is good."

The pair walked in silence to the restaurant and took a secluded table in the corner. With food and coffee ordered, Derek stared at Jacob expectantly.

"I was going to tell her…everything," Jacob finally stated.

"Going to?" Derek questioned, unfolding a napkin in his lap. "Start at the beginning. Pretend I don't know anything."

Jacob drew his thoughts together trying to figure out how to explain the betrayal he felt, recounting the events leading up to her rejection.

"She…cut me down like nothing was between us." Her harsh words echoed freshly in his mind. "I mean, I get it, the band comes first…"

"But?" Derek prompted.

"She was crying all night. I heard it through the walls."

Derek folded his hands on the table formally and enunciated his words carefully. "Did something happen?"

Jacob sensed the protector in his friend rising to the surface and shook his head vehemently. "No! God, no. Nothing like *that*."

Coffees appeared on the table before them, and Jacob focused on butchering his beverage with sugar and milk grateful for the reprieve. He waited to speak until testing a sip.

"She said we wouldn't work out. Wouldn't let me speak, and then she left." He paused as a snarl curled his upper lip. "And the next thing I know, I hear her crying in the shower through the wall. And I don't mean quietly— I mean full out sobbing like her heart's breaking for more than an hour. And after what she'd said, I couldn't go to her. I couldn't *do* anything."

He had sat there on his cold, hard, bathroom floor with one ear pressed to the wall, lost in his own pain and hers, impotent.

Their food arrived, and he stabbed at his eggs more viciously than necessary. Silence hung between them for several bites.

"Oh fuck," Derek mumbled suddenly. "You're in *love* with her."

Jacob chortled sadly, lifting a forkful of potatoes to his mouth. "What an idiot, right? You warned me."

Derek frowned, peeling open a yogurt. "You're not an idiot. But you've got your work cut out for you if you think you're going to win Rae over."

"Everything worth having is an uphill battle," Jacob countered.

Derek smirked. "I'll send you some hiking boots and maybe a machete to clear out some of the weeds."

Jacob chuckled. "You're a good friend."

Shrugging, the producer beamed at him. "It's what I do."

The words sunk into his brain, and he set down his silverware to straighten the napkin on his lap. "Why the hell did I give her the power to end this before it started?"

"Because you're a feminist," Derek replied easily.

"Well, yes…but don't we deserve a chance? To at least try?" he pleaded. "Don't *I* get a say?"

Derek nodded, sipping his juice.

"So go get her," came a familiar voice, startling both men. Joe pulled a chair from an empty table and sat down with them, ordering a coffee. He turned to Jacob.

"In what world did that sob fest sound like she doesn't want to be with you? GO GET HER," Joe repeated, fixing the younger man with a friendly glare. "Don't make me speak more than my daily quota."

The humor in his words caught Jacob off guard, and he laughed. Maybe he was right. He picked up his fork again, this time with determination. For the first time that day, his brain was still.

"Okay," Jacob agreed. "After food."

"Little tip—lot of privacy on the beach beds," Derek suggested. "*After* you persuade her in your most respectful way."

"Good to know," Jacob veritably purred in reply. He tucked into the food in front of him. "So, since it's the last night, I thought we might get the band together at the disco."

Joe and Derek agreed, and Jacob sent a group text to alert the others.

He wasted little time finishing up and returning to his room to psych himself up.

He paced as he practiced his speech, going over it again and again as if it were a monologue in a play. Caffeine coursed through his system, and he burst out the door toward the beach. He was going to tell her what he'd started to the night before. Even if she still turned him down, she had to at least listen to him. She owed him that much.

His feet sunk in the sand, slowing his progress, but he plowed ahead, each step firming up his resolution. How *dare* she make decisions for him? Why was she so certain that they would end in flames? He had plenty to offer. By the time he found the girls, blood was thrumming in his eardrums.

They were lounging in a single bed, bodies shaded from the scorching rays burning his scalp. Rae's back was to him, and he ogled her backside. Her suit had ridden up on one cheek, and all he wanted was to touch the fair skin…and bite it, and maybe even spank it if she was keen.

As he approached, Carmen spotted him, and he saw the three gathering the proverbial wagons. Rae sat up, hiding her gorgeous ass.

He wasted no time with formalities. "Walk with me, please," he growled, extending a hand to Rae.

She shrank back behind Carmen.

Perhaps that was a bit strong for a first approach at telling her he wanted to worship her. He wiped a hand over his face then cleared his throat. Forcing a smile and stowing his hands in his pockets, he tried again.

"Please come enjoy the ocean breeze with me," he murmured. "I have some things I need to say."

This time, when he held out his hand, she took it, fingers trembling in his palm. He squeezed them lightly to reassure her. So, she wasn't *immune* to him. He exhaled relief.

Rae stumbled out of the cabana, and Jacob caught her, righting her gently. He started toward the ocean, steps slow until he was sure she would follow. His shoulders relaxed when she did, and he waited till they reached the privacy of the shoreline to speak.

It took several tries before he blurted, "I don't want to wreck the band either." He slapped his forehead and pinched the bridge of his nose. "Nope. That is not what I meant to say. I had a whole speech planned."

He kicked away a piece of seaweed that washed over his foot then stared into the ocean as they ambled in the surf.

After a few breaths, he continued, remembering how he had planned to start the conversation. "Look, the thing is, no matter what happens or doesn't happen between us, I could never hate you, I—"

"Jacob, listen—" Rae was turning three-quarters toward him, and he saw her defenses going up, preparing to "let him down gently."

"No," he interrupted sternly. "It's my turn. You had your say last night, and it broke both our hearts." The memory of her crying fueled his fire. "I heard you last night in the shower. Let me say my piece. Can you at least give me that?"

Rae nodded and pulled her cover-up tighter, tucking her hands into her elbows.

"Thank you." The words came out more frustrated than he intended, but he barreled ahead. "This band is important to me—more than you know. I *need* this to work. And I need you to be part of that. So understand that when I tell you that we should explore this, it is with full understanding of the risks."

Rae stopped, and he turned to face her. Her wide eyes were glossy at the edges.

He was grateful for the stillness as he met her eyes. "And now I'm going to tell you that we *should* try because I'm dead in love with you. Like sick to my stomach, sweaty palms, and all."

He wasn't sure he could bear it or that he would believe her if she contradicted him so he plowed ahead, giving her no opportunity.

"I know we're both…burning with complications. I know we're both scared and full of doubt. But why do we have to do this alone? Deal with this alone? Maybe if we deal with it *together,*" he emphasized the word, meeting her eyes, and touching her arm. "…it could be good and great and everything we hoped."

"And what if it's not?" she choked out.

"It could be *more*," he answered softly. Firmly. He laid his hand on her forearm, willing his sincerity to slip through him into her. "It could be the *most*; the *best* possible anything."

He paused, lifting her chin until their eyes met.

"Please, Rae, give me a chance," he begged. "Give *us* a chance." He placed her hand over his heart. It was pounding, and he wanted her to feel the physical effect she had on him that had nothing to do with sex and everything to do with wanting to be in her orbit.

She met his eyes, and her breathing sped up. Her lips parted, and he caressed her fingers splayed over his heart. His whole life depended on her next words.

Slowly, she pulled her hand away, tears rolling down her cheeks.

"I can't," she whimpered. "You don't…can't know how much I want to throw caution to the wind and kiss you until we can't see straight. But I *can't.* I will not ever give anyone that kind of power over me again. I've learned my lesson."

Jacob hated her tears, but this response he at least understood.

"Okay, Baby," he murmured, pulling her close. Her tears soaked his shoulder, her body quivering against him.

"It's okay," he soothed, gently rubbing her shoulders. He let her cry a bit longer, before he spoke again. "I'll give you space, but I'm not giving up on us. When you're ready, I'll be here."

"Jake," she whispered. "I may never be ready."

"Sunshine," he whispered back, kissing her forehead. "You're worth the wait."

Fresh tears poured over her cheeks, and he held her like he'd wanted to do the night before. He deposited her in her room after extracting a promise that she would rest.

Back in his room, Jacob plopped onto the end of his bed. There was hope at least.

He reached for his phone, and a missed call from Jason Barrett was blinking for his attention. He hadn't heard from the man for months. The fact that he'd called today was ironic.

Jacob pressed the return call button.

Jason answered on the first ring. "Hunter!" he sang.

"Barrett," Jacob answered. "What's up?"

"Oh, not much. Had some time. Talked to Danny last night and wanted to check in."

He groaned inwardly, wondering why Danny felt compelled to tell his business to the other guys from their former band. "Oh, how's he doing?"

"Don't act like you don't know." Jason laughed. "He told me he was at your place, and you're about to release some sick album."

He sighed relief that he didn't have to talk about Rae. "Yeah, I've been working with some new people," Jacob replied. He wanted to share it with Jason—wanted to show him how far he'd come on his own with the support of good people. But he refrained. The Jason-train tended to steam roll over things and then pick out anything good that survived. He wasn't willing to risk his people being poached.

"What's going on with you?" he asked.

Jason needed no encouragement to ramble on about the movie he was filming, name dropping his co-stars and complaining about a sore wrist from the last scene he'd filmed.

"So, listen," Jason continued. "Since I'm in town, I was thinking I might sneak out incognito if someone I knew was playing around LA."

Jacob cringed. "We don't have anything booked yet, man. I'm actually in the Caribbean right now with the band."

"First class, man. Good for you!"

"Thanks."

Jason's tone changed with his next statement. "Look, I'm serious about supporting you. Anything you need, cool?"

A light bulb flashed in his mind. "As a matter of fact, we're in need of a good agent. The kind that listens to the talent and treats their employees right," Jacob muttered. "We're gonna deep six ours soon."

"Man, I *told* you Meyers was a shit heel," Jason commiserated. "Let me get with Blake and see who we can dig up."

"Stellar." With Jason's and Blake's connections, he would probably have a few option packets discreetly waiting for him by the time he got home.

SIXTEEN

Rae was the last to arrive at the disco where the band convened on their last night. She spotted them in a corner booth and danced from the door to the table, arms over her head soliciting the hoots and hollers. Joe had positioned himself in the center rendering him "unable" to get out and dance, but Carmen was calling him out, poking his arm with every word.

She shook her head under the auspices of dancing, but she wanted to clear her thoughts. Jacob's affirmation still had her head spinning: she was worth waiting for.

Tuning into the band, she twirled in front of the table before coming to a stop. She winked at Derek where he lounged with one arm over Grace's shoulder.

"Shots!" Carmen cried.

Rae readily agreed and followed her to the bar. They returned with a platter of twelve brightly colored concoctions. Rae didn't hesitate once they were dispersed, slamming two in quick succession. The music was loud and made conversation nearly impossible. An unholy glee filled her as she sprinted to the DJ booth with Carmen on her heels.

Rae leaned against the console, allowing her ample cleavage to spill out as she made a request for one of Jacob's singles from his solo album, "Boys Night."

As the familiar notes took over the club, Rae and Carmen rushed to the table, dragging Jacob to his feet.

"You didn't," Jacob complained as they tried to pull him toward the dance floor.

"We most certainly did," Rae squealed.

Carmen poked a finger in his armpit, and he crumpled like a rag doll. "Quit pretending like you don't know how to shake your ass," Carmen chided.

Rae's breath caught in her throat as his silver gaze raked over her. In moments, she had him sandwiched between herself and Carmen. The shots had already loosened her shoulders, and she twirled in front of Jacob.

Behind him, Carmen winked at her and licked her lips. She ran her hand over his shoulder, reaching for Rae then dropped low, wagging her behind to the beat.

Rae let herself go, mimicking the behavior and backing her ass into him.

For the briefest of moments, Jacob's pelvis pressed against her, one of his hands stroking over her hip.

Rae moaned, letting the music swallow the sound and running a hand down the center of her body. She ground against him, trusting Carmen would pull her back if she went too far. She flirted glances at him as she moved, grinning at how his cheeks glowed red even in the dark.

She liked watching him squirm. She took hold of his hips, turning him to face Carmen and generally directing his movement. Rae wanted to blame the heat building inside her on the tropics, but she couldn't. The way he allowed her to control his movements flipped all her switches. She wanted to tug his belt loop, guide him back to her room, and bind him to her bed for as long as it pleased her.

A frown curled her lips as the song came to an end, and she wrapped her arms around him from behind. The flat of her palms ran over his chest, his nipples straining against his shirt. She fought not to tweak them, and pulled back as Carmen spun him in a circle between them then bowed gracefully.

His face was split with a grin as he returned the gesture, reaching to take her hand. Jacob spun her gracefully as they reached the table.

Carmen caught up, slapping her behind and snapping her out of the lusty trance.

Joe lifted a glass to them as they slipped into the booth, crowding him.

"Where are D and G?" Jacob asked.

Rae followed Joe's finger to the center of the dance floor where Derek had his head buried in Grace's neck, her back arched to give him access.

Rae lifted a brow. "And she called us out on the music?"

"Let her have it," Carmen chided leaning across Jacob who had settled between them. "At least she's not reporting back to Meyers every five minutes."

"Oh shit, you're right," Jacob agreed, spreading his arms across the back around both Carmen and Rae. "Progress!"

Rae couldn't take her eyes off the pair on the dance floor. She had seen Derek woo his share of dance partners at a variety of bars in the past, but this was different. If he felt their eyes on him, it didn't show. This display was strictly for his partner, and Rae's brows met her hairline. Maybe this was it for him. Her days as a wingman were over.

"Yep—there's tongue," Carmen announced.

"Gross!" the table chorused.

"There's not enough liquor in this bar to watch," Rae grumbled, looking away finally. "Who wants drinks?"

"Triples," Joe replied.

"Duh," Rae laughed, wriggling out of the booth. It was like a train wreck, and her eyes were glued to the couple on the dance floor. Derek's hand slipped over Grace's ass, her skirt rising. It was clear to anyone with eyes that they were consenting adults, but Rae felt the urge to protect their dignity.

She disappeared into the crowd, cup in hand as she wove between dancers to the entangled couple.

Derek's groan rumbled over the music, and Rae gagged a little. It was hard to believe there was ever a time where she had sexy thoughts about this man. He was wholly unaware of her standing behind him, armed with an ice cube. She shook her head, and without hesitation, dropped the frozen garnish down the back of his pants.

He jerked away from Grace yelping and grabbing at his ass for the offending item.

In the commotion, Rae captured Grace's wrist and dragged her back to the table.

Derek chased after them, shaking one leg. "Not cool, Rae," he yelled, rubbing the seat of his trousers as he caught up. His face was a mixture of fury and frustration as he retrieved Grace's hand.

"I thought it was exactly cold enough," she countered, then pivoted toward the bar to get the drinks she had promised the others.

The bartender mixed up a set of drinks dispassionately. "Where you at?" he asked.

Rae pointed to their group.

He waved her off. "I bring," he insisted.

"And strong, right?" she confirmed.

He held up a thumb to her and continued pouring.

Rae turned to study the group. Joe was snickering; Carmen's arms were overhead, puckering her lips like a duck. Derek was relaxed with one arm around Grace. Their movements were synchronized, each tiny tweak answered by the other. Her neck tilted—his elbow shifted. And they were laughing. And Jacob joined them.

His teeth glimmered in the dark, his eyes twinkling as he stared at Carmen. His relaxed posture made her breath catch in her throat. How was she going to live with him? To look at that face and not melt into him? She wanted to run her fingers through his hair and let the silky strands glide past her knuckles. She wanted to bury her nose in his neck and memorize what he smelled like first thing in the morning and ride him through the night.

The waiter passed her on the left with a tray of drinks, sliding them onto the table with a smile then disappearing. The empty seat was half covered by Jacob's hip and she slipped into it with a gentle push.

He glanced at her as she did so, squishing deeper into the booth to make room for her.

Yes. This man was trouble. He was definitely trouble.

~ ♫ ~ JACOB ~ ♫ ~

After another hour, the disco was too loud to talk, and Jacob ushered them to the rec room. The sounds of chirping bugs echoed off the tile walls and floors, soft music whispering underneath the din. The attached bar had closed hours ago, but no one seemed to mind as Carmen racked a set of billiards on the pool table.

Jacob placed one hand against the wall discreetly. His knees wobbled beneath him, the result of underestimating the last round of drinks Rae had procured. They had been deceptively strong, and his stubborn streak had forced him to shoot it the moment she'd cautioned them all. The banana-split flavor lingered on his gums, and he swabbed them with his tongue.

His balance wobbled as Rae leaned over the table to roll the cue ball to Joe. Jacob's eyes were glued to the sight. If it wasn't for the wall holding him up, he might have joined her. Maybe hitch her dress up to reveal what was beneath it and run his palms all over her creamy flesh. His imagination kept her bent over the table, wondering if she would splay herself across it or reach back to grab his neck.

Derek's knuckles rapped against his chest like a door knocker, pulling him from his lascivious rendezvous. The producer gestured to a quieter corner, and Jacob trailed after him.

"Hey. You guys seemed okay at the club. Did you talk?" the older man queried.

Scratching the back of his neck, Jacob smiled sadly. "We talked. I didn't have much luck pers—" He tripped over the word "persuading" twice. "Selling her on it."

Derek's frown was instantaneous, then he patted Jacob's shoulder. "Sorry, man. You want me to talk to her?"

His blue eyes were so sincere.

"Nah, she's not ready." He slapped Derek's forearm lightly, liking the noise it made, and offered a forgiving nod.

Derek crossed his arms and grumbled, "Man, if I could find her ex, I'd wring his neck for all the walls she built up to keep him out."

Jacob shook his head to reassure his friend, but the room spun, and he squeezed his eyes shut. When it stopped, he stood tall.

"Man, be cool, I've got this," he promised. "As far as I know, she's still moving in with me when her apartment lease is up."

"She *what?*"

Jacob closed his eyes again to avoid sensing the earth's rotation. Maybe he needed some water. "Yep. It'll be good," he assured.

"You're moving in together?" Derek repeated. "Is that a good idea?"

This time, Jacob remembered not to shake his head. He lifted a hand to his counterpart and closed his eyes to emphasize his point. "*Trust me.* My girl—"

"Boys!" yelled the woman in question from the table.

Jacob's whole body froze, and his eyes clamped onto hers.

She was holding a pool cue in one hand, one hip thrown out, and one hand in the air as she stared openly at them. "Either make out or come play with us," she demanded.

She called, and he answered. Her words echoed in his mind processing. Derek wasn't bad looking, but he never had the taste for boys, and he desperately wanted to taste Rae. As if pulled by an invisible string, he darted to the bassist's side.

Rae pressed a cue into his hand, and he leaned on it for balance. The others gathered around the table, breaking up the quiet. In her emerald dress, she was like a goddess. The cracking of the balls on the table should have drawn his attention, but he wasn't finished tracing the drape of the fabric as she twisted around the table with a pool stick. For a while, there was nothing but the click and clack of the game with an occasional gasp as Joe pulled off one impossible looking shot after another.

When she was playing her bass, Rae had a tendency to curl herself around it. As she lined up another shot, her body lengthened, arching gracefully as she found the right angle. One toe extended as she lifted one leg and posed like a ballerina, and Jacob started moving furniture around mentally to find a way to accommodate a pool table in his home before she moved in.

~ ♫ ~ **R A E** ~ ♫ ~

The next day dawned with a gentle rain that did nothing to abate the sunlight streaming from above as if Tulum would be sad to see them go but was determined to give them a reason to return.

Rae smiled as she filed into the airplane, passing the empty window seat beside Jacob to take the aisle seat next to Derek on the other side of the plane. She'd felt his warm gaze following her, but he did nothing else to compel her closer.

Derek's muscled arms filled his seat but didn't spill into hers as she tucked her bag under the seat in front of her. In coach, he would have been squeezing into her space, but Jacob had sprung for first-class, so everyone had plenty of room to stretch out. His thoughtfulness and generosity were disarming, and she caught herself staring at the headrest of his seat.

"I'm proud of you, Sunshine," Derek murmured, barely audible over the thrum of the cabin as people boarded, walking past them to economy.

His words caught her off guard. "For?" she asked, cinching the safety belt around her midsection.

"I know how much you dig the guy," Derek pointed out. "It can't be easy saying no to him. If you need help, I'm here for you."

Rae felt her muscles loosen even further as she settled into her seat, eyeing the others who were engaged in their own conversations.

"Thank you, D," she breathed. "I got Grace to agree with me, but I'm pretty sure Carmen's on Team Hunter in this. She doesn't see that when everything goes sour—"

"I got you," Derek cut in.

Their conversation paused as the airplane doors shut, and the flight attendants reviewed the safety procedures, and the flight lifted off.

Derek took the conversational initiative. "So Jacob tells me you're moving in when we get back. Is that true?"

Rae's lips puckered. "Are you going to tell me it's a bad idea?"

"Well—" Derek began.

"Because I already know it is. We were drunk when we discussed it, but I do need a place to live when we get back," she rambled. "My lease is up, and it's a crummy studio efficiency apartment. I never even unpacked, so I could shift it all to storage. That's the best idea, right?" Rae huffed, catching her breath as she stared into her friend's face looking for answers.

"Do you love him?" he asked quietly. His voice was soft, eyes boring into her.

"It doesn't matter," she sighed.

"It's the only thing that does matter," Derek countered. "If you love him and won't have a relationship, it'll shred you."

"Oh God!" she clapped her hands over her mouth, eyes wide. Derek was right. It would eviscerate them both. He had laid his heart out for her, and it was up to her how many boot prints she left on it. "I'll have to cancel on him and renew my lease."

Derek eyed her, mouth shut.

She sighed. She couldn't expect him to give her the answers, big brother or not. They needed to come from her.

"Hmm, or maybe I could…I don't know, turn him off by being the world's worst roommate?"

"Like leaving dirty dishes in the sink all the time?"

"I was thinking more like using his razor in the shower…or leaving dirty laundry on the sofa."

Derek burst into laughter, and they began to plot the most disgusting and ridiculous bad roommate habits they could think of until they landed at LAX.

S E V E N T E E N

Jacob paced his empty house—again. Working on the album had filled his house with life and music, and he had loved that. The vacation had been amazing. After all the chaos, the sound of his footsteps echoing amplified his loneliness.

It was too soon to call any of his bandmates—they would all be recovering from jetlag. He *definitely* couldn't call Rae yet. She needed time to at least process the love bomb he'd dropped on her. Although, that night at the club…oh yeah, she wanted him too. She needed time. He would have to show her he wasn't Alex. That piece of trash had broken her heart, and he was going to be the one who healed it.

Looking for advice, Jacob pulled out his cell and opened the Harmonizers group chat he had been part of since the invention of texting. His thumbs flew over the keys.

Jacob
I need band names.

Danny
so when do the others get to meet everyone? Oooh! We can have a party at Jake's place

Jacob
never - it's bad enough *you* did…I don't need everyone else up my nose

Craig
Aww, but it's so roomy   ;P

> **Jacob**
> har har, come on guys…names

> **Blake**
> why do you need a band name? It's not like y'all are like…equals

> **Danny**
> Especially since he's shacking up with the bass player soon

> **Jason**
> you know Jake wants his little family group

Jacob rubbed his eyes and set his phone down, ignoring the dings as their opinions rolled in. *Why* had he told Danny of all people? That man couldn't keep a secret to save his life. Well, not from their brothers anyway. With a sigh, he scrolled past Blake's objections, Jason's indignant commentary, and Craig's inappropriate jokes.

> **Jacob**
> GUYS! I love her and that's not up for debate! What I need are band names.

> **Jacob**
> Blake, I need you to help Grace. We're making her our manager. She needs connects and support in the worst way.

> **Jacob**
> J, thanks for the agent packets.

> **Jacob**
> Craig? SHUT UP. I love you man, but this shit is tender so back off.

> **Jacob**
> Danny? I'll bend your ear later. Thank you and goodnight.

> **Blake**
> wow, he hasn't been this bossy in years…it's about time Daddy J came back out to play!

> **Craig**
> maaaan, fine, I'll be good

Jason
just be careful, and of course I'll do anything I can to help. will get you some sick names

Danny
Call me anytime

Refusing to be left pacing with his thoughts, Jacob set himself to stripping Rae's guest room. He started with the sheets, then piece by piece, all décor was removed. He wanted her to claim it on day one—to make his house her home.

The doorbell startled him, but before he reached the hallway, the distinct sound of locks tumblers releasing reached him. He grumbled to himself, remembering that LA local, Blake, had a spare key.

"Helloooo," called his former bandmate as he strolled in.

Jacob arrived as Blake closed the door behind him. "Hey, man. Wasn't expecting you."

"You didn't think dropping a bomb like that was going to go without comment?" Blake chided. "You used the big 'L' word."

"I had hoped." Jacob sighed. "Look, I—"

"Nope. No excuses. It's me, okay?" Blake made himself at home, easing onto the corner of Jacob's couch and staring up at him.

"She doesn't want to be with me," Jacob explained. "I told her I'd wait for her." He shrugged. "End of story."

"End my ass! Tell me the whole thing, from the beginning! How you two met, all of it. All we got out of Dan was that she's in this new band of yours."

"Ours," Jacob corrected. "There's five of us."

"Okay. But you're avoiding the question. What about *the* girl?" Blake rolled his eyes and sighed dramatically. "Are you going to make me pull it out of you? Because you know I will."

Jacob flopped on the opposite end of the couch. "Man, it's not pretty."

"And that's why it's delicious," Blake cooed. "How did you meet?"

"My producer introduced us. She worked at the studio where he records. She laid down the bass."

Blake nodded. "Okay. Legit."

Encouraged by his interest, Jacob continued. "She's amazing. And she already understood the sound, so I got her to agree to be on the album. Kind of insisted on it."

"Was it love at first sight?"

He shrugged. "At first listen, absolutely. The first time I saw her…" He trailed off in thought. "Well, I was surprised because her name's Rae, and I was expecting a dude."

Blake chuckled. "That would've worked for me, but I can see how that would be startling for you."

Grinning, Jacob licked his lips. "Yeah, but it turns out, she's *hot*."

Blake arched a brow at him. "She's hot? That's all you've got?"

Jacob arched his eyebrows at the younger man. "You asked if it was love at first sight. Don't get me wrong. Her curves are in all the right places, but it wasn't until I watched her play…" He sighed, remembering. "Totally blown away by her passion."

"I know you play it close to the vest, Hunter, but I'm calling bullshit. You're so much deeper than that. You were up to your eyeballs in hot fans and girls in our videos, and you never fell for anyone because she was *hot*," Blake said. "Tell me about her. Who is she? Where did she come from? Does she have a good laugh?"

Jacob sighed, realizing he wasn't going to get out of this conversation. "She's about this tall," he gestured around his armpits. "And she's got dark hair, kinda straight and down to her ass. Brown eyes. And the way she plays the bass is otherworldly, but I said that already."

"You did. Tell me something other than what she looks like."

"She's new to writing music, surprisingly. She composed for the first time in my studio here." Jacob detailed the memory for his friend before peppering in their interactions on the tropical vacation.

"She centers you," Blake finally summed up after the conversation stretched on for hours.

Blinking, Jacob considered the words. "Yes. That's part of it." He smirked. "And I'm so attracted to her—like turn-my-world-inside-out-attracted."

"You're moving pretty quick, Hunter," Blake warned. "You've been close to her, but you've only known her a minute. Are you sure it's not lust?"

"It's not sex. She's not ready. But I'll wear her down."

Blake frowned. "She's not a quest in a video game, you know."

"Of course not. But she wants it, too. I know she does. And I'll do anything she asks."

"Anything? Is that why she's moving in?"

"Nope, that was all me," he admitted. "Her lease is up soon, and if we tour, she'll be renting an LA apartment for no reason that'll probably get robbed anyway."

Blake stared incredulously. "Did you trip on your cape when making the offer?"

Jacob stared back. "You think I'm trying to be a hero?"

"Aren't you?" Blake challenged.

"No. It's just the right thing to do. I'm asking a lot of these people to give up their lives to follow me."

"You're making them the offer of a lifetime," Blake countered. "Stop selling yourself short. They are lucky to attach their wagons to your train. I don't care what mistakes you think you've made in the past. You've bought them a vacation, paid them for their work…and now one of them's moving in with you?"

He sought out Blake's eyes. "Please don't try to talk me out of it."

"I won't. I just need to understand. It's my job, brother. If you're headed over a cliff, I gotta try to catch you."

Jacob smiled affectionately but couldn't bear to meet his friend's eyes. "I appreciate that. I know it's a long shot, and I could get my heart broken, but she's worth it."

Blake's lips pursed knowingly before he beamed. "All the best things in life are worth the fight."

~ ♫ ~ **RAE** ~ ♫ ~

Rae would have described Derek's birthday party as a nuclear explosion. Pete's house was jampacked with the entire band as well as his former band mates and spouses. Rae's brain had virtually melted watching them fight over tamales. After gorging themselves, the guys had started dancing, and Jacob miscalculated a move and crashed headfirst into the couch.

Her body spiked with adrenaline, certain he'd broken his neck, and she'd leaped to his side to berate his error. The look on his face had stopped her mid-rant before she had escaped to the backyard, embarrassed at her outburst. In that moment, she had forgotten anyone else was there. She had treated him like he was hers.

But Jacob wasn't hers, and he wouldn't be. He couldn't be. Rae had promised herself that Alex was the last relationship. And Jacob was too precious to get tangled up in her baggage.

To ice the proverbial birthday cake, Derek had begged her to ride home with Jacob so he could take Grace, her ride, back to his house after the party. She had agreed reluctantly, but only because he was so pretty when he asked.

Crossing her arms over herself defensively, Rae focused out the window as Jacob pulled away from the house. They'd barely spoken since the dancing fiasco, and she wasn't sure if she started talking if she'd continue scolding him or start apologizing.

A few minutes passed before Jacob spoke. "I'm not hurt," he promised. "The last time I tried to do that, I had no issues. I guess I didn't realize how long it had been."

His words diffused some of her anger, and she folded her hands in her lap. "I don't like you taking chances with yourself like that. What if you really got hurt?" she worried.

Jacob nodded. "You're right," he agreed. "I should be more careful in my advanced age."

She rolled her eyes. "Stop, or I'll think you're making fun of me. I was really worried."

He squeezed her hand briefly, then pulled away. "I'm not making fun. But I'm okay. You can stop."

Oh, but she wished she could. "I'm doing my best," she assured.

Several minutes passed quietly before he spoke again. "I spent some time earlier this week clearing out your room."

Rae squeezed her eyes shut then peeked out at him. "Are you sure this is a good idea?"

He nodded firmly. "Yes. You need a place to stay while we see what happens with the band, and I have the room."

"Oh sure. Shut me down with logic. I see how you are." She wanted to pressure him about all the reasons he'd offered that couldn't be summed up so rationally. She rested against the car door to stare at his profile, and all the worry she was trying to sweep away came burbling from her lips. "You're a good man, Jacob Hunter. A really good man. And some woman will make you a good partner someday. I wish it could be me, but I'm just too damaged. I wouldn't want to put you through that, and I can't put me through it either."

He glanced at her several times before speaking. "Someday soon, I want you to tell me all about your ex."

Rae sneered. "He is not worth a whole conversation."

"But you are," Jacob retorted. "You are worthy of more than a conversation. Maybe even a monologue."

He was relentless. What was she going to do if something happened on tour? The longer she put off telling him everything, the more time she'd spend comparing him to Alex. The longer he'd have to prove to her he was everything she'd thought Alex was. Better to make him understand why this couldn't continue and save all the wasted energy.

"Okay," she conceded. "I'll tell you all about it, but it's like ripping off a band-aid. Let me tell you the whole story before we get to the Q&A portion. Or I might not be able to get it out."

"I'm listening," he assured her.

She directed her eyes to the horizon. "So, we started dating freshman year in high school," she began. "He was so pretty back then. He had perfect hair and the coolest attitude. Hottest guy in the school as far as I was concerned. We went to concerts and played music till 3 a.m. over the phone. And he loved that I played the bass. He loved to show me off and bragged about his rock star girlfriend and how I was going be famous one day."

"I hate that we're about to make him right," Jacob interrupted.

She barked out a laugh. "Well, I could back out. I'm not the only bass player in LA," she offered.

"No ma'am," he disagreed. "Forgive my interruption. Continue."

She stared at his face in the passing streetlights. She would rather stay in the moment with her present than delve back into the past. But she had promised him the full story.

"We were inseparable," she continued. "We even shopped for clothes together so we looked more like a rock duo. He was my biggest fan and constantly told me so. He had my ego so pumped up…I lost myself in him and his idea of me. He was my first *everything*." She laughed mirthlessly.

The car skidded to a stop, and Rae braced herself against the dash. Her seatbelt ratcheted tightly across her chest, arresting her motion.

"Sorry," he muttered, clearing his throat. He motioned out the front window. "Red light."

She straightened, unbuckling the belt to un-ratchet it before plugging it back in. "Uh-huh," she allowed. "We were married for twelve years, and I've only been single for a couple years now. He really hurt me. I don't want to get hurt like that again." She choked for a second. "I don't know why I told you that."

"Please continue," he muttered.

"We got married the Saturday after I turned eighteen. He even insisted I keep my last name because it sounded more rock and roll. Looking back, it should have been a red flag. But I was so wrapped up in him—"

"We've all been in one of those," he soothed.

She arched a brow.

"Okay smarty," he teased. "Most people I know have been in those 'lose your sense of self' relationships. Including me."

"Fine," she acquiesced. "I don't have a monopoly on bad choices. Mine just lasted over a decade. After the wedding, we moved out here almost immediately. Then my parents died. I couldn't pick up my bass without crying, let alone play. I became a bartender to pay the bills, and that's when the fighting started."

"Oh, Rae," he sighed, squeezing her shoulder. "That's terrible. I'm so sorry you went through all that."

She waved the air in front of her to cover the tears threatening to spill over and cleared her throat. "Playing again and composing helps. Rebel Gloss got me through it, but I was still in a deep, dark hole. It was like they played for me when I couldn't. Then the Harmonizers came along…and your voice…it cut through all the grief. Brought me back."

A growl rumbled from his throat, and his fist gripped and regripped the steering wheel.

"Should I stop?" she asked, chewing her bottom lip.

"Not unless you want to. You lived through this; the *least* I can do is listen," he assured.

Taking a deep breath, she continued. "Alex would disappear for days at a time, and then come home drunk or strung out or both. I like a little liquid courage myself sometimes, but not like Alex. He'd drink till he couldn't stand up. I tried to get him help, and all he'd do is scream how I was supposed to be this rich rock star and support him, but instead I was some lazy bartender. Then one day I came home to find him in bed with two women and another man."

"Three other people?" Jacob choked. He gulped visibly, slipping into a parking spot in front of her apartment complex. The vehicle lurched forward, and her seatbelt tightened again.

"I haven't told anybody else that part but you," she explained. "Most people know he cheated and that I caught him, but not…the specifics." She shook her head to Etch-a-Sketch the image out of her mind. "He promised to go to NA and get therapy. He served me with divorce papers. On my birthday."

"Jesus, woman," Jacob cringed. He cut the engine and took her trembling hands in his. "That utter piece of *trash* isn't fit to lick the bottom of your boots."

She laughed shakily. His steady hands calmed her nerves, and heat flushed her whole body. She didn't know if she should look away or meet his gaze.

"I wish you hadn't had to live through all this pain," he murmured. "But the woman you are today is a result of all that trauma, and I love the woman you are."

"How can you be so sure of what you feel?" she demanded.

"Maybe that's a story for another day," he chuckled softly. "This is about you right now, not me. And for the record, if I ever cross paths with this asshole, I cannot promise not to beat the shit out of him."

"He's not worth the bloody knuckles," Rae insisted. "And you'll never meet him, so don't waste your time thinking about him." She wished she could take her own advice. She looked at his hands large around hers. "I believe you think you love me, but you don't know me, Jacob. And I know that dating is a way to do that. But I...I can't."

"Shhh," he whispered, placing a finger against her lips. "Call me tomorrow. We'll get lunch and talk moving plans, okay?"

She nodded, suddenly exhausted. It was difficult to fight him, especially when he showered her in tenderness and understanding. But she would protect them both.

EIGHTEEN

In the record label lobby, Carmen's knee was bouncing a mile a minute, and Rae rested a hand on it.

Jacob had an abrupt image of Rae and Carmen engaged in other activities that included him more intimately. His bassist looked amazing sitting there, pretending not to be nervous with one shoulder jauntily exposed. Her tight smile belied her calm exterior, and he reminded himself he wasn't alone in this endeavor.

They had been waiting for over thirty minutes. This was either a scare tactic, or they were being stood up. Even the receptionist was missing. He should be used to this by now. He wasn't Jason. He was the *other* guy from The Harmonizers. The cast off. He began pacing the miniscule lobby with a scant dozen steps from one side to the other.

Derek was stretched languidly on one of the couches, arms extended across the back smiling so hard it hurt Jacob. He was the only one not worried. He was even smiling, and it set Jacob's teeth on edge. Before he could stop himself, he paused to lecture the man. It was only fair he'd be as anxious as the others.

"I can't believe you bailed on wardrobe shopping yesterday," Jacob grumbled at the producer. "I had to call Blake to rescue us."

Rae leaned in Derek's direction, flipping her hair as she did. "Love you, D, but I'll trade you for Blake," she teased.

Derek shrugged them off. "It's not my first rodeo," he replied, gesturing to his outfit.

"Show off," Joe groused.

"You guys did an amazing job," Derek complimented. "Send Blake my compliments."

The producer's calm radiated from him, and Jacob tried another tack. "You got the CDs?" Jacob worried, chewing a thumbnail.

"Yes," Derek groaned.

His lips and teeth fiddled with the tiny hangnail that had been forming on his thumb, worrying the pointy cartilage he could almost grab between his teeth. If he could just pull it out, his nail bed would be free of the pesky flap.

"Nerves," Jacob explained.

He startled when Rae tugged his hand away, stunned into stillness. The flush of her pink cheeks as she rubbed soothing circles on his palm with her thumbs mesmerized him. She pressed her shoulder against his supportively.

He relaxed against Rae, taking slow, deep breaths. Even if they were being blacklisted because he wasn't worthy, at least Rae was by his side. She was gorgeous and talented, and even if a label wouldn't see him, he was sure he could get her a gig with some other band who could take her places he couldn't.

Carmen whirled toward Derek. "I can't believe you spent the weekend with Grace, and now we're here, and we can't talk about it," Carmen complained, scowling at Derek.

"Who says we can't?" Rae beamed, releasing Jacob's hand and pouncing to Carmen's side.

Without her reassuring grip, the childish ribbing made Jacob's skin crawl. Everyone had sex before. Most of them were never on the verge of a deal this important, and he wished they'd get their priorities straight.

"Can we focus on the band? Please?" Jacob begged.

Everyone nodded, and Jacob returned to pacing. Moments later, he noticed Rae next to him, matching every step. He stopped suddenly. "What are you doing?"

"Trying to cut through the tension," she offered. "Is it working?"

He chuckled. "I think so."

They were silent again for nearly a full minute before Joe's voice echoed around the room.

"Sonic Tension."

The two words sounded right together—meaningful. Like them.

"I think that's it," Derek proclaimed.

"Me too," Carmen added.

"Yes," Rae confirmed.

They looked at Jacob, holding their breath. He chewed on the words for a moment, a smile curving the corners of his mouth. The one thing they lacked walking into the meeting was a band name.

"Can we put it on the CDs before we go in?" Jacob fretted.

Rae produced a black permanent marker from her purse and waved it around. "Someone else has to write."

Carmen grabbed it as Derek pulled jewel cases from his bag. They huddled around the low coffee table like an assembly line, Rae opening, Carmen writing, and Derek straightening each disc before snapping them shut. They finished the last one as the door to the offices opened, a young man in a t-shirt, jeans, and a vest filling the doorframe.

"They're ready for you," he announced.

This was it. Jacob strode forward, listening to the swoosh of plastic cases sliding against each other followed by the snap of the latch on Derek's bag. He grabbed Rae's hand at the last second, tugging her beside him.

A semi-circle of windows ringed the meeting room. An array of pastries and fruit lined a small buffet, and the table was set with glasses and pitchers of water. Half a dozen people rose when the band entered.

"Welcome," an older man greeted as they filed in.

"Good morning," Jacob replied, shaking his hand firmly. "We're Sonic Tension."

Handshakes were made all around, and the meeting started slowly. The main greeter spoke for a long time about who the label represented and the clout they held within the industry. However, when they shared their demo, the conversation moved into light speed.

It was approaching noon when Rae led the way toward the lobby.

Jacob had hardly noticed the hours passing, but his stomach rumbled with more than excitement. Jacob wanted one of the others to pinch him to make sure he hadn't dreamed the outcome, but he was determined to wait till they were a safe distance away before admitting his delight over the label's offer. After all, they hadn't walked away professionally quiet just to show all their cards to anyone looking out a fourth-floor window.

Beside him swaggered Derek, jaw twitching as he walked, eyes focused forward. Ahead of them, Carmen linked arms with Rae, Joe on their heels. As they reached the third corner from the building, Derek and Jacob finally exchanged glances.

Derek's eyes were wide, and one corner of his mouth stretched to his ear.

Jacob couldn't help but match it, and they did their best power walking impression as they rushed into the parking garage. Jacob didn't quite make it fully inside before he yelled, "YES!"

He turned to the others, fist-pumping the air and high-fiving first Derek, then Joe, then Carmen, and finally Rae.

Lightning crackled between their fingertips, and he beamed at her. She was going to be that rock star she had always dreamed of. And he was going to be by her side when it happened.

A group hug followed, and there may have been a few tears, but Jacob would never tell on Carmen or himself.

"I have never had a label be so receptive," Derek gasped.

"That was amazing. And it was the first," Joe gloated.

"We've got to call Grace," Rae insisted, whipping the phone from her pocket, thumbs already scrolling.

"She's at work," Derek cautioned. "She can't take that call in front of Meyers."

Rae grumbled, looking up at him with one thumb hovering over the screen.

"We can text her a picture," Carmen suggested. "Jacob, you've got the longest arms." She pressed Rae's phone into his hand and stretched her arms out to pull the others in.

A general murmur of approval found them squeezing around Jacob in a split second. Jacob lifted one arm as high as he could reach, angling the camera to fit all the faces in the frame. Bodies jostled around him until every face fit into the screen. He was grateful Rae had jumped in front of them all, or else he might not have been able to hide his current state of excitement.

He snapped the picture and returned the phone. The label had virtually gushed. They had offered tour support, press, marketing, and an advance that had even made his stomach flip. And best of all, they had looked at his talent as an asset.

"Greetings from Sonic Tension," Rae enunciated as her thumbs tapped over the screen and bouncing lightly from one foot to the other.

Jacob glanced at his watch. "I think we've got enough time to eat and strategize for the next meeting if we hurry," he suggested.

Carmen recommended a restaurant, and they raced to the cars, the guys in Derek's BMW, and the ladies following behind in Carmen's pink vintage Pontiac Astre. They were surprised at the quantity of food they were able to consume while still talking.

Derek stopped eating first. "Do what you want, but I don't want to risk falling asleep in our next meeting."

"Grace should have been with us today," Carmen mused. "She set us up good for that last one."

Rae and Joe nodded agreement.

"And she was able to do that 'cause Meyers has the contacts," Derek reminded.

Jacob leaned against the table. "So you all know…while we were in Tulum, I officially told her that I wanted her to be our manager. I know it was a unilateral decision, and I probably should have asked…" he began.

"Thank fuck," Joe replied.

Rae burst out laughing at his response. "I second that."

Carmen and Derek raised their hands as well.

Jacob joined their laughter. "Well, to make that happen, we're gonna have to land one of these labels. And I want to include her in our contract. Are we agreed?" He raised his hand in the air like a student with a question. Four other hands shot up without hesitation.

Joe looked at his watch. "We gotta go, guys. We can play the first label off the second. I think we can close a deal today."

"Let's let them stew," Jacob countered. "I'm as anxious as you guys to land this, but as long as we get them an answer by tomorrow—we'll get our best deal. And we'll make them go through Grace. Get her started with us at the very beginning," Jacob added.

They bounded from the tight booth and wiggled through LA traffic until they reached the second label of the day.

It was approaching four o'clock when they emerged from their second meeting, riding the highs. The afternoon meeting had been a near repeat of the morning, and they were going to have a difficult decision to make that night. They huddled between their cars in a nearby parking garage, hugging and happy-dancing.

"Oh, that felt good," Jacob exhaled.

Across from him, Rae concurred. "Validating."

Their toes were touching as they faced each other. Now that the day's business was complete, Jacob allowed himself to watch as Rae tucked one hand around her midsection and the other fussed with the charm on her necklace.

Carmen paced the length of her bumper as they bathed in the afterglow. "When are we playing this gig you threw in their faces?" she prodded.

"Early August," Derek replied. "We need time to practice and tighten up the setlist."

Rae through her chest out as she grew a few inches. "The one we promised *The Oubliette* when we held the auditions there," Rae reminded.

Jacob beamed. For as much shit as Derek gave Rae about her bartending gig, it had paid off in spades first with audition space, and now with a first gig to laude over the labels.

Joe groaned. "Practice. I know we wrote the songs and all, but if there's one thing I've learned it's that we have *got* to practice. Until we're playing it in our literal sleep."

"Yes," Jacob said, pointing to Joe with one hand and his nose with the other. "That. We need to practice."

"And not in the studio," Carmen chimed in. "We're going to need practice space. Playing in the studio is too comfortable. We've got to get used to performing. Break in our leather pants."

"Grace to the rescue!" Rae called. "Quick, let's send her another picture and see when she gets out." They squeezed in again, Joe throwing a thumbs up, Carmen pulling a rock star pose, Rae beaming, Derek stretching out his tongue, and Jacob struggling to get it all in one frame.

Jacob pulled out of the group, passing the phone back to their bassist. Pressed close to her in photo, the myriad of ways to celebrate with Rae had taken control of his lower half. He stared at the cars parked nearby, studying the patterns of bird droppings to quiet his brain.

"She hasn't seen the last one yet. Look," Rae announced, something broaching concern in her voice. Jacob studied her as she passed her phone around.

The photo they'd sent around noon still showed as undelivered.

"That's unlike her," Jacob agreed. "She's hella quick on these phones."

"Lemme call the work cell," Derek offered. He stepped away from the group toward the railings, holding a finger to his opposite ear.

Jacob glanced from Derek to Rae, watching her begin to twitch. First it was her hands which she tucked in her elbows. Then she leaned lightly against Carmen's car door. Her body wiggled, eyes glued to the producer.

When Rae popped a thumbnail between her lips, he looked at Derek. He was staring at the phone in his palm, stock-still.

"Uh…D?" Carmen questioned, walking over to him.

Derek was unresponsive.

Rae sprang into action, rushing to his side with Carmen hot on her trail.

"What's going on?" Joe questioned.

Derek looked like someone had slapped him as he met Jacob's eyes. "I called Grace's work cell." He paused for too long then added, "They say there's no Grace at the agency."

"What?" Rae exploded.

Jacob was glad he had moved closer. Rae's knees bent, her back tensing, preparing for a lunge, but he caught her before she could launch herself at Derek. All they needed was for one or both of them to go sailing off the third-floor.

"Don't hurt the messenger," Jacob soothed, lightly tugging her into his embrace. There was no resistance as he held her. His chin rested neatly on top of her head, like she was made for him. Her shoulders felt like rocks against his chest as she stared at Derek, one hand extended limply in his direction.

"Do you think she quit?" Joe asked.

"No—she left my place early this morning all dressed for the office," Derek responded. He was curling in on himself as well, thumb tapping his chin as he contemplated the news. "We even skipped breakfast so she could pick up his dry cleaning. That doesn't sound like someone ready to quit." He lifted his phone again.

Rae tensed in his arms, pulling free and craning toward Derek.

"Voicemail," Derek replied, launching himself from the railings. He stalked toward the driver's door of his car.

"Where are you going?" Jacob questioned, letting go of Rae. He sprinted to the BMW's passenger side, lifting the handle, afraid Derek might drive off without him.

"To her place and hope that's where she is," he snarled.

"I'm going too!" Rae demanded.

"Fuck that," Carmen growled. "We'll all go. Hop in whoever's going with me," she announced then looked at Derek. "Hit the gas. I can keep up."

Within moments, the pair of cars was speeding across town. As they climbed the steps to her apartment, Derek called her phone. They could hear the ringing from outside as Rae banged on her door without hesitation or restraint.

"Grace, let us in," she shouted.

It took about five minutes before the tumblers turned in the locks, and there was a collective gasp of relief.

Grace poked her head out, squinting against the sunlight.

"Hi," she greeted softly. Her face was splotchy red, eyes swollen, and she combed her fingers through her tangled hair. "What are you all doing here?"

Rae barreled into the apartment, nearly bowling the unsteady assistant over. "Why are you here? Why aren't you at work?"

Grace stumbled, hanging onto the door as the others filed in. "I thought you said I worked too much," Grace replied.

"I called the office," Derek announced, stopping beside her. "And they said you don't work there in so many words."

She closed the door and turned to face them, a bright, interested smile filling her face as she asked, "How did the meetings go? You had two, right?"

Rae, Carmen, and Joe scoffed at the dodge and crossed their arms over their chests. Derek wrapped an arm around her, guiding her to the couch. Rae darted after them and perched on the coffee table to face her.

What had Meyers done? Would he call the labels and have their deals revoked? Jacob didn't realize he was growling till Joe caught his gaze. He stopped himself, as everyone else settled around the room to listen to what happened. Jacob remained standing behind the loveseat to listen, body tight with frustration.

Derek led the charge coaxing the story out of her. Apparently, a photo of the two had surfaced online after the charity ball they'd attended together that weekend, and Meyers had fired her the moment she walked into the office.

For all the situations Jacob had seen their new assistant in, he had never seen her cry before, and he didn't like it. Moreover, he didn't like the ugly storm cloud gathering around Rae as she tried to commandeer the situation. He was going to have to step in to collect Rae so Derek could do his job as the boyfriend. Jacob had a sneaking suspicion that what Grace needed most, Rae couldn't deliver.

He sighed, perching on one arm of the loveseat Carmen occupied, within reach of Rae. "Well, that makes this easier. It's just a job," he encouraged.

"Yes," Grace acknowledged, sucking back the tears. "I've been telling myself that all day. It's just a job."

"And a shit one. We promise to be better to you than Meyers," Joe offered. "I don't even have a dog."

Grace burst out laughing, uncharacteristically loud. She clamped her hand over her mouth.

Jacob recognized the behavior. She was drunk. The band drank a lot after their sessions—sometimes during, but not once had Grace ever joined in. He had seen her tipsy on vacation, but the woman in the producer's arms was more than three sheets to the wind.

He could only imagine the lecture she'd received. No wonder she hadn't answered their first text. She was down the well by then, he assumed. After the two meetings with the labels, he was done with Meyers. The man had done nothing but meddle and talk down to his assistant. He had tried to keep Joe off their candidates list, and he couldn't imagine the album without the drummer's influence.

He was done with Meyers, Jacob concluded. He refused to live on a razor's edge waiting to do something the man didn't like before being cut off the same way.

He started toward the kitchenette, phone in hand as the others continued talking. He found Meyer's contact and tapped, listening to the line ringing. It took only a moment before the oily salesman answered.

"Meyers," he greeted, turning his back on the others. "Jacob Hunter."

Grace stage whispered to him, begging him to hang up, but he retreated deeper into the kitchen.

"Hunter." The confusion was evident in the agent's voice. "Everything okay?"

"No. I've decided to find another agent," he announced.

"Now, Hunter…" Meyers crooned. "Let's discuss this. Don't be rash. I'm sure whatever it is, we can work through it."

"No, I'm not interested in discussing this with you. I'd like the paperwork to my lawyer by morning."

"What can I do to change your mind?" Meyers begged. The sound of his office chair creaking punctuated his words. "At least tell me why the change of heart. I've done everything you asked, loaned you my personal assistant, even got you those label interviews."

"By morning," Jacob repeated.

Meyers continued to plead his case, and Jacob pulled the phone away from his ear. With a simple tap, he ended the call.

Grace blanched. "That wasn't necessary."

"It was," he and Rae insisted in unison. His eyes went to the half bottle of vodka on the counter. He lifted it in her direction. "You drank all this today?" he asked.

"Nowhere else to be," she replied with a shrug.

Rae's eyes bugged as her head whipped between the bottle and the other woman, and Jacob knew the time to intercede had come as Rae began ordering everyone around the room.

Derek shifted between the two, and Jacob stepped up behind her, laying a hand on her shoulder. He pressed his lips to her ear. "It's Derek's turn, baby. Let's go."

Carmen hugged Grace tightly. "I'm sorry you had such an ass for a boss, but his loss is our gain." She pulled away, grinning brazenly at the laptop displaying the offending photo. "You should frame that." She winked and headed out the door.

Joe was next with a hug, and Jacob lined up behind him. He squeezed her comfortingly, hanging onto her shoulders till he could align their gazes.

"I thought I was going to have to wait two weeks to hire you, so this is good news," he encouraged. He would take care of her and promised her so in a few more words despite her protests.

It took several tries to get Rae out of the apartment, but Jacob didn't mind. It gave him an excuse to gather her under his arm and hold her in the back seat of Carmen's car. She sloshed the bottle of vodka Derek had pressed into her palms from one end then slowly to the other.

"Don't you spill that in my car and get me in trouble for having an open container," Carmen admonished from the driver's seat.

"Oh. I should've poured it out," Rae apologized.

"And waste perfectly good vodka? I don't think so," Carmen

denounced.

Rae chuckled, and Jacob kissed the top of her head before he could stop himself.

She sighed in his arms, looked up at him, then patted his knee resting the bottle in the floorboard.

"You're a good friend for wanting to take care of her," Jacob told her.

Rae made an unhappy noise in return, eyes darting to the bottle.

"You have to give Romeo a chance to be the hero," Joe comforted from the passenger seat. "There are many demons to be slain by his sword."

The resulting laughter filled the car.

"Let's finish it off at my place while we discuss business," Jacob urged. "If we don't, Grace might, and we can't let that happen."

"And what a boring drunk," Carmen complained. "Just passing out like that. Amateur."

Joe laughed first, followed by Rae, and Jacob shifted to stretch his legs out. The bassist relaxed against him, hugging him around the middle and closing her eyes for the rest of the drive.

~ ♫ ~ RAE ~ ♫ ~

Two weeks later, Rae was sipping a beer with Derek and Jacob in Jacob's living room. Well, her living room now technically, too. Her tired limbs protested. While Derek and Jacob had done the lion's share of the lifting, she had been packing everything into cardboard for the journey for what felt like an eternity. She had tried to enlist Grace's help just for the company, but the woman was up to her eyeballs gathering celebrity guests for their VIP area. Moving house seemed very mundane in comparison.

It had taken longer to drive from her apartment to Jacob's than it had to unload her life. On the drive over, she'd checked Derek for cords to see where he'd plugged himself into the engine. He talked a mile a minute the whole way, relaying all the things Grace was lining up for Sonic Tension. She was grateful for the actual moving when they arrived just to hear herself think.

"Easiest move ever," Derek announced with a laugh as the three stared at each other.

Rae wanted to disagree but couldn't. Derek had pulled to her door at nine. She had been walking boxes down the stairs since she'd gotten up. He arrived with a moving dolly like a genius, and all the boxes were in the bed in short order. Then he'd played Speed Racer through the city. Once they'd arrived, the guys had taken over, and the only thing Rae had touched was her bass.

"You guys are such softies. I could've carried the boxes," she protested.

"We know you could've. But I've got a date, and I'm hoping if I work up a sweat, Grace'll give me a sponge bath."

Rae nearly spilled her beer at the thought of him prancing naked into Grace's bathtub. "No! No visuals, please."

Derek smirked, nodding toward Jacob with a wink.

When he finished his beer, she shoved him out the door calling her thanks after him.

And suddenly, she was alone with her new…roomie. His hair was tousled from the work, but otherwise, he was unscathed. She considered calling Derek back, but it was too late.

Jacob's silver eyes crinkled at the corners. "Let's go put your bass away. I have something I want you to hear." He reached for her hand.

Staring at his palm, she considered. If they touched, she wasn't sure she could resist him. The smile that played over his face looked innocent enough, as though he had a present for her other than all his manly parts surrendered for her pleasure. She rested her fingers against his and allowed herself to be led to the studio.

"What is it?" Rae asked, setting her bass in a stand near the console.

"Since we only had one ballad for the album, Derek and I have been working on a couple. We did it by ourselves, so there could be room for improvement, but—"

"Play it," Rae insisted, interrupting his ramble.

Jacob pressed a button on the computer screen, and a haunting piano refrain filled the room. After a few bars, Jacob's voice joined in, clear and strong.

Tears pricked at Rae's eyes as he sang. The lyrics bypassed all her worries and fear, tapping directly into her brain. Jacob's voice ramped up from a delicate explanation of his feelings to rasp and fray as he begged the listener to tear down the wall they'd built and let him in. He promised to fill her life with joy and rebuild the wreckage. He vowed to heal her.

By the end, her face was streaked in tear tracks, but she didn't bother to wipe them away as she looked up at the singer in awe.

Jacob chewed his bottom lip nervously, one brow arched in question.

Rae wanted to sob uncontrollably. But the picture he'd painted of the gentle care he wanted to lavish upon her sounded exactly like the balm she desperately wanted. But she couldn't tell him that.

"That was amazing," she complimented breathlessly. "Where did it come—"

"Stop," he cut in. "You know it's for you…about us."

Wiping her eyes, she bridged the distance between them. He remained seated, and she touched her knee lightly against his.

"This is how you feel? The lyrics? The music?" she murmured, looking down into his silver-blue eyes, heart pounding.

"Yes," he breathed, swallowing hard.

"Kiss me," she ordered as the rubber bands holding the shards of her heart snapped. But instead of falling apart, kintsugi gold welded her back together.

Jacob remained frozen to the spot.

"Please," she entreated. After all the times she told him no, she was sure her request was jarring.

Slowly with an audible exhale, Jacob stood, taking her face in his hands. With a painful slowness, he dipped his head and gently brushed his lips against hers.

Rae shuddered, hands splayed across his chest as she deepened the kiss, moaning as his grip tightened. Everywhere their bodies touched, she tingled. She lost herself in the kiss. The touch of his tongue against hers, her pulse racing as he nipped the corner of her lower lip, it was everything.

When they parted, he rested his forehead on hers, hands gliding down to her waist.

"So…you liked the song?" he purred.

She chuckled breathlessly. "Proud of yourself, are you?"

"Maybe a little," he admitted.

She swayed against him, slow dancing even though the music had long since stopped. "So…how does this work?" she asked softly.

"Well, first, I was thinking more kissing," he murmured, licking his lips. "Maybe I take you out to dinner? I don't know. Whatever you want, Baby."

"More kissing sounds perfect." She sighed, her breath ghosting over his lips. She gasped as his grip tightened on her jeans, and he leaned in again.

Rae slipped her hands into his hair. The intimate gesture of burying her fingers in the soft tendrils sent chills across her body, skin puckering in delight. Desire filled her belly, and she arched against him, holding onto his head for dear life.

His hands were groping her ass shamelessly as he ground his hips against hers, whimpering his need into her mouth.

She wanted nothing more than to throw caution to the wind, strip off their clothes and ride him into next week. But the emotions flashing through her reminded her of the first sparks of a relationship with her ex-husband.

His fingers slipped under the edge of her shirt and walked gently up her back. Skin to skin contact had her nerves singing, muscles beginning to tense in concern. What if he took what he wanted and then left? Conquest complete. This wasn't a fling. She wanted more than his body, despite herself. Fear wormed under her skin, her passion cooling.

Shaking, she pulled away slightly and stared into his eyes. If he truly meant what he'd sang to her, he would comply with her wishes.

"Not yet, okay? Clothes stay on," she instructed. She felt him try to nod, but the way she clenched his hair prevented the motion.

"Yes, Mistress," he gasped, angling his hips away, eyes searching hers for further guidance.

Relaxing her grip, she pushed down on his shoulders. Gracefully, he dropped to his knees and buried his face into her belly.

"Mistress?" she asked, tilting his face up to hers.

"If it pleases you," he murmured hopefully. "If *I* please you."

Rae considered his words. How had he known she needed to have control? More importantly, after the carnage Alex had left in his wake, was she ready to accept responsibility for Jacob? Was she ready to care for him?

She ran her fingers through his hair the way she had wanted to since the day they met. Keeping him was not a question of want. It was more a question of practicality.

"Maybe not in public?" she suggested, kneeling to face him. "I'm not…ready for that level. I'm still working on trusting myself."

"As you wish." He smiled, sitting back on his heels. "Know that I am ready and waiting for anything you want. *Anything.*"

"Right now, I want to listen to that gorgeous song again." She grinned, eyes sparkling. "Then maybe some food? Can we order in?"

Jacob choked out a sob, wrapping his arms around her, and she relaxed into his embrace. She was home, and she suddenly believed she could run a marathon or climb a mountain just to proclaim to the world that she had found her place. Except that would mean leaving his side, and she wasn't ready for that.

Jacob rose, lifting her with him as he did.

"Yes, mist…ma'am," he replied, kissing her knuckles as he led her back to the soundboard.

She giggled as he pulled her into his lap, tapping buttons before pulling her close. Snuggling up, she buried her face in the crook of his neck as he began to sing along, rubbing her back tenderly.

NINETEEN

ae knelt in front of her instrument case near the front door, pointing at each item and ticking off her mental list. She had spare strings, bandages, and a variety of accessories she might need. She thought she had everything, but if she showed up to Sonic Tension's first live gig without something, she would simply die. Her *Oubliette* coworkers would never let her live it down.

Jacob was pacing from the studio to the dining room and back ticking things off on his right hand then continuing to the left. She watched as he shook his head and started over.

Since she moved in, their lives had settled into a game of how far she was willing to take things between practice with the band. Carmen had ratcheted up the level of shit by a thousand degrees between takes, checking her for hickies and scratch marks regularly. Jacob had never sung so well, and she swore Derek had found the fountain of youth.

She zipped the case shut and backed away. She was sure she had forgotten something, but that's why they had Grace.

"Ready," she announced, chewing her bottom lip.

"Can't leave for another twenty minutes, or we'll be too early," he informed her as he came to a stop in front of her.

"Staff'll be there to let us in," Rae countered, shuffling from one foot to the other. "And I might have an in, you know."

His face softened into a smile. "Nervous?"

"Like you're not?"

He licked his lips and looked at her. "Right," he murmured.

That was the only warning she got before he yanked her to him and kissed her until they were both breathless. She lost herself in the playful nibbles he made of her lips. With lightning speed, he yanked her legs up to part around his hips, and she crossed her ankles over his ass to keep from falling.

The friction between them ramped up like fire and gasoline, and she grabbed the back of his head, feeling his scalp tight beneath her grip.

Jacob growled against her, pressing her back to the wall.

Rae gasped in delight, breaking the kiss and pulling his head to her ample cleavage. "Show clothes," she warned.

His nose nuzzled the edge of her shirt, and his fingers dug into her ass.

She was definitely going to need a change of at least underclothes, but Rae didn't care, pushing into him with wild abandon.

Unsure how much time had passed by the time they raced across the finish line, fully clothed, her body sagged as he rested her feet on the floor. His silver eyes searched her face for assurance.

"Whew," she breathed. "Where did that come from?"

"It's always there, waiting," he replied, smirking.

Rae could barely remember why they were headed to *The Oubliette* let alone be nervous as Jacob drove. After a quick parting kiss, Rae headed toward the stage with her equipment, and Jacob peeled off in the opposite direction.

Rae's body was tingly from their release of nerves and the comfortably quiet car ride to the venue. Moving in with Jacob may have been the smartest thing she'd ever done. She was impressed at her own easy gait nearing the stage where she would make her LA debut.

As she approached the stage, Carmen fell into step beside her. "Finally," she muttered with a sly wink. "I saw you two come in together. Should I check you for scratch marks when you put on your show clothes?"

"Still no," Rae countered. "We're not there yet." She glanced over her shoulder till her eyes landed on Jacob who was talking to Kendra and pointing.

"Are you torturing him because it's fun?" Carmen questioned.

Rae cringed, hackles raising instantly. "Not remotely," she snapped, then exhaled slowly and spoke again. "The last time I rushed, I wound up with my ass-hat ex."

Carmen's face mimicked the horror Rae felt inside. "Sorry. I keep forgetting you've been married before. You are far too young and vivacious to have an asshole like him in your past."

"Thank you," Rae purred. She hopped onto the stage, setting her case down.

The floor showed years of entertainment on its surface, the black non-slip surface worn through to the plywood beneath. Her heart raced at the sight, and a tremor ran through her fingers as she unzipped the case. As a bartender, she'd probably watched over one hundred bands going through this same ritual: straggling in, getting to know the venue, setting up their instruments. This time, she was the straggler, and her heart squeezed in excitement.

"Dad," she whispered as she extracted her bass and placed it on its stand. A myriad of conversation spilled out to her father in a sort of prayer. She wished he was here. She wished he had been able to perform live instead of only at the studio. She hoped she would live up to his standard tonight.

She may not have her father, but she wouldn't be alone. Joe's drum kit shone under the house lights, their black surface glimmering as she moved. Carmen's retro guitar was positioned its rack near the microphone stand. A set of keyboards and a mixing board were stacked on the opposite side of the stage. She took a spin around the performance area, imagining the path she would make during the show, stage flirting with Joe, Carmen, and even Derek.

She scanned the venue for her virtual brother and spied him leaning against a tall table in the VIP section with Jacob, chatting amiably, each with half a bottle of water. As if alerted to her gaze, Jacob turned, meeting her eyes across the way and offered a smile. Instinctively, her lower lip folded between her teeth as he turned away. It was time to focus on the music and not her partner.

From the corner of her eye, she caught movement and turned to see a young man in a baggy black T-shirt and loose cargo pants running a lead to her bass.

"Excuse me," she snapped. "What do you think you're doing?" In an instant, she put herself between him and her instrument.

"This is Bret," Grace soothed from out of nowhere. "I hired a couple techs to help set up and tear down so you guys can enjoy this. He comes highly recommended and will be especially careful with your bass."

Rae whirled to see her friend joining her on stage. She almost didn't recognize Grace. Tight, straight legged jeans made her legs look a mile long as she strode closer, an asymmetrical tank fluttering around her belt loops confidently. A cropped leatherette jacket finished the ensemble. Her slouched ankle boots clacked against the stage floor as she rushed to Rae's side.

The tech in question offered a friendly wave to Rae and tipped an invisible hat to Grace before completing his task.

Rae decided it was the hair that made Grace look like a new woman. It flowed long around her shoulders, slightly unkempt and perfectly rock and roll. Her smile was even relaxed as she arrived.

"Things seem to be progressing *happily* for you," she stated conspiratorially.

"And you too, Ms. Band Manager. Look at these duds!" she praised, lifting the hem of Grace's shirt.

"Derek took me shopping," she confessed. "And then he threw out most of my business attire." Grace cleared her throat. "What I came to tell you was that I have a little rolling rack in the bathroom for you and Carmen. She's in there changing now. After the show, change into your street clothes, and leave the show clothes on the rack. I'll have them cleaned and ready for the next show."

Rae gave a short scream. "No more dry cleaning!" she yelped.

Grace laughed and waved her off then gently pushed Rae toward backstage. "I have people for that. Go. Get changed. We've got VIPs showing up for the warm-up set in thirty and you'll want to have soundcheck done before they get here."

Rae's eyes widened, wondering who the VIPs could be as she headed off to get ready. It didn't matter. She was ready for this. Ready for Jacob. Ready for everything.

~ ♫ ~ JACOB ~ ♫ ~

It was all Jacob could do to get through soundcheck without touching Rae. Her long, wavy, hair was like a vanilla scented cloud swaying behind her every step. Her luscious lips were coated a dangerous deep red that both warned one to stay away and begged to be bitten. Afterward, he stumbled off the stage and into the men's room to wipe the sweat off the back of his neck with a damp paper towel. He wanted to hide, but he had to get back out there. He'd seen the VIPs trickling in as they finished, and he couldn't expect Derek to host the event without him.

He leaned on the sink, staring into his own eyes in the mirror. "Keep your hands to yourself, Hunter. She will tell you when it is time. You gave up control on this. Chill out and enjoy the ride."

He still couldn't believe he'd given her full control over him. Surrender was both frustrating and magical in equal measures. But if he wanted her, and he did more than air, he would restrain himself.

He emerged from the restroom and beat a path to the VIP area. Grace was funneling guests toward the raised lounge where Derek was passing out handshakes and smiles.

Jacob recognized Derek's former bandmates as they passed through the club entrance. They looked lost, mumbling to one another as they eyed the general admission tables and began to congregate toward one near the back. Pete and Ryan gripped a pair of tables to pull them together. This would never do.

He interceded quickly. "Guys, no! Come on. We've got a table for you in VIP," Jacob insisted.

"You do?" Leo questioned, his jaw slack.

"Of course! You're Derek's brothers, and family doesn't sit in general admission," Jacob explained. "Come on. Don't make Grace blow a gasket trying to show you how important you are. Look at her over there! Her eyes are about to fall out of their sockets, and she's creating a southern swell with all that arm waving."

The group burst into laughter, and Nancy took hold of his arm as he guided them to the private balcony. They paused to greet the band manager before Jacob pushed them all, including Derek, into the lounge to visit.

"I got this," he assured Derek before positioning himself at the base of the stairs.

"Thank you," Grace mouthed clearly from several feet away. She gestured a grateful bow with her hands pressed in prayer pose.

Jacob nodded back to her, before the moment was over, and she was introducing herself to the next batch of incoming guests.

Roughly fifteen minutes later, Grace ushered the band through a secret passage backstage to mic up. Jacob caught a glimpse of the front of house, shocked that general admission was swarming and full. The bar was surrounded three people deep waiting to place orders, and raised trays indicated servers delivering drinks to the sardines in front.

"Dude, it's full," Jacob mumbled incredulously to Derek as they entered their shared dressing room.

"We have a lot of friends," the keyboardist replied, smirking.

Jacob smiled back wistfully, disappointed that he hadn't seen his former band mates. He'd expected at least Blake to show up. He wasn't surprised. That was how he'd wound up forming this new band, after all.

He adjusted his in-ear monitors and allowed a crew member to attach the box for his wireless mic to the back of his pants. He watched jealously as a tech clipped a similar black box into the back of Rae's red leather skirt. He calmed himself, noting how professional the tech was and how his hands never once slipped down to squeeze her shiny behind the way *he* wanted to.

"Let's do this!" Derek hollered, stalking to the stage. Inspired by his cry, he and the others followed, bursting onto the scene.

Taking center stage as the house lights dimmed, Jacob looked at the ground as a pair of lights blasted him.

Drenched in hot light, gasping for breath, he threw one arm wide and tried to eye everyone in the room all at once.

"Hey, everybody! Thanks for coming out tonight," he yelled.

Joe was already clicking in the downbeat of the first song.

"We're Sonic Tension!" he bellowed.

For one glorious moment, the room was filled with screaming and clapping, and they launched into their set. Jacob lost himself in the music but could barely hear himself over the cheering. The next hour flew by, and Jacob barely felt the time pass. Despite not knowing the words, the crowd was picking up on the choruses, and the people down in front were singing along.

When they were finished, Grace met them at the edge of the stage. "The techs will break down the gear as if their lives depended on it," she snapped at them all. "Dry off and then it's up to VIP to greet all the celebrities that are going out of their minds to shake your hands." She flitted away once they complied.

This was not the largest venue Jacob had played. The stadiums he and The Harmonizers had sold out were tens of thousands of people. But the high he felt as he toweled off in the back room was the same. If Derek and Joe hadn't been high-fiving and screaming, he might have stayed in front of a mirror for the rest of the night.

Derek spritzed cologne over the back of his neck. "Let's go, you filthy rock star!" he demanded. "Don't make me send my girl in after you."

The threat did the trick, snapping Jacob from his reverie. As good as performing felt, the night wasn't over.

People in VIP were practically sitting on top of each other to make room and laughing amicably. He scanned the crowd to see who else had arrived as the band approached the stairwell. Danny, Blake and his partner were in the corner, Craig and Jason were nearby, engaged in conversation with a tall man. There was no telling who the man was from his back, but Craig and Jason looked nearly worshipful as they gazed up at him.

Rae slammed into his back with a whimper, and he caught her before she could fall.

"You okay?" he whispered against her ear.

"It's Nigel Davies," she stuttered.

The name sounded familiar, but he couldn't place it.

"Rebel Gloss. Bass player," she supplied. Her tiny hands latched onto him, and Jacob felt like a preening peacock as he ascended the last stairs with his arm around her.

Television host Paul Nightly practically pounced as they made the top step, grabbing his hand and shaking it.

"Jacob, man that was awesome!" Paul enthused. He flung an arm around the singer half pulling him away.

Jacob resisted, keeping his arm firmly around Rae. He and Paul went back, and he knew the man's MO was to take control of the conversation by dividing and conquering bands individually. He thanked the host and began introducing the band. They chatted until Grace appeared to pull them out of the stairwell.

Derek nearly knocked him down, pulling Grace to his chest. He kissed her hard and fast, grabbing her ass audaciously in front of God and everyone.

"Well, that escalated quickly," Joe groaned behind them. "Can we go back to them being too dumb to know they're nuts about each other?"

Jacob chuckled and nosed Rae lightly behind her ear, kissing the space tenderly.

He felt the tremble in her body before he met her eyes. She was ready to fly free, and he lifted his arm to allow her escape.

~ ♫ ~ RAE ~ ♫ ~

Rae floated to the bar where Kendra was working. She had done it— survived her first gig and had barely missed a note. There had been a shaky pair between one song, and another where the amp had crackled weirdly, but no one else heard it. The crowd of unknowns on the floor had danced the whole time, shouting and generally having an amazing time. During one of the last songs, she had noticed the audience swelling each time she slapped the bass.

Her jelly knees wobbled as she realized she was standing in the same room as Nigel Davies and all the Harmonizers. She scolded herself for bolting to the bar, but she needed some liquid courage before she faced the enormity of whose hand she would soon be shaking.

By the time she arrived, Kendra had her preferred drink ready. With one hand, Rae grabbed the edge of the bar then knocked back the whiskey shot with the other. She tapped her glass twice for two more which she also slugged in quick succession.

Kendra's eyes followed her as she took the empty glass away. "So, you finally…"

"Why is everyone saying that tonight?" Rae pouted. Her brain only had capacity for one thing at the moment, and thoughts of how she hadn't ravished Jacob yet were only bringing her down. "No, not yet. We're not there yet!"

"Riiiight. That's why he can't keep his eyes off you?"

"Sadly, the lady speaks the truth." Jacob grinned before asking for a beer.

Kendra drew back, fulfilling his request before prepping more drinks. She smiled at Rae. "You still have to glad hand and make conversation."

Rae nodded. "Trying to get rid of the nerves."

As Kendra passed drinks to another server, Jacob leaned close to her ear. His body heat crawled over her, his breath turning her to a quivering pile of goosebumps.

"There are other ways to release the tension," he whispered against her ear, trailing one finger down her back. Her knees weakened, and he stabilized her discreetly with a grin. He trailed the finger back up to her shoulder. She swallowed back a whimper. If he kept this up, she would surrender to him right there on the bar, and she wasn't sure she cared if the whole world watched.

Someone pressed against her other side, arm to arm. Rae looked beside her with half lidded eyes seeing Carmen backed against the bar, elbows on its edge. She was beaming.

"Turn around," she mumbled quickly.

A tall, older man swaggered towards them, his dark hair flopping with every step. His smile nearly blotted out his eyes as he approached, extending a friendly hand toward them.

"Hey, we haven't met, but congratulations! That was quite a show." His British accent made the compliment sing.

Jacob took the man's extended hand with a smile. "Thanks."

"Nigel Davies. Friend of Joe's," he explained.

"Thanks for coming out tonight," Jacob murmured. "You didn't fly in for this did you?"

"No, no. Moved to the states years ago."

Behind him, Rae pressed to Jacob's back, and she felt her teeth resting against his shoulder. She couldn't tear her eyes from the legendary bassist shaking her bandmate's hand! Was he going to shake hers next? Was she dreaming again?

"I'm glad I came, though," Nigel continued. "Joe was bragging about you guys to our mate Charlie, and he demanded I come check you out." He gestured over his shoulder to where Joe was engaged in animated conversation with an older woman. "My wife wants to know when we can buy the CD." He laughed.

"Wow, that's exceptionally kind of you," Jacob burbled. "They should be released soon. Let me put you in touch with our manager, Grace, and she can make sure you get one."

"We've met. She's a workhorse! And is this your bassist?" He looked over Jacob's shoulder and pinned her with his gaze.

Jacob pulled her forward gently by the wrist, winking discreetly at her.

"Yes, this is Rae," he introduced.

She moved forward on fawn-legs, using Jacob as her touchstone.

"Amazing work," Nigel complimented. "You killed it out there. Really like the level of melody you've got. Where did you come up with that?"

Rae's mouth was dry, and she felt like she was having an out of body experience when he shook her hand. She stuttered momentarily, then exclaimed, "I've been inspired by a lot of bands."

Nigel laughed. "Joe told us you and your manager are big fans. Next time we're in town, I'll send some passes over so I can introduce you," he offered. He tipped an invisible hat to them and squeezed Rae's shoulder.

"I won't monopolize your time. But if this is your debut, I'm keeping my eye out for you guys. Great job!" he encouraged.

As he wandered off, Rae dropped on a nearby stool. "Jake, Jake, Jake…do you know who that was?" Rae stared after the veteran Rebel Gloss bassist, watching as he peered over most of the crowd, searching for someone.

"I have an idea," he answered, settling next to her.

Her insides were writhing with tension. She had the Nigel Davies seal of approval. No amount of lust was worth not working the rest of the crowd. She had a job to do now. And one for later.

She leaned into Jacob's ear, letting her lips brush it as she swore, "You're getting laid tonight."

Then got up and walked back over to where Carmen was holding court with Derek's crew, practically sitting on Leo's lap.

Rae barely had a moment for them, squeezing their shoulders and begging to visit another time as she thanked them all for showing their support. She couldn't believe the variety and caliber of special guests in the section. There was a reporter from *Rolling Stone*, several popular reporters from radio and television, movie stars, other musicians…Rae could hardly keep up. She had no idea how unassuming, mousy little Grace had pulled together the guest list.

She made eyes at Jacob across the room, laughing at a mundane joke someone made just to get his attention. He stared back, winking and playing the game as well, and she watched his brilliant smile over and over as he flashed it at each new meeting. By the time they met at his car, neither could speak.

As Jacob sped through the streets of Los Angeles, Rae smoothed her hands along her red leather skirt. Her heart thudded in her chest as she imagined all the ways this night would go. Tentatively, she reached over to him and squeezed his leg.

"I won't change my mind," she promised. "No need to speed."

"It's not that," he said with a laugh. "I'm afraid I'll split my pants before we get to the house."

Rae stared at his lap, wishing it wasn't so dark, and squirmed in her seat.

"Oh yeah?" she asked, slipping her hand between his legs. "All that's for me?"

"God, woman," he groaned, twitching in her grip as the car swerved within its lane.

Miraculously, they made it to the house in one piece, even parked inside the garage and made it to the living room before she had pulled him by his collar, kissing him hard. He stumbled, pressing her into a wall. She latched herself around him, whimpering into his mouth and drowning in the hunger of his kiss.

His grip tightened, and liquid desire pooled in her belly and between her legs, stronger and more demanding than she had ever known. She shrieked as he whirled and pinned her to the couch, sliding her skirt up.

"Like that, baby?" he growled softly, nipping at her earlobe. Without a word she pushed him away and stood.

"Like this?" she whispered huskily, slowly peeling off her top and skirt to reveal black silk beneath.

"Please, baby," he begged, reaching out for her. "I need to touch you, feel you under my hands and mouth. Please."

"As you wish." She smirked, climbing onto his lap and undulating her hips.

"God," he hissed, gripping her waist and thrusting up blindly. "I want to pound you into the floor," he snarled, biting at her lips and neck. "But first, I'm going to lick and suck and bite all over until you come, screaming my name."

As he spoke, he suited word to deed. Once he had made good on his threat, and she was shaking with her orgasm, he carried her to his bedroom where they further explored until sunrise found them passed out and tangled in his sheets.

~ ♫ ~ JACOB ~ ♫ ~

Jacob woke around noon, Rae still unconscious beside him. Her face was soft in the afternoon sun, all her walls gone. He had broken down every barrier, indulging her every wish. He scooted on his hip, his ass still chafing after their erotic escapades.

But he couldn't lie there anymore. He was hungry and achy, and his body needed to stretch. Slipping into boxers, he grabbed his phone routinely to see if anything important had happened the night before.

He chuckled to himself. As if anything more important than the woman in his bed existed.

He was not expecting the hundreds of messages on his phone. So many of them were congratulatory, and he sifted through to see if there was anything he absolutely had to see. There were dozens of booking requests for local clubs, radio shows, or other appearances, which he forwarded to Grace.

As he puttered around the kitchen, his thoughts drifted to the previous night. The show had gone so much better than he had imagined. After…after was like descending into madness to find an oasis of calm. He had spent hours pleasuring the woman he loved and receiving pleasure in return. As frantic as they had started, it quickly morphed into worshiping each other's bodies tenderly and thoroughly.

With a contented sigh, he grabbed orange juice from the fridge and poured a glass. The barest hint of a kiss on the back of his neck jarred him out of his reverie, and he nearly flung the juice across the kitchen. He set everything on the counter, pushing his glass away from the edge before turning to face her.

"Mmmm," he murmured, eyes raking over her gloriously naked body. "Good morning, gorgeous."

"Right back at ya." She giggled, wrapping her arms around his neck and kissing him soundly. "Yummy." She released a happy sigh.

"Hungry, Babe?"

"For you? Always," she purred, right before her stomach growled.

He chuckled and watched fondly as she headed over to the fridge. It was impossible not to react to her naked body bent over in exploration. Her hips beckoned him closer, and he answered the call, pressing his silk boxers against her.

Rae's gasp rippled through his body, and he placed his hands on her hips. She shut the fridge door and backed up against him very deliberately.

"Go get a condom," she ordered. "And ditch the boxers."

Slapping her ass sharply, he raced to the bedroom to do that. When he returned with the requested item, she was licking her fingers. "I had a little snack to tide me over."

"You're going to need it," he growled happily, and set her on the empty kitchen island. It was the perfect height for what he wanted, and he confessed at the altar until she was screaming with release. Her body was languid on the counter, but he was far from finished as he stood and claimed her with a groan of relief.

This was where he belonged. Wrapped inside her, he was home. Everything was in this moment made one with her. He had the music, he had the support, and he had her.

TWENTY

An hour later, Rae snuggled beside Jacob on the couch nestled under throw blankets. Rae reached for her phone, relaxing against him. Her long hair was unbound, making a pillow on his thigh. A red number appeared in the top right corner of her app, and she shouted.

"Lord! I have over a hundred unread messages!" she groaned.

"Lucky." He chuckled. "I had three times that many."

"Show off."

"They're all about the band," he noted. "I've been forwarding them all to Grace, but they keep coming. I think we were a hit."

"Oh, good idea," Rae said, looking through her messages as well. "I'll forward mine, too."

Before the pair could get completely lost in the onslaught of emails, Jacob's phone rang. Carmen's picture popped on the screen, and he answered, pressing the speakerphone button.

"What's up?" he asked.

"Turn your TV on now and go to channel 6," Carmen demanded.

Confused, Jacob grabbed up the remote and did as told. A commercial was playing, and Jacob grumbled. "What am I looking at?" he asked.

"The news anchor teased a clip of what *Jacob Hunter was up to lately*, so you're lucky there was a break. I called D&G first, and they're not answering, so we're trying to record it." Carmen's voice muffled, and she heard a man in the background promising that he was working on it. "Who still uses VHS?" she grumbled, then stopped as the program began again.

Rae squealed, wondering who Carmen had left the show with, unable to shake the niggling feeling she should know the familiar voice.

A bouncy, brunette newscaster was talking fast. Rae vaguely recalled seeing her in the sea of bodies in VIP. "Last night, Jacob Hunter, former member of *The Harmonizers*, performed at a local club with a backup band under the name *Sonic Tension.* The VIP lounge was full, and the club was rocking."

The screen cut to footage of their performance.

"The crowd was going wild, but it leaves fans wondering where this puts a future reunion for *The Harmonizers*." The clip was over, and another reporter switched topics to another story.

"What the hell?" Carmen barked. "Back up band?"

"I didn't do that," Jacob defended.

"We know," both Carmen and Rae replied.

"Well, that sucked, but at least we made the news and they got the band name right." Jacob sighed. "Is your email blowing up like ours?"

"Yeah. Your street team has shaky video all over the place, especially socials," Carmen confirmed, chuckling.

"I was counting on it," Jacob replied. "I'm sending anything relevant to Grace. I have a feeling we'll be talking again soon."

"Okay—go get back in your groove. Talk later."

The phone disconnected and Jacob shook his head. "Live wire."

Rae nodded with a smile, then stretched. "Poor Grace is gonna have her hands full."

"Yes, but she's a workhorse. Nigel Davies said so." He laughed. "Right before he proclaimed that you kicked ass."

Rae's eyes darkened. "Round two," she growled, throwing off their blankets and crawling to his lap.

Around six o'clock that evening, Rae tried to get comfortable at the dining table. She should have showered before the band descended on them, but sleep had been more important. They were lucky she had combed her hair and made such a neat braid. While she knew the gathering was important, all she wanted to do was trace the muscles of Jacob's torso all the way south one more time. She might have missed something the last several times.

Jacob sat at the head of the table, and she purposefully kept her eyes off of him as Grace circled the table dropping a heavy packet of papers in front of each of them.

Joe picked it up warily, measuring its thickness with a frown. "What is this?"

"This," Grace indicated, holding up her copy, "Is a summary of all the contacts you made last night and the offers you've received for radio and TV appearances. And there are at least a dozen clubs that want *Sonic Tension* to play."

Rae scanned the pages as she flipped them. There had to be over two hundred pages, front and back. The others were pausing at various places, and she exchanged incredulous glances with them.

"In one night?" Jacob marveled.

Grace nodded, proudly. "Paul Nightly is practically begging for an appearance. You got multiple offers from smaller labels who didn't know you were already signed. All the major radio stations want an interview. If you can choose, like, the top five interviews and venues, I can start setting up a local tour tomorrow. You belong to me now, and you will make the appearances I schedule."

Carmen squealed, and Rae tried to pick her jaw up off the floor.

Grace stopped pacing and faced them. "Fuck Meyers and his contacts!" she exclaimed. "All you needed was to play the music! We don't need that bastard!"

Joe's chair teetered for a moment before tipping backwards, eyes glued on the manager.

Carmen, Jacob, and Rae stared at her from across the table, and Joe did so from the floor.

"Did she just…" Carmen blinked, then shook her head and gawked.

"I think she did," Rae whispered.

Derek looked amused, reaching out to pet Grace's elbow. "Oh, this is *nothing*. Trust me.'"

"Dirty!" Rae scolded playfully, but she couldn't hold back her joy at the sight of her almost-brother affectionately touching his woman. He was always a positive guy, but the comfort level he exhibited now was different. Whole. Confident.

She glanced at Jacob, understanding Derek's ease instinctually.

Unaware of her scrutiny, Jacob was glued to the packet, pausing at charts and tables. Rae looked over his shoulder.

"You did this today?" Jacob balked.

Grace laughed. "Well, yeah. Since I saw it all coming in this morning."

"Yes, and thank you so much for everyone sending her stuff that she was already copied on so she could weed those out," Derek complained, laying his head back in the chair like a bored teenager. "That's all she's been doing today. *All*!"

"Stop," Grace frowned at him. "It's not like I started on it until after breakfast."

Derek stared at the ceiling and crossed his arms. "Are we nearly done?" he moaned. "I have *things* I want to do." He looked pointedly at Grace.

Ignoring him, Jacob announced, "I think Paul Nightly is a good place to start."

"And we can't ignore Rock Jock Radio," Joe chimed in.

Rae started ticking off the venues in order of importance, and Grace took notes. The entire group started talking over each other, and finally, Grace held up her hands.

"I can't hear it all at once. Look this over. I want an email from each of you *tonight* about your preferences, etc. Tomorrow, when all the venues are open, I'll start calling around and making appointments. Are you ready for a club tour?"

"Yes," Rae answered without hesitation. She eyed the others who followed suit, beaming when Jacob winked at her.

"We're ready. Get the label in on this though. Let them do the heavy lifting," he instructed.

"Will do," Grace promised.

"Does that mean we can go?" Derek asked, eyes wide and begging.

Jacob cocked an eyebrow at the man with a knowing smile, and Rae dropped lightly into his lap.

"Yes—go. I assume you've read all this?" Jacob chuckled.

Derek nodded as he stood. "Come on, baby," the producer bubbled, squeezing her shoulders.

Grace patted his hand. "Let me gather my things," she mumbled, blushing.

"I'll help," he offered, grabbing her papers and tucking the disheveled pile under one arm. "Ready to go."

"Keep your pants on, I'm coming," Grace grumbled, tugging her purse strap over one arm.

"Whoa! Grace! TMI!" Carmen groaned.

The woman turned purple then scampered toward the door, Derek leering as she darted past him. He raced after her in the next moment.

As the back patio door slipped open and shut, Jacob whined. "I was all for them getting together, but they are like freaking rabbits." He sighed, shaking his head.

Rae looked at him incredulously. "Really?" she asked, squirming in his lap.

He gave her a blank look as though he had no idea what she was talking about.

"Finally?" Carmen asked Rae. At the bassist's wicked grin, she crowed. "Come on Joe, let's go do our homework!"

Once everyone was gone, Rae turned around and straddled his lap, rolling her hips seductively.

"I think we can do better than rabbits, hmm?" she drawled, leaning down to kiss him breathless.

~ ♪ ~ JACOB ~ ♪ ~

Nearly a month later, the band were in talks to open for Rebel Gloss on a mini tour of the US and Canada. Grace and Rae barely said a word as the group walked into the conference room where they were scheduled to meet the band and make final decisions.

Around the table, the members stood chatting, the singer and bassist staring out over the LA skyline, the synthesist seated and facing out the window, and their drummer sat chatting with the band manager.

Their singer, Charlie, turned on a dime as the door opened.

"They're here," he enthused. "Joe, man! How've you been?" he asked, dashing around the table to greet them with a hug for Joe and a warm handshake for Jacob and Derek. He hugged Carmen immediately followed by Rae and Grace.

After introductions, Nigel remained leaning against the windows with arms akimbo. "The album is great, and Grace got it to me so fast. I've been trying to describe to the guys the energy at your show. And I really like how you switch singers depending on the song."

Before the conversation could continue, several corporate employees from their respective labels filed in, restarting the introductions. This part was almost worse than landing a label. Now it was down to talking financials and business, and he wouldn't remember anyone's name anyway. Both bands settled around the table, and Jacob was shocked to see how all the Rebel Gloss members participated in the conversation, asking smart financial questions without hesitation.

Perhaps if he'd paid more attention during his solo record deals, he might have caught some of the loopholes that the British band across from him seemed to weed out like breathing. They knew what they wanted, and they said everything right up front. Once in a while, they glanced at Jacob and the others for approval.

He thought briefly that he should be jealous of the way Rae was staring at each of them, as they spoke, meekly nodding or squeaking out a yes when they spoke to her directly. She caught him watching her, and any fear that she would leave him for her saints of rock and roll evaporated.

Their band manager spoke succinctly, and it reminded him distinctly of Grace and her no-nonsense approach. At first glance, the woman looked equally shy, but she was well groomed and comfortable in a

Rebel Gloss themed t-shirt and sneakers. She cut straight to the chase. "The tour kicks off in about a month. We've sent your label the details of where we'll be staying and what you'll need for transportation. Are you guys up for it?"

A resounding "Yes" answered her.

"Excellent!" Charlie agreed, bouncing up to shake hands across the table.

Nigel joined him. "Here's to a great tour," he offered. "I'm excited to work with you lot," he added.

"So are we." Derek grinned.

The corporate stooges flowed out of the room once all the necessary signatures were acquired. Rebel Gloss left first, leaving Sonic Tension alone in the conference room. They were silent, Carmen peeking out the door. She closed it suddenly.

"We did it! We've hit the big time," she squealed, doing a silly little dance on the spot.

"We're big time adjacent." Jacob laughed. "But this is amazing exposure. I'm looking forward to the day we get to audition opening bands."

Jacob cheered with the others, squeezing Rae unabashedly.

Grace turned, in Derek's embrace, to address the others. "We have a lot of work to do to be ready. We're going to need more wardrobe. You guys can't wear the same thing every night. You'll need to check your leases and get your affairs in order. We'll be gone for six months."

"Do we get a tour bus?" Rae asked.

"Two, I think. I'll see what the label will spring for," Grace hedged. "As long as you understand that it comes out of your paychecks."

"We've done hundreds of thousands in record sales in three weeks," Jacob answered. "I think we'll be taken care of."

"Money!" the drummer cheered.

Jacob lifted a hand for them to still, feeling his vision go watery as he looked at each of their faces. "Thank you. Good work. We made it."

After another round of group hugging, they made their way out of the room toward the exit silently, splitting off to different cars.

"Charlie hugged me," Rae whispered once she and Jacob were in the car.

He glanced at her coming down from her celebrity crush high. She was like a kid who'd received a pony for Christmas and had no words to express her gratitude or excitement. It was utterly adorable.

Her voice was far away when she asked, "Jake, what do you do when all your dreams come true?"

He had been wondering that himself lately. He chuckled, kissing her temple before latching his seatbelt over himself.

"You make new dreams," he murmured, his throat tight as he felt dreams of his own being born in his heart. Every single one revolved around her.

"How?" she asked as he pulled out of the parking garage and onto the street. "I mean…I…in this moment, I couldn't imagine more. I'm in an excellent band full of talented and good people. We're about to tour with my all-time favorite band that I've loved since I was ten years old. I'm in love with the best man on the planet. Everything is just…perfect."

Jacob nearly swallowed his tongue. Had she said she was in love?

"Baby?" he murmured.

"Yes?" she asked, smiling at him.

"Did you say—"

"Caught that, did you?" She bit her lip and smirked. "Been meaning to tell you for a while, I just…kept chickening out for some reason. But today, I couldn't hold it back anymore. I love you, Jacob, and I can't wait to make new dreams with you."

He could barely focus on his driving. Reaching blindly for her hand, he squeezed it. "I love you, too."

~ ♫ ~ R A E ~ ♫ ~

Opening night of their first official tour was pure chaos. Close to one hundred people were rushing back and forth around the venue, climbing ropes, shimmying over catwalks, and ducking beneath the stage for last minute checks.

Grace walked in on Carmen and Rae veritably bouncing in the room.

"Finally!" Carmen growled, yanking the rolling cart away from the wardrobe woman who'd pushed it in, squeezing past the manager.

"Thank you," Grace called after the retreating person then turned to Carmen. "Calm down. You've got plenty of time. Soundcheck went well. The techs are handling the lighting."

"And extra strings," Rae reminded, chewing on her thumb nervously.

"It's all arranged." Grace nodded. "Worry about getting dressed now. You know how to do this."

"Not with Charlie fucking Duval in the next fucking room," Rae grumbled, pulling her outfit for the night off the rack. The lead singer was probably putting on his pants and strutting in front of the mirror too! She threw her head back in despair. How was she supposed to work a zipper with Rebel Gloss naked and mere feet away?

"They're way farther away than that," Grace chuckled. "Focus on your part." Advice dispensed, she left them to change.

Rae stuck her tongue out at the closed door petulantly, winking at Carmen as she cackled. Once dressed, she wandered backstage searching for a longer hallway to pace. Her fingers were practicing difficult transitions, and she was scolding herself for falling apart. This wasn't their first or even their tenth gig by now. But tonight she was opening for her favorite band of all time to a crowd of people who just wanted to see Nigel play the effing bass! How could she compete with that?

She stared at a gap in the railings, watching fans finding their seats. She could hear more of them than she could see. However, a man was arguing with one of the security staff. One of the people Grace had introduced them all to so they knew who was watching their backs. His name was Martin. He was surrounded by two other venue guards, and still the man on the far side of the gate gestured boldly.

And Rae knew him.

Rae almost swallowed her tongue, and naked members of Rebel Gloss were the last thing on her mind. She jumped around the corner, pressing her back to the wall. Eyes squeezed shut, she mumbled.

"Feel the hard wall. Smell the stinky air 'cause someone refused to wear deodorant. Come on, Rae! You have five senses. Where are the other three?"

A touch on her hip jerked her back to the present moment, and she yelped, holding up her fists wildly. Her eyes flew open, goosebumps erupting all over her skin. It was Jacob.

"Oh, it's you," she groaned with relief as her eyes locked with his.

"Whoa there!" He grinned. "Jumpy much?"

"Keep your voice down," she hissed. "Alex is downstairs, chatting up the bouncer." She closed her eyes again and rested her forehead on his chest as he stiffened, leaning to look.

"I've got this," Jacob growled softly and kissed the top of her head before releasing her.

Rae grabbed for him to stop him, but it was too late. He was already out of reach, and she bit her fist as she watched him go.

She swore he'd gotten taller, stalking to the security guard and patting him on the back. Rae sneaked closer to listen, shrinking against the wall as she did.

"What's up, man?" He forced himself to smile. He turned the gaze on the other man knowingly, pleasant but cold.

"Oh hey, Mr. Hunter," the bouncer replied, smiling. "This is Alex. Says he knows Ms. Duncan." Martin shrugged, folding his hands formidably in front of himself. "Told him nobody gets upstairs without a pass."

"Know her?" Alex chuckled, running a hand through sandy blonde hair.

Rae snarled at the gesture. It was his rock-star move, trying to shame people for not knowing who he was. But from the ratty hoody and torn jeans he sported, she could tell he was on a bender. His cheeks were gaunt, and she wondered how she'd ever found him attractive as he turned wild eyes on Jacob. "She's my wife."

"*Ex*-wife," Jacob enunciated.

Rae shivered at his tone, the subtle aggression causing butterflies to flit through her belly. Something in his tone promised he wouldn't be so nice if Alex continued.

"Semantics." Alex smiled, showing all his teeth and waving a dismissive hand. "If you'll let her know I'm here—"

"She's moved on," Jacob declared. "And I think you should too." He nodded at Martin.

Alex's eyes narrowed, and he smirked. "Yeah, right," he scoffed. He put one hand on his hip, jutting them forward. "DeeDee knows what—"

"She hates that name." Jacob cut him off again. "Rae doesn't need you, and she never did. The things you did to her were toxic. She's moved on to people who worship her. You don't even know what you lost. You're a fool. You're only coming around now because you think there's money in it. If any of the band catch you trying to contact her again, there's going to be jail time."

With each word, Rae stood a bit taller, watching Alex's rigid posture. Jacob turned to the guard.

"Escort this trash out of the building."

Rae scrambled back into the safety of the adjacent hallway, hands trembling. Everyone she ever knew always threatened what they would do if they ever met her ex. But Jacob had. And he'd handled it smartly and without fear. No greeting. No sympathy for his humanity. He'd simply put the man in his place.

Relief oozed out of her, and she shook out her hands as Jacob jogged toward her. She could hear Alex's protests as he was bodily removed from the venue, and she puffed out a sigh. He pulled her into his arms, holding on tightly.

"You were so brave," she whimpered.

"That was intense," he agreed. "I have to assume he was an Adonis and much nicer when you married him, 'cause he's a douche bag now!"

Rae laughed. "Something like that." She allowed him to hold her, pressing her face to his chest. Jacob smelled like summer sunshine, apples, and...*man.* She bit a nipple through his shirt, and he jumped with a shriek.

"Hey, stop it," Derek hollered from down the hall.

Jacob waved him off. "I'm wearing pants," he retorted.

"What a shame," she noted, then her face scrunched. "Why does that matter?"

"New rule—no PDAs without pants," Jacob explained.

Shaking her head, Rae eased out of his embrace, turning to face their bandmate. "I'm pretty sure I don't want to know."

"You don't," Jacob confirmed.

"You ready for the show?" Derek asked.

"Now that Alex has been kicked out, yeah," Jacob beamed.

"He was here?" Derek frowned. His eyes darted past them.

"But Big Daddy chased him off," Rae replied, nodding and patting his torso appreciatively.

Derek's eyebrows shot up. "Big Daddy?"

Rae shrugged, wondering if she had time to repay her thanks in a quiet corner. She could reapply her lipstick afterwards.

Derek pulled his cell out of his pocket. "I'll tell Grace, have her see to it."

Grace was rounding the corner with Joe and Carmen in tow. "Oh, thank God, I found you all. You have three minutes," she barked, grabbing her phone when it dinged in her pocket. She glanced at Derek then pocketed his phone as well. "Got it. I'll let everyone know once you're up there."

Rae's stomach dropped out when she looked past Grace and saw Charlie and Nigel striding toward them.

"Hey, guys," Nigel greeted, "We know you're about to go on, but we wanted to wish you luck."

Jacob was already bouncing, and he smiled at the two older men. "Thanks."

The exchange was cut short as techies started suiting up Carmen and Rae with their instruments.

"You guys are gonna do great," Charlie encouraged. "We have THE best fans. They're going to love you."

"It's time," Grace announced, gesturing for them to go.

The opening chords of the show reverberated off the stadium walls, and the band began winning over the crowd. Jacob's voice wove a spell around the audience. Derek chimed in on backup vocals, his face contorted in an effort not to laugh as Carmen rode up on him with her guitar. Rae and Joe seemed to be competing for who could drive the beat.

Rae thought she was winning. She was on stage, playing her bass, opening for her favorite band, all her favorite people within yards of her, and next to the man she loved who loved her back. It seemed impossible, and maybe she was dreaming, but if she was, she begged the powers-that-be not to wake her up.

THE END

ABOUT THE AUTHORS

Laura Christian was raised in St. Louis, MO but now resides in the great state of Texas with her husband, a Siamese cat and a Jack Russel Terrier. In her spare time, Laura enjoys reading, sewing, knitting, painting, and mostly playing Fortnite with her besties.

Gihan Salem resides in the great state of Texas, making a home with her husband, adopted daughter, grandson, and a bevy of affectionate cats. She has been writing for many years for fun and takes great joy in all things Star Wars. Gihan is a trained audio tech and loves music and the arts. When not writing, she can be found reading, gaming, or following BTS.

To learn more about the author and other publications, please visit www.thelaurachristian.com for more.